They stepped through the shimmer into the thicker, darker fog. It still had elements of yellow and brown, but Kirilli's corpse was gone. A single satchel lay on the ground near the puddle, and the knife was half-in and half-out of the blood.

"What did you do?" Judita asked.

"She tried to kill me," Cilka said. "What would you have me do?"

Judita stared at her, and then at the woman, in great shock.

"This shouldn't have been able to happen," she said.

"And yet it did," Cilka said.

The woman was collapsing against Cilka, the woman's legs unable to hold her up.

"She speaks with power," Cilka said. "She stopped Kirilli in his tracks."

"I know what she is," Judita said, not looking at Cilka. Judita was looking at the woman. "You should have killed her."

"What?" Cilka couldn't believe she had heard that. "Why?"

"Because she has more power than we do," Judita said. "And when she wakes up, we won't be able to stop her."

THE FEY SERIES
(READING ORDER)

ALSO BY
KRISTINE KATHRYN RUSCH

MORE FROM THE FEY

Destiny: A Story of The Fey

Lessons From The Writing of The Fey

THE DIVING SERIES

Diving into the Wreck: A Diving Novel

City of Ruins: A Diving Novel

Becalmed: A Diving Universe Novella

The Application of Hope: A Diving Universe Novella

Boneyards: A Diving Novel

Skirmishes: A Diving Novel

The Runabout: A Diving Novel

The Falls: A Diving Universe Novel

Searching for the Fleet: A Diving Novel

The Spires of Denon: A Diving Universe Novella

The Renegat: A Diving Universe Novel

Escaping Amnthra: A Diving Universe Novella

The Court-Martial of the Renegat Renegades

Thieves: A Diving Novel

Squishy's Teams: A Diving Universe Novel

The Chase: A Diving Novel

Maelstrom: A Diving Universe Novella

Writing as Kris Nelscott

THE SMOKEY DALTON SERIES

A Dangerous Road

Smoke-Filled Rooms

Thin Walls

Stone Cribs

War at Home

Days of Rage

Street Justice

AND

Protectors

Writing as Kristine Grayson

The Charming Trilogy, Vol. 1

The Charming Trilogy, Vol. 2

The Fates Trilogy

The Daughters of Zeus Trilogy

THE KIRILLI MATTER

THE FIRST BOOK OF THE
QAVNERIAN PROTECTORATE

KRISTINE KATHRYN RUSCH

WMG
PUBLISHING

The Kirilli Matter

Copyright © 2023 by Kristine Kathryn Rusch

Published by WMG Publishing

Cover and layout copyright © 2023 by WMG Publishing

Cover design by WMG Publishing

Cover illustration by Echo Chernik

Background art © cappa | Depositphotos

Figure art © Ravven and © Cheshire Studios

Vehicle art © Alina Lytvyn "Vex"

ISBN-13 (trade paperback): 978-1-56146-817-1

ISBN-13 (hardcover): 978-1-56146-843-0

This one is for the fans, who have waited so patiently for me to get off my ever-loving butt.

THE KIRILLI MATTER

PART ONE
A MYSTERIOUS DEATH

NOW

CHAPTER
ONE

Augustus Kirilli scurried out the doors of the accounting offices of Kirilli, Capalidi, Konstandt, and B'Levin, one satchel under his right arm, and the other clutched in his left hand. The satchels were heavy, stuffed with artifacts and notebooks and maps. He hadn't gotten a good look at any of it, but the magic they gave off was powerful.

Twilight gave Kirilli cover, but it also caused yellow-tinged shadows to form on the walls of nearby buildings. The air reeked of burning coal—a sharp, almost sulfuric smell that caught in the back of the throat and made it hard to swallow.

He hurried down the exterior stairs onto the sidewalk, glancing at the lightstone streetlamps as he did so. The ones nearest him were lit. Normally, they gave off a soft white glow, but on this night, the glow was yellow and gray.

There was no wind, which meant the city would have a real pea-souper. He hated nights like this. They made Trinovante seem like a foreign place, somewhere he barely recognized.

People scuttled from place to place, not wanting to be outside, which was good for him, at least. He had to cross through the financial district on the way home. Usually, there were dozens of people walking past, heads down, carrying satchels similar to his own, so busy that they didn't seem to know what to do next.

But they did keep an eye out for anything abnormal, and a fat, well-dressed man carrying two satchels was definitely out of the ordinary.

Or maybe he just felt conspicuous. He usually carried a single satchel—a much nicer one than either of these—with solid iron clasps and a sturdy frame.

The ones he carried right now had no real frame at all. They were just leather pouches with a lot of pockets, crammed full.

They weren't his.

He had promised to take care of them and get them somewhere safe.

For the past night, they remained locked in his office, which was safe enough. But now, he needed to take them home. He was having breakfast with his daughter in the morning, and he would explain the satchels to her.

He would also have her help him hide them, so someone else knew where they were.

Before hiding the satchels, he had opened the heaviest one, thinking to move some of the materials to the other satchel.

Instead, he had stopped and stared. He had found materials handwritten with faded ink. Some of them appeared to be spells, which made his hands shake. Others were chemical formulas, which he could just barely read.

Numbers ran across dozens of pages like a cipher, or worse, and he didn't have time to figure them out.

Then he found the map, hand drawn on parchment, obviously very old. It showed the Hidden River as it flowed out of Gangeeta into Byrü. The river had a dozen different names, one for each country it flowed through.

Now, the countries were all in the Qavneria Protectorate. Over the centuries, the leaders of the Protectorate decided to make all of the place names within the Protectorate uniform— and for the purposes of Protectorate maps, drawn now, they were.

But when this map was made, that decision clearly hadn't yet happened. All of the names of the Hidden River were inked across it, in a flowing hand, the names changing as the river crossed borders.

Eventually, it became the Hidden River, just before it disappeared under a stone formation leading into the Razbitay Mountain Range.

This map showed the Hidden River as it flowed through the Razbitay Range, twisting and turning past villages that were long gone and mostly forgotten. The river completely encircled Mount Vitaki, as if the mount was a castle and the river was its moat.

The map's artist made flourishes here, little drawings that served as some kind of comment, in a language Kirilli didn't know. The entire map sparkled and gleamed as if it were drawn yesterday instead of centuries ago.

Kirilli's stomach fluttered as he looked at the map. He had other similar maps at home, but they didn't show the Hidden River or the Forbidden Valley. His maps started at what was now the City of Razbitay, which was unnamed on all the maps, and then showed underground passages running through the Razbitay Mountain Range.

He hadn't looked at the maps since his father had given them to him decades ago. His father had been dying and told Kirilli that the maps were part of his heritage, that he had to keep them safe and protect them from anyone who showed an unhealthy interest.

Then his father insisted that Kirilli take his place on the Board of Regents for Higher Education in Qavner, a position that would give him control over all knowledge in the country. And his father had warned him to keep a particularly strong eye on Serebro Academy.

They cause trouble there, his father had said, and he had been right.

The Thaumaturgical Purges had started at the Academy while his father was alive, but they had become violent and terrifying during Kirilli's early tenure on the board, culminating in the murders and burnings that marked what most people thought of as the Thaumaturgical Purges, but which were really just the climactic end to a shameful chapter in Qavner's history.

Kirilli clutched the satchels tightly. There were maps in the other satchel as well, but he hadn't looked at them. That first map had scared him enough.

As he hurried across the street, he felt as if every single eye was on him. The magic wound its way around his torso, and he pulled the satchels even tighter, wishing they would stay closed.

Soon it would be dark, and the magic would be visible to everyone, making his trip home dangerous. The worst of the

Purges was over. No one killed because of magic anymore, but no one approved of it either.

Kirilli stopped, panting. He had been walking fast, almost running, something his tubby body had not done since childhood a long, long, *long* time ago.

He had to catch his breath.

"Professor!"

He turned before he even had time to think. He hadn't been a professor for decades, not since he'd left his position at the Academy to run his father's business. But old habits died hard. Apparently, somewhere inside him, he still considered himself a professor.

But he didn't recognize the person behind him. In fact, he was having trouble seeing them clearly in the yellow fog. He couldn't determine a gender, and something in their posture suggested youth. Anyone who had been one of his students would have been middle-aged now, at the youngest.

The person was tall but slight, and moved easily. They took a step closer, and Kirilli realized the reason he couldn't see their face wasn't the fog. It was a hood that covered all but a rather pointed chin.

"You forgot your satchel!" they called, and held up what really did appear to be his satchel.

Anger threaded through him. He had deliberately left his satchel in his office.

His *locked* office.

He wasn't even sure how to respond to this. He needed to get the other two satchels home. His personal satchel had financial papers for two different local firms in it, as well as some meeting notes from the board of directors for Kirilli, Capalidi,

Konstandt, & B'Levin, materials that no one outside of the company should see.

He made himself take a deep breath, and then he regretted it. His lungs filled with foul, thick, coal-smelling air. He resisted the urge to cough.

At least that short moment gave him some clarity.

He couldn't see the satchel very well. It might have been his or it might not have.

And he wasn't a professor. So maybe the stranger in the fog wasn't yelling at him.

He hurried forward.

"Professor! Wait!"

Well, that cleared *that* up. The person was yelling at him.

Kirilli hurried even faster, his right foot landing in a puddle left over from rain the day before. His shoe and pants leg were soaked, and the water was cold. It was probably as filthy as the air, something he would worry about when he got home.

"Professor!"

It almost seemed to him as if there was menace in that person's tone. A warning, maybe.

"*Stop!*" the person yelled. Their voice was distorted, as if it were underwater.

Kirilli was in the middle of a stride. He couldn't move either leg, or even straighten out his right foot. He was balanced precariously on his right toes, his left heel barely touching the ground before him.

He should have been wobbling—his balance hadn't been good for years—but he wasn't. He tried to adjust the satchels, maybe slide the one under his arm to his hand, but he couldn't.

He couldn't move at all.

A shiver ran through him. This had all the feeling of a nightmare—the thick yellow fog, the impossible-to-see person, the inability to move.

He would have added the urgency as well, but the urgency was real. He couldn't let go of these satchels.

Footsteps resounded behind him. They got closer. He tried to finish his stride, but it almost felt like he couldn't remember how to walk.

Scratch that: he couldn't remember how to move any part of his body. He couldn't even glance sideways, so that he could see who was coming up beside him.

At least he could breathe. And think. Parts of him were working, but other parts weren't.

What did his father use to say?

Thaumaturges have weapons at their disposal that make them very, very dangerous. Avoid them at all costs, my son.

Weapons.

Kirilli made himself concentrate. His father had said that the weapons were powerful, but could be defeated.

Kirilli just needed to remember how.

They change your reality, his father had said. *You must reimagine it. Never lose the imagination, my son. It is a bigger tool than you'd think.*

Reimagine his reality. The street, without the fog. The familiar street, with the usual people on it. The familiar street, at this time of day, with just a hint of grayish smoke in the air, and a chill that came with the season.

Kirilli's fingers, wrapped around the satchel handle. The other satchel, digging into his ribcage and the fleshy part of his underarm.

The air, filtering into his lungs. Not foul. Just scented ever so slightly with that tang that meant a lot of people were arriving home and lighting their coal-burning stoves.

Voices, laughter, the bounce of carriages on the nearby road. The occasional whinny of a horse, startled by a windstone vehicle running silently by with its vents open.

Something popped around him and he finished his stride, his legs aching, his toes in pain, the calf of his left leg throbbing. He had to hurry, to run, to get away.

He started to, when a hand gripped his right arm, dislodging the satchel underneath.

"Big mistake, professor," the voice said.

Now, he could see the face—long and narrow, with a long nose, slightly upturned, black eyes and—raven's wings instead of eyebrows? Not possible.

"You must have confused me with someone else," Kirilli said, actually using his professorial voice, one he hadn't used in decades. "I'm not a professor."

"Any longer." The person spoke softly. "You forgot to add 'any longer.'"

The satchel was slipping. To catch it, Kirilli would have to drop the satchel in his left hand, and he didn't dare. He needed to hang onto both of them.

He tried to yank himself away, twisting his entire body as he did so. The satchel tumbled to the sidewalk. He could grab the handle now with his right hand if he could get himself out of the person's powerful grip.

Kirilli twisted again, trying to get away, to bend, to reach for the satchel—as the person kicked it away.

"I believe that has items which belong to us, professor," the person said. "How about a trade? My satchel for yours."

"Let me go!" Kirilli sounded pathetic. Weak. He hated that feeling.

He imagined the person's hand, losing its grip. He willed the person away from him.

And, to his surprise, the person stumbled backwards.

Kirilli ran toward the fallen satchel, planning to grab the handle and keep running. He wasn't going to scream for help until he had grabbed that satchel.

It lay on the edge of the road, perilously close to a pile of horse dung and a deep puddle. He had nearly reached it when something jabbed into his back.

He turned, saw the person's arm, hand—a knife, dripping blood. His blood?

His breath was labored suddenly, and his knees wobbled. His legs wouldn't hold him.

He stumbled, reached for the handle of the satchel. Surely, he could keep going. Surely this was just a moment, just something that would pass. Maybe even an illusion, like that nightmare he felt himself a part of.

Something hit his back with a meaty thunk. He couldn't help himself. He turned, saw the person standing back, arm extended, but no knife.

The knife had to be in Kirilli's back. In the middle of his back.

Pain zigzagged through him.

He fell onto his knees, the satchel in his left hand landing on the road even though his fingers still gripped the handle.

He willed himself to move forward, but that feeling of

power that had come with the first willing, the one that had sent the person backwards, was gone.

Kirilli didn't feel like himself anymore. His body wouldn't listen. He opened his mouth to yell for help, but instead, tumbled forward, face landing on the first satchel, the stench of horse dung overriding the odor of the yellow fog which had returned, if it had ever really left.

"I'll take that, professor," the person said, and lifted him up by his collar, just enough to slide the satchel out from underneath him. Then the person wrapped Kirilli's fingers around the satchel the person had originally carried—theoretically, Kirilli's satchel—and picked up the fallen satchel, the one Kirilli had been reaching for.

"It didn't have to be this hard," the person said. Then cackled, a sound that almost had too much joy in it. "Or maybe it did. And maybe you should have remained a professor, instead of involving yourself in ancient history."

Footsteps crossed behind Kirilli, then receded. The fog grew thicker. The stench choked his lungs. Kirilli knew he had to stand up, but he couldn't. Not right now.

There was blood in the nearby puddle, blood making the puddle larger. Surely someone would notice that.

Surely someone would help him.

Although as his body twitched uncontrollably, he wondered if (or maybe he knew that) any help would be too late.

CHAPTER

TWO

The morning did not look like morning, even though the sun should have risen fifteen minutes ago. The sky was yellowish green, mixed with the grays usually found in the worst of winter twilight.

Procurator Cilka Lupei stood in the middle of the street, clutching a steaming mug of tea that her assistant had kindly brought for her, not that Cilka wanted it. The tea would taste like the fog, thick with sulfur and rot.

Cilka had a thin headache that would build as the day went on, just as it had every single day since the fog had returned to Trinovante. By the end of the day, she would have a raging headache and nothing would resolve it, not a good night's sleep, not a good meal—nothing, except, maybe, a trip to the country-side where this kind of fog wouldn't follow.

The government said the fog had traveled in from the coast along the river, and then remained here with nowhere to go,

13

picking up the smoke from coal fires that everyone burned when the air grew chill.

Maybe that was right, but Cilka had reason to doubt it. The Trinovante of her childhood never had fogs like this. Her parents had burned coal. *Everyone* had burned coal, even back then. But the air didn't clog up and fill with yellow-brown gunk whenever a fog seeped in from the south.

The stone buildings of the financial district had once been white. When she was young, they'd been gray. Now, thanks to pea-soup fogs like this one, the buildings were gray with yellow and orange streaks, moisture marks that no one tried to clean off.

This fog seemed even stranger. There was mud-black threaded through it. The mud-black had been a feature for the past few weeks, and she hated it.

She wrapped her left arm around her torso, trying to stay warm. She was wearing her heaviest coat, made of rich wool that would probably retain the stink of this outing. She wished she could set down the tea, but she knew better. She would either lose the mug in the dank darkness or she would spill the tea on the area where the crime had been committed.

Not that she was close to that area—or so the others believed. It was still a good half a block away.

The buildings huddled around each other as if they were gossips who didn't want to be overheard. The streets themselves wound through the buildings, growing narrow in the oldest parts, and wide as a boulevard in the newer parts.

This was one of the in-between sections. Old and new intersected, leaving trails and confusion, poorly marked street signs and local knowledge the only way possible for a person to navigate the strangeness. This district was one of several in the old part of Trinovante that had not been laid out on a grid, but rather had been designed by whim and chance—sometimes circling to avoid a bit of property owned by someone special, and sometimes cutting across areas that had once been river channels.

The river channels had been stopped up long ago, then seeded with more stone than needed. The roads in that section often had an uphill slant as well as their curve, so that they sometimes seemed like part of the taller buildings.

She used to walk a beat here, back when she was a watchman, and she had hated it. The people were not kind, the area confusing, and the lights—well, they'd been gaslight back then. The gaslight created shadows everywhere, so the area was never brightly lit.

Once she had been promoted, she had done her best to avoid this part of the city. She had only been back a few times, and never in a fog like this one.

Three watchmen, which was probably two too many, stood in a triangle formation at the end of the street. She could barely see them, gray shapes in the fog. Only their distinctive caps, which had long bills and water-resistant wool crowns, made it clear who they were.

Her stomach clenched. The hastily eaten piece of bread that she'd had before she got here either wasn't sitting well or she had been hungrier than she thought.

"Come along this way, mum," said the constable beside her. "It's not far."

He was a young man, with eyes that were an odd shade of gold. His hair was dark and uncovered. He carried his own cap, not quite as distinctive as the caps worn by the watchmen. His uniform was similar though, dark blue with gold piping. His did not have the wear that an older constable's would. Most only received two uniforms as part of their duties. If they needed another, they would have to pay for it out of their fairly meager salaries.

She knew that because she'd worn the same uniform once, and struggled to keep both uniforms clean in a city known for its filth.

"Thank you," she said, even though she could see for herself that it was not far.

She stifled the urge to sneeze, and kept pace with the young constable. His stride was long, but so was hers. She was unusually tall for a citizen of Trinovante. She had once had thick black hair, which had, fortunately, turned white. Back then she had also had unruly upswept eyebrows, but after she became an adult, she plucked them, drawing a line in with a charcoal pencil. It made her eyes stand out and look larger than they were, but at least people were looking at her eyes, and not at her upswept features, which made everyone nervous. People with features like hers, the rumors went, had magic, and magic was dangerous.

No one was looking at her features right now. Everyone was dealing with the chill and smelly fog. None of them really wanted to be here, and neither did she. She didn't belong here anymore.

Perhaps that was what bothered her the most. She wasn't supposed to be in the field.

But Desmond M'ndue had asked for her specifically. He was the chief constable now. They had worked together as watchmen, stayed in touch even though their careers went in different directions and, as old friends, knew much too much about each other.

That was one reason why this trip into the financial district unnerved her on a low-key level. Desmond had thought her the perfect person to handle it.

Technically, she didn't take orders from him. She ran her own Procuratorate, sending out procurators herself, handling investigations and prosecutions and all other manner of criminal activity. She liaised with the court on many issues, prosecuted even more, and discovered all kinds of hidden activities using methods she never wanted to discuss.

But Desmond had seen her develop those methods, years ago, and he never said a single word to anyone about how she worked. He had kept her secrets, and now that he needed her, she really didn't dare say no.

She arrived beside the watchmen, three men younger than the constable who led her there. She handed one of them her tea, and would conveniently forget to grab the mug before leaving.

Then she peered at the body.

It was male and portly, wearing a coat much more expensive than hers. A hand extended forward, fingers wrapped oddly around a leather satchel, legs at a strange but somehow familiar angle.

Blood had pooled and darkened. This man had been dead for hours. There was a pile of horse dung, squashed with a handful of footprints, near his face. The footprints looked like they had come from boots, and if she sniffed around—quite literally—she suspected she would find that at least one of the watchmen had obliviously stepped in the horse manure.

Which meant that they had probably walked all over the area around the body, although she didn't see any bloody footprints.

A knife was lodged deep in the body's back, bent upward at an angle that took it under the ribs and into the heart.

She had trained to be a doctor in her youth, so she'd explored the interior of bodies, giving her a body of knowledge that most investigators did not have.

She also had another skill, one few other investigators still working had. She had subtle magic, which allowed her to understand the corpse's leg position. She needed to examine the legs closer, but at first glance, they seemed to have been ensorcelled.

She pressed her hands together and wished she had worn gloves. Now that she no longer held the mug, her hands had grown cold.

"Do we know who he is?" she asked, leaving the question general. The watchmen could answer if they wanted or the constable could.

It was the young constable who spoke.

"So sorry, mum," he said. "I was to tell ye, and I dinna remember. 'Tis the Kirilli of Kirilli, Capalidi, Konstandt, & B'Levin."

She started. She knew Augustus Kirilli. He was a talented accountant, a man who had an uncanny way with numbers, and whom she had called on more than once to aid her in her investigations.

She crouched and looked at his face, mostly turned away from her, showing a vulnerable ear, a loose jaw, and some flab around his neck. His hair was alarmingly thin on that side of his head, and wet from the fog.

Almost everything that would have made him recognizable

to her was buried deep in the cobblestone and the blood. Only his portly frame and expensive clothing looked familiar, and those two things were not unusual in the financial district.

She crouched, wishing she had privacy. Because she didn't quite understand what she saw here.

Kirilli's legs suggested that he had been ensorcelled mid-step, frozen in place, as it were, and was somehow breaking free. But she had never thought of Kirilli as someone who knew magic, despite his way with numbers. He had actively tried to avoid it. Whenever someone brought up the word "magic," even in casual conversation, he had put up a pudgy hand and smiled.

I'm not going to participate in discussions like this, he would say, and walk away.

Some said that was because he had become a member of the Board of Regents for Higher Education in Qavner. Anyone connected to educators had to be particularly cautious when it came to discussions of magic and sorcery and thaumaturgy.

Others claimed it was because his family had suffered through a long history of magical events, and others claimed it was because his family had *caused* those magical events.

But she had never listened to the gossip with close attention, particularly when those claims could be leveled at anyone in Trinovante with a degree of power and respectability.

She had managed to avoid those accusations, but only because she did her best to be invisible. She didn't go to parties. She didn't participate in major conferences. She didn't do public speaking.

If an organization wanted representation from her Procuratorate, she would send someone else, particularly someone who had just finished a high-profile investigation or who had some kind of positive physical attribute that the press would focus on.

Not someone who looked like her.

She braced a hand on one knee and leaned slightly to one side. Kirilli's legs looked like they had come out of a spell, but his hands were wrong too. Or at least the hand she could see.

His fingers should have gripped the satchel's handle tightly or they should have been far from the handle, if the satchel had slipped his grasp.

Instead, his fingers rested on the handle as if he couldn't decide whether or not to pick it up. His wrist was at an odd angle, not like it had fallen there, but like it had been placed.

"You want that we help?" the constable asked.

"Not yet," she said.

She wanted to look some more. There was something about the way his other arm fell that caught her eye. The forearm was trapped below his torso, with a gap under his armpit, almost as if something else had been between his arm and the body.

She leaned closer, peering at that gap. His coat was pressed against his bicep, and pulled tightly against his chest. Something had been under his arm, something that was now gone.

She stood, shifted positions so that she could move closer to that knife. The hilt was made of white stone, with a bit of gold wrapped around it for design. There were indentations for fingers, so that whoever gripped the knife could do so extremely tightly.

With a slow movement, she put her right hand next to the hilt, but didn't touch it. Her fingers were too small to fit comfortably in those indentations. If she used that knife, it would slip.

This was someone's personal knife, maybe even a signature knife.

And, since there was evidence of magic, the knife itself might be ensorcelled.

She swore quietly.

"I don't want anyone to touch the body or the knife," she said to the constable. "Back your team out of here. I'll stay."

"Alone, mum?"

"Yes," she said. "Here, on this square block, I need to be alone. But do not let anyone else into the area. Do you understand?"

He nodded in that slow way people had when they grasped the words, but didn't really know why those words were spoken.

She wasn't going to explain herself. So before he could ask more questions, she said, "I want you to send a message to Chief Constable M'ndue. I need Ilyn. He'll know what I mean."

"Ilyn," the constable repeated in a somewhat bewildered tone, for which she was grateful. Because that meant he had not heard of Judita Ilyn.

"Yes," Cilka said. "Tell him to be quick."

"Yes, mum." The young constable waved an arm at his team, indicating they should come with him. Then he paused. "I should leave someone here to protect you."

By the rules of the constabulary, he should. And if circumstances were different, she would ask him to. But she didn't dare. It was lucky no one had touched the body or the knife.

So far, no one else had died.

"I will be safe enough," Cilka said.

She hoped.

CHAPTER

THREE

The fog had grown thick. Augusta Kirilli sat in the ostentatious carriage her father insisted she travel in, and adjusted her long skirts. She hated the carriage. The interior pretended at comfort with its plush seats and velvet curtains, but the wheels bumped along the cobblestone roads, and the horses seemed to pull at an uneven gait.

Worse, she felt horribly out of control. When she was in her windstone vehicle, she could see everything through the windscreens, even with the top up. And the wheels were made of some bouncy material whose name she had forgotten that seemed to smooth out the cobblestone.

But her father didn't approve of the windstone vehicle. He hated that she had purchased it herself, using the money that she received from the family trust, and had threatened to revoke her access.

Of course he wouldn't do that. She was her father's favorite. Her siblings never showed the interest she had in the family's

23

heritage. Only Benedeto came close, and, she suspected, that was because he had known that their father was a traditional man who wanted his eldest son to inherit.

Over the years, though, her father had changed his mind. Augusta—who preferred Gussie—had taken the time to learn every detail of family history. She also had shown an interest in the Regents, unlike Benedeto or the younger siblings.

Her father had noted that. He had planned to talk with her about it. But they had never made time.

The message he had sent requesting this morning's breakfast had referenced the Regents, and stated that it was time to discuss her legacy.

Something was up. She just wasn't sure what it was.

The clip-clop of the horses' hooves stopped, and the carriage rocked. She pulled back the curtain and looked out into the fog. It wasn't quite as thick here, but it was still in pea-soup territory.

What surprised her was that they had stopped on the road, not in the carriageway leading to the manor. She threw open the window, preparing to ask the driver, Fanis Zeitsev, when she saw strange shapes in the fog.

They seemed centered around the pathway leading into the family's manor. Something about those shapes sent a shiver through her.

Suddenly, the carriage moved forward. The horses turned onto the carriageway. She could see their regal heads bobbing as they moved, apparently unconcerned about whatever was going on at the manor.

The carriageway veered slightly to the right on the far side of the property. The carriage house was near the back, but the horses slowed before the carriage got close.

Then the carriage stopped.

Gussie grabbed the door handle, and turned it, stepping out before Zeitsev even got down.

"Oh, lor', miss," he said as he peered down at her. "Ya hafta lemme go investigate, ya do."

That was why her father wanted her to travel in a carriage, so that someone would take care of her, should there be an emergency. Not that Zeitsev would have been the best protection. He wasn't a big man. He was wiry and fast, but in a fight, she would have expected him to lose.

"I'm coming with you," she said.

"No, miss." He clambered down.

He glanced over at the manor. She followed his gaze, but didn't see what he was looking at. From this vantage, she couldn't even see the shapes in the fog. "Ya need ta get back inside the carriage."

"No," she said.

"Yer father'll have my head," Zeitsev said. His eyes moved back and forth, as if he was looking for something. He seemed edgy.

She had never seen him seem edgy before.

"I'll talk to him," she said.

Zeitsev shook his head once. He knew her well enough to know that he wouldn't win an argument with her.

He looked at the horses, as if weighing what was going to happen next. She expected him to go to them and secure them, and he probably would have if she was staying. But she wasn't.

Leaving them made them vulnerable. They were well-behaved but if there was a loud noise, they would startle. And someone could steal them.

Perhaps he didn't think anyone was lurking.

Or maybe he didn't believe he had the time.

"Ya stay behind me now," he said.

She would do that, even though it wouldn't do a lot of good. She was half a head taller than he was.

He took the path that led to the front door of the manor, which surprised her. She would have thought that he was going to head to the servants' entrance or the entrance into the back garden, and maybe recruit some of the staff to help him.

Instead, he walked on the grass growing alongside the dirt, and with one hand, he indicated that she needed to as well.

She didn't want to. She was wearing slippers that matched her outfit, something she had thought twice about before she put them on. They were embroidered and made mostly of fabric, nothing like the sturdy boots she usually wore.

But her father wanted her to be more ladylike, and she was willing to do that for a peaceful breakfast with him. So much for peaceful now. Her feet were going to get soaked. The fog always made the grass wet.

Still, she walked in Zeitsev's footprints, because he had already flattened the grass. She was struggling not to hold her breath as she tried to peer through the fog.

She couldn't really see much, and she couldn't hear anything except water dripping off the building—which always happened in fogs this dense.

The air smelled of sulfur, so this fog had its roots in the coal that the locals were burning. But there was an orange-yellow edge up front and a brand-new blackness that she had never seen before. It all seemed almost unnatural to her.

The path curved toward the manor. Zeitsev led her between

two ornamental trees, and then he held out an arm, indicating that she needed to stop.

She did, heart pounding. She hated the nerves crawling through her. She had thought she could handle anything, and maybe she could, but she hadn't expected nerves for no reason.

The manor loomed large ahead of them, its edges blurry in the fog. The path went around some waist-high ornamental bushes. Zeitsev looked behind them as he walked, as if he expected someone to be hiding there.

The steady dripping sound was getting on her nerves, as was Zeitsev's caution. She had no idea why he had kept whatever this was secret from her. She hoped he had his reasons.

He finally reached the fork in the path. One part of the fork led to the road, and the other part eventually hooked up with the path leading to the manor itself. That path was curved, glistening in the fog.

"Yer stayin' here," he said.

"But—"

"Ya dunna argue with me," he said.

He put a finger to his lips, reminding her to remain silent, and then he started forward.

She wished he hadn't. She finally thought to ask him if she should secure the horses.

But she didn't.

Instead, she watched him make his way through the fog. It was dense and unmoving, and he left a little open trail that created an arched pocket of air that she could actually see through.

That arched pocket led to the front door.

She moved slightly toward the street so that she could see better, and what she saw made her gasp.

The front door was a statement that had been designed to be seen from the street. The door wasn't really a door, but a double set of doors, so wide that the carriage could fit through them. They were surrounded by reddish-brown wood from the Razbitay Mountain Range. The wooden frame extended another arm's length on three sides.

The doors had been carved in the Razbitay Range by artisans there, hired by her great-grandparents. The doors had incredible detail, woven branches, leaves, faces peering through them that were—it eventually became clear—the Kirilli family as it existed a hundred or so years ago.

The Kirilli family crest was in the middle, visible only when the doors were closed. The crest was curious: no one knew its origins. Her great-grandparents did not invent it. The crest had been a part of the Kirilli family as long as there had been a Kirilli family.

The crest was a broadsword, resting on its hilt. A heart—the romantic kind, not the actual organ—hovered above its tip. Above the heart, an ornate crown floated.

From some perspectives (and in some designs), the design looked like the sword was a body, the heart the head, and the crown rested on top.

The only thing that differed design to design was the crown. Sometimes when it was painted, it was gold, with a large number of spikes along the top, and jewels embedded throughout. Other times, it was a simple design, silver, without much ornamentation, although it often matched the sword. And in some representations, it was made of bent tree branches of a kind that she didn't recognize.

On the doors, the crown was ornate. The jeweled areas dipped back, but the rest of the crest was designed in bas-relief—the sword, heart, and crown sticking out. The crest was not embellished with a design around it, like it sometimes was on maps and on clothing. Nor were there any words added to the crest.

It just was the centerpiece of the entrance, stunning, a statement of power and command, which was repeated in tiny patterns along the edges of the reddish-brown shutters around the windows.

But not anymore.

The shapes she had seen in the fog were broken segments of the front entrance. It sprawled all over the landing at the top of the stairs. One of the railings had fallen away.

She thought she saw some shutters hanging on bushes, but she wasn't sure. That part of the manor was still covered in fog.

Zeitsev was standing at the base of the stairs, looking up. His entire posture was hesitant.

She almost shouted at him, then changed her mind. She was not going to stay put.

She walked up the path quietly. At least the slippers were good for something. She stopped just behind him.

"I'm here," she said softly.

He jumped, clearly startled.

"I told ya ta stay back, miss," he said.

"I know," she said, "but I couldn't."

He stared at her, then looked at the door.

"I dinna see anyone in there," he said. "We should go for help."

That would be the sensible thing to do, but her father was in there. He had been expecting her to join him for a late breakfast. That meant at least part of the staff was with him.

Her heart twisted. She cared about all of those people.

"Go for a constable," she said. "I'm going to see if I can find my father."

"No, miss," Zeitsev said. "Ya canna. Ya need ta stay here."

She shook her head. She needed to see what happened.

She needed to find her father.

She needed to know if he was okay.

FOUR

The relative warmth of the daylight had not burned off the fog. If anything, the fog had grown more brown, more yellow. And thicker, as if it was becoming more dense.

Cilka didn't like any of it. And she was beginning to question the wisdom of letting the constables and watchmen leave her alone with the corpse of Augustus Kirilli.

Not that the corpse had done anything. It remained the same. She had crouched down three more times to examine it, wishing she could turn it over and examine its front.

But she had sent for Judita Ilyn, and Judita would want everything as close to the way that Cilka found it as possible.

Cilka was about to give up, thinking that maybe the constable she had spoken to hadn't relayed her message to Desmond, when a figure floated out of the fog.

The figure was small and dressed in a black cape with the

hood up. No feet were visible. Even the arms weren't immediately apparent.

And then the image resolved itself into a small woman with a familiar halting gait.

Judita.

As she got closer, she let her hood drop, revealing her shock of white hair. Her hair always looked like it had exploded out of her head. Her face was long and angular, but her hair made her head seem round.

She stopped walking a good six feet away.

"I am coming no closer," she said. She had a stentorian voice, designed to carry, which was one reason why Cilka had asked that the watchmen and constabulary be more than a block away.

She also hadn't wanted them to see anything Judita did, not realizing at the time that the fog would have prevented anyone from seeing anything unless they were right near the corpse.

"Am I in trouble?" Cilka asked.

She didn't mean personally. She meant with the magic that surrounded the corpse.

"Did you touch it?" Judita asked.

"No," Cilka said.

"Then I think you will be all right. We will check when we are done."

Cilka nodded, feeling something like despair and then willing it away. If she had to decontaminate, then she had to decontaminate, no matter how awful the procedure would be.

"Do you know what happened here?" Judita asked.

"Only what the scene could tell me," Cilka said. "It told me that magic was involved, but I am not you. I cannot recreate. I can only read the signs."

Judita clasped her small hands in front of her cape. Her mouth was thin, as if she were biting down on her lower lip. Her eyes seemed brighter than usual, her nose longer. It had an unusual hook at the end, which had always made her seem older than she was.

Judita must have sensed some kind of urgency. Or perhaps Desmond had pushed her. He had worked with Judita too, even though he didn't like her much. He tended to hire people who had similar upswept features and no fear of the word *magic*.

"You would like to view this death?" Judita asked.

"Yes," Cilka said.

"You know what you ask," Judita said. Cilka couldn't tell if that was a question or a statement.

Of course, Cilka knew what she asked. She had watched Judita work before.

Maybe the sentence was a warning. Maybe there was something she didn't know.

"Am I asking something different than we've done before?" Cilka asked.

"I thought you could read the scene," Judita said.

"I read enough to see he had been trapped by magic and had broken free," Judita said. "I know that there is something wrong with both the satchel and the knife. I know that something else is missing from his person, but I do not know what it is."

As she said that, she realized just how meager her knowledge was. She had grown soft in her job at the Procuratorate.

"Then you do not see the trail?" Judita asked.

Cilka almost asked *What trail?* but that was the same as an admonition. She did not see anything.

"No," she said.

"Ah, that explains it, then," Judita said. "And the fog? What do you see?"

"Only that it has become more dense and dark as the day progresses," Cilka said.

"It is darker here than anywhere else in the city," Judita said. "It is incorporating the magic around the body."

Cilka took an involuntary step backwards. She was right beside the body, which was, apparently, too close.

"How far back should I move?" she asked, determined to keep the panic out of her voice.

"You should not move at all," Judita said. "You will take the magic with you."

"I sent constables and watchmen who were near the body away from it," Cilka said.

"I am aware," Judita said. "I have sent an assistant to deal with them."

Whatever that meant. Cilka didn't ask. If there was a serious problem, then Desmond would have to handle it.

Cilka was in charge of this corpse, this investigation, and, apparently, this growing puddle of magic.

"Is the magic seeping from the corpse?" she asked.

"You are asking me if Kirilli had magic?" Judita asked.

Cilka supposed she was. Magic seeped from corpses, especially those killed in a violent or unresolved manner.

But she really hadn't been asking that. At its heart, she had been asking if whatever had caused his death was still in the area, still exerting some kind of influence.

"No," Cilka said. "I was asking whether or not whatever killed him is still here."

"Yes and no," Judita said. "Parts of it are still here."

It. Cilka didn't like the sound of that.

"If you recreate what happened—"

"We are in trouble," Judita said. "I will not recreate. I will view. That will keep us safer."

Cilka had seen this kind of magic before. She knew that the entire crime scene would come to life.

"And if I'm in the way?" she asked.

"It will flow through you," Judita said.

Cilka couldn't think of anything more unpleasant. She wasn't going to go through something like that. She'd let a watchman see one of those recreations decades ago. The man still had nightmares. He had left his work and gone to the northern desert where there was no fog, and too much daylight. Even that made him uncomfortable.

"I'm stepping back," Cilka said, mentally adding, *any trailing magic be damned*.

"I do not recommend it," Judita said.

"For me or for others?" Cilka asked.

Judita's hands pressed deeper into her cape. Her eyes narrowed just a bit before she said, "Others. As you well know."

Judita had taught her to always put others first. But Cilka's work had taught her that she couldn't always do that. Sometimes she had to put herself first, so that she could continue in her job.

Or maybe just continue living.

She stepped several yards back.

The fog moved with her, the brown, blacks, and yellows

creating almost a rope in the mist. The darkness was attached to the corpse as well as to her.

She hadn't touched the dead body, but might as well have. The effects were the same.

Or at least, she thought the effects were the same. If they would have been worse had she touched the corpse, then she couldn't imagine what that would be.

She shivered, and she didn't think that response was due to the chill and the damp.

"A little to your left," Judita said.

Apparently, even without recreating the crime scene, Judita knew how far it extended. And now that Cilka had stepped back from it, Judita was helping her step out of the way of the action.

Cilka took three steps to her left. The fog felt thinner here, even as the tendrils of yellow, black, and brown enveloped her.

Dammit. She should have called Judita earlier, the moment Desmond had sent for her. He wouldn't have contacted Cilka without seeing the magical elements himself. Would he?

"Brace yourself," Judita said. "There's something potent here."

Cilka had no idea how to brace herself. She widened her stance a bit, so that it would be hard for something to knock her over. She unwrapped her arms from her torso, even though she wanted to keep hugging herself.

And she stood up as straight as she could, imagining herself a tree that had grown deep roots in the middle of the street. That way, if some force tried to knock her down, she would have a moment or more to gather herself before she needed to fight against it.

She resisted the urge to take a deep breath, though. She

didn't want to inhale any of more of this fog than she already had.

"I'm ready," she said to Judita.

Judita raised her arms.

The fog shimmered. The browns vanished, the blacks faded, and the yellows paled, as if they had lost their potency. The light seemed brighter, even though Cilka could tell from the angle of the brightness that the sun above the fog was setting.

She had to remind herself that she was seeing the past, although it felt like she was in the middle of it all.

The street had resolved itself into a busy workaday street. Horse-drawn carriages shared the road with the windstone vehicles moving silently along the cobblestone. People were pouring out of the nearby buildings, which looked straighter than they had earlier. Taller, like they were newer, even though Cilka knew they were not.

Judita—barely visible through the shimmer—inclined her head toward Cilka. It took Cilka a moment to realize that Judita wanted her to turn around.

Of course she did. The crime did not start here. It ended here.

It must have started farther away.

Cilka turned, saw that the shimmer continued for more than two blocks, ending almost like a swirl of fog around the grayish white square building that housed Kirilli, Capalidi, Konstandt, and B'Levin.

Cilka had gone in that building a dozen times. It was cold, covered in marble and heavy black wood trim. She had never been comfortable there.

The door to the office opened, and Augustus Kirilli scurried out.

Even though she should have expected it, his movement—alive and well, at least for the moment—shocked her.

He was wearing the same outfit—a long heavy wool coat over black suit pants and shiny black dress shoes. The clothing made him look rounder, and part of her wondered how he could scurry at all, given the shine on his shoes and the way he danced forward, almost on his toes.

He was a man in a hurry, a man who couldn't run anymore, if he ever could have.

She was too far away to see his face, but if she had to guess, she would have thought from his movements that he was terrified.

He carried two satchels, one under his right arm and the other clutched in his left hand. Their content made both of them fat, almost like they would burst if he wasn't very careful.

The satchels themselves looked like they had gone through hard times, and if the material inside didn't make them fall apart, then the sheer pressure of Kirilli's arm might do so all on its own.

He hurried down the road, looking both ways as he did so, then focusing intently on something before him.

Cilka had to step aside before the shade of Kirilli ran into her. Judita had told her that Cilka would be fine here, but Judita had been wrong.

Neither of them had known that Kirilli would veer all over the sidewalk in his haste to get away from the building he owned.

Cilka had never seen him look so panicked. He had never

struck her as the type of person who ever panicked. But his mood here was unusual and all the more frightening because of it.

"Professor!" The word sounded garbled, as if it had come from a great distance.

Kirilli stopped, and looked toward the sound of that voice, then shook his head a little.

Cilka had no idea why Kirilli would think the person had yelled at him. Kirilli wasn't a professor at all—or had he been?

She couldn't remember. His history before he had founded Kirilli, Capalidi, Konstandt, and B'Levin was opaque to her. She might have to look it up.

A person-sized hole appeared in the fog, but Cilka couldn't see what had filled that hole. The person-sized hole was tall and narrow, but that was all she could tell from an absence of the actual person.

The very thought of that absence chilled her. She had never seen anything like that.

"You forgot your satchel!"

She had to concentrate to parse the words. They sounded almost unfamiliar, as if the sentence emerging from the person-sized hole was in another language.

But she managed to put the words into place and as she did, a satchel rose out of the person-sized hole.

That satchel looked like the kind of satchel Kirilli would carry. Expensive, made of leather, with gold or metal clasps that could hold anything.

She glanced toward Kirilli, who looked furious. He took a large breath, almost like he was going to shout back at the person shouting at him.

Instead, Kirilli's skin turned a yellowish green. His throat convulsed as if he was going to cough or perhaps even vomit. Then he turned away, as if the interaction hadn't happened at all.

He tucked his own satchel tighter under his right arm, then walked faster than he had before.

"Professor!" This time the word was sharp and clear and commanding. "Wait!"

Kirilli neared the spot where he would die. His leg went deep into a puddle, covering his shoe and his pant leg.

Cilka had to move a little toward the corpse to keep an eye on the Kirilli of the past.

"Professor!"

The person-sized hole had moved closer to Kirilli. Cilka thought she saw arms extended from the hole's sides. Person-sized arms, creating a void in the fog.

"*Stop!*"

The word rang out and echoed, repeating over and over and over again. Cilka felt compelled to remain still, even though she had never been a professor, and never would be one.

She shook herself, and as she did, the word emerged as letters, written in the fog, in brown, black, and yellow cursive, traveling toward Kirilli.

Cilka stepped backwards, as far from the brown, black, and yellow cursive tendrils as she could get. They blocked her view of Judita and of the person-shaped hole, but Cilka could see Kirilli clearly.

He had stopped mid-stride—the toes of his right foot on the ground, and the heel of his left barely touching the street before him. His hair—what there was of it—trailed away from his skull, as if a wind had blown it, and then it had frozen in place.

Cilka ran around him, careful to stay away from the tendrils. They had encased him. She could still see his face, though. His expression was determined, but it didn't reach his eyes. They were moving from side to side, as if they were the only thing that Kirilli had control over.

The brown, black, and yellow tendrils grew thicker, imprisoning all but his head.

The person-sized hole reappeared and almost resolved itself. For a moment, she thought she saw a face, a sharp chin, black snapping eyes, and then that face vanished into the nothingness she had seen earlier.

But Kirilli was starting to move. His entire body was vibrating, and the tendrils were falling off of him as if they had been repelled.

The person-sized hole grew closer, as if the person inside of it was running toward Kirilli. Cilka backed even farther away. She didn't want whatever was in that hole to get anywhere near her.

Then Kirilli burst forward, finished the stride and nearly stumbled. The tendrils burst, their particles filling the fog, making parts of it black, parts yellow, and other parts brown.

Cilka shuddered. Was that what she had been standing in?

The person-sized hole had arrived behind him, and Cilka had no idea how that had happened. She hadn't seen the hole move closer. It had been far away, and suddenly, it was right behind Kirilli.

A hand jutted out of the person-sized hole and grabbed Kirilli's right arm.

"Big mistake, professor."

Kirilli looked into the emptiness that was the person-sized hole, and frowned deeply. He didn't look frightened, but he did look startled, as if he wasn't expecting to see what he had seen.

"You must have confused me with someone else," Kirilli said. He sounded powerful, confident, even though his body was hunched, and he gripped the satchel so tightly in his left hand that the muscles on the back stood out. "I'm not a professor."

"Any longer," the person inside that hole said. The voice had become clear, almost too clear. Its firmness pierced Cilka's ears. "You forgot to add 'any longer.'"

Those words sounded threatening, but Cilka did not have an opportunity to figure out why.

Kirilli twisted away from the hand that still held him, and the satchel under his right arm toppled to the ground. Kirilli looked at it as if it contained gold.

He bent over, reaching for it, and a leg came out of that person-sized hole, kicking the satchel away. It spun on the road, stopping at the very edge of a puddle.

"I believe that has items which belong to us, professor. How about a trade? My satchel for yours."

The words seemed even sharper, more piercing. Cilka resisted the urge to put her hands over her ears, partly because she was afraid her ears might be bleeding.

A second hand emerged from the person-sized hole, dangling the more expensive satchel in front of Kirilli's face.

Kirilli didn't even seem to see that satchel.

"*Let me go!*" Kirilli's voice had a similar power to that "stop" command that person-sized hole had given earlier.

Kirilli's words echoed and reverberated, clearing the blacks, browns, and yellows out of the fog, and then clearing the fog itself. It became bits of mist, water droplets hanging in the air.

A person appeared—whip-thin and wiry, with an even thinner face, a hooked chin, and upswept cheekbones that matched the black upswept eyebrows.

Cilka used an old constabulary technique. She memorized the face. She had never seen it before, not with the deep-set dark eyes and the matching black hair. The lips were thin and darker than she'd ever seen. The hair was pulled away from the face, revealing small ears with pointed tips.

Something about the face was familiar. She didn't know the person—this woman. This *young* woman—but she had seen her before.

In drawings, when she had studied with Desmond and Judita, decades ago. When they had found an entire treasure chest filled with thaumaturgical texts and handwritten histories, punctuated by drawings of people who looked just like this woman, only not as young.

Angrier, and not as young.

The young woman looked through the mist at Cilka, and her eyes grew wide.

The woman couldn't have seen Cilka. The woman was a construct, there in the past, not in the present, but if Cilka had to testify about it, she would have sworn that the woman *had* seen her, that the woman had looked directly at Cilka, and that Cilka had surprised the woman.

Because she could see Cilka or because she was looking at Cilka?

Cilka didn't know. She couldn't tell, at all.

Kirilli broke the moment. He ran toward the satchel on the ground, his gait haphazard and off-balance. He wasn't built for running and bending at the same time, but he was trying it.

He wouldn't make it. Cilka knew he wouldn't make it, because if he sprawled forward, he would end up near that puddle and some horse dung, just like the place where his body was right now, even as she watched this.

But the woman who had been yelling at Kirilli was still staring at Cilka. The woman wasn't in the scene anymore. The woman held a knife—the very knife that was in Kirilli's back—but now, the woman was advancing toward Cilka, with the knife out.

"Who *are* you?" the woman asked. "What do you want?"

Cilka didn't understand this, but she wasn't going to fight it. That was Judita's job. So Cilka was going to act the way she always did when someone wanted to hurt her. She held her ground.

"What's in the satchels?" she asked.

"It doesn't matter," the woman said. "I have them now."

"Do you?" Cilka asked, wondering if she could grab them and run off with them. This entire illusion should have shattered, but it hadn't. It continued, but not in the way that Judita had clearly intended it to.

"I will, once I take care of you," the woman said and lunged at her.

Kirilli stumbled forward, nearly falling, but he grabbed the second satchel and then kept running.

Cilka saw all of that out of the corner of her eye as she dodged the knife. She heard Judita's voice, screaming her name, screaming and screaming, but Cilka only had eyes for that knife.

It kept slashing at her and missing her. The woman wasn't used to wielding a knife. The fact that she had killed Kirilli had more to do with the magical power than the weapon itself.

But Cilka had been trained in street fighting. She moved sideways, away from the angle of the knife and the downward motion, and then she elbowed the woman as hard as she could in the stomach.

The woman hadn't expected it. The woman expelled air with a loud *oof*, and bent over. Cilka clasped her hands together and brought them down as hard as she could on the back of the other woman's neck, adding to the woman's downward momentum.

The woman fell to her knees, put out the hand with the satchel to catch herself, and continued to clutch the knife.

So Cilka kicked the woman in the buttocks, and she toppled onto her stomach, her knife hand splayed forward. Cilka stomped on the woman's wrist so hard that Cilka heard it snap.

The woman screamed in pain and raised her remaining hand, the other satchel on the ground, forgotten. The woman curled her fingers and started to say something, and Cilka knew instinctively that she couldn't let the woman do that.

So Cilka stomped on the side of the woman's face, crushing her jaw. The woman screamed again, only the scream included a gurgle.

Then Cilka kicked the knife away. It landed in that puddle where Kirilli's body should have been.

Cilka grabbed the woman's free hand and yanked it backwards, grabbing the shackles that Cilka always carried around her waist, and locking one on the woman's wrist. Then Cilka grabbed the other wrist, the one she had shattered, and ignored the woman's gurgling scream as Cilka pulled that arm back.

The skin around the wrist felt like a bag of marbles, but Cilka didn't care. She put the other U-shaped shackle around that skin bag and locked it tight. She doubted the woman could pull out of it, because even as Cilka attached the edges of the shackle together, the woman's arm started swelling. Soon, the flesh would surround the metal.

The woman was breathing heavily now, not screaming, not shouting. Blood was dripping onto the street and sliding into that puddle, heading toward the horse dung.

Cilka pulled the woman upright so that she wouldn't choke. The woman snorted and coughed, spraying blood everywhere. Her face was already black and blue.

Her eyes were half-open. She wasn't really conscious. Pulling the injured hand backwards had clearly been too much for her.

The fog was white and clear. The shimmer had vanished, and so had Kirilli. Cilka couldn't see him at all.

Judita's voice, calling her name, centered Cilka. She yanked the woman to her feet. She staggered, and nearly fell, but Cilka managed to hold the woman, dragging her forward, toward Judita.

They stepped through the shimmer into the thicker, darker fog. It still had elements of yellow and brown, but Kirilli's corpse was gone. A single satchel lay on the ground near the puddle, and the knife was half-in and half-out of the blood.

"What did you do?" Judita asked.

"She tried to kill me," Cilka said. "What would you have me do?"

Judita stared at her, and then at the woman, in great shock.

"This shouldn't have been able to happen," she said.

"And yet it did," Cilka said.

The woman was collapsing against Cilka, the woman's legs unable to hold her up.

"She speaks with power," Cilka said. "She stopped Kirilli in his tracks."

"I know what she is," Judita said, not looking at Cilka. Judita was looking at the woman. "You should have killed her."

"What?" Cilka couldn't believe she had heard that. "Why?"

"Because she has more power than we do," Judita said. "And when she wakes up, we won't be able to stop her."

CHAPTER
FIVE

Zeitsev closed his eyes for a brief moment, as if he was trying to get control of himself. The fog swirled around him, yellow and gray with a touch of orange. The air stank of sulfur and something rotted.

Gussie's stomach turned. She had never seen the kind of destruction that marked the door. Even during the worst of the Thaumaturgical Purges, her family had protected that entrance. They had hidden the artifacts and developed extremely strong locks for some of the rooms, like her father's office—once her grandfather's office.

She hoped her father was locked in there now.

But the estate was extremely quiet. She could still hear the water dripping off the trees.

Zeitsev opened his eyes, and adjusted his driving cap. He said, "If I dinna come out ten minutes after I go in, ya need to take the carriage and head for the constabulary."

"No," she said. "If you don't come out—"

"Promise me, miss," he said. "And do it quick, because we're wasting time."

Suddenly, she understood what he meant. If her father was in there, and he was injured, then every moment they argued was a moment he didn't have before help arrived.

"All right," she said. "But you hurry."

He nodded, then headed for the short stairs leading to the landing. He had to be careful not to kick any parts of the entrance.

Gussie wrapped her arms around herself, using every bit of her willpower not to follow him.

He stepped over something—a broken part of the door?—and then vanished inside.

The dripping seemed louder. In the distance, she thought she heard voices, and the clip-clop of hooves on cobblestone. She had lived through enough pea-soupers to know that some sounds carried.

But why wouldn't their neighbors have heard the sounds created by the destruction of the entrance? It had to have been very loud.

There was no wind, and the fog was creeping back, almost like a door easing closed.

She was about to walk up the stairs anyway—never mind what Zeitsev told her—when he poked his head through the ruined entrance. His driving cap was askew, and his expression grim.

Gussie's arms tightened around herself.

"My father...?" she asked.

"Is na here. Nor's anyone else that I can see," Zeitsev said. "I called, but na soul answered."

A chill ran through her that had nothing to do with the cold fog. Someone was always inside the manor. The staff was always somewhere nearby, even on days that most of them had off.

They wouldn't have had this day, though. She was supposed to be there for breakfast, and her father always treated that as something special.

Apparently, Zeitsev took her silence for a question.

"Ya can come in," he said, voice trembling just a bit, "but I dinna think ya should."

Gussie's spine straightened. She made herself take a deep breath, hoping—wishing—that would calm her nerves. It didn't, of course. Nothing seemed to. Her heart was pounding against her chest so hard that it felt like it might break through.

Zeitsev's head had disappeared back inside the manor. The fog swirled like angry ghosts around the steps. Sometimes she could see the steps and sometimes she couldn't. Even the manor itself disappeared in the swirls, almost like…magic.

The word made her shudder. Her father's voice always caught when he said that word. Her mother wouldn't allow it to be spoken in their home. Gussie's grandfather, on the other hand, believed that magic would save them every time, even though he lost friends to the Purges.

As Gussie got closer to the manor, she realized that it looked really odd, and not just because of the destruction. The building seemed to tilt slightly. She knew that was an illusion, but it unnerved her all the same.

Or rather, the destruction did.

The entire morning did.

Where was her father if he was not inside? He should have been there all night. He would have sent her a message if he wanted to cancel the breakfast, but setting it up had been so difficult, she knew he would never have done that.

Zeitsev poked his head out again, just a little, as if he was checking on her. She swallowed against a dry throat, and started up the stairs. The wood was slick from the fog. Water seemed to pool on everything except that left-side banister. She leaned away from it, careful not to touch it.

It was coated with something reddish and drippy, which seemed poisonous somehow.

She took her skirts in one hand, raising them just enough that she wouldn't trip on them, and climbed up. She wanted to grab the banister, but she didn't. The appearance of the other banister made her so uncomfortable that she didn't want to so much as brush against it.

She made herself focus on the entrance, or what was left of it. The lock had been broken separately, as if someone had taken the back end of a hammer or a fireplace poker to the handle itself.

The place where the doors met, where the family crest had been, where it stood out like a beautifully carved wooden statue, had been demolished.

There was nothing left of that part of the entrance. The wood had been broken in such a way that absolutely no part of the images remained.

As she reached the second step, she could see Zeitsev hovering inside.

He looked even smaller against the darkness of the interior, like a boy still in his teens. He kept moving through the entry way, checking to his right, and then to his left, before glancing out the door again.

Not only did he seem nervous and frightened to be inside, but he also seemed to be worried that someone else would join them.

She reached the landing, leaning forward just enough to keep her balance. The wood was slicker than she expected.

Zeitsev turned toward her, and before he masked it, an expression of relief crossed his face. He extended his gloved hand.

"You'll have to climb over," he said, then shook his hand just a little, in emphasis. She took it. The glove was made of soft cloth, and felt warm against her cold skin. She raised her skirts even more, and stepped one leg over the lip of the door.

Her slipper caught on broken pieces of wood, scattered all over the floor. The wood shifted, and Zeitsev had to hold her even tighter. She nearly lost her balance.

Only the fact that she was straddling the door itself kept her from falling.

She regained her balance, then nodded at him. He loosened his grip just a bit, probably as uncomfortable with the touch as she was.

She finally started to move again, only to realize her skirt had snagged on the jagged bits of wood. If only she were one of those modern women who occasionally wore trousers. But she didn't have a profession, like some of those women, and she had been raised to be proper, so she always wore skirts.

She was regretting that now.

Zeitsev's hand tightened around hers, holding her in position, just in case the trapped fabric made her fall. But there was so much fabric that the skirt had a lot of give.

She was able to move forward, and pull her other leg inside, before detaching the skirt. Slivers of wood clung to the fabric, and her finger poked through a hole that hadn't been there before.

She deliberately looked down before putting her other foot on the floor. She had to step wide to avoid the shattered pieces of wood. Zeitsev started to kick some away.

"Don't," she said. She didn't want him to move anything. She could see a spot to set her foot.

She leaned into his hand, hoping that he could keep her upright. Then she set her foot down in that little broken area.

Zeitsev let go of her hand as if any additional contact would reflect badly on him. She resisted the urge to wipe her fingers against her skirt, but she didn't dare, not only so that she wouldn't offend him, but those slivers of wood might lodge in her hands, and that would be painful.

She made herself look up. The entry was dark. The light-stone fixtures appeared to be broken.

She blinked hard, trying to get her eyes to adjust. It took a moment, and then when they did, she wished they hadn't.

Holes had been punched into the walls, as if someone had randomly stuck a fist into the wood. The entry table had been knocked on its side.

She saw no evidence at all of the lovely pottery her grandfather had brought back from his various trips to the Razbitay Mountains. The hair rose on the nape of her neck. Her father never let anyone touch that pottery, telling Gussie that it was too expensive.

Even though her grandfather had always said the pottery was valuable, he had never discussed its monetary worth. Instead, he had said the pieces were all rare, and if they broke, entire worlds would disappear.

"Is every room like this?" she asked.

"I haven't been to every room," Zeitsev said. "But what I walked through was."

The sulfuric stench of the fog had followed her inside, combining with a foul odor, as if someone had knocked over a dozen chamber pots. The stench made her eyes water, and made her wonder if whoever had done all of this had also befouled the damage in other ways.

She wasn't going to think about that, not yet. She picked her way across the floor. Walking was slow. Not every part of the floor was covered with broken or damaged wood, but she had to wend her way around furniture that had been upended.

No pottery, though. No art either. The maps her grandfather had framed weren't on the walls, but they weren't on the floor either. The rugs that had covered the slate flooring were gone as well as the tapestries her grandmother had hung near the entry to the front parlor.

Zeitsev shadowed Gussie, looking around as if he still expected someone to jump out of the darkness. Her heart was pounding hard.

She had to find her father.

He would be in one of two places—either in his study or in his bedroom upstairs.

She didn't want to face the upstairs, not first, anyway. She turned down the corridor, away from the closed parlor door, and hurried toward her father's study.

It was off in a hallway that was difficult to find—or so she had always thought.

But the damage continued here—holes in the wall, shattered end tables, and missing decorations. Some of the lightstone fixtures remained in place, but they too didn't seem to be working.

A number of them—maybe half—were gone altogether, pulled out of the walls.

Someone should have found her by now. Micah, maybe. He took his duties as the family butler with a seriousness that bordered on comical. Gussie and her siblings used to joke that they could just think about visiting their father, and Micah would be waiting at the door, hands clasped behind him.

Gussie wasn't even sure if Micah had ever taken a day to himself.

The maids should have been cleaning up the mess. Someone should have been boarding up the windows or trying to cover the doors.

But no one moved.

The interior of the manor was as still as the dark windless day outside.

Zeitsev was breathing heavily, as if keeping up with her was hard work. Their footsteps resounded on the slate flooring, a sound that was unfamiliar to her, since the flooring was usually covered with rugs.

Anyone nearby could hear them coming.

The corridor was dark without the lightstones, but the paintings on the ceiling had a natural luminescence. Her grandfather had been so proud of those paintings. They showed the night sky as he had seen it in his travels. He had hired a famous artist whose name she had forgotten to paint the night scenes, and to make sure the sky was filled with stars.

The stars lit her way now, barely.

She rounded the last corner and froze. The study door was smashed too, in the exact same way as the front door had been.

The study door also had the family crest carved into it. Not as elaborately as the entrance, and not in bas-relief, but etched so beautifully that the design seemed to come alive when light from the lightstone fell across it.

This time, no one had even tried to fiddle with the latch. Whoever it was had gone in through the hole in the door itself.

Gussie's throat closed and she had trouble taking a breath. She had to force herself to breathe, even though the rancid smell was making her dizzy.

"I'll go in first, miss." Zeitsev stepped past her.

She put a hand on his arm.

"No," she said with more courage than she felt. "I'll go."

She stepped across the hole in the door, just like she had done with the front door. This time, she manipulated her skirt so that it wouldn't catch. But she really wasn't looking at the skirt; she was peering inside her father's study.

The shapes didn't line up the way that she had expected. She had been in her father's study in the dark—or near-dark, anyway—and it had never looked like this.

Of course, there hadn't been a hole in the door before either. That changed the lighting all by itself.

Her slipper didn't land on the ruined wood this time, which surprised her. Then she realized that whoever had destroyed the door had moved the wood out of the way, so that they could walk on the floor without tripping.

She brought her other leg into the study. She had stopped shivering. Sometime in the last few minutes, she had come to accept the idea that if something was going to happen to her, it would happen. She could only change it by leaving, and she was unwilling to do that, at least until she figured out what had happened to her father.

She turned toward the corner table her father always kept near the door. Miraculously the small table hadn't been overturned. Even the strange spidery plant on the table's lower shelf remained. She could see its tentacles reaching across the floor, as if the debris around them enticed them.

The plant had always given her the shudders, and it was even more so now. She felt along the edges of the table, until she found the lightstone lantern that her grandfather had fashioned to carry through his treks in the Razbitay Mountains.

The lantern's iron handle bit into her hand, but as she lifted the lantern, the light inside it began to glow, just like it was designed to.

She let out a small breath, glad something was working as intended.

The light gradually increased. First she saw the corner where the lightstone had spent most of the past six decades, then the light expanded so that she saw the area around the door.

Nothing on the study side had been touched. It looked like it always had, if she didn't count the hole in the door, and the debris someone had piled next to the door frame.

Tiny portraits and miniature paintings covered the narrow wall space on each side of the door. The matching mirrors, one on each side of the door, had been covered with black cloth, which she found both odd and ominous.

Covering mirrors was an old mountain habit, done when someone died, so that their spirit couldn't return from the dead.

The mountain folk believed that spirits traveled through the mirror, and entered the real world through even the smallest piece of mirrored glass.

"Is all right, miss?" Zeitsev asked.

No, all is not all right. She clamped on her annoyance, knowing it for what it was—an underlying terror that she didn't even want to acknowledge.

"Give me a moment." She needed to absorb what was going on here, alone. If he continually spoke to her, she wouldn't be able to concentrate.

The tiny plants hanging in their strange planters remained as well. The planters hung between the portraits and miniatures, exactly where her grandmother had placed them all.

Her grandmother had brought the plants back and had instructed her father how to care for them. He, in turn, had instructed Gussie, saying that the plants were delicate, and only responded to the touch of a few.

Right now the plants seemed to be facing her, their leaves rotating in her direction. Even the pink and blue flowers had turned their tiny blooms toward her.

She acknowledged them, not wanting to do much more while Zeitsev was there. She had no idea how he stood on magic and thaumaturgy. While she didn't believe she had many skills in that area, some folks were inclined to believe that a person who spoke to plants was either crazy or oddly gifted.

The other corner table was also in its place, the dusty thick vines of the constrictor plant forming a curtain over the table's lower shelf.

As she crouched, ready to move the vines, they parted on their own, revealing the books her grandfather had written about his travels—not the ones that had been published, but the ones his publisher had deemed too fantastical to see print.

Those books were little more than notebooks, written in her grandfather's hand. She had memorized each page as a child, but hadn't read them since.

Somehow, she expected them to be gone. Clearly, whoever had been in here hadn't even known they existed.

She held up the lantern and pivoted slowly. The remaining three walls were bare. The portraits, paintings, maps, and tapestries had been yanked off. Some lay in a pile on the floor. But that pile didn't seem to have enough items in it.

Most of the items there were tapestries, and maybe there were some portraits beneath it all.

It would take her forever to go through this mess.

Her father's desk was still in the center of the room. That huge thing, made of ironwood, was impossible to lift or even shove aside. It had been built in place, out of little pieces of ironwood which had somehow then fused themselves into a single unit.

The desk did move when the entire floor moved. Her father had shown her that once. There was a lever in one of the drawers that moved the desk to one side. Beneath it was an ironwood safe. It had locks and a combination. The combination was what her father called a perfect number, 496. She had remembered it only because he had spent her whole life claiming that was his favorite perfect number—followed by some kind of mathematical gobbledygook that she didn't understand at all.

He had told her the combination and had given her the keys. The keys opened the drawers, which were made of metal, not ironwood. Her father had wanted that so that he could open the drawers easily, and so that he could lock them.

He always had the keys on him. Gussie's spare set was in the safe at Gussie's house so she could open the drawers in case of emergency.

She supposed this counted as an emergency—if she couldn't find him.

She would have to go home to get them, though. If necessary.

The lightstone's glow grew. It had gotten to the point where she couldn't hold the lantern at eye level. She needed to move it down. If she set it on the table, the lightstone would go out.

She used to know how to change that setting; her father had shown her years ago. But she couldn't remember it now, under stress. If anything, her heart was beating faster than it ever had before.

She had to keep reminding herself to breathe.

Something clanked behind her. She whirled, to see Zeitsev climbing inside the room. Irritation flared, but she pushed it back. She couldn't focus on him—not right now, anyway.

In fact, the room itself was hard to focus on. The occasional tables, most made of wood, had been knocked over, and many of them stomped. The items that had been on those tables might have been on the floor, but she couldn't really tell in all the pottery shards and broken glass.

Here, as in the hallway, the rugs were gone. But the curtains remained, pulled against what would have been the light of day if the damned fog wasn't enshrouding the building.

Her father's chair, large and imposing, just like he was, had been pulled back, as if someone had sat in it and had gone through the items on the desk.

Her father would never have left that chair out. When he left his study, he always made sure that the chair was shoved under the desk, the drawers were closed and locked, and the desktop was clear.

The desktop *was* clear. That was the only thing that even looked familiar in the middle of all of this chaos.

"Gooorrrr," Zeitsev said. She'd heard him say something like that before, always a sound of surprise. She never knew if that was a real word in a language she didn't understand, or if it was just some noise he made when he was startled or shocked.

She didn't feel like asking right now. She didn't even want him in here. His emotions were interfering with hers.

"Perhaps you should see if any of the staff are here," she said, trying to keep her voice low.

"No, miss," he said. "I'll be beside ya. This is a strange one, it is."

She suppressed a sigh. She didn't want him here, but she didn't know how to tell him. He was being logical. And she had gone beyond logic.

"Still," she said. "I'm not dressed for exploration in this..."

She wanted to say horrid chaos, but for some reason, she was afraid to use those words together. The air inside this study had a tingle that she recognized, but from where she couldn't remember.

Then her brain served up the memory—old and half-forgotten.

Her grandfather—a large, imposing man with a shock of

white hair and a mustache that trailed down to his collarbones—entering a room, laughing, and grabbing for Gussie.

My best girl, he said, and shoved his large hands under her ribcage. She had giggled and squealed, glad to be around him.

Even the air tingled, as if someone had sprinkled diamonds all around him, and those diamonds caressed her skin.

He had picked her up and put his velvety cheek against hers. She tugged on his mustache and he pretended outrage, upon which her father told him to put Gussie down, because they had business to attend.

Business...

"Miss?" Zeitsev asked. "Are you all right?"

She blinked. The lightstone lantern's brightness had increased, so that the entire room was bathed in light. The light was as clear as a midday sun in the middle of summer.

No, she wasn't all right. She wasn't at all. But not just because of the mess here, but also because she had been on the verge of realizing something, and Zeitsev's words had shattered that feeling.

That feeling, which had come with some lost time. The lightstone shouldn't have been that bright yet. She should have seen a gradual change.

She didn't answer Zeitsev, which was probably a tiny bit cruel, but she didn't want to engage him right now. She wanted that feeling back. There was something buried in the memory, something she hadn't realized was there, something she needed to grab...

She tried, but that feeling—whatever it had been—was gone. The irritation she had felt toward Zeitsev flared, and she wanted to yell at him.

Or maybe she just wanted to yell, because someone—maybe a group of someones—had destroyed her father's home.

Her home.

The home she had grown up in.

She squared her shoulders and carried the lantern—which seemed heavier than it had before—with her as she picked her way over the shattered wood, the chunks of ruined pottery, and the tiny slivers of broken glass. She finally reached the side of her father's desk.

The chair was completely surrounded by debris, which meant it had been pushed back before everything shattered.

She took a few more steps forward. If she had real courage, she would have sat in the chair, but her father had never allowed that. He didn't want anyone else sitting there—even though someone clearly had.

The table under the window behind the desk was ruined. The table hadn't been toppled, but it had been crushed, maybe by the same thing (a large hammer?) that had destroyed the door.

Whoever had destroyed the table had done so to break open the drawer underneath the tabletop. That drawer hung askew, its bottom in place, but one side completely destroyed.

If anything had been inside the drawer, it was gone now, either because it had slid to the floor or because someone had taken the contents with them.

She didn't know what her father had kept inside all of the drawers in the room, the ones in the chests that had lined the far wall, or the ones in the other tables.

And she certainly didn't know what he kept in the drawers of the desk itself.

She made herself look at them, expecting them to be open or pulled out and damaged, just like the drawer on the table.

But they weren't. They were closed.

They were dented, though, as if that hammer or whatever it had been had pounded against them as well.

Only in this case, the pounding had made no difference. The desk held and the metal drawers held, which meant the safe held.

The desk had managed to hold all of her father's secrets.

Her stomach twisted at that thought. Did that mean whoever had done all this damage was coming back, maybe with a better tool?

"We need to find the staff," she said.

Zeitsev shook his head. "We need to leave, miss. It's not safe. This's for the constabulary, it is."

"No," she said. "We must find the staff first."

If they waited for the constabulary, then the people who did this might return first. And if that was the case, then those people might have figured a way into the desk.

If they were willing to do such damage to her family home, her father's study, maybe even her father, what would they do to her and Zeitsev?

"Let's go," she said, with a lot more strength than she had ever imagined.

The time for shaking and shivering in fear was over.

It was time to take action.

Whatever that meant.

CHAPTER
SIX

Cilka was still standing in the street, the fog pressing down like a live thing. She held the woman against her torso. The woman's weight was double what it should have been because she was fully unconscious now. The pain she experienced from the wrist Cilka had broken and the jaw Cilka had crushed had to have been intense.

The woman's breath was whistling through her nose—or maybe through her half-open mouth. Cilka wasn't sure how long she could hold the woman upright.

Judita was staring at the woman as if unable to believe what she was seeing.

No one else was on the street. The knife was near the puddle, and the satchel the woman had been carrying was on the ground.

Kirilli—or Kirilli's corpse—was nowhere in sight.

And the fog was thinning. The yellow, black, and brown droplets were disappearing altogether. Now the fog felt like a normal pea-souper, with some coal smoke in the air, but nothing quite as noxious as before.

Cilka could actually see buildings half a block away, which she hadn't been able to see before Judita had opened up some kind of magical window.

"What does this mean, that she's here and Kirilli is gone?" Cilka asked.

Judita's gaze finally met hers. "She's stronger than I am."

A shiver ran through Cilka. Judita was the most powerful thaumaturge that Cilka had ever met—certainly more powerful than all of the thaumaturges still alive and secretly working.

Judita was one of the few with enough courage to learn spells, use her powers, figure out how to blend into a world that had decided to hate her and all she stood for.

"Do you know her?" Cilka asked.

Judita hadn't taken her gaze off the woman. Judita was tense, as if she was ready to spring at any moment. Maybe even launch herself at the woman.

Did Judita expect the woman to regain consciousness? Speak to them somehow? Perform a spell?

Cilka wasn't sure how the woman could perform a spell without her voice and her hands. But Cilka's knowledge of magic was small and limited, interrupted by the Purges and the terror that had happened long ago.

Unlike Judita, Cilka hadn't wanted to perform magic secretly. She hadn't wanted to take classes or talk with others. She didn't want to risk not only losing her job, but losing her life.

Still, she could see magic—just like she had seen the evidence of it when she had looked at Kirilli's corpse.

She shifted the woman in her arms. Something had to be done with her..

"No," Judita said after a very long pause. "I don't know her."

But there was something in her tone that belied that.

"What do you know?" Cilka asked.

Judita's gaze seemed even more intense than it had a moment ago. She squared her shoulders, opened her hands as if she was going to call up some kind of light spell, and took one braced step forward.

The fog got even thinner. The smoky coal smell remained, but almost like an afterthought, as if everyone in the city had suddenly stopped using their coal-burners.

Yet the air had gotten colder. And the woman was slipping slowly out of Cilka's grasp.

"She shouldn't be here," Judita said.

"I know," Cilka said. "Something happened when you recreated the—"

"She walked through it," Judita said. "She walked through the past into our present."

Maybe, Cilka wanted to say, but didn't. Maybe the woman had walked through, but more than that happened. Kirilli had run away. Kirilli who, a moment earlier, had been a corpse, lying in his own blood, a corpse that had been on its stomach for *hours.*

And now he was alive.

"Walking through," Judita said, "that took magic."

Cilka knew that the change was magically caused. She didn't need that part explained.

"It took a lot of magic," Judita said. "More than I have. I have no idea how she did it."

"That's not what you know." Cilka adjusted the woman in her arms, bending her tiring knees. Cilka needed to know what Judita was thinking before deciding what to do with this woman.

All that Cilka knew right now was that she couldn't leave the woman with the watchmen or put her in the constabulary's jail cells. That might lead to more chaos.

Cilka didn't want to bring a doctor to her, because a doctor might find a way to repair the jaw or give the woman the use of her hands.

"She shouldn't be here," Judita repeated.

"I *know*," Cilka said.

"No, you don't." Judita's skin had gone a grayish pale that had nothing to do with the fog. "You don't understand at all. Her kind, we wiped them out."

Cilka blinked. "We...what?"

"Not me. Not you," Judita said. "On Dorovich, when they invaded. We defeated them. We wiped them out."

Judita sounded like a crazy woman. She wasn't talking about Qavner. She was talking about *Dorovich*. The continent. The Qavnerian Protectorate only covered part of the continent. So why was Judita saying "we"?

The woman slipped. Cilka nearly dropped her.

"We have to do something with her," Cilka said. "I can't hold her much longer."

Part of her hoped that Judita would do a small spell, something to help Cilka's flagging strength. Because Cilka only had a few choices now: she could keep holding the woman until she toppled over, she could set the woman down again, or send Judita to one of the watchmen a few blocks away for help.

But really, Cilka didn't want to send Judita away. Cilka didn't want to be alone with this woman.

Cilka was afraid of her—and she couldn't remember the last time she had been afraid of anything.

"Yes," Judita said in a very flat voice. "We have to do something with her."

"I hope you have ideas," Cilka said. "Because I—"

"We have to kill her," Judita said.

"What? No," Cilka said. "We need to figure out how to contain her, and then we need to learn what she knows, what she was after. We have to figure out where she came from and—"

"All very good investigative questions," Judita said. "But you don't investigate these people. You slaughter them."

That flat tone didn't even sound like Judita. It sounded odd, as if she was speaking from far away.

The same way that this woman's voice had sounded when she had been shouting at Kirilli.

Cilka looked sideways at the woman's face. Her eyelashes were fluttering. She was waking up and once she did, she was going to do something.

Or maybe she was already doing something now. Maybe that was why Judita sounded so far away.

Cilka wrapped her arm around the woman's chest, holding her up. With her other hand, Cilka grabbed the woman's shattered wrist, and yanked up against the shackles.

She screamed before collapsing against Cilka.

Cilka staggered backwards, barely able to keep standing. Her knees buckled, and she had to will herself to remain upright.

Judita moved forward and grabbed the woman under the arms, mouth turned downward in distaste. Judita clearly didn't want to touch her.

Judita's assistance took some of the pressure off Cilka, and she was able to stand up. But she didn't remove her hand from the remains of the woman's wrist. Cilka kept pulling upward, knowing that she was doing even more damage than she had done before, and not caring.

The woman had nearly magicked them, or something. She was sly, this one, and dangerous, just like Judita had said.

"You need to tell me how to contain her," Cilka said.

"There is no containing her," Judita said. "You saw that. And our people—we're no longer able to handle someone like her."

It was amazing the lengths she went to avoid the word *magical*. Someone *magical* like her.

But Judita was right. The woman had done something to change what they saw. The corpse was gone now. Kirilli was alive. He had run off.

Cilka did not know—did not even expect—that a thaumaturge could raise the dead. She had had no idea that was possible and if she was honest with herself, it scared her greatly.

She had been nervous when she called in Judita. Now Cilka was terrified.

"We had to have dealt with people like her in the past," Cilka said. "There has to be ways of imprisoning her."

Judita peered at her around the woman's shoulder. The woman's jaw was swelling and her skin was turning an odd shade of purplish gray.

"I don't know of any," Judita said, again in that flat tone.

Cilka wondered if that tone meant that Judita was lying. It certainly didn't sound like her.

"We don't have time to research them," Cilka said more to herself than to Judita. "Surely, there's someone who knows what to do."

Judita shook her head slowly. "I didn't realize there were people like her in Dorovich. I don't know if anyone knew that. I would have heard."

But Cilka was no longer certain Judita would have heard. Cilka had the odd feeling that she couldn't trust Judita at all—a woman she had routinely trusted with her life.

Was that lack of trust something this strange woman was causing, the way she made voices sound far away and the way she made corpses rise? Or was there something else going on entirely?

"Can you hold her?" Judita asked.

"I can hold her upright," Cilka said, "but I can't move her from here."

"All right." Judita let go of the woman, and Cilka staggered again. She nearly lost her grip on the woman's shattered wrist. "Set her down."

"On the ground?" Cilka said. "If I do, she could choke on the blood from her shattered jaw."

"Then put her in a position where that won't happen," Judita said, as if that was something easy to do.

Judita was backing away, and as she did so, she wiped her hands on her robe.

"You can't leave me here with her," Cilka said.

"I'm not leaving," Judita said as she bent over and picked up the knife.

CHAPTER
SEVEN

The lightstone lantern's illumination was so bright it reflected off both walls of the hallway. Gussie doubted the lightstone sconces had ever been this bright. If they had, the cleaning staff would have noticed the old scuff marks and they would have seen that the filth from the city itself outlined the areas where portraits, paintings, miniatures, and tapestries had hung.

It felt like walking among ghosts. Or maybe stepping on corpses, as much of the hallway was littered with broken bits of precious items. As she stepped over piles of glassware and shards of vases, she realized that whoever had done this had shattered anything that could hold something.

Vases, intricately carved boxes, earthenware pitchers, glassware that was opaque in some way—all destroyed. Drawers forced open, and some tapestries—the ones she had loved that had pockets or extra thick centers, covered with yarn or extra weavings—ripped apart.

She couldn't mourn for any of it, even though part of her felt a prick of sadness every time she recognized something that could not be repaired.

What had happened here might end up being important. Or it might be a small coda to a large crime. If her father was dead, then all of this mattered only in the periphery.

If he was alive, well, then he would handle all of this. He would be heartbroken, but he would soldier on, because that was what he did.

She would support him, as she had done when her mother died. Gussie's father had managed to keep moving forward every single day, but he hadn't been the competent man she had counted on. Every now and then, he had stopped whatever he was doing and stared at nothing at all.

Gussie had enabled those moments. She had kept the staff away from him at those times, or she had walked him home from his office. A few times, she had gone to his partners, and asked them to take a little of the most difficult work away from him.

He had thought he had been clearheaded, but he had not been.

That would have to be a lesson to her. If she got through this —*when* she got through this—she would need to understand that at times, clarity would be sacrificed for expediency.

She passed room after room, opening doors before Zeitsev could stop her. He was behind her, picking his way across too, but the difference between them was that he would actually step into the rooms.

Some were perfectly preserved. Her mother's favorite parlor, with its rag rugs and comfortable furniture, was untouched.

Even the early samplers that Gussie and her sisters had made, before they all realized they had no talent for needlework, remained on the walls.

Her sisters. Gussie had given them no thought at all. She had three. When they had come of age, they had received their inheritance, which was both property and money. Two had married, and the other—Helia—well, she was as stubborn as Gussie.

All of her siblings were stubborn in their own way. And wealthy in their own right. They had all received the inheritance from their father, and had also gotten a token amount from the Kirilli family trust.

Gussie also had a small income from her grandparents' estate. She had been her grandfather's favorite, and he had bestowed the income on her, so long as she never told anyone where the money came from.

He had done so before his death, setting it up so that the money came from a trust that the estate managers never saw.

Should you marry, my girl, he had said, *I don't want some handsome young ambitious fellow to stifle that glorious mind of yours. And, in case you cannot tell, I don't want you to marry. Let your siblings carry on the bloodline. That's the work of a broodmare. You are no broodmare. You are special, my girl. This income will guarantee you remain special and will have all of the opportunities that I can give you.*

She had never taken advantage of those opportunities, at least not in the way her grandfather had wanted her to. She had floated free, untethered to a man, family, work, or anything meaningful. She had her charities, and little else.

Gussie opened another door to find a storage room she hadn't even known existed. It smelled of ginger and cloves and other spices she could not entirely identify, partly because a pile of spices and flour and sugar covered the floor near one of the shelves. Someone had knocked the food storage bins around, but the destruction in this room was small compared with the destruction in the family quarters.

With her left hand, she shoved the lantern into the room to illuminate the corners. Just more storage and a bit of breakage. Nothing more.

A footprint, outlined in flour, led out of the room. A man's boot, large with a distinctive tread. It seemed to exist all by itself, as if someone had hopped away from the destruction.

She backed out, and continued down the hall. The destruction was easing as the hallway narrowed. The flooring changed from slate to uneven wooden slats, and the walls were not painted.

The back of the house. For a moment, she had thought that the person who had done this damage hadn't come here, but then she saw whispers of that flour-covered footprint heading toward the kitchen.

The hallway contained a slightly greasy odor of roast beef, probably from dinner the previous night. Food smells got trapped here, but usually, they dissipated as new food smells were created.

That there was no breakfast odor—no smoked herring or white-fish, no eggs or bacon, no bread, no cinnamon cakes—bothered her deeply. She had been coming here to join her father for breakfast.

Instead, that lower layer of stench had followed her in here. Or perhaps it simply coated her nostrils, supplanting any other smell.

The nervousness she thought she had put behind her rose up again, and she mentally beat it into place. She glanced over her shoulder to see if Zeitsev was still following her.

He emerged from her mother's sewing room, even more hunched than he had been before, as if this journey—this search—was tiring him. When he saw Gussie looking at him, he touched the brim of his cap in acknowledgement.

Somewhere along the way, he had realized that she didn't want to talk. At first, it had been because she didn't want his emotions to contaminate hers, but now, she had the odd sense that she needed to remain quiet.

She didn't want to startle anyone.

She rounded the corner, and nearly walked into a closed door. She stopped, startled. She had had no idea that there was a door here, although it made some kind of sense.

This was where the kitchen officially began, even though she had to go just a bit farther in the narrow hallway to get to the two large ovens, the cast iron ranges with their firepits underneath, and the long mixing, cutting, and sorting table that centered the entire room.

Part of her had been looking forward to arriving there. The kitchen, with its myriad heavenly smells, had always seemed like a safe haven to her.

That the haven was now barred sent a shiver through her.

She didn't even try the door. Instead, she turned one last time to see Zeitsev. But he wasn't in the hallway.

She was going to have to go back and get him. She did not want to go into the kitchen alone.

Just as she was about to start back toward him, he emerged

from the storage area. He was looking down at the white footprint, hopping its way toward the kitchen.

She looked down again. She had been so startled by the closed door, she hadn't checked to see if that footprint had continued forward.

It had. Half of it still appeared underneath the closed door. Presumably the other half was inside the kitchen corridor itself.

Gussie continued toward Zeitsev. He had never served indoors, so he had no idea that a closed kitchen door had never happened, not during Gussie's entire life.

She didn't want to tell him in front of that door, either, just in case someone was on the other side.

She put a finger to her lips, then reached his side. He smelled sharply of sweat, and that was when she realized he was even more terrified than she was.

"The door shouldn't be closed," she whispered.

His eyes got wider, and he nodded, once, then took a deep breath, as if bracing himself. His nerves would affect her, if she wasn't careful. So she walked back to the kitchen door, with purpose, the lantern now in her right hand.

She realized she didn't even know if the door pushed in or out. She glanced at the hinges, and saw that there weren't any.

Pocket doors. Of course. She set the lantern down, and stuck her right index finger in the holder, then shoved the doors sideways as quickly and as hard as she could.

They squealed. Of course, they did. They hadn't been used in a generation.

She froze. The people who had closed the doors would hear that. And they had probably planned it that way. She had a choice now: she could go forward or she could run back down the corridor with Zeitsev, and hope they got away.

That wasn't a choice. Now that she had made it this far, her fear was turning to fury.

Someone had destroyed the interior of her father's house. That someone was going to pay.

Zeitsev hadn't caught up to her yet. She glanced over her shoulder. He was frozen in place, just like she had been for a moment. Only it was clear that his fear was holding him prisoner.

She didn't have time for him. She didn't have time for any of this. She needed to know what happened and why.

She leaned forward just a little, and listened. Nothing. No footsteps, no whispers, no creaks and moans of the floorboards as someone stepped on them, trying to be silent.

Unless whoever it was happened to be very good at hiding, there was no one in the kitchen.

She picked up the lantern which, if she needed it, could also be a weapon. Then she lifted her chin and strode into the kitchen corridor, like her mother used to do when something had gone wrong with a meal.

Unlike the rest of the manor, the sconces here remained in place. Their light came on as she walked by, and the lantern light slowly faded, just like it was supposed to.

The air smelled odd.

This smell was making her lip curl, and putting her on edge. Something about it was almost feral, wild, a stench that she associated with the worst parts of Trinovante, where garbage covered the streets, and the closely built apartment towers lacked plumbing to handle the demands of the tenants.

The stench got worse the deeper into the corridor she went. Her breath was coming shallowly, partly because of the smell, and partly because she was afraid of what it portended.

But she kept moving until she rounded the final corner.

A wave of heat hit her. The fires in the oven had burned out, but only recently. The ovens glowed, but not the dark red she'd seen on feast days. The ovens were cooling, a pattern she recognized from her childhood.

The remaining heat had an oily feel, which instantly coated her skin. And buried in that heat was even more stink, the smell of burning meat.

The wide table that covered the entire room was empty. Nothing sat on top of it, not food, not cut vegetables, not bread.

Nothing except crumbs and crumpled bits of something brown, something that looked like curled hair.

Pots sat on the ranges, but water wasn't boiling in them. The smell didn't come from the pots, although the bottoms of at least two of them looked like they had been burned by a high flame.

She was about to go in deeper when she saw the first pair of feet, splayed outward at odd angles.

Part of her wanted to turn around, but the rest of her needed to know if those feet belonged to her father. The shoes said the feet belonged to a man, but the shoes were scuffed, something her father's shoes never were.

"Miss!"

Zeitsev had followed her after all.

"We need to leave and get the constabulary," he said.

She didn't turn around. "You go," she said.

"Miss, beg pardon, but ya dinna want ta do this."

She had no idea what she didn't want to do, except that she didn't want to ask him what he meant.

She finished rounding the corner, near the feet, and she stopped. It took a moment for her brain to register what she saw.

She had found the staff—at least morning staff. Micah, the butler, who had been with the family since she was a child, was sprawled on the floor, his head twisted at an odd angle.

A footmen had fallen against one of the ovens, his usually pristine waistcoat smoking slightly.

He, she realized, was probably source of the burned meat smell.

Ten members of the staff were all tied to each other. Two of them had been tied to the legs of the table, apparently keeping the entire group in place. Or they had once, since they were dead, their heads either bent forward or back, but all of them with copious amounts of blood on their uniforms. Drying blood. Blood that had reached and seeped into the floorboards.

Blood, that had, apparently, come from the slits in their necks.

Even more bodies were sprawled along the floor.

She had known half of them all of her life. The cook, who insisted on being called Cook, instead of by her name. (*Me name is for me family, miss. I be Cook here, and don't ye forget it.*) Micah, who had always been so kind to her when Gussie had ended up in parts of the house that didn't concern her. Lizet, who ran the maid staff with an iron fist. Her hair was frizzed, and draped around her face, something Gussie had never seen.

The others, in various states of disarray, from clothing to hair to their feet and shoes. They were the younger men, the footmen and the hall boys. She didn't know most of them. They'd been hired after she left.

Like the maids—as she was guessing from their clothing. And the assistant cooks.

This was a slaughter. She had no idea how it could have happened. There were so many of them. But they had been killed.

Still, it would have taken more than one person to do this—all of the damage and all of the death. More than the possessor of the single footprint.

Then she let out a small breath.

Her father wasn't here. The staff was dead—everyone who worked inside the building—but no outdoor staff. No grooms, no chauffeurs, no gardeners.

She looked over her shoulder.

Zeitsev stood on the other side of the table, so that he couldn't see the bodies. His skin had turned an odd shade of coppery green. He looked like a man who was trying hard not to be sick.

"I thought I told you to go get the constabulary," she said.

"I canna leave ya, Miss," he said.

She raised her head once, nodded, and almost told him, in a fatuous sort of way, that she wouldn't be alone.

But she didn't say it. She felt a little guilty for even thinking it.

They were gone, all of them, these people who cushioned her father's everyday life. They had been killed in his service.

And he was missing.

She let out a small sigh, astonished that she wasn't upset. Maybe she would be later.

"All right," she said to Zeitsev. "You shall drive me to the nearest constabulary."

Zeitsev looked relieved. He needed to leave here. She probably did too, but she didn't feel ready.

She looked at the kitchen she had once loved.

Whoever she found at the constabulary had to be worthy of an investigation involving her father.

An investigation that, she knew, could still go very, very wrong.

EIGHT

Cilka's arms were getting tired, particularly the arm pulling up on the woman's broken wrist. She was unconscious, heavy against Cilka. Cilka's legs were so tired, and she was lightheaded, either from the difficulty holding the woman or from the conversation she'd been having with Judita or from the fog, which was thinning and had lost its noxious odor.

Now the noxious odor was coming from the unconscious woman. She smelled of blood, mostly, and sweat and something sharp and spicy Cilka had never smelled before.

Judita hefted the knife, as if she was testing its weight. It looked different than it had in Kirilli's back. It was watery almost, as if it had lost solidity. Or maybe that was just an illusion, based on the bright shiny silver color of the knife and the wavy pattern of its design.

"Put that down, Judita," Cilka said, with as much force as she could muster.

Judita didn't even seem to hear her. Judita held the knife in the flat of her hand, continuing to bounce it up and down ever so slightly as if she expected its heft to change. It didn't. Nothing changed.

The fog started moving in again. The movement was noticeable. A moment earlier, the fog had been thin enough to see the financial buildings a block away, huddling together as if they were cold.

Now, the buildings were not visible, and the fog was growing thicker and whiter. Near the knife, the fog had regained its burned yellow color. The smell was starting to come back. Not just the coal-stink, which Cilka was used to, but the rotten odor that made her lips curl.

"This knife," Judita said, looking down on it, almost talking to it. "This knife wasn't made here."

Cilka could have told her that. Cilka had never seen a knife like it, and she had seen a lot of weaponry in her career.

The woman twitched ever so slightly, and the movement made Cilka's knees buckle again. She nearly dropped the woman.

"Judita," Cilka said. "I can't hold her any longer."

She regretted the words the moment they left her mouth.

Judita's head snapped upward, and she whirled toward Cilka. Judita gripped the knife in her fist and with a single movement, stabbed upwards, into the woman's chest.

She let out an *ooof* of air. It whistled. Her eyes fluttered and opened wide.

"You..." she said, her voice barely strong enough to be audible. "You do not..."

Cilka tried to move the woman away, but now that she was

awake, she was fighting. And she shouldn't have been, because Cilka was trying to save her, although she wasn't entirely sure why.

Judita hadn't let go of the knife. She yanked it out of the woman with such force that her entire body jerked. Blood gushed as the blade came out.

"You..." she whispered.

Cilka had the sense that the woman wasn't trying to tell Judita anything. Cilka had the sense that the woman was trying to curse Judita.

Judita stabbed the woman again, this time bringing the knife down her breastbone toward the center of her chest.

Cilka thought she heard the blade hit something. A shudder ran along Judita's arm, confirming that.

She pulled the blade out and stabbed again. The blade chunked into the woman's flesh.

"Stop it!" Cilka said. "Stop!"

She didn't want to be a part of this, and yet she was. The sound was horrible, the way the woman's body jerked and twitched was horrible.

The blood stench grew. Cilka's arm, the one she had wrapped under the woman's armpits, had become slimy wet, probably with blood.

Cilka had never been party to a murder before. She had never held the victim upright; she had never pulled an arm back and caused extreme pain, leaving the victim mostly unconscious.

That thought made her drop the woman's wrist. Her damaged arm swung and Judita screamed—not the scream of the frightened or startled—but a scream of rage.

She stepped backwards, then saw the damaged arm swinging

at her, and let out a small growl. She moved in again, arm upraised, knife bloodless and glinting.

How could it be bloodless when the woman was gushing great gouts of blood?

"You don't belong here," Judita shouted and stabbed downward.

This time, Cilka managed to move the woman out of the way of the blade, for what good that did. Because Cilka's legs twisted, and the woman's body weight grew, and she fell forward. Cilka fell with the woman, toppling onto the street where Kirilli's body had been.

Cilka scrambled upwards, afraid Judita would accidentally stab her. Judita's eyes were glazed. As the woman tumbled, Judita followed, looking like she was going to climb on top of the woman and stab again.

"Judita!" Cilka shouted. "Stop! You have to stop!"

Judita didn't stop, though. She hunched over the woman, bringing the knife back to stab again. Cilka braced herself, despite the pain in her legs, and kicked Judita in the stomach, sending her backwards into the puddle and the pile of horse dung.

The knife clattered, falling back into the position it had been in moments before.

Judita sat there, looking stunned. Cilka stood over the woman, her clothes a mass of blood. The woman's face was grayish white, eyes slitted and partially open.

She was dead.

They would find nothing out about this woman ever, because Judita had murdered her in cold blood.

But was it cold blood? Or did the woman really pose a

threat? She seemed to. If Cilka had gone after the woman, it would have been self-defense. But Cilka hadn't. She had held the woman while Judita had attacked.

The yellow in the fog was receding once more, just as the fog was. The sun finally appeared, pale grayish white against a half-hidden sky. The buildings were returning, and it seemed to Cilka that they were leaning forward, as if they wanted to see the action.

Judita let out a shaky breath. Her gaze moved from the dead woman to Cilka's face.

Blood droplets covered Judita's chin and cheeks. Spray decorated her eyes and forehead. The pattern looked almost deliberate, as if someone had painted her fury onto her skin.

"I had to do that," she said, her voice shaking. "You know that."

But Cilka didn't know that. She didn't know that at all.

NINE

Kirilli ran. He hadn't run in decades, and yet he was managing it now, terrified he was going to trip. His legs ached, and his chest ached worse and he was wondering if he was going to have some kind of seizure. Maybe his heart would just stop, or maybe it would pound its way through his chest.

The pea-souper seemed to be fading as he got out of the financial district. The familiar streets wound in their little curves, around the most expensive houses with the largest properties.

The light was strange. He had left the office at twilight, but this looked brighter somehow. And wrong.

Everything felt wrong.

His breath wheezed out of his lungs. He was afraid he was going to be sick, but he didn't dare stop.

Someone had distracted the stranger. Someone who shouldn't have been there, according to the stranger.

Kirilli hadn't seen anyone, but then, he really hadn't been looking. He had concentrated on grabbing the satchel he had almost lost, and then on getting home.

That stranger—had Kirilli seen a knife in that stranger's hand?

Kirilli wheezed so hard that he doubled over. He couldn't run anymore, and he wasn't that far from his home.

He grabbed the pole of a lightstone streetlamp, feeling the shimmer of lightstone power run through his body. The streetlamp was holding him, but it was also illuminating him. If that stranger came after him, they would see Kirilli under the light, like a theatrical spotlight, as if Kirilli were on some stage somewhere, about to command the attention of the entire room.

He had to move. It didn't matter how tired he was, how his legs felt like jelly and how his entire body didn't feel like his anymore.

His back ached, just below his ribcage, and it wasn't one of those dull aches. It was a sharp, stabbing ache, the kind that came after something had sliced the skin.

But nothing had touched him. No one had touched him.

He made himself let go of the streetlamp. He stepped outside of the circle of light, and peered back into the fog. He didn't see anyone.

His heart wasn't slowing down. It was still racing, even though he had stopped. His mouth was dry.

He hadn't been this terrified in years.

He needed to get home. He would put the satchels and the maps and all of the documents and artifacts in the safe in his office. Only he and Gussie knew how to open it. Only he and Gussie even knew where it was.

Then he blinked. The fog was lifting, and the sun was in the east, not the west.

He had no idea how that could be.

But he knew what lost time meant. It meant there was magic in the air.

He didn't know how he could have lost time, but he had to move on the assumption that he had.

Which meant that Gussie might already be at his house.

His heart rate spiked, and he gasped in pain. What if the stranger knew where Kirilli lived? What if the stranger knew the side paths to getting there? What if the stranger went after Gussie?

But Kirilli had checked: the stranger wasn't behind him, and when he fled, the stranger had been dealing with someone else— the person who shouldn't have been there.

Surely, the stranger would know that Kirilli was going home, but maybe the stranger didn't know where Kirilli lived.

Which didn't seem likely since the stranger knew that Kirilli had been a professor, and that Kirilli usually carried a single, more expensive satchel.

If the stranger did indeed know where Kirilli lived, then Kirilli only had a short time to get home, stash these satchels, and leave.

And he would leave, maybe with Gussie at his side. He would flee—not to one of his other houses, because if the stranger knew about this one, surely, he would know about the others.

No, Kirilli would go to Serebro and rent a room.

Or maybe not. Because the stranger might expect him to go to Serebro or the Academy, to talk with the other Regents.

Kirilli staggered forward, feeling not himself. Maybe it was the run. Maybe it was the lost time. Maybe the stranger had done something to him, something that Kirilli wasn't completely aware of yet.

He was only a few blocks away from his home, though, so if he hurried, he would get there.

But he couldn't run.

So he walked quickly down the familiar streets, seeing lights on inside the large houses that he passed. Not evening lights, which usually glowed in front parlors and sitting rooms, but daytime lights, lights for a foggy day, in the morning rooms and kitchens.

That odd sense that he was missing something more than time, that this entire day was unreal somehow, caught him, but he wouldn't let it stop him.

He needed to keep moving, so he did, walking as quickly as he could, even though his breath was whistling in his throat. His chest hurt from his attempt at breathing, but that slice in his back—whatever *that* was—that pain had grown sharper and sharper.

He couldn't reach around to touch it, not with satchels under one arm and in the other hand. But something was going on back there. There was the slice-ache, and then there was the feeling that his entire lower back was smeared with blood.

He didn't want to think about that, even though he was having trouble clearing it from his mind. He kept seeing flashes of a blood pool, right near his nose, and horse dung, not too far away. Twice, he'd had to shake his head to clear it—and that helped, sort of.

Finally, he reached his street. His house stood in the very

center which was usually a point of pride for him. But the house looked strange to him on this odd day.

There should have been lights in the fog, whether parlor lights or sitting room lights or kitchen lights or morning lights.

He saw none of them.

His daughter's carriage, the one he paid for, stood in the drive just in front of the carriage house, with the horses still in their harnesses. Zeitsev, her driver, was better than that with the animals. That was one reason that Kirilli (and not Gussie) had hired him.

Zeitsev usually didn't leave the animals unattended, and he certainly wouldn't have left them rigged up, so someone could steal the carriage. The carriage wasn't even hidden.

Maybe someone had left the carriage there, so that they could escape easily.

He didn't know why the word *escape* had come to him. Maybe because he was running (staggering) from that stranger.

Whatever the reason, it felt good to be home.

Or at least, it did, until he ventured up the sidewalk to the front door, and saw that it had been completely smashed.

The carvings his grandfather had made specially to honor the history of the Kirilli family had been shattered. Kirilli could see nothing of them. The doors were closed though, although someone had smashed the lock.

He ran up the stairs, and crawled inside the ruined doors, startled that he could move so easily when running had been hard before. He tightened his grip on the satchels, and carefully picked his way across the floor.

Everything of value in the front entry was destroyed. The carvings, the tapestries, the statues—all of the wonderful small glass items his father had brought back from the Razbitay Mountains—destroyed or stolen.

Kirilli's heart was in his throat. He had felt sick only a few moments earlier—physically sick—but that was easing now that he was home. He didn't feel physically sick; he felt heartbroken.

This entire manor had displayed his family's collections, built over more than a hundred years. The Kirillis who came before him had been explorers, adventurers, people who *discovered* things.

He had abandoned that tradition for numbers because he loved them, but he had still honored everything his family had done. He had donated items to museums (oh, thank all that was good that he had donated to museums because that meant some items hadn't been destroyed), and volunteered other items to scholars for study.

He had managed to save countless items in the family Vault, items that he should have turned in during the Thaumaturgical Purges, but he did not. He preserved them. Only Gussie knew where they were.

Gussie.

He looked around the ruined house. Her carriage had been outside. The horses were impatient. Which meant Gussie was here.

He hovered for a moment between the different hallways, uncertain where, exactly, to go. Should he search for Gussie? Or secure the satchels first?

Kirilli glanced down the other hallways. He couldn't hear anything, but ever since he had seen that stranger, Kirilli's hearing hadn't worked as well as usual. At first he had thought it was due to his concentration—he'd done his best to focus on escape—but now that he was in the house, he noted that every sound seemed like it had come from very far away.

He didn't know what that meant, exactly, except that Gussie might have been moving in one of the other rooms and he couldn't hear her.

His back ached, and the satchels felt very heavy.

He needed to put them in the safe—if he could. If only he could get to the Vault. Maybe if Zeitsev and Gussie were all right, they could drive him there later.

He made himself hurry down the hallway to his office, hoping he would see Gussie, or Zeitsev, or anyone on the staff. No one was around, but maybe they were fighting whoever had done this damage. Or maybe the constabulary had already come and everyone was gathered in the gardens or the kitchen, figuring out what to do next.

Kirilli tried very hard not to see the damage around him. He didn't focus on the broken glass or the shattered wood or the bits of statues. Kirilli wasn't sure his heart could take all of that loss.

He finally reached his study door and cringed when he saw the exact same kind of destruction he had seen on the front doors. These doors were irreplaceable. He couldn't just hire someone to carve the images again, even though they had been drawn and photographed and written up in countless books and journals.

The artist who had carved the doors had a special touch. In the right light, the bas-relief images would almost come alive. Sometimes, at night with the study door open, Kirilli thought he had seen the heads move and heard rustling sounds, almost like they were whispering to each other.

He had told no one that, although his late wife—Gussie's mother—refused to go to the study at night because she said that the faces terrified her. He had let her believe that what she had seen was just a product of her wild imagination, and nothing more.

He had always regretted that.

He stepped over the damage in that door as well, got halfway inside the room, and stopped. The air shivered with malevolence, almost like a presence remained here, something that was going to destroy him too.

The malevolence had destroyed almost everything in the room, but hadn't managed to move the ironwood desk. There was a trick to that desk, one Kirilli had kept close. He doubted even Gussie knew of it, because he had been waiting to teach her.

The safe, also made of ironwood, was below that desk, built into the floor, and reinforced.

But he didn't want to go farther into the room, not with that malevolence in there.

Maybe he was making this all up. But he didn't think so. The ache in his back had grown worse. His skin was sticky, as if it had been coated with something. And his heart ached, not just from the destruction, but also from everything he had seen.

He couldn't go into the study. He pulled his leg back into the hallway.

He had to find his daughter, but he wasn't going to call for her until he was away from the study.

He didn't want whatever was in there to get to her too.

They were picking their way out the way they came in, one cautious step at a time. Gussie took the lead. Zeitsev didn't seem like himself. The last thing she wanted to see was a man losing his breakfast right in front of her.

She mentally shook her head at herself. She had just seen the bodies of people she had known all her life. They died horribly, and that hadn't made her sick. But she was afraid that Zeitsev's nausea would infect her.

Maybe it would make the deaths real to her. The smell and mess, that hadn't convinced her. She felt separated from herself, as if she was now a completely different person.

Maybe she was, after this day.

Or maybe she was just realistic. They were dead.

There was a chance—a small one—that her father was alive.

Gussie led Zeitsev through the kitchen hallway. They had left the door to the main hallway half-open, and she slipped through it, glancing over her shoulder at Zeitsev.

He was staggering along, right hand out, trailing the wall for balance. His skin was still that grayish-green color, and his head was bowed.

Zeitsev clearly wasn't the man her father had thought he was. That Gussie had thought he was. Zeitsev had been fine at the beginning of this crisis, but he was doing poorly now.

And then she frowned.

Maybe he had known the staff—not as *staff*, but as friends.

She felt something twinge inside her. Her throat closed, and her eyes pricked, and she willed that feeling to stop. She would not cry right now. She did not dare. She would have no reaction until she had time for a reaction, and she did not have time for it right now.

She would have time later—days later, maybe, but later.

Something rustled ahead of her, followed by the clatter of wood and the tinkling of glass.

Someone else was in the house, someone who was not moving cautiously.

She waved her other hand behind her, hoping Zeitsev saw the movement. She didn't want to tell him that another person was in the house; she wanted him to be quiet, though, even if he could do nothing else.

Within just a few steps, she reached the branch where this hallway turned toward the parlors or the study. And there, in the half-light of a dying lightstone, her father stood, clutching one satchel and hugging another to his torso with his other arm.

He looked wonderful, in his wool coat, his regular trousers, his slightly portly self.

For a moment, he shimmered, as if he wasn't quite there. A

trick of the light, maybe. Or maybe, since she had wanted to see him, she did.

That would explain how normal he looked.

For that reason, she didn't call out to him. Instead, she stepped into his line of sight, figuring if her eyes were playing tricks on her, then this movement would certainly stop that—and she would see the person before her clearly.

"Gussie?" Her father's voice sounded breathless, gurgly, as if he were speaking through a window.

"Papa!" she said and ran to him, throwing her arms around him. He wobbled a little, and almost fell. The satchel under his arm slipped, but he managed to catch it with his hand.

He wrapped his other arm around her, though, and pulled her close. The satchel he held against his chest felt like a barrier between them. His coat scratched her chin, his arm was strong around her. She couldn't smell his familiar scent though, and for that she blamed the horrors she had just walked through.

"What happened here?" her father asked.

"I thought you knew," she said. "I thought maybe you were here when it all took place."

"No." He let her go and then leaned back so that he could see her face. His face was translucent, the color of the fog.

She let her hands drop. They felt odd, almost sticky. She looked down at them. They were coated in something reddish black.

Blood. They were coated in blood.

"Papa, turn around," she said.

"Gussie, there's no—"

"Turn around," she repeated. "I think you're bleeding."

"Oh." The word was mostly air. "I wondered."

He turned. The entire back of his coat was soaked. How could someone lose that much blood and still be standing?

"Papa, we have to get you to a chair," she said. "In your study, perhaps."

"No." He sounded almost frightened. "Do not go there. Something is in there."

Something?

"You mean someone," she said.

"No," he said. "Some*thing*."

She thought she had felt something in that study—a tingle, an expectation—and terror. Yes, she'd felt a lot of terror, but she had attributed it to the destruction of the manor.

And that tingle...something about it had made her think of her grandfather. She wouldn't have called him a something.

Her father peered at her, as if he thought she hadn't understood him. He leaned toward her, and added, "There's something wrong in this house."

"Yes." Zeitsev spoke from behind them, his voice shaky. "The staff has been slaughtered."

"Slaughtered?" Her father stood up straight and looked over Gussie's shoulder at Zeitsev. The news clearly startled and upset her father.

"Tied up. Killed. In the kitchen." Zeitsev's voice grew stronger with each word. "Are you sure you don't know what happened to them?"

Her father shook his head. "I left work and..." He looked at Gussie, a measuring look, that protective look he had used many times before. "And then I came here."

"Why were you at work all night, Papa?" she asked.

"I wasn't. I hadn't been. I left at the usual time..." But his voice trailed off as if his own words surprised him.

He shook his head slightly, almost a denial of what he had said. His frown grew.

"I left at the usual time," he repeated.

Gussie had trouble drawing breath, not because she was tired or injured, but because he was scaring her. The bodies, they hadn't scared her. This place had, and now her father.

He blinked at her. He looked even fainter than he had before. She could see the wall through his face.

He shoved the satchels at her.

"Take these," he said.

She took them as he shoved them, mostly because she didn't have a choice. They were heavier than his usual satchel but frailer, as if they might come apart in her hands. And the handles felt weird—one handle slick with blood or sweat, the other dry and cold.

He watched her hold them, that frown almost all that was left of his face.

"Protect them, Gussie," he said, his voice even more echoey and far away.

"Protect them how?" she asked.

"The Vault," he said, sounding even farther away. "And the safe. You know the safe?"

"Yes," she said, wishing she didn't have to acknowledge it out loud. Her father trusted Zeitsev, but she didn't. Not on something that concerned money or the safe.

She didn't trust any of the staff that way. And then she shuddered.

The staff was gone.

She wouldn't let herself focus on that.

She started to reach for her father, but the damn satchels got in the way. He had been so concerned about them, though, that she didn't want to let them go.

"We need to get you some help," she said, flailing her arms with those heavy satchels just a bit.

Her father shook his head. "I'm not sure there is help."

His gaze met hers. Did she see fear? In her father? That wasn't something she was used to. Had she ever seen it? She wasn't sure. She didn't think so.

"Right now, though," he said, "you need to take the satchels away from here. *You* need to get away from here."

"What's going on, Papa?" she asked.

He shook his head again. "I don't know, exactly." His voice sounded so small, so distant, and he was almost clear. "I don't know, Gussie. Something bad. Something I hadn't thought possible, but your grandfather did. He used to say…"

And then her father's voice faded to nothingness. His lips moved, but she couldn't hear him.

"Papa?" she said, the panic breaking through. "I can't hear you. Please, speak up, Papa."

He looked confused, as if he couldn't hear her either. He looked to one side as if he heard something else.

She wasn't going to let that break her concentration.

"Papa!" she said, trying to get his attention.

He was frowning, leaning toward her. His body was just an outline now. Through him, she could see the barren wall, with its nails and hangers and bits of the picture frames.

He was vanishing.

People didn't vanish.

"*Papa*!" she shouted.

He got so close to her that she should have felt the warmth of his skin and the pressure of his breath. Instead, she felt a slight breeze and nothing more.

"Go," he whispered. "Leave. Take the satchels."

His mouth continued to move, but the words got lost again. She couldn't hear anything.

"Please repeat that, Papa. About the satchels."

He shook his head, then waved his hand. The hand seemed to brush her sleeve, but it really didn't. Not at all. She couldn't feel him.

Not the satchel, he seemed to be saying. She thought she recognized what his mouth was telling her. *The*..."maps. Compare the maps. There's something important..."

And the words vanished again. She wasn't even sure what he meant by maps, but she supposed it would be clear at some point.

"Come with us, Papa," she said grabbing for his arm. "Please, come—"

Run! he mouthed. *I'll be okay*.

But he didn't seem to be. Nothing seemed to be okay.

"He wants us ta leave," Zeitsev said. "We hafta go. If they chased him here, then they'll get us. And do to us what they done ta the staff."

"Did they chase you, Papa?" she asked.

Her father shrugged. The movement was more of a disturbance in the air than anything she could see clearly.

Go! he mouthed. *Please. Go.*

Then he made a shoving gesture with his hands. But she didn't want to leave him.

She couldn't leave him.

Zeitsev grabbed her arm and pulled her away. She stumbled over some broken wood, and then slipped on a tapestry.

She caught herself, nearly falling on top of everything, and then turned back to her father. She would pull him out of here if it took everything she had.

Only he wasn't there. He was gone as if he had never been.

There was no way he could have gotten past her, no way he could still be in the hallway either. He had to have gone back into the study.

She peered through the door, and saw nothing and no one. The air tingled like it had before. Her father wasn't there.

He wasn't anywhere.

She almost thought he was a ghost, but he couldn't have been because she was still holding the satchels. Satchels she had never seen before.

She looked down at her hands. They were still dark with blood.

Her father's blood.

What had just happened?

Her stomach flipped on itself.

"Papa," she said. "Papa, come back."

Zeitsev pulled on her arm again. "Please, Miss Augusta. Please. Something bad's happening here. We hafta leave."

She let him drag her away from the room, and down the hallway.

Something bad wasn't just happening there now. Something

bad *had* happened there. During the night or early in the morning. And if she didn't get out soon, something else bad would happen, to her or Zeitsev or both of them.

"Okay," she said, her heart aching, her voice trembling. "Let's go."

CHAPTER
ELEVEN

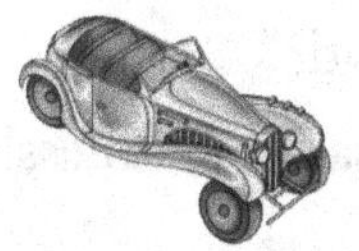

What a mess. Cilka had come here to figure out what caused Kirilli's death. Numbers of people had seen him, lying on the street, his arm out, a knife in his back.

But now, he was gone, and there was another person on the street, with multiple stab wounds, a tall thin woman who clearly was not Kirilli.

And Judita and Cilka were covered in that woman's blood.

At least Cilka had sent the watchmen and the constabulary away. At least no one had seen the circumstances of that woman's death.

But Cilka would have to explain it. She would also have to figure out what to do with the corpse.

"This is a magic I do not understand," Cilka said, deliberately using the word *magic*.

Judita, still sitting on the street only yards from the woman's

111

body, winced when Cilka said the word, as if speaking the word was worse than actually murdering someone.

Cilka made herself take a deep calming breath. She was so furious that she might make mistakes if she didn't keep a tight control on herself.

Cilka continued, keeping her gaze on Judita's.

"Is this woman," Cilka said, waving her hand at the current corpse, "going to stay dead?"

"I hope so," Judita said breathlessly. Apparently, she wasn't working on staying calm.

"You don't know?" Cilka asked.

"Of course, I don't know," Judita said. "I'm not sure what happened in the first place."

She braced one hand on the street, and eased herself upward. She was older than Cilka realized. She had never seen Judita act like an old woman before.

Maybe she was just sore, the way she got up. Maybe the push backwards had hurt her.

Cilka stepped around the body. The woman had crumpled over herself into a heap of clothing. Her face was turned sideways so that Cilka could see those half-open eyes, but the rest of the woman looked smaller than it had before.

Her wrist—the one Cilka had destroyed—was bent at such an odd angle that it looked like the hand was on sideways.

"Did the knife cause this?" she asked. "Is it magical?"

"I don't know," Judita repeated with an edge in her voice. "The knife is..."

Her voice trailed off. Cilka raised her head and looked at the woman she had called friend—at least until the events of this morning.

"Is what?" Cilka asked. There was an edge in her voice as well, only she knew what that edge was.

It was fury. Complete and utter fury.

"Too light," Judita said. "I don't know what it's made of. Some kind of metal maybe. Or…"

Cilka wanted to slap her to make her finish her sentences. Judita didn't usually sound this unsure of anything.

"Or *what*?" Cilka asked.

"Or…some other material," Judita said. "Something we've never seen before."

Judita bent over and picked up the knife, hefting it again. Then she turned it, holding it at the spot where the hilt hit the blade.

"Take it," she said.

Cilka didn't want to. She was half afraid that she would touch it and go on a killing frenzy.

She told herself the idea was fanciful, but it wasn't really. Everything she'd seen this morning had been fanciful. Everything.

But she needed to know what was happening, and she had to trust Judita to get out of the way if Cilka tried to hurt her.

Cilka extended her hand, and slowly wrapped her fingers around the hilt. It was warm, the metal thin, like a filigree necklace, but her fingers didn't fit into the grooves. The knife was clearly made for someone else.

Judita let go of the knife. The loss of her hand barely made a difference. The knife was as light as paper, but perfectly balanced.

Cilka was tempted to touch the edge of the blade just to see how sharp it was, but she didn't. Technically, the blade should have been coated in blood. It looked clean, but that didn't mean it *was* clean.

Cilka hefted the knife, just like Judita had. Cilka now understood that hefting the knife wasn't something she was doing to see what the knife weighed, but because the knife was featherlight when it looked like it should be heavy.

"Well," Judita said with relief in her voice, "you didn't try to kill me."

"Did you think I would?" The fury in Cilka's voice startled her. She knew she was angry, but she hadn't realized just how deeply.

"I didn't know, honestly," Judita said.

"You were going to blame your killing frenzy on the *knife*?" Cilka asked, even though she had been willing to do that just moments before.

"Frenzy." Judita looked at her. The drying blood was growing dark, like spots on Judita's face—almost like a tattoo that had been made of her own fury. "I hadn't thought of it as a frenzy."

She lowered her voice, and looked down at the corpse.

"Cilka," she said quietly. "It wasn't a frenzy."

"It sure looked like one," Cilka said.

Judita shook her head. "It was fear. I know what that woman is."

"Are you ever going to tell me?" Cilka asked.

Judita nodded. "I'm going to have to now, since everything has changed."

Cilka didn't acknowledge that sentence. She wasn't sure what to say next. She crouched, and set the knife behind her, away from the dead woman just in case she did rise up and try to kill them.

Cilka's heart was pounding.

"What do we do with her?" she asked Judita.

"We cremate her," Judita said. "And soon."

Cilka looked at the corpse. The eyes were clouding over. The woman looked less malevolent without the shine in her eyes.

Cilka had no idea how they would get her to a crematorium. She would have to ask for help. She wasn't sure how to explain that, or if she should even try.

And the knife. They would have to deal with the knife.

She crouched beside the corpse. There wasn't going to be an investigation, so it didn't matter if she touched it. And she had already pulled the body close to her, so Cilka didn't need to worry about the—magic? essence?—contaminating her. If it was going to, then it already had happened.

She pushed the woman's blood-covered hooded cloak to one side revealing a belt around her waist. The woman had attached a sheath for the knife to the belt. Cilka removed the sheath, stuck the knife into it, and then put the sheath on her own belt.

She was already covered with the woman's blood, so more on her clothing didn't matter at all.

A couple of other pocket-sized things were attached to the woman's belt, holders for something or other. After a moment of indecision, Cilka unhooked the woman's belt and tossed it onto the road.

"What are you doing?" Judita asked. She sounded shocked.

"Gathering evidence," Cilka said. Not evidence for any kind of investigation, but to find out what this woman was.

Cilka felt along the crusty edges of the cloak, and found

pockets on either side of the woman's waist. The pockets contained tiny, unexpected items—feathers, unrecognizable coins, reddish rocks, and buttons. Cilka cleaned them out and put the items in her own pocket.

Then she leaned back and looked at the woman's pants. Maybe she had more pockets there.

Judita was watching her, a frown on her face. "You don't know what those things are or how they're used," she said. "You have no idea if they could hurt you or not. You don't want to—"

Cilka stopped listening. She had never seen pants like these. They appeared to be some kind of soft leather, but she wasn't certain. They had an element of unreality to them. There were no fasteners, nothing to make them easy to remove. Maybe the buttons were on the side that the woman had fallen on.

"Cilka!" Judita sounded almost panicked.

Cilka looked up. A hole the size of a plate had formed in the fog near her head. She scurried away from it. The fog swirled around it, as if the hole were a real thing.

Then hands—brown hands on long arms, covered in the same fabric as the pants the corpse wore—reached through the fog, and grabbed the corpse's cloak.

Judita didn't move. Neither did Cilka. She wasn't going to call attention to herself, although she did want to see what was through that hole. The arms seemed brighter than the fog, almost as if they were covered in sunlight.

The fingers curled around the cloak, tugging at it. It didn't move the corpse.

So two hands appeared above the corpse and cupped the air. The corpse rose, as if it were being pulled by invisible strings. Then the hands grasped it under the shoulders.

The woman's head lolled back, her broken jaw wobbling with each movement. The hands tugged the corpse into the hole. The head disappeared, then the shoulders, the torso, the legs.

Judita reached toward the corpse, as if she was going to grab it, but Cilka shook her head.

Getting rid of the corpse would make everything easier for Cilka. She wouldn't have to explain any of it. She wasn't even sure she wanted to tell Desmond.

The feet disappeared into the hole, and then the fog stopped swirling. It moved inward, closing the hole, the way that water would sometimes fill a newly formed deep spot in the middle of a puddle.

Finally the hole disappeared entirely, and the fog evened out, which Cilka hadn't even known that fog could do.

The hair rose on the back of her neck. She was still covered in the woman's blood. Cilka had the woman's knife on her hip, and the woman's treasured items in her own pockets.

But Cilka no longer had the dead body. Even the puddle of blood on the street was disappearing.

"We've lost two corpses in the space of an hour," she said to Judita.

Judita shook her head. She pointed at the puddle that she had fallen into not long before.

On its edge, an image was forming. Another body, prone, one arm extended, the other slightly away from the body.

Cilka's breath caught.

That was Kirilli's corpse.

She didn't move. The outlines of the corpse formed and then filled in. The body was in the exact same position it had been in before. But there was no satchel near his hand, and no knife in his back.

The knife was in a sheath against her hip. And the satchel—a different satchel—rested near his head.

"I don't like this," Judita said.

Were they supposed to like this? Cilka didn't know. She glanced at the place where the hole had been, but could see no evidence of it. In fact, she wasn't even sure exactly where it had been.

She stepped around the place where the woman's body had been. Cilka took the handful of steps toward Kirilli's body, and crouched beside it.

She started to reach toward him, then stopped. Her hand was covered with the blood of that woman. The blood was drying, but it was still there.

Cilka wiped that hand on the lower part of her pants, the only area that wasn't sticky wet with blood.

Then she gingerly touched Kirilli's shoulder, half expecting him to sit up and laugh and tell her it had all been a mistake.

But Kirilli wasn't the kind of man who made those sorts of mistakes. Any kind of mistake, if he could help it. And he wasn't the kind of man who played tricks on people, particularly elaborate ones.

And she wasn't sure she had ever seen him laugh.

His shoulder was stiff and the coat cold and damp. She put her hand around the shoulder joint, and shook him, just to be safe.

Or rather, she tried to shake him, but rigor had set in and his entire body shook when she tried to move his shoulder.

He had been dead a long time.

If she didn't have a knife against her hip and blood all over her clothing, she would have thought the last hour was a hallucination. But it hadn't been.

Kirilli had come to life, run off, and now was back, as a corpse. The person who had originally killed him had nearly stabbed Cilka, and she had kicked and stomped and maimed her —and Judita had killed her. And then the woman had disappeared.

Shortly thereafter, Kirilli reappeared. Or rather, his corpse had.

"Did he come through that hole?" Cilka asked Judita.

Judita shook her head. She looked both uncertain and frightened.

"You don't know what kind of magic this is, do you?" Cilka asked.

"Oh," Judita said in that hollow voice she'd been using all along. "On the contrary. I do."

"So tell me," Cilka said.

Judita's entire face squinched up, as if she thought of something distasteful—and maybe she had.

"The magic," she said, her voice trembling. "It comes from the Fey."

CHAPTER
TWELVE

Atrü sank to the plank floor, his hands covered in blood. Hadley was crumpled against him, face unrecogniz- able, wrists twisted at an odd angle, her hooded cloak soaked.

The small windowless room stank of sulfur and manure. Sirocco crouched in front of the hole she had made in the air, her fingers working strange Weather Sprite magick, her narrow face furrowed with concentration and panic.

Gem, their Domestic, scurried about behind them, trying to find pillows and blankets and all manner of Healing equipment.

"Just stop moving," Atrü snarled. He couldn't think. He hadn't Seen this. He had Seen everything up to the death of Augustus Kirilli. Atrü had Seen that moment when he had his hands on the satchels, satchels that were stuffed with documents and the all-important maps.

He just hadn't Seen that moment when the satchels and the maps literally vanished.

121

Hadley's eyes were open, her face—what there was left of it —gray. She had shut the Link when she had gotten captured, as her pain ratcheted up. No matter how hard Atrü tried, he couldn't reopen the Link.

He had known that Hadley was in serious trouble, and that they had to reach her somehow. In his panic, Atrü turned to Sirocco, begging her for help.

No Visionary should ever beg a Weather Sprite for help, but Atrü had to do so or Hadley would die.

Hadley had died anyway.

Atrü placed a hand on Hadley's shoulder, wishing it had all gone differently, wishing he had the ability to bring Hadley back —the ability that someone had shown in Trinovante.

Something strange had happened in the past hour, something Atrü didn't entirely understand.

He had known—all of the Fey knew—that the people of Dorovich had powerful magick, but this magick had been unrecognizable.

Whenever the Fey had encountered the magickal before, the magick made sense.

This did not, not entirely.

Atrü leaned against the wall, but he found no comfort in its roughness. The team had found this rental on the edge of Trinovante. Atrü had liked it because the landlord didn't really care about it. The upkeep was spotty, and the neighborhood sparse.

Gem had complained about it. She had done her best to make it feel somewhat homey, particularly from the street. If the landlord had come by, he would have been reassured that the house had good care.

She had used Domestic magick to camouflage what they were doing. It was a small thing, but it mattered.

All of it mattered when they had no real backup.

Gem wasn't using her magick now. She was in and out of the room, carrying more and more blankets and baskets, as if she could actually do something to make Hadley better. Gem had found pillows she had stashed and some cleaning rags and an entire box of potions. She hadn't stopped moving since Hadley returned.

"Gem," Atrü snapped. "I said stop."

"I might find something in here," Gem said. "Maybe if I wipe the magick off her—"

"You might open that portal again, whatever it was." Atrü turned just enough so that he could see Gem.

Gem was slender and young. She wore her black hair braided and wrapped around the top of her head. Her robes, multicolored and multilayered, swished about her.

The sound should have been comforting, but it wasn't, mostly because she was devastated.

She just didn't realize it yet.

Atrü let out a small sigh, then glanced at Sirocco. The toll all of this had taken on her was severe. Her long narrow face was lined, the shadows under her eyes deep, and her hair, which normally looked like it was blowing in an imaginary wind, hung limply around her face.

She hadn't looked like that the day before, when she had opened a portal into the financial district. They had known that Augustus Kirilli would leave his office at the end of business, and they wanted to be ready.

Their Dream Rider, Slumber, had touched Kirilli's mind,

and believed that he had received maps which didn't belong to him. Slumber believed Kirilli would put them somewhere for safekeeping.

This mission had been three objectives. First, find the maps and liberate them before Kirilli stashed them away; second, get him to tell them where the other maps were; and third, make sure that the rumors of his family's magick were just that —rumors.

If the Kirillis themselves had actual magick, then Atrü's team needed to kill all of them.

Finding magick in this strange country was difficult. At some point, the Qavnerians had scared themselves and outlawed magick. Omriseu, this team's best Spy, believed that magick practices were stronger in the farthermost reaches of the Qavnerian Protectorate near Mount Vitaki, but he had no way to confirm that.

In a debrief a few days ago, Omriseu had made note of all of the ways that the Qavnerians—and those in Trinovante in particular—had suppressed their own abilities.

But apparently not all of them suppressed their abilities, given what had happened this morning. This strange and horrid defeat.

Atrü started to run a hand over his face, then stopped when he saw the blood. He had to wash himself off—once they figured out what to do with Hadley's body.

Sirocco was watching Atrü, as if she expected something from him. Or maybe she was just deeply exhausted.

She had used a lot of her magick in the past two days. She had changed the weather in the financial district so that Hadley could go in and take the satchels from Augustus Kirilli. Sirocco had maintained that fog for hours, then let it recede into a normal Trinovante evening fog.

This morning, though, when everything changed, Sirocco had to bring the fog back—partly so that she could reopen the portal to the street where Kirilli had been killed.

Atrü put his hands back on Hadley's shoulders. They seemed frail and thin. Had Hadley always been frail and thin? She had looked so much larger than she had been.

But then, Enchanters often looked bigger than they actually were.

Even lower-level Enchanters, like Hadley.

The Black King's son, Rugar, had not sent his best people to Dorovich. He had sent several teams, all of them to scout out the current situation in Dorovich and find a way for the Fey to defeat the Dorovician magick.

It had been centuries since the Fey were here—except for a few traders now and then—and a lot had changed. The continent had split into well-defined countries, and then the countries had been overrun by the Qavnerian Protectorate, which controlled most of the continent.

The Qavnerians claimed they let each country continue to rule itself, but the claim was false. The individual countries handled their own cultural issues, but anything that ran contrary to Qavnerian law or Qavnerian practices was taken care of in front of Qavnerian legal entities.

Hadley had been the one guiding Omriseu, asking questions he had to find the answers to. The Dorovicians had a Place of Power, but they lost track of it, over time.

The Fey had used that Place of Power centuries ago, and most of the troops who had gone through it had gone mad or died along the way. That was when the Fey learned they could not approach another Place of Power from inside their own Place of Power.

They had to conquer Places of Power from the outside in.

Atrü had thought that all it would take was some study to figure out where the Dorovician Place of Power was. But he hadn't counted on—hadn't known—that the Dorovician didn't know what they had, which meant they didn't know where it was.

The Kirilli family had found something in the Razbitay Mountains and had removed many items from that something —selling them or giving them away. There had been a fanatical run on the items—everyone in the entire Qavnerian Protectorate wanted one—until the items created problems.

The rumors that Rugar had heard all the way across the Infrin Sea, in Nye, had turned out to be true. The Dorovicians had magical tools and they were scattered throughout the continent.

Rugar wanted those magickal tools, which the Qavnerians called "artifacts," destroyed before the Fey showed up. He had fought against cultures that used magickal tools before, and found them dangerous. The tools themselves could take an average fighter and give them an incredible advantage.

But it was Hadley who first discovered the maps, Hadley who broke cover and sent a message to the other Enchanters who were on teams headed to Dorovich, Hadley who had warned them about the Kirilli family artifacts. None of the Enchanters were powerful, but they were all young, and they had been raised together, which meant that they were Linked.

Atrü groaned. The others might have felt the severing of

their Links. They might have questions. Or they might think that this team had failed completely, when Atrü still had a lot of work left to do.

His cheeks warmed. He didn't want word to get back to Rugar that the team had failed. Atrü had come here to prove that he was worthy of a leadership position in Rugar's army, especially when Rugar's forces traveled to Dorovich.

Rugar was planning all of this, so that he could prove to his father that he was worthy of the Black Throne.

Sometimes Atrü thought that Rugar wanted to convince his father to step aside. Rugar couldn't force his father to do anything—violence among family members created the Blood against Blood, particularly if the Black Family killed one another. The last time the Black Family had warred on itself, it caused a raging madness that made families slaughter each other throughout the Fey Empire.

The Fey Empire had been small when this happened.

It was not small now.

Atrü shuddered. There was competition among the teams, so he could easily see one team reporting false—or at least incomplete—information to Rugar. It would take months, maybe even years, to correct that.

But Atrü couldn't think about that now. He had to focus on the task at hand. And the task was nowhere near complete.

Somehow, through a magick they didn't understand, they had lost the maps.

Sirocco clasped her hands together, as if they hurt. They were shaking. Her skin was gray also, and she looked like she might collapse.

She was staring at Hadley.

"I don't understand this," Sirocco said.

Neither did Atrü.

Hadley had been laughing not five hours ago about her successful mission. She had figured that since the Qavnerians had magickal tools, she would make one too.

She had finally created a knife, one made from bone and sinew, and formed to her hand. That knife was imbued with Hadley's magick. If anyone else used the knife, she had said to Atrü, it wouldn't have magick. It would only have its sharpened blade. A potent weapon, but not one as powerful as the knife was when Hadley wielded it.

And now, the knife had killed her.

After the mission, Hadley had pulled the maps out of the satchels, noting the incredible magic rising off the parchment. Although she hadn't been entirely sure that what she was holding was parchment.

She had set the maps on the table when suddenly a portal opened right in front of her.

Atrü had been standing beside her. He had seen nothing in that portal, just a mirror-like reflection of himself and Hadley. But she had seen something else.

She froze for a half second, the laugh dying in her throat. Then she took a step forward and said, "Professor!"

And then she pulled the hood over her head. A hood that hadn't been there at all. Her cloak had been hanging on a peg in the main room.

With a whoosh, the maps vanished and the satchels disappeared, and Hadley took another step forward, the knife clutched in her hand.

In her other hand, she held a different satchel, one that Gem had made to exactly match the one that Kirilli usually kept in his office. Only Hadley had filled Gem's satchel with magickal traps, the kind that could hold a man or make him confess to something or make him forget exactly where he was. The kind that might kill him, if conditions were right.

The team had put that satchel together over a long night, arguing about what should go into it, how exactly they might use its contents to capture Kirilli if Hadley didn't manage it. How that satchel might lead them to other bits of Dorovician magick.

"Hadley!" Atrü had said. "What's going on?"

But Hadley hadn't heard him. Instead, she had held up the satchel. "You forgot your satchel!"

"Hadley," Atrü had said, reaching for her. "Stop."

But Hadley had continued to step away from him, yelling about a professor, and then that command: *Stop!*

It had been unfocused and diffuse. It had frozen Atrü in place for a moment, until he had figured out what was happening.

Hadley was a young Enchanter. Sometimes she forgot how to cast a directed spell. But she hadn't made that mistake in Dorovich. She'd been disciplined.

Only at that moment, her discipline had slipped. Everything had changed and Atrü hadn't been sure why.

That portal had ceased to reflect anything. It had become darkness. Magickal fog had slipped through, the smell of sulfur and rot mixing with the warm baking smells of Gem's kitchen.

Only at that moment, Sirocco hadn't been creating a magickal fog. She had been standing in the doorway, hand to her mouth.

"Atrü," she had said. "What kind of magick is this?"

He hadn't known—he still didn't know.

And he hadn't had time to think about it, not in that moment. Hadley had stepped through that portal, her voice becoming faint.

The portal expanded for just a moment, showing a fog-covered street at twilight, a chubby man looking over his shoulder, and some kind of blinding lights winking on along the street corners.

And then the portal had winked out.

Atrü had regained his motion, Sirocco had yelled, "No!" and that had brought most of the team running.

They frantically tried to reopen the portal. Atrü could feel where the magick had been, but he didn't have the ability to open it. He had finally Linked to Hadley, who fought him from inside her own mind, telling him to go away, she needed to concentrate—and then she had been captured by one of the Qavnerians, a woman who seemed as frightened as Atrü felt.

That woman had physically defeated Hadley, and as the fight continued, Hadley had kicked Atrü out of her mind, sending him tumbling back across the Link. He had fallen into himself, and Hadley had slammed doors shut.

The next fifteen minutes or so had been futile, people with the wrong kind of magick trying to figure out a way to get to whatever was happening.

Finally Sirocco had come up with the idea of opening a weather portal...and by then, Hadley was dead.

Atrü let out a breath, remembering his training. A defeat was a moment in time. It was an incident. It was a setback. It was only permanent if the defeated made it so.

He still had much of his team. He needed to regroup, to figure out what, exactly, happened.

He was the leader, after all. He had to calm them, remind them that even though this didn't feel like a battlefield, it was.

He stood.

"We knew there was magick here," he said. "The Fey tried to take Dorovich a long, long time ago and failed. Now, we're seeing a hint as to why."

Gem clutched one of the pillows to her chest. She looked at Hadley, still in the same position on the floor.

"It's not a hint," Gem said. "This is a disaster."

A few minutes ago, Atrü would have agreed with her. But using a word like *disaster* only made everything worse. They had to get through this.

"We continue the mission," Atrü said, not directly answering Gem at all, "or we split up and blend in with the locals, becoming part of this community ourselves."

"Or go back to the harbor and see if we can get passage home," Gem said.

Sirocco let out a hiss, revealing her shock. Then she looked at Atrü.

He wasn't going to be harsh: Gem was very young and this was probably her first setback. She had just lost someone she cared about. She wasn't thinking clearly.

"You want to go back to Nye?" he asked quietly.

She nodded, her eyes filling with tears.

"And what will you tell the Black King's son? That you failed? The Fey do not fail. They suffer a setback, regroup, and try again."

"It took us hundreds of years to come back," Gem said, the tears still lining her eyes. Her voice sounded full.

She wasn't quite right. The Fey had come to Dorovich several times over the centuries. They had mostly sent Spies. The Spies had learned a few things, saw the changes, and then had gone back. But the Black King—all of the Black rulers who had led the Fey in that interim—had not decided to come here.

Rugar wasn't Black King yet. He was using this to build his reputation, to show his father that the Black King had been wrong about waiting to come to Dorovich. Rugar had believed that the Fey shouldn't have stopped at Nye, that they should have continued their mission to take over the world immediately, without the "rest and rebuilding" that his father was insisting on.

"It's not safe to go back," Sirocco said softly. "If we retreat, we bring shame."

"Or we get killed as Failures," Atrü said.

"And if we just disappear?" Gem asked. "Then what?"

"Then we have made a valiant fight," Sirocco said, not looking at Gem at all. Sirocco was looking at Hadley.

Atrü frowned at Hadley's body, wanting to crouch and talk to her, reason with her. Hadley had decided to go after the Kirilli because she felt they had no choice. Their Assassin had died on the voyage to Dorovich, nearly a year before. He had warned Atrü from the beginning that he didn't do well on ships, and then he had proven it. He had never gotten his sea legs, and one afternoon—to all of their horror—he had tripped and fallen off the side of the ship, dying before anyone could save him.

He wouldn't have died if he had fallen off a Fey vessel, but they had taken a Tashil ship. The Tashil had tossed two floating cushions at him, but he had flailed around, terrified to be in the water, and hadn't listened to any instructions.

He had drowned.

Atrü had overheard some of the team discussing the accident, saying it was a sign that this entire mission would go bad. But Atrü had Seen those satchels, the maps, and heard his team's joyous laughter. It had been one of his earliest Visions, shortly after he had gotten his Sight.

He had been so certain they would have a victory here, so certain that everything would go right that he had forgotten one of the first lessons a Visionary received: Visions were always incomplete. And sometimes Visionaries interpreted them incorrectly, using what they wanted to have happen instead of trying to understand what was really happening.

He supposed he could blame that misunderstanding on his youth at the time of the Vision, but that wouldn't be true. The Vision had finally come into focus when he had gotten this assignment.

And—to be fair to himself—he had told Rugar about the Vision. Rugar had been the one who had actually used the word "victory." He had also said it was a sign—a sign that the Fey needed to go to Dorovich.

Atrü had trusted Rugar. Rugar was a much more powerful Visionary than anyone else Atrü had ever met. Most Visionaries were lucky to have a handful of partial Visions over their lifetime. Rugar had had dozens by the time he was twenty.

That was a feature of the Black King's family. Their Sight was better than everyone else's.

But apparently, the Black King's son was as prone to misinterpreting a Vision as a young and inexperienced Visionary.

"Um, Atrü?" Gem was looking beyond him, at the door into this sealed-off room.

Atrü turned slightly, and saw the rest of the team. They were crowded around the door, peering down at Hadley. The rest of the team was there—six Infantry, two Spies, and the Dream Rider, Slumber.

Atrü hadn't told them yet about Hadley's death. He hadn't really even thought of them, and all they would be facing.

He wondered how much they had heard, wondered if they had heard that splitting up and assimilating was an option. The Qavnerians often pushed back against people with Fey features, but that was due to the Qavnerian fear of magick. They knew that tall slender people with upswept features and pointed ears often had magickal abilities that couldn't always be trusted.

The fact that there were such people, born every day in Dorovich, pointed to the Fey losses of the past.

Atrü had no idea how many Fey had come to Dorovich over the centuries. Hadley hadn't been able to find out in her limited research on the voyage over. She had brought some Nyeian histories of the six continents—much of which seemed to be fanciful, not at all based in truth—but it had given her a start in understanding the cultures here in Dorovich.

And many of the cultures included an abhorrence of anyone who looked slightly Fey.

"What happened?" Omriseu asked. He looked like so many Spies. His features didn't quite move, but they were hard to focus on. He could change his appearance for a short period of time, looking more like someone from Qavner than someone Fey.

Around the team, though, he wore his own face, which was

slightly blurry and nondescript. Everything about him was slight and hard to see. Spies were like that; it was part of their magick, part of what made them blend into any crowd they walked into.

They also asked pointed questions to get information, questions the listener often forgot—due to one of the Spy's best assets, a magickal ability to make certain memories disappear, if the spell happened within moments of the memory's occurrence.

Well, Omriseu had just asked a pointed question. And this time, no one was going to forget it.

"The magick here makes no sense," Atrü said softly. He then explained to the team what had happened—how Hadley had walked through that portal, interacted with investigators, and somehow the man she had killed hours before came back to life.

The Infantry didn't say anything. They stayed out of the room, hanging around the edges of the door, like Infantry often did during discussions of magick. They had none. They were good fighters, smart people, and often knew how to get out of a physically bad situation, but they couldn't use any kind of magick to save themselves.

So they listened rather than participated. Two of them— both men—were still young. Sometimes Infantry members came into their magick later. It was never a lot of magick if it came that late, but it would usually be enough to move whoever the person was from Infantry into the field based on their magickal abilities.

Slumber leaned against the wall, much like Atrü was doing. Slumber had his arms wrapped around his torso, his dark eyes narrowed. He had tried twice since they had arrived to induce dreams into a sleeping host, so that the team could invade the house, only to lose control within the first hour. But he had managed to enter the mind of Augustus Kirilli two nights ago.

Atrü had trusted what Slumber had learned. And it had proven right.

It had also proven to be the first step in this disaster.

Atrü looked away. Atrü didn't need any more reminders of the fact that Rugar had not included his best people in the teams. Rugar's reasoning had been clear: he hadn't wanted to lose his best. His argument to the teams had been even clearer: if they wanted to prove that they were among the best at what they did, then they needed to do so on this mission to Dorovich.

Atrü had known it was a long shot, not just for him, but for his team. He was a minor Visionary, which meant that he would never rise to the ranks of people like Rugar. But Atrü might be able to lead his only fighting unit at some point, or maybe even become a trusted adviser. Particularly if he gained enough understanding of Dorovich to be able help Rugar plan an invasion.

"Did the Kirilli do this?" Qurzi asked.

Qurzi was the other Spy on the team. He was smaller than Omriseu, and even more indistinct. Atrü kept forgetting he was there. Qurzi had not wanted to come on this trip, but had been ordered to do so by his parents, who were accomplished Spies. He had inherited their abilities, but not their willingness to use them in service of the Fey.

Atrü had to order Qurzi to go on missions—when Atrü remembered that he was around.

"We don't know what happened exactly," Atrü said.

"It wasn't the Kirilli," Sirocco said, almost at the same time. "He was dead. This was something that a woman did."

So Sirocco had seen something as she had reached through that portal, but not as much as Atrü had seen.

Atrü looked at Sirocco. Her expression was defiant, almost angry.

"Be honest with the team, at least," she said, as if she blamed him. He did not know why she would blame him. He hadn't caused Hadley to go back to that street.

"I'm not sure what you mean," Atrü said. "I was inside a Link, trying to fight my way out, experiencing what Hadley was experiencing."

More or less, anyway. Hadley had blocked off her pain receptors, so that Atrü couldn't feel what she had been feeling. And then she had closed her Links entirely, when she realized that she might not survive.

All of that happened quickly, and hadn't allowed Atrü to look through Hadley's eyes and clearly see what was going on.

Sirocco gave him an annoyed glance, then said to the team, "There were two strange women on site when I opened the portal. One of them was holding Hadley and Hadley was unconscious. But the other looked Fey."

"She wasn't Fey," Atrü said. "Hadley would have treated her differently."

Sirocco's eyes narrowed. "I said she looked Fey. I didn't say that she *was* Fey."

"What does that mean?" Rodderc asked. He was larger than anyone else in the room. His shoulders were broad, his arms and legs so muscular that they often reminded Atrü of tree trunks.

Atrü took a deep breath. Any question Rodderc asked deserved a thorough answer. Rodderc had become the leader of the Infantry in this small team. He had done a good job of it too.

They'd managed to get into a lot of places and destroy a lot of magickal items.

"A lot of people in Trinovante look Fey," Omriseu answered before Sirocco could. "They must have Fey ancestry."

"Yes, that might be it," Sirocco said. "Her clothing was not Fey, nor was her manner. But she seemed to have a lot of power."

"Fey ancestry," Gem said quietly. "Is that why you think we can abandon our mission and blend in?"

She had directed that question at Atrü.

"Yes," he said. "We've done it before."

Meaning the Fey had, after the disastrous trip through the Place of Power centuries ago.

"Which means that the magick here is powerful." Rodderc sounded surprised. "I had not realized that two different cultures had blended their magicks here."

"I told you that," Omriseu said. "When I told you what I found as I went through the city."

Rodderc shrugged. "I thought you meant the artifacts that we were destroying. I thought they were remnants of a past that no longer applied."

"It clearly applies." Qurzi said quietly. His head was bent toward Hadley, although his features were still blurred. Atrü couldn't tell if Qurzi was looking directly at her body or not.

"I wouldn't have thought that they could harness our magick," Omriseu said. "I had found no evidence of it. Had you, Qurzi?"

Qurzi bowed his head slightly. "I hadn't looked for it."

Atrü wanted to yell at him, to say, *That was the reason you were here, that you would find things you* weren't *looking for. You were supposed to observe and report.*

But Atrü didn't. He couldn't. Not right now.

"It's hard to figure out their magick," Omriseu said to the entire team. "Magick is not discussed and is mostly banned. It's done in secret. I have no idea how two women could have done magick in a public street."

"They cleared the street," Atrü said. He knew that because Hadley had seen it, and had somehow registered it. "I'm not sure who had the magick, the woman who killed Hadley or the other woman."

The one he hadn't seen clearly.

"They both did," Sirocco said. "But one does not know what she has, while the other has complete control of her power. She saw us, Atrü. She'll be looking for us."

A shiver ran through him. They needed some kind of shield now. He didn't know who could build it.

"Can you protect this house?" he asked Gem.

She frowned, then glanced at Hadley, then looked back at Atrü. It clearly took a moment for the question to register in Gem's mind.

"You need to make a Shadowlands," she said.

Shadowlands were a military device, something Visionaries could build in a region using their Vision. It was like building a box that no one could see from the outside. Expert and powerful Visionaries could build Shadowlands that could house an entire army.

Atrü could build a Shadowlands that could hide the satchel that Hadley had been carrying. And maybe not even that.

"I can't make one for us," Atrü said.

"Can't or won't?" Gem asked, with an edge he'd never heard from her before.

"Can't," he said. "It's beyond my ability."

She exhaled with something like a moan. "I can't protect this house by myself. That's not what Domestic magick is."

"That's precisely what Domestic magick is," Rodderc said, before Atrü could reply. Atrü wouldn't have been so confrontational, particularly not now, not while Gem was grieving.

"You don't understand magick," Gem said.

Rodderc gave her a thin, cold smile, one that sent another shiver through Atrü's spine. He wouldn't want Rodderc to look at him like that.

"I know more about magick than the magickal," Rodderc said. "That's what those of us without magick do. We learn magick, first in hopes that we will come into ours one day and we'll need to learn how to recognize it, and later so that we know who to consult when we need magickal help. You need to protect us, Gem. You need to protect this house."

She shook her head. "I don't know how."

Sirocco swore. "I'll do it for now," she said.

"No," Atrü said. "Hiding the house in fog or creating some kind of weather barrier won't help at all. If that woman has Fey powers, she won't come into the house through the outside. She'll use that portal. You'll have to make sure it's completely shut."

"Both portals," Rodderc said. "That Fey-like woman opened a portal here before you opened your second one."

"All three portals," Qurzi said. "You opened one first. She might have traveled along that."

Atrü hadn't thought of that, but Qurzi was right. Qurzi might've been an awful Spy, but he did seem to see other things a lot more clearly than the rest of the team.

"Three portals," Sirocco said, shaking her head. "All I can do without an Enchanter, a Spell Warder, a real Visionary—"

And at that moment, she glared at Atrü, who started to defend himself and then stopped. She was right; a real Visionary could build a proper Shadowlands.

"—or a Domestic who knows what they're doing," Sirocco continued, "is...well, I can ice the portals shut."

"Then do it," said Yris. She was another of the Infantry, as tall as Rodderc, but not nearly as wide and muscular. Yet she had a grip that could destroy almost anything.

"They can still follow the magick in the portal," Rodderc said, "especially if one of them created a portal."

Atrü nodded. He knew that.

"If they travel inside the portal, they'll find it blocked," Sirocco said.

"And if they have the ability to look outside of that portal," Atrü said, "they'll see the exterior of the house."

"If they understand Fey magick," Sirocco said, "they'll recognize any weather that hides it as being something I did."

Atrü made himself look down at Hadley's body. It seemed to have shrunken in on itself, and Hadley hadn't been large to begin with.

"We're going to have to move," Rodderc said, just before Atrü could say the same thing.

"That's not easy," Qurzi said. "We'll need to rent another place, and finding one, with our limited resources..."

He let his voice trail off.

Atrü shook his head. "Our resources aren't limited any longer."

Sirocco frowned at him. "What changed?"

"We changed," Rodderc said. "We brought back valuables."

And they had only reported it to Atrü, because he was the leader. He hadn't thought to share with anyone.

"We don't need to rent another place," Yris said. "That last manor we went to—it had a lot of outbuildings. And since there's no longer any staff, I say we take over one of those."

Yris was perfectly trained Infantry. Take over the enemy's property; hold it and defend it and make it Fey.

Atrü frowned, thinking about that.

"Was the last manor the Kirilli place?" Sirocco asked.

"Yes." Yris's smile was feral. "The staff is gone."

"But the Kirilli is not," Sirocco said. "He reanimated and ran away from the scene."

"If that's the case," Gem said quietly, "then there's unstable magick in that manor. We shouldn't go there."

"It's not the only place we visited with outbuildings," Yris said, looking annoyed. "We found a number of them—"

"And since their owners all had magickal tools," Atrü said, "we should probably avoid that. Omriseu, I need you to find us another residence, and quickly. Rodderc will give you some coin, so that you can pay for it."

"Yes, sir." Omriseu slipped out of the room, followed by Rodderc.

Atrü trusted Omriseu. He was the one who had found this building.

"Sirocco," Atrü said, "you need to ice the portals."

She nodded, then went into the kitchen, clearly to take care of the portal that she did not create first. She moved slowly, and Atrü wondered how much more magick she could use.

Gem crouched beside Hadley's body, and touched the shoulder.

"She's really gone," Gem said, more to herself than to anyone else.

Atrü did not respond. There was no reason to. Gem would have to deal with the loss on her own, like Fey usually did.

"What do we do with her?" The voice came from beside Atrü and it took all of his strength not to start with alarm.

He turned slightly, and saw the edges of Qurzi's face, but not his actual features. Having him that close was uncomfortable.

Atrü did not move aside, however. He assumed that Qurzi wasn't talking about Gem, who was just beginning to understand that Hadley was dead.

"I mean," Qurzi said, "we don't have any Tenders or any Red Caps. They usually take care of things like this."

In peacetime, the Tenders managed the dead. But they rarely traveled with an army and they certainly weren't part of this team.

In wartime, Red Caps stripped the enemy dead of their flesh and bone, so that Spell Warders had something to work with. That was not how it worked with Fey dead, but he wasn't sure exactly how it did work.

The team had been lucky with their Assassin. His body remained in the sea.

Atrü would have to decide now what to do with Hadley. Here, in Dorovich, bodies were either burned or buried. Neither choice seemed like a good one. And the ones that were burned were usually those of lesser folk—people who had fallen on hard times or who had been jailed.

For a moment, Atrü was tempted to take Hadley's body to one of the undertakers in Trinovante, until he remembered that the Dorovicians seemed to have some magick of their own.

If they understood how the bodies of the magickal dead could be useful, then he didn't want to volunteer one of theirs.

A thread of irritation went through him. Normally, he would have consulted with Hadley about what to do with the magickal dead.

They had no good options. They couldn't cremate her on their own. And they were nowhere near the Hidden River or the Infrin Sea.

"Let me take care of her," Gem said. Apparently she had heard the conversation.

Atrü wasn't sure if she understood what she was saying. "We have no Tenders," he said, referring to Domestics who took care of bodies. "We're not set up to handle a body—"

"I know," Gem said. "But I am. That's part of training for Healers."

She looked at Hadley, then ran a hand along the side of her face.

"Not everyone a Healer touches survives, you know," Gem said.

He had known that, but he hadn't thought it through. Of course. The Domestics often took care of the non-war dead, with the help of Red Caps.

"You'll need assistance," Atrü said, not sure what he was volunteering one of his people for.

"No," she said. "I prefer to do this alone. It's the least I can do for her."

Atrü felt more relief than he should have. "All right. The rest of us will gather our things. We need to be ready to leave here as soon as Omriseu has found us a new place to go."

Gem nodded, but she didn't seem to hear him. Or maybe she just didn't care.

"I should assist her," Vidso, one of the Infantry, said.

"She said she didn't want help," Atrü said.

"She'll need someone strong," Vidso said.

Atrü couldn't argue with that. He certainly didn't want to deal with the dead. So, he would let the two of them work it out.

He needed a plan. He also needed to remember that they had done a lot before they lost Hadley. The Infantry had destroyed a lot of magickal items. They had brought back wealth.

He didn't have the maps any longer, but he hadn't even known the maps existed before arriving here. If he got his team together—if he got himself together—he would be able track down the maps, maybe get them back.

Maybe if he figured out who had given them to the Kirilli in the first place, he might be able to find even more maps.

Or maybe his team could find those two women. One of them would know where the Kirilli went.

Then Atrü smiled. Yes. That was what he would do. He would have his team track down the women. They would know what happened to Kirilli and the maps.

After all, they had cost Hadley her life.

He felt stronger now. He had a goal. He knew what he was going to do next.

He was glad he had remembered his teachings. A defeat was

only a defeat if he allowed it to be. Otherwise it was a setback. A moment in time, followed by another moment in time.

And that second moment would contain victory.

PART TWO
NOW

CHAPTER
THIRTEEN

Zeitsev half-pulled, half-carried Gussie to the door of the manor. This, this was why her father had hired Zeitsev. He hadn't been thinking clearly until her father had shown up, and then Zeitsev took over everything.

Gussie was glad of that. She wasn't seeing the hallway or the destruction. She could barely see anything. But she clung tightly to the two satchels that her father had given her. She held them, even though her hands were sticky with blood.

His blood.

She kept thinking he was still back in his study, but Zeitsev said he wasn't. Zeitsev was getting her to move.

And to think she had mentally chastised him for reacting poorly to the kitchen. She was reacting poorly to seeing her father, and she knew it.

She had to break out of it.

Her father had given her the satchels. She needed to get them to the Vault.

149

And for that, she had to go alone.

Zeitsev had almost gotten her to the door.

"Please, miss," he said. "Please. We hafta leave, we do. Now."

He'd been saying a version of that since her father vanished. Sometimes Zeitsev added, "He's gone, miss. We're na gonna see him agin."

She wasn't sure why she wanted to stay. She felt like she needed to go back to the study, open the desk, look underneath at the safe her father kept there, maybe move the plants or look in her grandfather's journals.

Something was drawing her back there, and she was having trouble fighting it. She had a memory of feeling this way before. When her grandfather visited. No, stayed. He had stayed in the house. This had been his house, and that had been his study and he would smile at her when she came to the door.

My precious Augusta, he would say. *Let me show you—*

"Miss, I'm gonna carry ya, I am," Zeitsev said. "I need ta. Because that fog, it's breakin', and when it does, if some'n' is watching the place, they'll see ya, and they'll know they dinna get everyone, and they'll come for us. Those satchels, they're important. Your Da said so. Ya hafta get them out of here."

Her father. The satchels. Those words snapped her out of the memory of her grandfather. But it hadn't felt like a memory. It had felt real.

Gussie frowned. It had felt real like her father had felt real. And her father *had* been real. She was coated in his blood.

She made herself turn away from the end of the corridor where the study was. She wouldn't let herself look at the fork which led to the kitchen. She stepped over the destruction.

Zeitsev was right. He was thinking clearly now and she was

not. Maybe that was because he was scared, but maybe (her brain said in her grandfather's voice) it was because she had touched something magical.

Her father shouldn't have been here.

Her father was dead, and yet he managed to find her. He managed to give her something she needed to protect.

"You're right," she said to Zeitsev. "I'm sorry. There's something wrong with this place, and it caught me."

Zeitsev looked at her like she was crazy. She could almost hear his thoughts: of course there was something wrong here. The kitchen was full of the bodies of the dead staff, and the ghost of her father (her dead father—the shade of her father? Her father's spirit? Something...) had visited them, and given her satchels, things she had to protect.

The entire place was ruined, everything her grandparents had brought from their trips to the Razbitay Mountains had been destroyed, and she had spoken of it as if there had been a small bit of smoke in the air.

Of course. Everything was wrong.

Thin light poured in through the destroyed front entrance. Dust motes floated in the air. Micah would be appalled to see them. Micah would—

Her brain stopped and stuttered over the rest of that thought. Micah. He had been a fixture for her entire life.

She started to shake.

"Miss," Zeitsev said, and she could hear the pleading in his voice.

"I'm sorry," she said. "You're right. We have to leave."

She stepped in front of him, her slippers catching on some loose boards. She nearly tripped, but she caught herself before she had to drop one of the satchels on the floor. She couldn't do that. She didn't dare set them down.

And she couldn't give them to Zeitsev. Her father had entrusted her with them. They might have had some magic that enabled him to reach her side.

If that was the case, she didn't want Zeitsev to get infected by it.

Or to report it.

A desperate chuckle rose in her throat, but she managed to suppress it. Everything about the satchels was magic, and Zeitsev had seen it all. He had seen her father fade away. He had seen the satchels remain.

If Zeitsev felt the need to report the magic, so be it. She had no idea if that report would overshadow the report of those horrid deaths.

Zeitsev remained beside her. When her slipper caught on that board, he hovered, but didn't touch her. Touching her would have been improper, especially now that she was moving on her own.

He had gotten her this far. She had to go the rest of the way on her own.

She skirted around the piles of debris, resisting the urge to run her hands through it, to see what was ruined and what she could save.

It was that urge—the urge to touch everything that felt off.

She needed to get outside. She—

Stopped. The sense of her grandfather grew. She could almost see him. And behind him, she could feel her grandmother's presence, even though Gussie had never really known her grandmother.

But considering the events of the morning—considering that Gussie had just watched her injured father disappear—she wouldn't be surprised if she did see her grandparents.

"Miss," Zeitsev said. "What's holding ya up? We hafta…"

She didn't hear the rest, because his question caught her. Something was holding her up.

"We have to go back to the study," she said.

"Miss, we dinna have time," he said.

"I know that." She sounded curt. But she couldn't help herself. "But I left something there. I need to get it."

"It can wait, miss," Zeitsev said.

"No, it can't." She started back down the corridor. "I'll meet you at the carriage."

She wished she wasn't carrying the satchels. They seemed even heavier than they had before.

Finally, she was walking quickly. She stepped around the piles of debris. She didn't feel like she was slogging through thick air.

Footsteps echoed behind her.

She glanced over her shoulder. Zeitsev was following her, looking both angry and terrified at the same time.

"Miss—"

"The faster I go there, the quicker I leave," she said. "Why don't you go to the carriage? I'll join you."

"I'm na leavin' ya, miss. I'm na."

She wasn't going to be able to get rid of him. And she wasn't sure why she wanted to, just like she wasn't sure why she needed to get to the study.

It only took a few minutes to make her way to those

damaged doors. One of the lightstone lanterns was gleaming, even though she hadn't touched it.

"Goooor," Zeitsev said as he came up beside her. "Who dun that?"

My grandfather, Gussie almost said, but didn't because she knew how it would sound. She wasn't even sure where the sentence came from, although part of her knew it was probably true.

Her grandfather was guiding her here. That was why she hadn't been able to leave.

She stepped over the broken door, lifting the satchels. After she got inside, she tucked one of the satchels under her arm, and hurried to the table with the plants. They parted for her, revealing her grandfather's notebooks.

She let out a sigh of relief. They were still here.

Although she had no idea who would have taken them. Or why she thought anyone would.

But she had to get them out of here, and quickly.

She looked about, and saw another satchel half buried under some broken paintings. The satchel looked like one of her father's, sturdy and well-made.

She picked it up, and thrust it at Zeitsev.

"Hold this open for me," she said.

He didn't reach for it. "Hold what?"

"This satchel." She shook it at him. "I need you to hold it."

"I dinna see a satchel," he said. "Yer na holdin' anathin'."

Her father faded. Her grandfather led her here. The satchels had appeared out of thin air before.

She had to believe that Zeitsev was telling the truth.

"Fine," she said with great irritation—not really at him, but at everything. Irritation was easier than sheer terror or grief or complete confusion.

She set the newly found satchel on top of the desk, and grabbed a notebook, setting it inside of the satchel. There were ten notebooks that she could see. She had no idea if they would all fit, but she was going to try.

"What're ya doin', miss?" Zeitsev said. "There's nathin' there."

"I see something, even if you don't," she said. "I'm nearly done. Watch the door."

He moved away from her with seeming relief. He turned his back and faced the door. As he did, two more lightstone lanterns flared.

Gussie could see the lower shelf now. There were more notebooks.

"I can't carry much more," she muttered.

"Wha—?" Zeitsev asked.

"Nothing," she said, louder. She grabbed the remaining notebooks, and somehow, they all fit inside the satchel. It would be heavy, but apparently she had to be the one to carry it, since Zeitsev couldn't even see it.

The plants closed their tendrils again, covering the shelf, and the light in the lanterns faded. The room was growing colder, and the air felt distinctly different, as if a friendly presence had left.

"Miss, please." Zeitsev clearly felt it too.

"I'm ready," she said. The third satchel was very heavy. The one under her arm threatened to slip. And the other one felt glued to her hand.

She wasn't sure how she would get them out of here, but she felt like she had to.

"Yer ready?" he asked.

"Yes," she said.

"Ya'll be followin' me this time," he said. "And no arguin'."

"All right." She felt different too. She had finally reached the same urgency he felt. Maybe more.

Her father had said there was a bad presence in the study. That couldn't have been her grandfather, could it? Her father wouldn't have thought his own father was evil, would he?

But the study felt distinctly different now, and she had to get out of it. She resisted the urge to run—not that she could have with her long skirts and the satchels and all of the ruined belongings all over the floor.

Zeitsev helped her through the broken door, mostly by standing beside her and placing a hand near her, so that she trusted him if she fell.

And then they walked side by side toward the entrance.

Somehow, she managed without dropping the satchel under her arm, or tripping against some debris, or damaging her feet in those thin slippers.

She and Zeitsev reached the entrance. The damage looked worse than before, but that might've been because of the pale sunlight filtering through. The fog wasn't gone, but it had thinned, taking much of its stench with it.

Zeitsev was watching her as if he couldn't quite understand what she was doing. She had a hunch he could see her right hand, curved around the new satchel's handle, but he couldn't see the handle itself.

She knew how strange it all seemed. It seemed strange to her too. But she couldn't think about it. If she did, she'd have to acknowledge the magic, and she didn't want to do that.

The very idea of it made her heart hurt.

Or perhaps that was the thought of her father, fading away. *Go*, he had said. *Take the satchels.*

To the Vault.

She would take all three there. And compare the maps, whatever that meant.

The debris near the door was unstable. Some of it looked like it had toppled while she was in the manor. Had her father done that? He'd been solid when she first saw him, after all. Or had someone else done it?

Her heart skipped a beat.

She wove her way around the stacks of debris, the remains of this place she had loved so much, and then she got to the broken entrance. She would have to step over it while balancing the satchels.

Zeitsev paused beside her. He seemed to want to say something, but he didn't. Because she had already made it clear that he couldn't take the satchels—or, at least, the ones he could see.

She maneuvered her right hand to the front of her skirt, and shifted the satchel she was holding just enough to grip the skirt with her thumb and forefinger to get over that broken bottom of the door. And then, she'd have to make sure she didn't tumble down the stairs.

At least she was wearing slippers, not shoes with heels.

It was hard to maintain her grip on the skirt, with the fat satchel bumping against her knees. It would take all of her balance to get outside, and even then, her skirt might catch.

She couldn't think about it. She just had to do it.

She had to step over the broken part with one leg, pause, untangle herself, and then use the other leg.

First, she peered through the entrance. The pale light illuminated the trees that lined the walk. They looked like scrawny men, stuck in positions of terror, arms upraised.

Her heart pounded even harder. She had never really been fanciful before; she wasn't sure why she had become fanciful now.

Perhaps because she was so deep down terrified of whatever had happened to her.

She stepped into the area just in front of the entrance, lifted her skirts higher, and stepped with her right leg to the outside.

The air was colder, but fresher. The sulfuric smell of coal was easing. An ever-so-slight breeze seemed to be clearing out the fog. She supposed she should be grateful, but right now, she didn't want anyone to be able to see her clearly.

The satchels made her feel exposed.

She leaned forward, redistributing the weight of the satchels, trying not to let the one under her arm slide, and then eased her left leg out of the broken entrance door. She was almost free when the back of her skirt caught.

She couldn't turn to grab it, and she couldn't move forward.

"I'm sorry," she said to Zeitsev. "I need you to free my skirt."

It was unseemly for an unmarried man to touch her skirt. It was also unseemly for the man who drove the carriage to touch her in anyway at all.

As if that mattered, with all the death and destruction around them.

But still, he hesitated.

She supposed she could just rip free, but she didn't want to do that.

"Please," she said.

He nodded, looking pained, and then he bent over, his hands picking and adjusting. She couldn't quite see what he was doing, but she could feel the tug on her skirt ease.

"Now, miss," he said.

"Thank you." She stepped the rest of the way out, feeling lighter than she had, as if she had lost a burden. She made her way down the stairs leading to the walk, so that Zeitsev had enough room to make his own exit.

He did so quickly. Then he came up behind her, scanning the grounds just like she had done.

"We need ta hurry," he said, and he didn't have to explain. She had the same feeling.

She couldn't agree more. She walked as quickly as she could, with the extra weight of the satchels. In particular, the new one, with her grandfather's notebooks, slowed her down. It tugged her sideways, and took most of her strength to keep it off the ground.

It wasn't until she reached the carriage house and saw the carriage, along with the patient horses that she realized just how relieved she was. She had worried that someone would have taken them.

Zeitsev stepped around her.

"I'll set up, miss," he said, and reached the carriage in no time. He disappeared around the side, making low conversation with the horses.

The last few yards were, for her, extremely difficult. She was tiring. The weight of the satchels exhausted her. The ones her father had given her tingled. She didn't know if the tingling really came from the satchels or just from the way she was holding them, but she couldn't stop to find out.

She reached the carriage door, but it was closed. She wasn't going to be able to open it.

"I'm going to need assistance," she said to Zeitsev.

"One moment, miss," he said from somewhere around the horses.

She didn't really have a moment. She was so tired that she wanted to lean against the carriage. But she wasn't going to.

Finally, he emerged from the side. His gaze went to her hands, then to her face.

"I'll get the door for ya, miss," he said, and she felt more gratitude toward him than she expected. He was showing a lot of restraint today, more than she had probably shown.

He climbed up the two steps, then pulled open the door. He climbed down and extended his hand, as if he expected her to take it.

She shook her head a little. She was going to have to set the satchels down now. There was no other way into the carriage.

She reached up and put the satchel with her grandfather's notebooks inside, her heart pounding as she did so. She was half afraid that if she let it go, it would disappear on her. But it did not.

Then she took the satchel from under her arm, and slid that satchel beside the new one. She hadn't realized just how over-stuffed the satchels her father had given her were. They also looked like they were going to burst.

Something made her continue to cling to the third satchel.

She gripped the little railing built into the door, and pulled herself onto the steps, her skirts swirling around her slippered feet.

She stopped, and looked back at Zeitsev.

"I'm going to need you to take me home," she said.

His gaze went to the satchels, then back to her face. "I'd like ta go ta the constabulary first," he said.

"If only we could. But I have to honor my father's wishes. I need to secure these satchels. He..." She wasn't sure how to finish that sentence. *He risked his life for those satchels* wasn't quite accurate, although she didn't know that for sure. *He had brought them to me from beyond the grave* strained even her own credulity. *He...*

"...gave everything to bring them to me," she said.

Zeitsev frowned, but he seemed to understand. He had seen the strangeness too. He nodded, then backed away.

"If someone's followin' us, I'm goin' ta the constabulary," he said, almost defiantly.

"That would make sense." She was willing to acquiesce to that, because if someone was following them, she didn't want to lead that someone to the Vault.

She climbed the rest of the way into the carriage, and sat on the edge of one of the seats. Her right hand ached from holding the satchel so tightly.

She leaned her head back and closed her eyes, just for a minute, unwilling to analyze any of that.

The carriage lurched as the horses took their first steps. The carriage path went in a half circle so that the horses didn't have to be led around.

Even though she trusted Zeitsev, she still opened her eyes and peered out the carriage window, just to make sure they were on track.

He had taken the carriage down the side path, away from the manor. She wouldn't have thought to do that, even though it was the quickest way to her home.

They were going through a copse of trees, and then they'd pass the stone fence, and get onto the road.

There was no fog here, just thin sunlight, reflecting off the damp leaves. She'd think it all pretty if she wasn't so wrung out. Now, the pretty seemed almost to mock her.

Compare the maps, her father had said. *There's something important...*

Not just get them to the Vault, but figure out what the maps were. She hadn't remembered any maps in his office, not like this. Nor did she completely understand what she was going to compare the maps to.

All she knew was that when she got to her own home, she had to be ready to keep moving. Her father's command to go to the Vault was the most important thing she had to do with the rest of her day.

The carriage moved a little too slowly for her. She wanted to lean her head out the window to see if anyone was following them, but she didn't. Instead, she pulled the curtains and sat in complete darkness.

She knew better than to sleep—sleeping wasn't safe right now—but she didn't open the satchels either. She just needed to rest. She needed a moment to think, to recover, to be with all of the strangeness that had occurred.

You're the strong one, Augusta, her grandfather used to say. *You're the one this whole family rests on.*

Gussie, darling, her father had said, just days before. *I need to talk to you. I need you to consider taking my place.*

Papa, I don't understand numbers like you do. I can't take your place at the firm, she had said, trying to hold him off.

At the Regents, Gussie, he had said. *There've always been Kirillis on the board. Strange things are happening. I need you to learn what I know.*

I'll never know what you know, she had said.

Gussie, please, he'd said. *It's important.*

And she had given in, not just because he had said it was important, but because she had a sense that she was betraying her grandfather by arguing with her father.

Her grandfather's presence had been near her all week, and she hadn't known why.

She looked at the satchel, filled with his notebooks. She had never felt the urge to read them, not since she was a little girl and she had snuck into the study, opening the notebooks and looking at all the drawings.

Not yet, child, her grandmother had said, taking the pretty drawings away from her. *Someday we'll explain these to you, but not yet.*

Someday had never come.

And now, she was on her own.

She only hoped she was smart enough to figure out what they'd been trying to tell her, what was so important about the notebooks, the satchels, the Vault.

And the Regents.

The ironic thing was that she thought she would have time.

Her father had felt an urgency, but she had put him off.

"I'm sorry, Papa," she whispered, but she couldn't feel him.

He was really and truly gone.

And the apology had come much too late.

FOURTEEN

Sirocco's hands were shaking. She stood in the room where Hadley's body had rested until Rodderc and Gem figured out what to do with it.

Sirocco hadn't helped them with that decision. She had seen enough. Weather Sprites weren't supposed to look at the aftermath of war. Weather Sprites were supposed to make conditions favorable for the Fey.

Sometimes that meant sunlight on a day that should have had none. Sometimes it meant snow on an elevation that never usually received any. Sometimes it meant fog to hide whatever the Fey were doing.

It didn't usually mean opening a portal and dragging one of their number—an Enchanter—away from the people who killed her.

Sirocco wiped her hands against her robes, for probably the fifteenth time in the last hour. She had gone into the small excuse for a kitchen after Atrü had given them all assignments, and she had washed her hands. Over and over again.

Touching blood had made her squeamish. Especially the blood of someone she knew.

She couldn't quite call Hadley a friend. No one made friends with Enchanters. They were unpredictable and difficult, even ones with as little magick as Hadley had had.

Still, they had all relied on Hadley. Hadley could do things none of the rest of them could do. Most of the team had no magick at all. Just brute strength, which had proven useful so far, but wasn't what they needed now, in the face of real magick users.

Sirocco rubbed her hands together. They were dry and chapped.

She was here to prevent those Qavnerian magick users from coming through the portals.

She was starting in this room, because, she figured, this was the portal that the Qavnerians all knew about. This, and the one that the Qavnerian magick user had created.

Sirocco took a deep breath to steady herself.

One portal at a time.

She hated this room. It was small, an enclosed box without windows and with a single door. There was some kind of overhead light that Omriseu had called a lightstone lamp, and before they could touch it, he had destroyed it.

They used candles in here most of the time, except when Gem was here. She created little lights out of glassware she had found. The problem was that she was so new to her training, she couldn't make the lights work for anyone else.

Those lights still burned. Gem had placed a lot of them in

the room that morning, and had relit them when she was working with Hadley's body. Gem had said she didn't want Hadley to rest in the dark.

Gem had gone a little crazy with Hadley's death, a fact that Sirocco didn't want to think about.

She didn't want to think about a lot of things, but she wasn't being very successful at keeping them out of her brain.

The room didn't help, with its faint scent of blood and rot. There were no chairs here either. They, and the only table, had been moved the night before when Hadley had created her portal to attack the Kirilli.

Sirocco shuddered. She had hated this room from the moment the team had moved into this sorry excuse for a house.

Omriseu had done a good job finding it. The house was on the outskirts of Trinovante, in an area where few people lived. The house was also big enough for the entire team, if the Infantry bunked three to a room. They didn't seem to mind.

Slumber never slept at the same time as the team, so he didn't get a room to himself. He was supposed to be out, practicing his magick, since his training was haphazard.

Sirocco had her own room, and so did Gem, and Hadley had as well. Atrü believed they needed it for their magick. The Spies shared a room, and Atrü had stayed in here, which wasn't a bedroom per se, but had the benefit of no windows and a single door.

Maybe he thought it felt like a Shadowlands. Shadowlands didn't seem to bother Visionaries like they bothered some of the Fey.

But Atrü couldn't create a Shadowlands. If he had been able

to, they wouldn't have had to waste their coin on someplace like this.

Sirocco squared her shoulders, and tilted her head back. She was wasting time, deliberately. She wanted rest. She'd been creating fogs for more than a week. And then there had been the trauma of the morning, the sudden need to form a new portal, and a slow, underlying terror that had been building since the strange Qavnerian magick had somehow snagged Hadley, the strongest of all of them.

Sirocco took a deep breath, and reached into her magick, feeling the air for the portal she had opened to rescue Hadley.

That portal was the newest one, and in some ways, the most painful. Sirocco had simply thrown her entire magickal self into creating in, panic substituting for planning and good judgment.

Which meant that this portal was strong and visible to anyone. Even though she created it, she couldn't destroy it. Her magick allowed her to open doors to create weather events, which she hadn't done here. When the weather events ended, the portal was supposed to fade—slowly, and over time.

Since this portal was created in panic and she hadn't thought to send a weather event through it, she had no idea if it would fade. Or, if it did fade, when.

Sirocco had closed the portal, but that wasn't the same as making it vanish. Certain members of the magickal Fey could open that portal without Sirocco's help, and clearly, from what had happened that morning, some Qavnerians—magickal Qavnerians—had the same power.

Ever since Atrü had assigned her the job of permanently closing the portals, she had tried to think of a spell she could do

—or maybe one of the Spies or Slumber or Gem could do—to close or destroy the portals.

Spy magick didn't work like that, and Dream Riders entered the brain, not the physical world. Seasoned Domestics could probably have figured out how to isolate the portals, but Gem was the opposite of seasoned.

She was so new that her own magick frightened her sometimes.

Sirocco's spells were all weather related, which was why she had thought of ice first. As she washed her hands (for the thousandth time), she had wondered if she could create some kind of unbearable heat around the portal, but that would have an impact on this room—and the other rooms with portals.

So...ice it was.

She raised her hands, and whipped them through the air. She had to pull moisture from it, as much moisture as she could find. She didn't dare use real water, because that ice might actually melt.

She wanted this ice to remain until the portal itself faded away. That required her to perform an indefinite spell, something she hadn't done since she trained a dozen years ago.

Fortunately for everyone concerned, she could remember her training in minute detail—unlike Gem, who apparently had never considered that spells didn't come directly from instructors. Gem was having to do her best to remember what she learned.

Sirocco would never forget.

But she had never used ice like this.

Although she had been taught how to use ice as a weapon. There were dozens of Weather Sprite spells that created thick ice that could encase anything real—a building, a carriage, another person—and those spells could last for days.

Maybe that was all she needed. A spell that could last for days. Because, if Atrü got his way, Omriseu would find them a new home and they would be gone by late tomorrow.

Sirocco couldn't count on that, though. She had to build the ice. Then she could check on it in a week or so, and see if the portal was gone.

Her hands had gathered more than enough water from the air—she hoped, anyway.

She had never encased anything magickal in ice before, but she had to believe it used the same principle.

Water from the air, stirred and formed into ice crystals which then adhered to each other.

She envisioned the ice sheet, made it an ice block, and attached it to the outside of the portal.

Someone could come through that portal, but they would encounter ice so thick that it would act like a wall.

A frozen wall—something they couldn't fight against.

Unless they had heat magick—and they knew how to use it.

She made herself focus.

If she made the ice extremely thick, then the heat magick would take hours, if not days to work.

She finished, opened her eyes, and stepped back.

It looked like there was a floating ice sculpture in the center of the room. The ice sculpture was taller than Sirocco and as wide as a cinderblock.

To make sure it stayed, she extended the ice all the way to the floor.

The room was already getting cold.

She hadn't thought of that, and what a problem that would be. She still had to ice two more portals—the one that Hadley had opened to go after the Kirilli, and the one that the Qavnerian had pulled Hadley through.

And then there was the original portal for the fog, which Sirocco had created in her own bedroom.

She staggered forward just a little, already tired from the day. She hoped Omriseu found the team a new home, because this one was going to get very cold and uncomfortable quite quickly.

Then she wiped her hands on her robes again, and smiled to herself.

The ice sculpture worked better than she had thought.

At least Rugar had known that a team like this needed a good Weather Sprite. When she saw him next, she would tell him about the things she had to do to correct the problems that the incompetents created.

If they got out of this.

She banished that thought from her mind.

Of course they would get out of this.

They had no other choice.

FIFTEEN

The fog was receding. Cilka could see gaps in it, almost like that opening that had appeared before her just a few short minutes ago.

Kirilli's corpse still remained on the street. She kept checking because it had disappeared once before. She could see the constables now, outlined against the fog's grayness. Before she hadn't been able to see them at all.

Judita stood a little too close to her, face tight, eyes intense. She wasn't covered in blood the way that Cilka was. It was almost as if the events of the last hour hadn't physically touched Judita at all.

Emotionally was a different matter. Judita seemed like a completely different woman than the one who had arrived here at Cilka's behest.

Cilka certainly felt different. She resisted the urge to wipe the blood off her face. All she would do was smear it. She needed to deal with Kirilli's corpse, and then she had to figure out just what was happening here.

Judita had just told her that this magic was Fey magic, which was ridiculous. Cilka had heard of the Fey—everyone alive had heard of the Fey. They were a power-hungry group of conquerors who had run roughshod over three continents—Vion, where they originated, Etanien, and Galinas, where they had settled.

Although some in the government believed the Fey were going to continue conquering until they had captured the entire world. Governmental discussions were often about preventing Fey invasions, not that the Fey had made a move to leave Nye for years.

Some in the government felt they had time, that the Fey had to conquer Leut before they ever got to Dorovich. But others believed the Fey would come to Dorovich first.

Cilka had a distant memory from her earliest schooling that the Fey had already come to Dorovich, although not Qavner. And their arrival had occurred long before there was anything like the Qavnerian Protectorate. All she knew was that there had been a battle or two, and that the Fey had not conquered Dorovich.

She couldn't remember the details of the Fey incursion, which wasn't uncommon for her and ancient history. It simply didn't interest her.

"Fey magic," she said and shook her head. She didn't really believe Judita. Fey magic was what people said when they wanted to scare children away from something dangerous or something that a child shouldn't touch.

Fey magic was a kind of terror fiction, something that hadn't existed in Dorovich for centuries, but which everyone seemed to be afraid of.

Even back in the Purges, there were factions that believed they weren't eradicating natural magic; they were eradicating *Fey magic*.

Cilka tried very hard not to pay attention to any of it.

"You have to listen to me on this," Judita said. "Fey magic—"

"Is not something I want to discuss right now. We'll talk about that later." And they would. Cilka had learned long ago to ignore Judita at her own peril. "Right now, I need to move this corpse and figure out what is in this satchel."

Judita looked over her shoulder. "That satchel might not be the important one. The two he was carrying when he was attacked—those were the important ones."

Cilka agreed. But those two weren't here right now. And they hadn't been here the first time Augustus Kirilli had died.

That thought made her shiver. She had never had that thought about anything before.

"Where do you think he took those satchels?" Cilka asked.

"He shouldn't have been able to take them anywhere," Judita said. "That's why I think this is Fey magic—"

Cilka held up a hand, stopping her. Cilka didn't want to hear it, not right now.

"I know he shouldn't have," Cilka said. "The fact is that he did."

Judita's mouth thinned, as if she was holding back words. After a few seconds, she nodded, but she didn't say anything.

"I think he took them home," Cilka said. "He'd left his office in a hurry and he was walking in the direction of his house.

Unless he had somewhere else to store them that we don't know about, they're there."

Judita's frown grew deeper. "You're thinking this is spirit magic."

Cilka wasn't thinking of the magic at all, but she would discuss it in these terms.

"It would be logical," she said, and as she thought about it, it *was* logical.

Spirits remained when they had unfinished business. Sometimes magic allowed them to finish that business.

Perhaps the delivery of the satchels was Kirilli's unfinished business. The magic that Judita had ignited when she tried to view the scene of the crime had given his spirit just enough power to take the satchels to his home.

But that didn't explain the loss of the corpse or the fact that initially, as Judita opened the scene, the corpse had remained in position. It was only when the stranger had seen Cilka that everything changed.

"It's going to take work to figure out what happened here," Judita said. "That's not work I can do alone. We'll need a circle."

A magical circle. On the street. In the financial district. They would all be tempting fate—unless Cilka could get Desmond to approve it, maybe even participate in it.

"Obviously, we can't do it right now," Cilka said. "I need to deal with—"

She almost said "the real-life implications" but what she and Judita had just gone through was real life. Inexplicable, maybe, but real all the same.

"—the body, the satchel, the crime that was committed

here." Then Cilka ran a hand along the outside of her clothing. "I also need to clean up."

Judita's prodigious frown became something even deeper. It had a power all its own.

"There will be residual magic," she said. "We can't leave this as it is."

Thin sunlight was coming through the fog—not burning it away so much as taking advantage of the fact that the fog was thinning.

Cilka couldn't see magic the way that Judita could, but Cilka was much more practical than Judita. They might have to seal off part of the street. There would be no other way to keep the people who worked in this area away from it otherwise.

"You'll have to show me which parts need to be blocked off," Cilka said. "And quickly."

"It's not the best use of our time," Judita said. "The Fey are here, which means—"

"I don't care what it means," Cilka said. "We have practical considerations. You'll have to abide by them."

Judita glared at her. It felt, for the first time since they'd known each other, that they were on opposite sides, but what, exactly, that meant, Cilka didn't know.

All she knew was that she had a job to do first. Then they would worry about the magic.

She knew it was all of a piece, but her work dictated that she do some things in a particular order.

She wasn't going to explain that to Judita. Judita would argue with her, and all the argument would do was waste time.

"Show me what I have to block off," Cilka said.

Judita squared her shoulders. She shook her head as if she

didn't even approve of the question—and maybe she didn't. But it didn't matter.

"I'd prefer it if you block off the entire street," Judita said.

Cilka actually considered it. She looked around at the buildings, their shapes indistinct in the thinning fog, and wondered what it would take to close the street.

Maybe less work than closing off parts of the street. People would rebel against closing parts of the street—maybe even walk through the magical area. But people would have to avoid the street altogether if she put some watchmen and vehicles at the entrances to this block.

"Will that be enough?" she asked.

Judita leaned back slightly. Cilka could feel her surprise. Judita had clearly expected Cilka to argue with her more.

"I mean," Cilka continued, "Augustus Kirilli initially came from his office. He was tracked on the street, and then—"

She waved a hand at the body, the satchel, the area where the opening had been.

"—then *this* happened," she said.

"And he ran away." Judita looked at the corpse and then the street beyond. "I don't know. Give me a moment."

She walked around the corpse, much slower than Cilka wanted her to. Cilka wanted Judita to deal with all of this immediately. Maybe this was immediate in Judita's mind, but Cilka could feel some kind of internal clock ticking.

Maybe that was what Judita felt too. Something was going wrong and they had a very limited time to resolve it.

Judita walked parallel to the course that Kirilli had taken. Or, at least, that Cilka remembered him taking. She hadn't really watched him. She'd been grappling with his assailant.

Cilka wanted to call out to Judita, to say, *Don't use magic here, especially to "see" what had happened*, but Cilka had to trust her. Judita understood magic better than Cilka did.

After what they had just experienced, Judita would be sensible, right?

Cilka's heart pounded, though. She had no idea if there would be a magical trail. She had no idea what she would do if one ran all the way to Kirilli's neighborhood.

Judita stopped almost a full block away. Then she retraced her steps, her head partially down, her expression thoughtful.

When she reached Cilka, she said, "I'm not sure I understand what's going on here."

"You might be wrong about Fey magic?" Cilka couldn't resist asking.

Judita shook her head once. Just once. "We both might be wrong. Or we might be seeing something entirely new."

"What does that mean?" Cilka asked.

"There is a splash of magic around the corpse," Judita said. "The kind of splash you would see if he had been holding a sack filled with water and landed on it. The magic sprayed forward. It was thick and deep, and may have absorbed into the street."

"May have?" Cilka repeated.

"We need the circle," Judita said. "We would need the circle for most of your questions."

Cilka nodded. She wasn't going to start that argument again.

Judita glanced over her shoulder, then shrugged.

"Beyond that spray, that splash," she said. "There is no magical trail from the corpse out of the financial district."

"None?" Cilka asked.

"None I recognize." Judita frowned at the corpse, waved a hand slightly, but (fortunately) didn't cast any kind of spell. "There are magical streams, but there are always magical streams. Right now, I don't dare examine them closely. I'd be using too much magic."

That would make sense. Cilka couldn't see any at all.

"But if what you postulated was true," Judita said, "that Kirilli was operating with spirit magic, then it makes sense that there would be no magical trail. The magic is attached to the spirit, not to the location."

Her hand twitched again, as if she was going to try to reveal more magic.

Cilka held up a hand, reminding Judita to stop.

"Don't worry," Judita said, more to the corpse than to Cilka. "I'm not going to use any magic here. There are too many crosscurrents. That's what I missed earlier. There is a lot of magic in this area, and some of it I do not recognize. I just hope it won't fade by the time we get around to that circle."

Cilka did not respond to that. She did not appreciate the pressure.

"What about between here and Kirilli's office?" she asked.

Judita shook her head. "Nothing from the office. But the area around us, from the place where the stranger first appeared, that has a lot of magic."

Finally, Cilka's questions were answered.

"All right," she said. "That means if I block off this street, then no one can walk into the magical crosscurrents."

"Unless the crosscurrents expand," Judita said.

Cilka ignored that too. "My next question is a practical one. Can we easily remove the corpse without disturbing the crosscurrents?"

Judita put a hand over her mouth as she contemplated Kirilli's corpse. Then she moved ever so slightly, and Cilka felt a surge of panic.

"You won't have to use magic, will you?" Cilka asked.

Judita gave her an almost angry sideways glance. It was becoming clear that whatever had just happened—and Cilka still wasn't entirely sure—had separated them greatly.

Maybe permanently.

Judita didn't even answer the question, which made Cilka even more nervous. The fact that Judita didn't know exactly what had caused that window to open, that Judita was willing to label it Fey and then examine whether it was spirit magic in the same conversation, did not give Cilka much confidence in any answer Judita gave her.

The problem was that Cilka had no one else to ask, and they had to get this body off the street. Soon.

Judita walked past the body and crouched, studying the satchel as if it had all of the answers. Then she braced her hands on her thighs and pushed herself up.

She seemed tired now, older than she had just an hour before.

Her face was haggard as she turned toward Cilka, which made Cilka wonder if Judita had used magic. Magic sometimes drained a person.

"The satchel and the body are covered in magic," Judita said. "But the magic is faint, and I'm not sure where it originated. It doesn't appear to be mine or yours or even from that portal or that...creature...we saw."

Cilka wanted to say that they hadn't seen a creature; they

had seen and fought with a person, and they had killed that person.

"I wonder if the magic came from Augustus Kirilli himself," Judita said.

Cilka frowned. She supposed that was likely, but she couldn't quite see it.

Judita took Cilka's silence as a disagreement.

"He did break out of that spell, the one that commanded him to stop," Judita said.

Cilka nodded. If the magic came from Kirilli, it would travel with him, and she could do nothing about it.

"I'm going to move him, then," she said.

"Use the iron tombs," Judita said.

Cilka started. She hadn't thought of those in years. No one talked about them.

During the Purges, the dead who were thought to be magical were placed in iron caskets while they awaited processing. Some were cremated. Others tossed far out to sea. And some, considered incorrectly accused, were buried in family plots.

Cilka had visited there a few times and the tombs had always terrified her. At that point in her life, she had been a woman who did not terrify easily.

Apparently that was changing.

"You think he's a threat?" Cilka asked.

"I don't know what's happening here," Judita said. "But it's better if we're all protected."

Cilka would have wagered that Judita never thought of the iron tombs as protection before. She must have been terrified as well.

"It'll prevent the Fey from stealing him," Judita said.

And suddenly all became clear. Judita hadn't made the suggestion to lock Kirilli and his magic away. She had made the suggestion to keep the Fey from stealing his body.

Cilka had no idea why anyone would do that, but she was out of her depth right now, and she knew it.

"Put the satchel there too," Judita said.

Cilka nodded. "I will."

Judita relaxed ever so slightly.

"I will contact you later, as I said," Cilka said. "We'll make plans then."

Judita tilted her head, looking at Cilka as if she'd never seen her before. Which was fair, because Cilka was beginning to believe she had never really seen Judita before. Or maybe she had never really understood Judita. That was probably more accurate.

"You cannot wait too long," Judita said. It didn't sound like a warning; it sounded like a threat.

"Or what?" Cilka asked.

Judita paused, as if she was choosing her words carefully. "Or the danger will increase."

That, Cilka believed. She felt it too.

"I won't wait too long," she said. "I promise."

She only hoped that she would be able to fulfill the promise. Everything felt up in the air right now. Everything, including Cilka's understanding of the world around her.

And that, she knew, was as dangerous as anything else.

CHAPTER
SIXTEEN

Gem sat cross-legged in the newly turned dirt in the yard of the horrible house that Omriseu had found for them. She watched the back door, the one into the kitchen, waiting for it to close behind Rodderc.

He looked at her with concern, but she gave him a fake smile and nodded, as if everything was all right.

Everything was *not* all right. Everything was awful and she had failed miserably, but she hadn't known what else to do.

He smiled back at her, then let himself into the kitchen, barely fitting through the entry. The door banged closed behind him.

Gem breathed shallowly, the cold foggy air that Sirocco had wrapped around the house clogging Gem's nose and throat. Her lower lip trembled, so she bit it, hard, and the pain brought tears to her eyes.

Oh, who was she fooling? The tears had already been there.

She kept breathing as shallowly as she could, even though she was gulping air. Her entire body was trying to sob, and she wouldn't let it.

She hadn't been in love with Hadley—it wasn't good or right for a Domestic and an Enchanter to love each other; their magicks were too different—but she had wanted to love her.

Hadley had wanted something too. Their glances lingered too long, their smiles at each other were a bit too bright. The room lit up whenever Hadley entered, and even Hadley's bad moods were glorious.

And now she was dead. Horribly dead, her beautiful face mangled, her body badly bruised.

Gem couldn't even perform the proper magickal rituals, the ones Domestics were trained in. Gem should have extracted as much magick as possible from Hadley, maybe even caught her spirit—if the death had been recent.

But Gem hadn't had the tools to do that, and even if she had, she wouldn't have had anywhere to store the magick. There were no Spell Warders here to take recovered magick and maybe assign it to a worthy successor. There were no members of the Black Family nearby who might need a magickal augmentation, even though most would have turned that kind of magick down.

There were no other Enchanters around who could take the spirit and extract the personal spells, maybe memorize them before they faded.

Everything that Hadley had been, everything that she had known, was gone, planted in the brownish-red dirt of a land that the Fey had no claim to.

Being buried wasn't the Fey way. But none of the Fey's methods could apply here. They couldn't drag Hadley's body with them to dispose of properly. They couldn't hide it and come back for it.

They couldn't figure out a way to preserve her. There was no one to do it. Domestic magick only went so far. It was Tenders who managed to perform miracles with the upper levels of Fey dead.

And there wasn't a Tender anywhere on this continent. So far as Gem knew, there were only three Domestics counting herself, and she had no way to contact the other two.

She inhaled sharply, a deep shuddery breath, as close to a sob as she could get.

Atrü would hate to know she was crying. Everyone would. They already saw Gem as incompetent and weak.

She just hadn't finished her training. She hadn't told anyone that. She so disliked her training partners that she had left early and walked back to Nir, the capitol city of Nye, claiming (when asked) that she had passed her training tests with the highest possible marks.

She had been gambling that no one would talk to the people who were supposed to train her. They had told her, repeatedly, that she wasn't Domestic material. It didn't matter how strong her magick was, her imagination was weak.

And then they'd pinch her when she did something wrong. She had thought she could live with that, but her skin had become a sea of bruises within a month.

The pinching had been a test too, although she hadn't realized that until she was back in Nir. The pinching was a non-lethal way to provoke her, to see what happened when she was in great pain or deeply angry.

She hadn't been angry. She had been defensive. She had

retreated inside herself, until she decided the verbal abuse and the pinching weren't worth the training.

Surely, she had thought, Domestic training would be gentle somewhere along the way.

But, as one of her friends mentioned in passing, nothing about the Fey was gentle. Domestic training pushed its practitioners to the limit, so that an unworthy person wouldn't become a Domestic.

Worthiness was measured not in magickal ability—which Gem had a great deal of—but in the ability to hold her temper. If a Domestic lost her temper and deliberately killed someone—even in a battle—then her magick would disappear.

It wasn't worth training a Domestic for years only to have her squander it in a moment of fury—or so her friend had said.

Gem had hated that. She had hated all of it.

But she loved making homes and creating comfort and making everything around her nice.

She had practiced it as best she could without the training. She might have been able to continue fooling people, if she hadn't been so terrified of getting caught.

That was why she had volunteered to go on this trip. She had thought it the best way to escape her past.

She hadn't realized that the gaps in her training had made her ineffective here. The gaps in her training might have led to the loss of everything that was special about Hadley, her knowledge, her magick, her essence.

Gem swallowed hard. The lump in her throat actually hurt. The tears had gathered under her chin, dripping onto the back of her hands.

The others couldn't see her like this. They would know just how weak she was.

The Fey did not cry over their dead. They preserved what they could, used as much as possible, remembered as best they could, and then got revenge if revenge was required.

Only Gem couldn't get revenge. It would destroy her magick.

All she could do was support the others in their quest for revenge.

She used her hands to brace herself, and then stood, not looking at the disturbed patch of ground. She wobbled a bit, steadied herself, and took a deep breath of fog and chill.

This time, the breath wasn't shaky. This time the breath was clear. The threat of tears was fading, although she had a hunch it would eventually return.

She waved a hand over the dirt to smooth it out. Then she created some tiny flowering plants to rest in the dirt, and made those plants promise they would bloom for a hundred years.

She didn't care what the Qavnerians thought of that. There had to be some kind of memorial for Hadley, even if it was one that no one but Gem understood.

Then she gathered herself, and focused on what she had to do next.

She had to assume that Omriseu would find them all a new place to live. He would have to do that soon, because Atrü believed those people who killed Hadley would find the team and try to destroy them.

The team couldn't hide here forever.

They didn't have a lot of possessions or equipment.

Everyone would be responsible for their own. She didn't want to touch any of the weapons that the Infantry brought, and she didn't dare touch anything belonging to Slumber, the Dream Rider. She had no idea how his magick worked, and she didn't want to get lost in it.

She also didn't know what they would do with Hadley's meager possessions. Gem would have to examine the entire room, and then bring Atrü in on the decision.

Before they left Nir, they had all been told to leave as much behind as possible. They only needed items that would augment their magick or were necessary for day-to-day survival.

Gem had brought clothing and Healing supplies, as well as herbs she wasn't certain she could get in Dorovich. The Infantry had all brought shields and swords. Atrü had a valise, as did Slumber. And it had appeared that Hadley brought nothing, although her room had been full of all sorts of items when Gem had visited a few times.

Gem put her hands on her knees and stood slowly. She felt very old, even though she was the youngest in the group. Old and tired and sad.

In addition to everyone's individual possessions, the team would have to bring the artifacts that the Infantry hadn't destroyed. They were displayed across a table in the room the team had been using as a living room. The artifacts were odd bits, sculptures and glassware and jewelry, instruments and books and silverware. No real weapons at all.

But Gem could feel the magick wafting off all of them, the kind of magick that terrified her. Even though some of the items looked like they belonged to a Domestic, she got a sense that none of these items were made for comfort.

They gave off an energy similar to the ones that she had seen on the Infantry's knives and swords. Things that, if she had to guess, seemed to have only one purpose—that of killing someone else.

She wasn't even sure she could pack those things up. She wasn't sure she could touch them.

She would have to tell Atrü that.

She knew he wouldn't want to leave those things behind.

Like they were going to leave Hadley.

Gem's heart constricted. Her lower lip trembled again, and she bit it so hard that she tasted blood.

The Fey are warriors, Hadley had told her after the Assassin died. *Warriors accept death. They live with it and move beyond it. You are too sentimental, Gem.*

I'm a Domestic, Gem had said. The Assassin's death had shaken her, even though she had greatly disliked him.

Being a Domestic is not an excuse for sentimentality, Hadley had said. *You need to heal people, sometimes in the worst circumstances. There is no time for emotion. Emotion is an indulgence, one we do not have time for on this mission.*

Gem nodded, as if Hadley was speaking to her right now.

No time for emotion. All Gem could do was make the right decisions.

The best decisions.

She gave the tiny plants one last glance. They were purple and red and bluish yellow, and they would be beautiful in a few days.

She wouldn't be here to see them grow, and that was all right.

"Sometimes, Hadley," Gem whispered, "sentimentality has its place."

Yes, Hadley would have said. *And that place is behind us.*

Gem nodded, and then let herself into the house. She had work to do, and she suspected that she would have to do it fast.

CHAPTER
SEVENTEEN

The carriage pulled onto Gussie's street and she felt herself relax. Home, to her, really wasn't the manor. It was the home she had chosen for herself, against her father's objections.

The house was small by Kirilli standards. Only four bedrooms, a front and back parlor, and a large carriage house in the back that doubled as a servants' quarters for her housekeeper, groom, gardener, and Zeitsev. She had had a second carriage house built after she moved in, but the carriage she stored there had nothing to do with horses.

That carriage house concealed her windstone vehicle which was, if she was being honest with herself, her pride and joy.

The neighborhood wasn't as grand as the neighborhood surrounding the Kirilli manor. The houses here were newer, smaller, and didn't need dozens of servants to keep them running.

From the interior of her house, she couldn't see any of the

other houses in the neighborhood. They had all been built that way, and she felt it gave her a certain measure of security.

She was no longer sure if that was true, but it felt true—even as part of her worried that whatever had happened at her father's home had happened here as well.

She leaned forward slightly as the horses clopped along the street. Nothing seemed out of the ordinary, except, perhaps, the light through the fog. The fog had grown progressively thicker over the past week, and last night through early this morning, it had been almost unbearable.

She hadn't realized how much she had grown accustomed to Trinovante in the fog—and how much she hated it.

She twisted her fingers around the thick fabric of her skirt, not letting herself think about things more serious than the fog or the security of the neighborhood.

The satchels at her feet beckoned her, but she didn't let herself touch them. She was worried that she would remove the maps that her father had mentioned and something about them (*the magic inside of them*, her inner voice whispered) might draw whoever had attacked the manor.

She didn't want that. She wasn't sure she'd be safe at the Vault either, but she would be safer there than she was in the carriage or than she would be in her home.

The carriage turned to the right and up the familiar bump that took it to the carriage house. She knew without looking how this path felt, where the wheels would catch in small ruts, how the horses would slow as they approached the end of their journey, how Zeitsev would handle them once they reached the carriage house.

The familiar wasn't putting her at ease, though. It was

making her tense. Part of her wondered whether or not this would be the last time she would experience something this familiar, small, and comforting.

The carriage stopped, rocking slightly like it always did as Zeitsev got down. He didn't come to her immediately, which was unusual. So unusual, in fact, that her heart rate increased.

Had he encountered something? Was there someone waiting for them after all?

Then he pulled open the door.

"Yer home, miss," he said, his voice filled with disapproval.

"Thank you." She picked up the satchels, knowing it would be a difficult climb to get down while she held them. But she still didn't want to give them to him.

He stayed to one side and supported her using her right elbow, his hand uncomfortably close to one of the satchels. She reached the ground and stepped away, her stomach churning—not because of him, but because of everything that had happened.

She set the satchels down and looked at her home.

The view of the house from here was the same. The fog had parted near it, so the edges of the three-story building were crisp and clean. The windows were intact, the shutters open. Nothing had disturbed the roses, climbing trellises on the outside of the walls. The garden seemed fine.

But she couldn't go inside. Not yet.

"I need you to do something for me," she said to Zeitsev. "I need you to bring the staff to me."

She felt like a coward making him go inside alone, but she had to guard the satchels. Or, at least, that was her excuse.

He frowned at her, seemingly questioning what she was asking.

"I'm going to give them the next few days off," she said. "I want them far away from anyone Kirilli. That goes for you, too."

He shook his head once, but didn't say much. He secured the horses, then walked around the carriage house.

She didn't usually need much—she was a pretty undemanding boss, at least as far as her family went—so when she was gone, the small staff often took time off.

She had been expected to be gone the entire morning. She would have expected Daisy, her housekeeper, to take a few hours to herself, then return to work to make sure the house was ready for Gussie's return.

Gussie shifted slightly, knowing she was covered in drying blood. Normally, she would have done something about it. On this day, though, she didn't have the time to worry about her appearance.

The groom emerged first, maybe because he'd heard the carriage. After acknowledging Gussie with a nod and a slight frown, he went to the horses, rubbing their noses and murmuring softly to them.

The horses suddenly seemed calmer. She hadn't realized they had been riled up as well. But she didn't pay attention to horses. She rode, but unwillingly. She found horses an inconvenience and a burden, which probably had a lot to do with several incidents she had suffered through as a child.

She shifted from foot to foot, trying not to show her impatience. She needed to get to the Vault, but she had to release the staff first.

She would not be able to live with herself if she didn't make sure they were safe.

Even though the amount of time this was taking was logical, she could barely beat back her anxiety. What if whoever had killed her father's staff was inside the house? Then she had sent Zeitsev to his death.

The gardener showed up as she had that thought, his clothing covered in dirt. He had a bag of bulbs over his shoulder, and was carrying a trowel. When he saw her, he looked surprised, and then concerned.

Then Zeitsev showed up, with Daisy at his side. She had an apron wrapped around her tall, slender form, her brown hair escaping its customary bun. She glanced at Zeitsev, then back at Gussie, clearly trying to keep her expression neutral.

All four of them—her entire staff—alive and well. Gussie felt a relief so profound that it almost brought her to tears.

She made herself take a deep calming breath, hoping no tears would escape.

"I have terrible news," she said. "My father..."

Despite her attempt at remaining calm, her voice broke. The groom looked at her as if he couldn't believe she felt emotion. The gardener's mask slipped, making him look somewhat alarmed.

She tried again. "My father..." She couldn't finish the sentence. "He, um..."

What could she say? That he was dead? She wasn't completely sure of that, which wasn't true. She just didn't have actual proof. But she knew. Deep down.

Still, speaking the words made it so.

She waved a hand, signifying that she was going to move on.

"Someone—a lot of someones, I think—attacked my father's manor. The staff..." and there her voice broke again. She swallowed hard and forced herself to finish. "...they didn't make it."

"All of them?" Daisy whispered. She had often worked closely with them on family projects.

"I'm sorry," Gussie said, a tear spilling out of her right eye and running down her cheek. She didn't wipe at the tear. She didn't want to call attention to it. She cleared her throat, and made herself continue. "I don't know who attacked them. Or why. Or what they wanted from the manor."

Was that her first lie? She wasn't certain. Because her father (the spirit of her father? Whom she had hugged, and whose blood covered her still?) had thought whatever they wanted was in the satchels.

The staff continued to watch her. Daisy's eyes were red and she was sniffling. The groom's mouth was in a very thin line. And the gardener was holding his trowel as if it was a sword.

"Because I don't know what happened to them exactly," Gussie said, "I don't know if whoever attacked them will come here."

She resisted the urge to look over her shoulder, to see if some stranger was coming down the street. She didn't hear horses or the rattle of a carriage, but that no longer mattered. Not with so many people starting to acquire windstone vehicles.

"But I can't risk your lives on an assumption," she said. "I give you two options. You can quit, and I will give you excellent references."

The gardener stiffened. The groom didn't move. Daisy was shaking her head.

"Or," Gussie said, "I will give you the next week off. Maybe by then the constabulary will know what happened and have the perpetrators in custody."

"Miss," Daisy said, "we canna leave you here alone."

"I'm not sure I'm going to be here either," Gussie said. "But I will promise you that I will not be alone. I will have someone with me."

After I go to the Vault, she thought but did not say. Her gaze caught Zeitsev's. His eyes narrowed. He knew she was lying about that.

"Please," Gussie said. "Leave this place. Take the week. If the investigation takes longer or if the threat remains, I will send someone to you to warn you to continue to stay away. So you need to let me know if you're quitting or if you're going to stay with family."

"I'm goin' ta my sister's," Daisy said. "I will be checkin' in here daily."

"No," Gussie said. "Please. Let us contact you."

Only there was no "us." Just her.

The groom shifted, then said, "I'll be stayin'. The horses need me."

The horses. She hadn't thought about the horses.

"Is there any place to take them?" she asked. "I don't want them here either."

"We'll think of somethin'," Zeitsev said quickly. "And I'll let ya know, miss, what we decide. And where we'll be stayin'."

It was clear; he was going to convince the groom to stay away.

"I got nowhere to go," the gardener said. "I don't have family."

Gussie had known that, and forgotten it. She had hired him when he moved to Trinovante from Serebro. He'd gone to the Academy and studied...whatever it was people studied when they liked plants.

Her mind was not as sharp as usual. She was managing too much.

"Ye'll come with me," Daisy said. "My sister'll take ya."

The gardener nodded, then said, "What about you, miss? Without your father, you're alone in the city."

She was. Her siblings were spread out all over Qavner. And she needed to let them know what was happening.

"I'll be all right," she said, knowing the words rang hollow. "I have an errand to run, as do you, Fanis."

She looked at Zeitsev. He shook his head once.

So she was going to force him.

"Fanis will be talking to the constabulary, and letting them know what we found at my father's manor." Gussie could say that. She just couldn't say what happened to her father.

"And you, miss?" Daisy asked, real concern in her voice. "What about you?"

Gussie took a deep breath. Taking action was making her calmer. "I made a promise to my father. I will do what he asked, and then figure out what's next for me."

"I'll be goin' with ya," Daisy said.

"No," Gussie said. "I promised him I would do this alone."

"Seems dangerous, given what you said." The gardener adjusted the bag over his shoulder.

"It is," Zeitsev said.

"I think anything connected to a Kirilli is dangerous right now," Gussie said. "I'll do what I can to be safe. I'll also protect you. I can't take you with me, because that will put you all in danger."

And the satchels as well. Because if anyone outside of the family knew where the Vault was, the information could be beaten out of them.

She wasn't going to say that. She wasn't going to say anything like that for fear of making it so.

"All right," she said. "Standing here is not helping any of us. We need to move."

And then, without looking at them again, she picked up the satchels and walked toward the second carriage house. She wasn't wearing her driving togs, but it didn't matter. She had to get the Vault as soon as possible.

She had waited long enough.

EIGHTEEN

Omriseu had on his businessman's face. He had worn it before, when he first found the house that the team lived in now. The face, the slightly constrictive clothes, and the ridiculously tight shoes felt normal to him now.

That was how Spy magick worked. He didn't pretend to be someone else. He augmented a new aspect of his own identity, one he hadn't realized he had before.

He was at the very edge of the financial district which, he was surprised to learn, had been mostly shut down due to the attack on Kirilli. Omriseu thought of it more as the death of Hadley, but he had to clear that thought from his mind.

For the next few hours, he was no longer Fey. He was from Trinovante, one of those mid-level professionals who didn't really have wealth, but wasn't poor either. He worked with people who had wealth, and he did what they asked, whether it pained him or not.

He needed a new house for the team, and quickly. Because he had to act quickly, he took the risk of reusing his cover story —that he was finding a place for his boss's adult children to live while they were on holiday leave from Serebro Academy.

Originally he had told the brokers that the house would be used off and on by a variety of people, and Omriseu wouldn't be able to vouch for the condition they left it in. For the brokers' trouble, he would give them double rent just so that they would look the other way.

And they did. They agreed to it.

Among the merchant classes in cultures like this one, money spoke the loudest. Omriseu had negotiated his way through a variety of different cities and cultures and behaviors, and he always found the merchant classes the easiest to manipulate. As long as they got paid, and paid well, they didn't care what anyone did.

Or really, who anyone was.

He stopped in front of a small rectangular building made of tan brick. The building sat between two monstrosities owned by big firms like Kirilli's firm, and almost got lost between them.

Originally, Omriseu had entered this place reluctantly, not realizing that a broker like this one—an independent one— wasn't trying to impress anyone, unlike the Kirilli firm. This firm was out to make money, not to play high stakes business with city leaders.

In other words, this place had turned out to be the exact kind of place that Omriseu had needed.

He glanced around the street, a bit uneasy at how empty it was. Most of the big buildings were dark. Watchmen stood on a handful of corners. The watchman (actually a woman, not a man) that he had passed to get here had nodded at him and smiled.

Omriseu had smiled back, because blending in was the most important thing he could do.

Fortunately for him, many people on Dorovich were tall. Tall people were accepted here as normal, which wasn't the case in some other cities Omriseu had visited.

He adjusted the white sleeves on his comfortable shirt, tugged the hem of his jacket and slicked back his hair. He had shortened and straightened it, making it lie flat against his scalp, which, the first time he had done so, felt quite strange.

He was getting used to this as well.

The outer door was open here, as if whoever was inside felt the need to have a bit of the remaining fog blow inside.

Omriseu felt a curious reluctance about following that fog into the building. He didn't want to negotiate another house, even though he had more than enough coin on him to do so. He even knew what house he wanted.

It had been his second choice and was only a few blocks from the first one. It had been larger, but it hadn't had a room without windows like the first one, a room he had thought would be very useful.

Maybe it had been, considering that was the room they had pulled Hadley's body into. Or maybe, as Gem suggested one evening, Omriseu had liked it because it reminded him of the confinement inside a Shadowlands.

If only Atrü actually had the abilities of a real Visionary, instead of the smattering of magick that minor Visionaries were lucky to have. Then the team could hide in a Shadowlands. They could have spied on the Kirilli, figured out who gave him those satchels, figured out whether or not he had magick, and protected themselves better since it was obvious now that Kirilli —or someone around him—had a lot of magick.

Omriseu's skin itched. It was an early sign that his identity was about to crack. He forced himself to concentrate. He would think about the others later, and that magick—that unexpected magick.

Omriseu took a deep breath and walked through that open door, feeling his persona harden as he did.

He saw the broker he had worked with before, a man named Yanni Komidas. Komidas was a round man who was going bald and not fighting it. His dark hair was combed back on either side of his head, but the top was completely bare.

His eyes were as round as his head, his lips protruded a bit too much—perhaps because his nose was smaller than it should have been for the architecture of his face.

He didn't quite smile when he saw Omriseu, but he tried.

"Strange day, huh?" Komidas asked, his voice booming.

He didn't have to speak loudly. The entry room, which usually had at least five people waiting in the various chairs, was startlingly empty.

Doors down the two hallways were closed, and Omriseu got the distinct sense that he and Komidas were the only two people in the entire building.

"I wouldn't be here if my boss hadn't insisted," Omriseu said, realizing as he spoke that his words were true no matter what identity he was using. "Their kids do not like the house we procured for them."

Komidas looked stricken. "Why not? Are there problems?"

"Aside from callow youth?" Omriseu said with a half-smile of his own. "No, none at all."

"I'm afraid I can't let you out of the lease," Komidas said.

"And I wouldn't argue for it," Omriseu said. "We paid your fee for the half year. As far as we're concerned, that deal is separate from this one. I was wondering if the house a few blocks away was still available."

Komidas walked around a desk and pulled open a drawer. It was a deep drawer with files inside, some of the paper sticking out as if someone couldn't be bothered to replace it all properly.

He pulled out one of the files, thumbed through it, and then peered over it at Omriseu, and recited an address.

"That's the house we're discussing, am I right?" Komidas asked.

"Yes," Omriseu said.

"Then it is still available," Komidas said.

"Can we have use of it as early as tomorrow? The eldest son and some of his friends are due to arrive from Serebro for some kind of break—"

"In the middle of the semester?" Komidas asked, shocked.

"When you have money," Omriseu said, "you can do whatever you want."

Komidas shook his head.

"I always seem to forget that," he said, and then gave a little chuckle with no mirth in it.

"Can we settle up now?" Omriseu said.

Komidas frowned, then nodded. "Of course. I don't want to be here any more than you do. The sooner we complete our business, the sooner I can close."

Komidas hadn't been waiting for Omriseu, but something about this moment had convinced Komidas to leave.

"I will see if we have a key here." He stood, pivoted and scurried down the hallway, his feet echoing on the wooden floorboards.

Omriseu had never seen this place so empty. He hadn't seen the financial district this empty either. It felt odd to be here, odd to be anywhere in the city.

The magick he had seen that morning didn't so much unnerve him as make him realize their little team was no match for anything that the Dorovicians threw at them. People with magick here had much more magick than their little team did, now that Hadley was gone.

The history of the Fey had shown that Dorovich had been difficult to conquer. The Fey had been turned back the first time they tried it. They had sent other teams here over the years to understand what went wrong, but nothing coordinated until Rugar had decided that enough was enough.

He so wanted to impress his father, but Omriseu was no longer certain that coming to Dorovich first was the way to do so.

If only there was a way to get back to Nye without declaring this mission a failure—

A rustle caught him and he turned. Komidas was staring at him as if he had never seen Omriseu before.

Omriseu must have lost his face. He was probably a bit of a blur.

It took him a moment to recapture his persona completely.

Then he smiled at Komidas. "Did you find a key?"

Komidas shook his head, as if what he had seen had been his

fault and not Omriseu thinking of his Fey life instead of his Trinovantian persona.

"Um, yes," Komidas said. "We have a key. All it will take is payment. While you gather that, I'll send a cleaning crew—"

"No need," Omriseu said. "I have payment right here. And we have our own cleaners."

That sounded odd. He hadn't said that to Komidas before either, so Omriseu had to cover quickly.

"I'm sorry to say that the current house was not cleaned to my boss's satisfaction." Omriseu shoved his hands in the pockets of his suitcoat, getting the money he had stored there. "I have no idea why he wants these places cleaned so thoroughly. His children will only mess them up."

"They'll need to be cleaned before you turn in the key," Komidas said as if Omriseu had forgotten.

Omriseu executed a fleeting and humorless smile. "Fortunately, that's not something we'll have to worry about for several months. Do you have a document for me to sign?"

"Ah, yes." Komidas had clearly forgotten. "Give me just a moment to fill it all out."

"Take all the time you need," Omriseu said.

He walked to the narrow windows beside the door. A different watchman walked by, but no one else did.

This district was eerily empty.

He didn't like that. He didn't like anything about Trinovante or Dorovich. There was little more he could do here. He could maybe find out the sources of the magick, but that might be a wasted effort.

He was afraid—and the thought caught him. Yes, afraid—

that no one on the team would return to Nye, and all of this information would be lost.

He squared his shoulders. He would give the key and the address to Atrü, and then Omriseu would claim that he had more investigating to do.

He would leave at that point. They didn't need him anyway. If their second stronghold got breached that would not be his concern. For all he cared, they could go back to the first.

By then, he would be long gone.

And it wasn't as if he was leaving them in some kind of lurch. They had another Spy.

Qurzi wasn't as capable, but this group didn't need capable.

They needed a miracle.

And Omriseu wasn't going to be it.

NINETEEN

It took longer to move Kirilli's body than Cilka expected. Two of the constables refused to touch it once they realized she wanted to take it to the iron tombs.

In the end, she sent for two different constables and a special wagon. She was in the buckboard of the wagon now, handling the horse herself, because she didn't want to explain how to get to the iron tombs.

The two constables—the new ones who had no idea where they were going—were sitting in the back with the dead body.

The streets were mostly empty this morning, even though the fog was nearly gone. It was white and wispy, the way fog used to be when Cilka was a child. She hadn't seen fog like this in a long, long time. The fog looked pearlescent and almost pretty.

Her hands felt damp on the reins. The horse, a comfortable animal that didn't mind the blinders, plodded along. The wagon bumped underneath her. The constables were quiet. Cilka made sure she was going slowly so that the body didn't slide back and forth. It was under a blanket, but she was still conscious of it.

She wanted to go faster, but she didn't dare. She had to remind herself that she was in no real hurry.

But a deep and uncomfortable part of her, a part that had been greatly unsettled by the events of the morning, disagreed. She *was* in a hurry.

She needed to get Augustus Kirilli's body to the iron tombs, and then she needed to see Desmond.

The iron tombs were built into the Ancient Rise just past the Waterfront District. The Ancient Rise was, as its name suggested, one of the oldest parts of Trinovante. The Ancient Rise circled around the old city and had once acted as a type of wall until a thousand years ago, someone had actually built a stone wall there.

The stone wall had been in ruins as long as Cilka was alive. Two stone pillars still stood near the widest part of the road. They had once held the wooden gate that would swing open for Trinovante's leaders and no one else—or so legend said.

The stone pillars had been worn down by time and weather, but the original design was still visible. Each one looked like a tall man, head bent slightly as he looked down at the gate—or where the gate had been. The neck and shoulders bent forward, the arms were in front of the torso, resting on the hilt of what some scholars believed had been a very ornate sword.

The legs disappeared into the base of the pillar, and there were no feet, but the entire effect was one of motion. The men were leaning and thinking. They seemed protective.

Other stone men—or maybe women—had similar posts around the Ancient Rise. They'd clearly been part of the stone fence. Even though the fence had mostly worn away, these pillars hadn't.

They were the subject of much scholarship, but not much was known about their origins. As some scholars had pointed out, the pillars looked vaguely fantastical. The man on the south side of the entrance had a pointed ear. The man on the north side had no point on his ear, but that was because the point appeared to have been broken off.

The very idea of that pointed ear made Cilka suddenly nervous. Kirilli's murderer had had pointed ears. Judita had called that person Fey, and Cilka knew, from her inadequate education, that the Fey had once come to Dorovich.

Why would Fey statues be used to guard the entrance to the old city? What had she failed to understand? These stone pillars were called the Stone Guardians on some maps, and she had always thought the name poetic.

But what if it hadn't been poetic at all?

The road got rougher the closer the wagon got the top of the Ancient Rise. The road was broken here, mostly because someone had tried to cover over the remains of the stone wall.

She always felt a slight burning vibration as she went over that part of the rise, as if she had put her hand on something that sizzled. The feeling sliced through her right now, and she resisted the urge to look behind her, in the bed of the wagon.

One of the constables grunted, though. She wasn't sure if that sound had come from his discomfort in the bumps in the road, or if he too felt that burning vibration.

And then a part of her wondered if the corpse had moved. Or sat up. Or changed.

She couldn't resist. She had to look over her shoulder.

The constables were leaning against the wagon's wooden sides, staring up at the Stone Guardians. They were youngish men, with dark hair peeking out from beneath their caps. They were both tall and lean, and didn't seem to mind the proximity to the corpse.

The blanket hadn't moved at all. It was still Kirilli-shaped.

The satchel had fallen on its side, but it remained on the edge of the blanket.

She saw all of that in an instant, then turned back around, feeling relieved. She let out a small breath, thankful that something, at least, was going her way.

The wagon reached the top of the rise. The view from here always surprised her. Today's view was no different. The pearlescent fog had gathered in the old city, making it impossible to see. The Rise ringed it. It looked like she was about to drive into a cloud, with nothing surrounding her.

A spire rose out of the fog in the very center of the old city, but that was the only real construction that she could see. The fog undulated, as if something pushed at it from underneath.

She gripped the reins tighter, and hoped the horse wasn't as unnerved as she was.

The road tipped downward, and the wagon headed into the fog. The air became cool and damp. It felt like she was driving into a thick mist.

She wished she had on a heavier coat. She shivered and tried not to remember how awful the fog had felt earlier, when she had arrived in the financial district, before she realized that the corpse she was seeing belonged to Augustus Kirilli.

The wagon bumped forward, but she could see better than expected. It was almost like the fog had created a protective white layer along the top and had thinned out underneath. The light here was diffuse, but clear enough, even though some of the buildings in the old city had clearly lit their outdoor lamps.

It wasn't hard to find her way to the iron tombs. They were part of the old cemetery, which covered only one small block on this side of the city. The cemetery itself had a very small above-ground component, but the rest was built into the Ancient Rise.

A lot of the Old City was built into the Ancient Rise, and even more of the Old City was built underneath it.

In fact, a lot of Trinovante—old and new—was underground, something she had never really reflected on until now.

Cilka turned the wagon to the right, heading to the cemetery. The clomp of the horse's hooves and the rattle of the wheels seemed to echo. There was no wind, which was probably why the fog remained here. Or maybe that thick white layer along the top of the bowl kept the wind out.

Not that there was ever much wind in the Old City. It was the most protected part of Trinovante. Once a desirable address, it was now a mishmash of old houses, even older buildings, and some historically rich sites.

She had always hated it here, which was why she shuddered when Judita told her the body had to come here—even though Cilka had known that Judita was right.

The cemetery wasn't too far away along this road. More stone pillars rose from the cemetery entrance. These pillars were undecorated, although they had a similar form to the ones on the top of the Ancient Rise.

Cilka really hadn't given the decoration much thought, assuming that whoever had founded the cemetery had put them there to echo the Stone Guardians at the top of the Rise.

She hunched as she rode between these stone pillars. They were attached to a wall that was made of the same stone. Only this wall was lower than most, more of a reminder that the cemetery was here rather than something to keep the unwanted out of the cemetery.

There was an iron gate attached to the stone pillars. The gate was open. When it was closed, it looked like a series of flowers and leaves blowing in the wind.

She had always thought it too pretty to be in front of a cemetery. Now, though, she only glanced at it, and part of her was happy that the gate was iron.

The horse went deeper into the cemetery, following the main path. She didn't really give the horse its head, but she wasn't really guiding it much either. Horses were sensible enough creatures. This one knew that only the main path was wide enough for the wagon.

The main path went through the oldest part of the cemetery. Graves rose out of the thin fog, some of them with headstones made of the same stone as the stone wall around the Ancient Rise. Those headstones echoed the Stone Guardian's design, either with a bowed head or with a tiny figure leaning over a sword.

A shiver ran through her. She was getting very cold, and the small realizations she was having weren't really helping.

She let out a sigh of relief as she saw the gated opening to the underground tombs. This gate, which matched the one in the front of the cemetery, was closed.

There was a special code that had to be typed into the numerical lock on the side of the gate, something the constables all had to memorize. Fortunately, she had checked with the two men she brought along to see if they knew this month's code.

They claimed they did.

She stopped the wagon just outside the gate, and shifted in her seat.

"One of you need to open the gate," she said.

The constable to her left, the younger one, raised a finger and touched the bill of his cap, acknowledging her.

Then he climbed over the side of the wagon and hurried to the gate. He crouched a bit so that he could easily see the numerical lock box. Then he pressed his fingers against it in the proper order, and lock clicked loudly.

The gate swung open, fog swirling around it.

As the gate swung inward, a series of lights went on in the underground cavern. The lights were built into the ceiling of the cavern and along the floor against the wall.

They were made of lightstone and would get brighter the longer she, and the wagon, were inside.

She waited until the constable climbed back into the wagon, and then she urged the horse forward. The path smoothed out here and the path wasn't as hardpacked, so the sound of the horse's hooves wasn't as dramatic.

The wagon no longer bumped either. Her eyes hurt at the growing light, but that was to be expected. She hadn't realized just how dark it had been growing in the Old City.

A smell rose around her, something fetid and dank, almost rank. She looked down, and saw that the dried blood on her clothing wasn't dry any longer. The blood was boiling—in fact, the blood was boiling off her coat.

She hadn't realized she still had that much blood on her, but she hadn't seen the point in cleaning it off since she was going to have to help the constables handle the body once they were inside the iron tombs.

"What in the name of all that's…" She stopped herself before finishing the oath. She was beginning to understand the power of words as well, something she had forgotten since her minimal magic training years ago.

"Dunno, missus," said the second constable, but he held his hands out. His gloved hands. Little droplets of blood rose from the gloves and exploded in the air, vanishing altogether.

The other constable—the one who had opened the gate—didn't seem to have any boiling blood on him. Which meant that the blood that was boiling probably hadn't belonged to Kirilli.

That blood had probably come from the assassin. The second constable had handled the satchel, which the assassin had left behind.

The boiling blood was rising off Cilka's coat and turning into droplets, just like the droplets off the second constable's gloves. The droplets weren't really exploding. They were forming a blood-like mist.

She turned just a little. That mist was floating behind them, a thin river of blackish red, disappearing through the open gate.

"Missus," the second constable said, sounding terrified.

"Just let it happen," Cilka said. She wasn't sure what caused it, but she wasn't going to fight it.

She looked down at herself, saw that wherever the growing light touched the blood stains came alive, and then rose out of her clothing, and then boiled.

She wasn't being burned. She didn't even feel hot. But the smell was turning her stomach.

She didn't urge the horse forward—she wanted this cleansing (or whatever it was) to cease before they went any deeper. Even though she had been coated with blood, she had wiped a lot of it off.

And the blood was finite. It would dissipate eventually.

Just as she had that thought, the blood droplets thinned. Nothing rose off the second constable's gloves.

She rose ever so slightly, so that the light could touch all of her—her backside, the backs of her pants. There wasn't as much blood there; she had held the assassin in front of her, after all.

But once she sat back down, she raised her feet so that the blood could come off her boots.

Another wave of blood droplets rose and burst, heading toward that mist that seemed to be fleeing from the cavern.

After a few minutes, the mist cleared.

"What was that?" the first constable asked, his voice shaking.

Cilka had ideas, but she didn't know for certain. It clearly had something to do with that assassin, and that assassin's magic. But she also figured that whatever had just been cleansed from her—and it really did feel like a cleansing—had been part of the reason Judita had told her to come here.

Maybe that meant these Fey couldn't get into the iron tombs. Maybe it meant that the Fey magic—whatever that was —didn't belong here.

It didn't explain the look of the Stone Guardians, but Cilka didn't care—not right now.

She felt a bit lighter than she had when she had entered this cavern, but that might have been the actual light from the lightstones. The light was as bright as midday sunlight now, illuminating the path ahead.

There was no decoration here. The path ahead was amazingly plain. But there were cubbies built into the wall, arches really, that housed artifacts, like the ones she'd seen in museums and in some of the older houses around Trinovante.

Some of those arches were glowing as well.

She got the horse to move forward. The iron tombs were on a lower level than this, down a long hill into what looked like—from here—a deep darkness.

But as the wagon plodded forward, the lights above and below illuminated. The light was warm. It baked the chill out of her body, made her feel a bit more calm and upbeat than she had felt all day.

That unsettled sensation was nearly gone now.

The path wove through some more arches, and she saw a lot more artifacts than she had ever noticed before. Some were on tables that had been built into the walls, others were in even wider cubbies, more like sealed entrances to somewhere, sealed entrances with shelves.

She didn't look around much—she kept her gaze forward, waiting for the iron tombs.

They showed up once the path leveled. The iron tombs were built into the ground, and they ran for what looked like miles.

She had never gone all the way to the back. But she did know from her time in the constabulary that the front tombs were reserved for corpses like Kirilli's, corpses that needed to be stored until someone determined exactly what to do with them.

One of the amazing things about the tombs, something that only the higher ranks in the constabulary knew, was that the bodies didn't decay in the tombs. They remained exactly as they were when they were placed in the tombs, even if they were stored in their tomb for months.

As with everything else that made no sense at the beginning, some scholars had done a study of this, and thought that the tombs themselves had some unusual properties. Some scientists had taken scrapings off the side of them, and used all methods of examination to see what the tombs were made of.

As far as she knew, they really were made of iron, although they did seem to have grown out of the ground rather than being built and stored in place.

She hadn't questioned them, not even as she moved up in the constabulary. She had simply accepted them, and then had forgotten them as she moved into her education as a Procurator.

Now, after everything she had seen today, she was questioning everything, including what the iron tombs were and what made them work.

She pulled up in front of the first row of iron tombs. She went toward the center of them, knowing that some closest to the path would be in use.

"Check to find an open one," she said to the first constable.

He nodded, and climbed out of the wagon a bit more quickly this time, as if he wanted to get away from her and from the second constable.

Maybe the blood had unnerved the young first constable. Or maybe he was just as ready to be done with this task as she was.

He bent over the edge of the wagon's bed after he got out, and removed one of the crowbars from the pile of tools that was under a tarp near the side. Then he walked to the tomb closest to the side of the wagon, and used the crowbar to move the cover.

The cover squealed as it slid. He peered inside, shook his head, and then worked the cover back into place.

He went from tomb to tomb, going deeper along the row, until he found one that apparently was empty.

He waved a hand at her, and she brought the wagon closer. The young constable was working the cover off, but going slowly.

"Help him," she said to the second constable.

He climbed off the side of the wagon, then walked over to the tomb. The two constables conferred for a moment, voices low. Then they returned to the wagon.

"It's empty, right?" she asked.

"Yes," the first constable said. "It doesn't even have any dust."

Which, come to think of it, the underground part of the cemetery was lacking as well. No dust, no dirt, no cobwebs. This place was clean and she wasn't sure how it maintained itself or if someone cleaned it.

There was so much she didn't know about Trinovante. She was beginning to think that she hadn't been paying attention at all, which bothered her. Her job—jobs, really, from the time she joined the constabulary to the day she became a Procurator—required her to see things clearly and understand them.

She had dismissed too much of the strangeness in Trinovante as simply *the way things were*. Yes, indeed, that was the way things were and always had been, but she had never acknowledged the way they were as strange in some places, like this cemetery.

The constables made their way back to the wagon. Now, she climbed off of it. She was going to supervise the placement of the body, but she wasn't going to touch it.

The second constable had already reached it. He still had his gloves on, but they looked clean, maybe cleaner than they had ever been. He waited for the first constable to get into position.

That young man had pulled out his gloves and was putting them on with great deliberation. He had initially carried the body into the wagon without them, but apparently something about this trip changed his mind about handling it.

"Ready," he said, clapping his gloved hands together.

"Missus?" the second constable said. "It doesn't seem proper, just putting him in the tomb with nothing more than a blanket."

"He won't be there long," she said. She had no other words of comfort for the second constable. She wasn't even sure if she was lying to him.

"I dunno like it down here," the second constable said. "It's cold and spare and it feels...odd."

It did feel odd, but Cilka wasn't finding it cold. As the light increased, the area around the tombs had warmed up considerably.

She didn't contradict the second constable, though. His discomfort was real, as was hers.

The constables half climbed into the back of the wagon, and grabbed Kirilli's corpse by its legs. The first constable kept adjusting the blanket so that Kirilli remained covered. Together the two men managed to lift the corpse out of the wagon.

They carried it—the second constable holding the feet and the first with his hands underneath the shoulders—toward the tomb. The body swayed as the men staggered. The blanket ran along the floor, threatening to slide off.

Cilka stood near the edge of the wagon, watching, half expecting Kirilli's corpse to revive again and go running among the tombs.

But the swaying was only because Kirilli had been a fat man, and now he was dead weight on top of his large size. As she watched the constables struggle, she wondered if she should have brought two more men. This corpse was proving quite a challenge for the two she had brought.

They finally reached the tomb. They rested the body against the bottom lip, the blanket draping the side like decoration.

Both constables were sweating and breathing hard. If she had been in their shoes, she would have shoved the body into the tomb and been done with it.

She had done that more than once, which would probably upset the second constable something awful.

But she said nothing. She let them handle the body, and do with it what they needed to do.

The first constable grabbed the shoulders again. The second took a deep breath and picked up the feet.

And then, very gently, the men moved the corpse to the center of the tomb. They lowered the corpse into the tomb.

The first constable stood up, and then put one hand on the small of his back.

The second constable was still bent over the tomb, apparently adjusting the blanket.

"Don't put the cover on just yet," Cilka said.

She reached into the back of the wagon and grabbed the satchel. The handle felt greasy, which surprised her. She probably should have been wearing gloves, just like the two constables, but she hadn't thought of it.

She tugged the satchel to her, surprised at its weight. She almost stopped and opened it, just to see what was in it, but Judita's voice rose in her mind.

There will be tricks, Judita's voice said. *Do not fall for them.*

Cilka couldn't remember Judita ever saying that to her, but it seemed like sensible advice, particularly considering what had happened so far on this day.

Cilka put one hand under the bottom of the satchel as she pulled it the rest of the way off the wagon. Even though she was prepared for the increased weight on one side, she still nearly toppled in that direction.

The satchel weighed five times what a normal satchel weighed, maybe more. She almost had to drag it on the ground to get it to the tomb.

But she didn't drag it. She grabbed the handle with both hands, and carried it in front of her, duckwalking toward the tomb.

Surprisingly, neither constable reached out to help her as she brought the satchel, but the second constable helped her with it once she reached the side of the tomb.

"We put it with him, right, missus?" the second constable said.

"Yes." For now anyway. But she didn't add that. "Put it by his feet."

She couldn't stand the idea of putting it near Kirilli's hand, like it had been when they found him. She didn't want him to wake up again and grab it. Not that he could. She wasn't sure anyone could get the cover off the tomb by himself.

Unless he had magic powers. Unless he had some kind of extraworldly help. And right now, she wouldn't put that past him. Or whatever she had encountered.

Besides, she had the sense that he might find whatever he needed inside that satchel.

Then she made herself calm down. The iron tombs were supposed to hold in magic—that was what she had learned long ago. But she had also never questioned putting some of the worst criminals inside an iron tomb.

Why else would the constables and any member of law enforcement have access to the tombs? Why would they need the tombs?

She let out a breath, and watched as the two men placed the satchel at the corpse's feet. On top of the blanket, which she hadn't directed the constables to do, but it was an action she approved of.

Then she stepped back and let them wrestle the cover into place. It was clearly heavy and difficult to maneuver. The cover grinded against the iron tomb, making a rumbly squealing noise that grated on her ears.

She took a step back.

It took the constables quite a bit of shoving and pushing and adjusting to get the cover in the proper place. Then it snapped into a position with an audible click.

They looked at it with surprise, as if they couldn't quite believe it had gone into place so quickly.

Then light shot out of the top, meeting the bright light from the lightstone above. The light was hot. Cilka could feel it from where she stood.

She had no idea how hot it would be up close. The constables both backed away from it. The second constable put his arms over his face, as if he was afraid of being burned.

The bright light faded, leaving something that looked like words scrolled on top of the cover.

Cilka had never seen that before—and she'd put quite a few bodies into iron tombs over the years.

She leaned forward, squinting, so that perhaps she could see what had been written there.

The letters were unfamiliar—and yet they weren't. She might have seen them in one of the museums around Trinovante, but she couldn't be certain.

The letters cut deeply into the cover. Near the letters, concentric circles formed. They rose up just a little, then faded into the cover.

The letters rose above the cover and floated past her. She had the sense that the letters formed words, but what those words were, she had no idea.

"What is that, missus?" the second constable asked in a whisper so loud they probably heard it outside.

She shook her head. "I've never seen it before."

Just like most things that had happened on this day. She had never seen any of it before.

The words traveled down the path, past the horse and wagon, past the other tombs, and toward the entrance.

The first constable followed them, peering around a corner as if he was worried that the words would come back and attack him.

Black spots danced in front of Cilka's eyes. Those spots seemed to be the inverse of the letters. She hoped they weren't the kind of magic that got inside a person and did some kind of unseen damage.

Because it was too late to guard against it, whatever it had been.

She felt shaky, and she couldn't be shaky. Not yet.

"All right," she said, walking back to the wagon as if nothing was amiss. "Let's get out of here."

"What did we just see, missus?" the second constable asked.

Some kind of mystery, she thought. Only her mind put an emphasis on the word "mystery" as if the mystery were a thing rather than a concept.

She was out of her depth here. She needed to talk to Judita. And Desmond, too. They both needed to know what was going on.

"I don't know," Cilka said honestly. Then she climbed up the buckboard and grabbed the reins.

She realized, as she did so, that the horse was curiously undisturbed by the noise, the lights, and the words that had floated past it. And it wasn't just because the horse had been wearing blinders.

It didn't seem disturbed by anything that had happened down here.

"Let's go back," she said to the constables.

They remained near the tomb, staring at its cover as if the cover revealed some great secret that they hadn't realized existed before.

"Gentlemen!" she snapped. "Now."

They both shook themselves as if they were waking from a long sleep. She didn't like that, but she wasn't sure what to do about it.

The men approached the wagon. The second constable shook his head.

"Never seen nothin' like that before," he said.

"Me either," she said.

"Are we gonna be all right, missus?" he asked.

How could she answer that? She didn't know from day to day if anyone was going to be all right.

"From this?" she asked, as if trying to clarify.

He just stared at her. He didn't nod.

"Yes," she said with as much confidence as she could muster. "We're going to be just fine."

CHAPTER

TWENTY

Slumber plastered himself against the interior wall of the kitchen as Gem let herself inside. Her nose was red, her eyes sallow, her cheeks shiny with tears.

She didn't seem to notice the iced up portal or the growing cold. Through the partially open doorway, Slumber could see Atrü. Slumber hoped Gem had gotten inside without letting Atrü see her tears. He hadn't been the most compassionate leader, and Slumber doubted that Atrü would be at all empathetic.

He certainly hadn't been with Slumber. Atrü had been disgusted with Slumber's level of training, even though Slumber had told him back in Nye that Slumber had never gone on a real mission before.

He was sorry he had come on this one.

Slumber slid across the wall and into the main room. No one on this team really liked him, so he had taken to being a dark

231

splotch in any room he was in. Most of the team had forgotten he was around.

Everyone except Rodderc, who would whip around and focus on Slumber whenever he saw him, then reassess, realizing that Slumber was *their* Dream Rider, and not some other Dream Rider who had come to disable or maybe kill one of them.

Every. Single. Time.

But Rodderc had gone with Slumber two nights ago, when he had dived into the brain of the Kirilli, and managed to get Slumber out of there when Slumber had been trapped.

The others should have seen that as a warning, but of course, they hadn't. No one listened to him.

To be fair, though, Slumber wasn't all that good at explaining himself. He hadn't told Atrü just how hard it had been to escape the Kirilli's brain. For a while, Slumber had feared he would be trapped there forever.

When Slumber had said that to Rodderc, Rodderc had said —bluntly and without any emotion at all—*that is the fault of your training*. Or maybe there had been an emotion. Maybe that was what passed for compassion in Rodderc's world.

Slumber remained flat against the wall in the main room. No one seemed to have noticed him. The Infantry were sprawled on the furniture, legs splayed, expressions grim. They were in the middle of a heated discussion, their voices low.

They were larger than Slumber, larger than most Fey. Yris sat on a chair, pretending at relaxation. Rodderc, Xevkin, and Urekyn were close to the artifacts, clearly discussing them. Vidso and Haevner sprawled on the ruined couch.

Rodderc was about to speak when he saw Slumber. Rodderc

started, like he had every other time. Then he nodded at Slumber, as if he expected Slumber to nod back.

Slumber didn't move. He was perfectly happy (well, not *happy*, but comfortable) being a splotch on the wall.

As Rodderc turned his gaze back on his Infantry, hard lines appeared on his face.

Apparently Yris didn't see them, because she said, "I still don't see why we can't use one of the outbuildings at some of those estates."

She was being sullen. She had reverted to sullen when Hadley died.

"We're not going to discuss it any longer," Rodderc said. "I want you all ready when Omriseu returns. We will leave this place as quickly as we can."

"What do we do with these?" Urekyn waved her large hand at the pile of artifacts on the table across from Slumber.

Those artifacts were curious things. They were all manner of shapes and sizes. They had forms that had seemed utterly useless to Slumber until he had slid into Augustus Kirilli's brain on the last night of Kirilli's life.

There, Slumber had seen some of the artifacts in use. The sculptures came alive and grabbed things. The lightstone lanterns caused some people to burn in the light, their skin turning so red that they were disabled. Some of those people even died.

The art made no sense to Slumber—not yet—but he figured there was a purpose. The dishes, the silverware, the glassware, also made no sense.

And, quite frankly, the musical instruments terrified him. A lute, resting on top of a pile of jewelry, seemed to glow. A violin vibrated so hard that Haevner had to move it away from the wall, otherwise there was a slight irritating hum in the room.

There were long boxes with strings inside, apparently for the stringed instruments. There were all manner of musical pipes, from some barely the size of a finger to others as long as Rodderc's arm.

The Infantry had also managed to seize small mountains of gold coins, which would come in useful, considering how much the entire city relied on those coins in trade for everything. Omriseu had taken pocketfuls of the correct coins to pay for another house.

Omriseu and Qurzi had both figured out how the money worked in this city. At least they were doing the job Spies were supposed to do. They knew more about the city—and Dorovich—than everyone else in the room.

Slumber knew a few things. He'd been practicing Dream Riding, since Atrü demanded he do so. But it was hard to discriminate between what was happening in someone's conscious mind and someone's subconscious mind.

Slumber could sort information more or less. It helped when a person's thought processes were organized.

Augustus Kirilli's processes had been organized.

He had been worried about the delivery of two satchels. Those satchels would have maps, and the maps needed to be safeguarded.

Which was the information that Slumber had brought back to the team, the information that Hadley had decided to act upon.

She had been afraid that the team might lose the opportunity to get their hands on something valuable. She hadn't been sure why they were valuable, but she had been confident that they were.

That night, after she had taken the maps, she had actually thanked Slumber for telling her about the opportunity. The maps had been spread out on the table in the small room, undulating and giving off more magickal energy than Slumber had seen in this tiny place.

At that moment, the entire team had thought they had won.

But they hadn't. And now they were going to flee because there might be someone out there more powerful than all of them combined.

"When Gem is ready," Rodderc said to Uryek, "we will pack these up. I believe they will be useful."

If they could figure out how to use them. Slumber had seen glimpses in Kirilli's mind, but hadn't been able to figure out how any of the items were used.

Slumber had worried about it, instead of manipulating Kirilli's dream so that Kirilli would give him information in a logical and easy-to-understand manner.

Kirilli had actually formed a small replica of himself in his mind. That replica had stood up, and stared at Slumber. *What the heck are you?* Kirilli had asked him, and this was where Rodderc said Slumber had erred.

I'm a Dream Rider, Slumber had said.

What is that? Kirilli had asked.

And that had been when Slumber realized he had made a mistake. He fumbled, inside his own magick and inside Kirilli's mind.

I'm not important, Slumber had said.

But you are nosy, Kirilli had said. Then he had waved a hand. *Begone.*

The *begone* had echoed the way that Chants sometimes did, and Slumber had tumbled backwards into the detritus in the back of Kirilli's brain. Slumber had lost track of everything he understood. The detritus in the back had had crates and crates of artifacts, as well as some iron sarcophagi that seemed to grow out of the walls.

Slumber had whimpered in terror, and that was when he had heard Rodderc call his name.

Slumber had focused on that, finding Kirilli's ears, and sliding out of one of them.

Rodderc had been standing in the hallway, which had been dangerous. The staff of the entire manor should have found him, but they hadn't.

Sometimes Slumber thought Rodderc had some magick.

Slumber had escaped, then he waved a flat hand at Rodderc to signal that all was fine. Then Slumber had slithered across the wall to the windows, and down the side of the manor.

Rodderc had climbed out through the same window, using some kind of rope. Slumber hadn't watched him, because Slumber had been trying to sort through what he had seen, and he had been trying to figure out how much he would tell Atrü.

Fortunately Atrü had no ability to sense failure (like some Visionaries did), so he hadn't sensed the shame that Slumber had felt when he got tossed into the back of Kirilli's mind.

Rodderc later told Slumber that he had been in there for hours, much longer than a Dream Rider should ever be inside another's head. That was when Rodderc had decided to intervene, figuring the Kirilli wouldn't wake up since he had been under the influence of a Dream Rider.

Rodderc's gamble had been correct, even if his assumption hadn't been. By the time Rodderc had called for Slumber, Slumber had no longer been in control of Kirilli's brain.

The memory of all of that made Slumber queasy. The entire last few days had. He had been questioning himself. If he hadn't told Hadley about the satchels, then she would still be alive. If he hadn't made so many mistakes, maybe they would have known how to use the maps.

Maybe they wouldn't have lost the maps.

"I think we should just leave them," Vidso said about the artifacts. "I think they're dangerous."

Rodderc straightened. "Of course they're dangerous. That's why Rugar sent us to destroy anything magickal. He wants to make sure this land is ready for his army. That's *our* job, or have you forgotten?"

"I haven't forgotten," Haevner said. He didn't seem bothered by Rodderc's temper.

Haevner should have been bothered by the artifacts. His face still bore the scars from the light that had fallen upon him when one of those lightstone lanterns kicked on.

But Haevner seemed to have come to terms with whatever it was that had hurt him. Or maybe he was still curious about those artifacts.

Although, Yris had said the previous night, that Haevner had been the one who had made certain everyone had destroyed as many artifacts as possible, when the Infantry had gone to the Kirilli manor.

"It's not our decision," Haevner said. "You act like it is. We need to assume we're moving the artifacts, until Atrü tells us differently."

"You think Atrü will make a good decision?" Yris asked, her voice slightly lower than it had been. She was talking about their leader, after all.

Haevner pivoted slightly in his chair and looked at Yris. Her body sprawled, but, Slumber was beginning to realize, she wasn't relaxed. Every muscle seemed very tense.

"It's not important whether or not he makes a good decision," Haevner said. "He is the one in charge."

Rodderc made a slight harumphing sound, as if he didn't really agree with that.

Slumber wasn't sure who he agreed with. They had a mission, and they seemed to have lost track of it. They weren't supposed to capture artifacts. They were supposed to destroy them.

Maybe he should have said nothing about the maps. Maybe he should have said only that they were more artifacts.

He wondered if everyone would have acted differently then.

"We treat them as if they're ours," Gem said. Her voice was thick, as if she had some phlegm in her throat.

Slumber had to shift his position on the wall so that he could see her. His movement caught Rodderc's eye, and made him start ever so slightly.

What had happened to Rodderc that Dream Riders made him so nervous?

"Until we hear otherwise," Gem said. "So we'll be packing them up."

"Ugh," Yris said. "I don't want to touch them a second time."

"I have gloves," Gem said. "I will get some for everyone."

"Do we still have the boxes that we brought them in?" Vidso asked Gem.

"I did not destroy anything," Gem said. "I'll need help carrying the boxes, though."

She slipped back into the kitchen.

Slumber stayed on the wall. He didn't want to touch any of those things. He had seen some of them in the back of Kirilli's mind. They had seemed bigger there—the sculptures in particular. They had been life-sized and they had reached for him.

Xevkin had told Hadley that the sculptures on the doors and shutters in the Kirilli estate had come alive, which confirmed the magick that Slumber had seen.

He hadn't told anyone about the artifacts in Kirilli's brain. The way that some of them glowed. The ghosts that seemed to haunt the goblets and bowls, using them as serving utensils. The musicians tuning up—which, thankfully he hadn't been able to hear.

He had fled from that, even if it had been in Kirilli's mind.

Slumber wondered if he should take a more Fey form, and then tell everyone what he saw.

He thought about it for a moment.

What would they do with the information? The Infantry had all touched the artifacts already. Some of them seemed to have a healthy fear of those artifacts, but the others just seemed to see them as things.

Slumber wished they had followed the instructions they had received. He wished they had destroyed everything. He didn't want those things in the next house.

Maybe he would talk to Atrü. Getting Atrü to listen to him would be difficult, but necessary.

Slumber pushed into the wall, wishing he could take it with him to support him. He always felt stronger when he was flat against a wall, looking like a spot to everyone else.

But all he was doing was absorbing the wall's strength, not using his own.

He had done some useful things here, even if no one else thought he had.

He slithered to one side, heading down the hallway to see if he could find Atrü. Maybe Atrü would listen to him.

Then Slumber would have laughed to himself if he could have, while being completely flat.

Of course, Atrü wouldn't listen to him. Atrü thought Slumber couldn't do anything right.

But Slumber had to try. It wasn't just Atrü's mission. It was all of theirs. And Atrü had to make a good decision this time.

Because lives were at stake.

The team's lives.

And if the artifacts awakened, Slumber wasn't sure anyone on the team would survive.

TWENTY-ONE

Gussie wouldn't let anyone help her take the satchels to her windstone vehicle. In fact, she wouldn't let anyone accompany her to the second carriage house, where the vehicle was stored.

Instead, she carried the satchels as she'd been carrying them for more than an hour now—one in her left hand, one under her arm, and another in her right hand. The satchel with the notebooks was the heaviest, and more than once, she thought of setting that one down, and balancing herself with the other two.

But every time she tried to put that thought into action, she felt her grandfather's presence as if he'd been sitting on her shoulder the entire time, guiding her.

The feeling both comforted her and made her nervous. Her brain wondered if the spirit she felt really belonged to her grandfather, and her heart felt wrapped in his love. She had missed him, just like she knew she would miss her father.

The second carriage house had a side door, at her insistence.

The door blended with the building so that stray people couldn't see it. Only she and Daisy had a key. Zeitsev hated the windstone vehicle or he would have gotten a key as well. But when he thought she wasn't listening, he called it "the contraption" and he claimed it would never replace the carriage.

Gussie had owned the windstone vehicle for nearly two years now, and in her mind, it had replaced the carriage, which she only used to please her father. Her heart twisted at that thought; she wouldn't have to please her father any longer.

He probably would oppose her taking the windstone vehicle to the Vault, even though all windstone vehicles were faster and more maneuverable than the type of carriage her family relied on.

She had to set one of the satchels down to unlock the side door. She set her grandfather's satchel on the tops of her feet, crushing her toes inside her slippers. But placing the satchel on her feet put the satchel between her legs and the door, making it difficult for anyone to steal it.

They would literally have to steal it right from under her. Still, she crowded the door as she unlocked it with her set of keys. Then she pocketed them, as she always did, before pushing the door open.

A long time ago, she had placed a series of lightstone lanterns inside this carriage house, as well as two lightstone fixtures. The lantern nearest the door activated when she touched it before picking up the satchel. Then she staggered her way into the carriage house—which really wasn't a house at all.

It was composed of two rooms—a large single room that had space for more than one windstone vehicle (she had dreams of her staff driving one to do errands, something no one was yet willing to do), and it had a back room filled with equipment that supported the vehicle, from new tires and vents that went underneath the chassis, just in case one of the vents got accidentally broken.

There were also a series of tools she didn't understand, but which the man who had sold her the windstone vehicle said were specific to that particular model. He claimed that anyone who came to repair the vehicle, should something go awry, would be happy to find that set of tools.

She had two driving coats in the back room, driving shoes, several driving caps, and driving goggles, but she didn't want to go inside that room with the satchels. She needed to get moving.

The vehicle itself gleamed before her. It had a sleek body that curved toward the ground. Its windscreens curved upward and inward, protecting the operator. She usually drove with the top down, but she wanted it up today. She would have to pull it up all on her own.

One of the reasons she had purchased this model was that it had compartments inside instead of two rows of seats. She opened the most hidden compartment now, and stuffed the satchels inside. Then she took the riding gloves that she stored on the front seat and slipped them on, so that she wouldn't cut herself on the top, as she had done the first time she had tried to pull it up on her own.

Once the top was up, no one would be able to see inside. Something about the angles and positions of the top changed the windscreens and made them opaque.

Some called that magic, but she thought it some kind of science, even though she did not understand it. Same with the way people described windstone propulsion.

The inventors of windstone technology claimed it was simple: all they had done was use windstone to create vents beneath the vehicle, vents that harnessed the wind and used it to propel the vehicle. Most people didn't understand how windstone worked, but the inventors, engineers, and some operators did.

Gussie didn't care how the vehicle worked, any more than she cared how lightstone lanterns worked; she only cared that they did.

The top receded with the touch of a button, activating a tube that pulled the canvas top inside, almost like a window shade got activated with the correct pull of the hand. Getting the top out, however, wasn't as easy. She had to tug it, and that tube liked to hold it in place.

She needed to brace herself against the side of the vehicle and slip her hands into the handholds in the middle. Then she had to use all her strength to yank the top free.

Once it came loose, if she maintained steady pressure, she could pull it over the entire vehicle, and hook the edges in place.

She made herself concentrate on the movement rather than its difficulty. A smooth, even pull, like unwinding fabric from a dowel, worked better than the starts and stops of a succession of yanks.

She worked carefully, holding her breath until she realized she was making herself lightheaded. In the past, she'd gotten the top halfway only to lose her grip on it.

This time, she was holding so tightly she wondered if her fingers were leaving divots in the material. She eased the material over the bar where she had lost control the first time she ever tried this, and managed to get the canvas to the latches on the side of the main windscreen.

The latches always seemed to rise out of the windscreens and reach for the top. Maybe it was just her exhaustion that created an illusion or maybe that was a form of wishful thinking. Or, maybe, there was a bit of magic in windstone vehicles. Before the Purges, everyone was convinced that windstone and lightstone had magical properties.

Now no one discussed it.

The latches clicked and the top was in place. The vehicle looked dark and mysterious, like it always did with the top on. Never before had she valued the way that the windscreens dimmed on the outside, and the operator remained anonymous.

She went to the double doors and unbarred them, pushing the right one until it remained open. Then she pushed the left.

The light had become pearlescent. The fog was still present, but receding with each passing moment. The sunlight was still thin, but she could see beyond the trees to the road. No vehicles lurked, no carriages waited, and no horses with riders seemed to be present.

She turned her back on all of it, and went inside the carriage house, opening the operator's door and sliding onto the seat. Then she pulled the door closed, tugged on the driver's cap she had left in the front seat, and wrapped the goggles around her face, even though she didn't really need them with the top up.

She wanted to wear them, because she didn't feel right operating the vehicle without them on.

She pushed the button that activated the windstone vents, felt the vehicle shudder as it gathered the air around it, creating wind. Then she used the driving stick near her right hand to make the vehicle back out of the carriage house.

She had to look behind her to do so. She twisted so that she could see the path, backing onto the wide part, and then turning the vehicle around, so she went out of the drive with the vehicle facing the street.

Usually, when she executed that maneuver, she stopped the vehicle for a short moment to close the carriage house doors herself. But she didn't have the time for that this afternoon. She had already wasted too much time since her father had found her and had given her the satchels.

She knew the route to the Vault; her father made her practice it monthly when she was a younger woman. He would take his small carriage pulled by a single horse. Along the route, he would pull to one side and allow her to take the reins. Then he would watch as she navigated the twisty streets of Trinovante.

Sometimes he would take the carriage to different parts of the city to make sure she always knew the quickest way to the Vault.

Someday you might have to hurry there, he'd say. *You need to know how to arrive fast.*

She used to make fun of him for that, calling him paranoid.

What could possibly be in that Vault that would require me to hurry? she would ask.

You might need something we store there, he would say. Or he would say, *You might need to hide something there.*

She had thought him dramatic. Sometimes she had even thought him crazy.

And yet, here she was, negotiating the bumpy drive as the windstone vehicle made its way to the street.

She paused before entering, looking closely at everything. Trees lined the opposite side, so she looked for hidden figures—horses, people, anything—and saw no one. She looked to the right. The fog had thinned enough that she could see the nearest cross street. No one waited there, and this part of the street was empty.

She looked to her left, saw the edge of her neighbor's great house, looking white and bloated in the odd light. No one lurked there, no carriages waited in their drive, and no windstone vehicles were parked against the side of the road.

On a whim, she looked up. Demigliders were illegal in the city limits, but that didn't stop some from using them.

The gray fog mixed with the pale sunlight made her squint. But she didn't even see birds above her. Just fog-covered sky.

Her heart beat hard, almost painfully, against her chest. Normally, she loved operating the vehicle, but today, her hands shook as she used the middle driving stick to turn the front wheels to the left. She had no idea what the vehicle's maximum speed was.

She was usually cautious when she drove it, not wanting to collide with something bigger. Today, though, she went faster than she normally did, especially on this street, where she saw no one.

She crossed two intersections, then twisted and looked behind her. No one followed, not a person on horseback, not a carriage, not another windstone vehicle. She was the only person on these back roads, just like she usually was.

She didn't relax, however. She wound her way around the neighborhood as if she was inspecting it. Some of the homes were newer than hers; others were old cottages that had been here so long that they predated the annexation of this section of the countryside into Trinovante.

Finally, she left, via a different side road than she usually did, just in case someone was used to following her around and waited at her normal spot.

Her mouth had gone dry. She wished now that she had gone inside the house to get some water and to change. Her clothes were starting to give off a faintly sour air, probably from the drying blood.

The roads remained mostly empty. She had to pass two carriages, which she did slowly, because she'd learned that the silent windstone vehicles spooked any horse not wearing blinders (and even some that were).

The Vault was on property that had been even farther outside of Trinovante back in the day. The property was vast and left mostly to its own devices.

Her father had warned her that the city would occasionally send notices, asking the owners to clean up the property. He— or rather, his firm, in the name of a "client"—would then hire someone to clean the first few yards around the road, leaving most everything else to grow over.

Her father had also hired different teams at different times to trim back the overgrowth as near what he called the carriage-way, but what was really another road. And he had them clip some of the more annoying branches and brambles near all the buildings.

The Vault was on what had once been the estate of Gussie's great-great-grandparents. They were not Kirillis. They were Rows, the parents of her great-grandmother, the woman who discovered a cave on Mount Vitaki that was filled with artifacts that started a revolution in design and attitudes throughout the Qavnerian Protectorate.

Some said that her actions also lead to the Purges, and whenever Gussie visited the Vault, which was more often than she had wanted to in the past decade, she could believe it.

That place had a feeling to it, as if it could vibrate its way into the clouds. She didn't know exactly what that feeling was, but she hated it.

She'd asked her father about it more than once, and he had looked at her as if she was crazy. *The estate is the estate is the estate*, he would say and shrug.

Only once did he acknowledge that something odd was going on there. He could never hire the same gardeners for the place twice. Sometimes he claimed that was because he didn't want to hire the same people, but occasionally he let it slip that several did not want to return because they had had a bad experience on the grounds.

Gussie had once said that they needed to go inside to have a bad experience, and her father had snapped at her.

If your brothers and sisters had half your intelligence and all of your courage, I would assign one of them this duty. Unfortunately for you, you are the Kirilli. *Or you will be when I'm gone.*

And now, apparently, she was.

Her heart twisted at the thought. She drove just a bit faster, as if she could outrun how she was feeling.

But she couldn't.

She had to weave around a bit more traffic—a man with a wagon pulled by what looked like a mule, a woman riding astride on horseback even though she wore skirts, and two men walking down the middle of the road as if they owned it.

It was the two men who caught her attention, and made her slow down just a bit. She had entered one of the more rural parts of Trinovante, where the countryside had somehow overtaken the city, even though the city claimed the land for its ever-growing maw.

She had to keep an eye out again for anyone following her, because the entrance to the estate was difficult to find. She didn't want to lead them there.

The main entrance to the Row estate was marked by over-grown stone columns that held a wooden door her father had kept up, but also kept locked. The stone fence around the property was high and moss-covered, giving the entire place an air of neglect.

That was by design; anyone who wanted to know where the old Row estate was would come here, and be unable to enter.

Her grandfather had changed the ownership records for the estate during the worst of the Purges. Her father had "sold" the property to two different entities, hiding the ownership behind a legal wall so impenetrable that Gussie doubted anyone in the city of Trinovante knew who really owned the property.

She had always thought the protections were overdone, but now she understood them. It wasn't as if she hadn't lived through some personal attacks because of her last name—Kirillis were both hated and feared in Trinovante—but they had never been attacked, not even in the worst of the Purges.

Or so family lore said. Given how vicious the Purges were, Gussie had often wondered if that was true.

Her hands were sweating inside her driving gloves. A bead of sweat ran down the side of her face as well. She was sweating because she was terrified, something that hadn't happened to her in a very long time.

She didn't know what she would do if she arrived to find the entire estate destroyed. Or the gigantic crypts that housed the entrance to the Vault.

Don't create trouble before it arrives, girl, her brain said in her grandfather's voice. Or maybe it actually was her grandfather's voice, since his spirit had haunted her all morning.

She drove past the main entrance without slowing. The stone fence looked as neglected as it had before. The stone columns were intact and, from what she could see as she sped past, the wooden gate in between them remained closed.

So...no battering rams, no destruction, as far as she could tell.

The road curved through tall trees that had blue-green cobwebby moss dripping down the branches. In most of the city, those ropes of moss got trimmed back, just like the branches got trimmed back if they covered too much of the roadway.

But here, no one touched them. She had never asked her father why; she wondered if he had paid the city cleanup crews to look the other way.

Some bits of dangling moss brushed against the roof of her vehicle, leaving a trail on the back windscreen. She could still see through it, but it was harder than it had been.

Part of the problem was also that the trees blocked the struggling sunlight. The fog was thicker here, but it was white—more mist than true fog.

It was rarely sunny on this patch of road, and the mist-fog rose off the ground, particularly on cool mornings.

The mist-fog's presence reminded her that it wasn't very late in the day. She had been supposed to meet her father early, by any standard, and she had arrived ahead of time. Hours had passed, but it was still midmorning, even though it felt like she had been awake for days.

The road veered steeply to the right, and then forked. That fork was the most difficult part of the drive, because she had to keep going right, even though that section of road disappeared into darkness.

Her father's horses were used to that part of the trip, but he had warned her that hers would not like it. He had wanted to take her carriage here more than once, but she had always made an excuse, because she planned to use the windstone vehicle whenever she came here.

She was glad she had made those plans. The white mist-fog had vanished, replaced by an unrelenting gloom. Had she been in a carriage, she would have had to rely on the horses to handle the darkness or stop and light the lanterns on the carriage's side.

But her windstone vehicle had round lightstone lanterns placed on the front grill. Whenever the windstone vehicle was active, the lightstone lanterns ignited automatically in deepening darkness.

They did so here, carving holes of light into the heavy darkness. It almost looked like the round streams of light were beating the darkness back.

She gripped the steering sticks tightly, her breath shallow. She was trying to breathe quietly, because she wanted to hear if another vehicle (or horse) was entering the road behind her.

It was hard to hear with her wheels spinning on the dirt, the wind howling through the vents.

The road dipped downward, just like it was supposed to, and damp from the trees above dripped onto the front windscreen. The windscreen could handle drops; it tossed them off as if they were made of air. If the drops became actual rain, though, she would have to activate the cleaning blades, which she did not want to do. They were fat and mostly useless and they squeaked as they went up and down, blocking part of her view through the screen.

Of course, rain would block *all* of her view.

The vehicle bobbed on the road. There were dips that she hadn't anticipated, almost holes in the road. It had clearly been a while since someone had maintained the road.

Then the downturn became an actual decline, and the darkness became less gloom, and more the kind of darkness caused by something blocking the light.

The vehicle had entered the tunnel that went underneath most of the property. The tunnel was wide and arched and made of gray stone of uniform size. The road turned from dirt to the same stone—wider than cobblestone and much more even.

Horses would have clopped over it, revealing the location, but the only sound the windstone vehicle made was a diminished howl as the outside wind stopped swirling through the vents. Now, away from the wind, the vehicle would use stored wind and some other propellant that she did not understand or, she was told, she would have to worry about.

She worried anyway. This tunnel was long, and it didn't open onto the property. It opened underneath the crypts. If the vehicle stalled, if the ceiling fell, if the tunnel closed, she would die here, because no one knew that this place existed.

No one except her father.

Tears pricked her eyes. Since she had shared this with her father only, that meant no one knew. No one at all.

She would have to tell one of her brothers, just in case something happened to her, like something happened to her father. The only brother she could really rely on was Benedeto, and he didn't live in Trinovante.

She was going to have to summon him anyway, because there were too many things for her to deal with. She would need Benedeto and maybe her brother Corrin or her sister Filippa, the sensible ones who at least had a chance of handling the murders and the destruction, and all the other problems that Gussie had been handed this morning.

The tunnel widened and as it did, the interior lightstone lamps ignited. They had registered the lightstones on the front of her vehicle—at least, that was how her father explained things.

She stopped the vehicle near the entrance and slid out, her heart pounding. She left the vehicle's door open so she could get back in quickly. The lightstone lanterns illuminated the entrance, which looked like smooth stone instead of the bricks that made up the rest of the tunnel.

In the dark, with a trick of an eye, it was hard to see the entrance doors, unless a person knew they were there.

The doors were intact, and her relief at that almost made her tear up. She would have had to turn around and leave if they weren't, and she had no idea what she would have done with the satchels if the Vault had been discovered or destroyed.

Still, she couldn't really take a deep breath. She was so nervous that everything felt difficult. Or maybe she was having a delayed reaction to her father's...death.

She winced, wishing she felt him on her shoulder instead of her grandfather. Even though her grandfather wasn't really present anymore either.

Her great-grandmother's family had built this Vault a long time ago—maybe more than a century or two—beneath the network of crypts that were on the estate. Her great-grandmother's family had been astonishingly wealthy, and her great-grandmother's discoveries had only added to that wealth.

Gussie had no idea how much the family was worth; all she knew was that there was enough money in trust for each family member. Her parents had had eight children, and some of them had their own children now.

Her father said that new trusts activated when new Kirillis were born. So there was money in holdings, and there was other money in trusts.

Fantastically wealthy was an understatement, and that really didn't count some of the riches that remained inside this Vault.

Her entire body was shivering. It was chilly in the tunnel, and the air smelled dusty. Not musty—there was no dampness underground despite the prolonged days of fog and before that the seemingly never-ending rain. Water didn't leak in here.

The tunnel almost felt like its own world, and the Vault itself definitely did.

She had never opened these entrance doors without her father's assistance. For the past several years, though, he had made her do it on her own, so she knew exactly what to do.

She glanced over her shoulder. The lightstone lamps were still lit, their light growing. There were no shadows in the tunnel behind her, and none in front of her either. The brightest light she had seen all day was in this tunnel, as if she were standing the middle of a field in bright summer sunshine.

That reassured her. Her grandfather (there he was again) had warned her that evil lurked in shadows, that sometimes, evil *was* a shadow that could haunt a person's dreams and then steal their very soul.

She had used to think such things were fantastical, but after what she had seen today, she was beginning to doubt that. There was a part of her that was starting to understand that every fantastical thing she had been told by her father and grandfather actually had some kind of basis in fact.

She turned back to the entrance. Unlike the entrance to her father's manor, the entrance here had no carvings, not even a handle to pull to yank the doors open.

She placed her palm on the center of the right door, about eye height. Then she placed her left palm equidistant from the right, and stared at the barely visible crack between the doors.

She had to remain perfectly still or this wouldn't work. Her pounding heart seemed to speed up, as if it was trying to escape this place.

Her father had taught her five nonsense words to say very slowly. Or at least, he had called them nonsense words.

She was beginning to doubt that they were nonsense. She had simply accepted too much, explained away too much, thought she had known too much, when in fact, what little she did know should have shown her that she knew absolutely nothing.

The nonsense words had to be spoken with different tones —the first low, the second almost nasal, the third low again, the fourth in her normal voice, and the fifth at a whisper.

She said them, maintaining the pace as if they were part of a piece of music. Her father had taught her that too—that there was a rhythm to these words—and she needed to speak them precisely.

Then she silently counted to thirty, trying not to go too quickly, like she had done the first time she had come here.

It isn't working, Daddy, she had said.

Not now, it won't, he had said. *You broke the rhythm. Now I'm going to have to do it.*

He had explained later that she didn't dare speak while she was waiting. He also advised that she not move.

So she didn't. Even though the silence—the waiting—the fact that she had her back to the tunnel, her vehicle, and the open door—made her feel as if she was even more vulnerable than she had been before.

Finally, the doors vibrated beneath her palms. A bit of dirt dislodged from the top of the doors, just like it always did. It no longer showered her with dirt, like it had the first few times her father had brought her here, but still, the dirt cascade was both annoying and unsettling.

The vibration continued, growing stronger, and then the doors slid open, their bottoms scraping on the stone floor beneath. The squeal had always reassured her father, but had made the hair on the back of her neck rise.

This day was no different. The doors shuddered open and the darkness of the Vault beckoned.

Fortunately, the vehicle's lightstone lanterns pushed back the dark just enough for her to see that the entrance was unencumbered, like usual. The unique smell of the Vault, dust and cinnamon and sunlight, floated out like an invitation.

The familiarity of it made her eyes tear up. She was going to cry at some point, but she didn't dare do so right now. She still had a lot to do, and none of that counted figuring out what happened to her father and what happened to the entire staff at the manor.

She scurried around the side of the vehicle and peered into the tunnel. She could hear nothing except her own breathing and the beating of her own heart.

No one had followed her so far. And yet she felt like someone was. She had no idea why she had that feeling, but, she realized as she acknowledged the feeling, maybe she shouldn't trust her feelings at all.

Right now, her heart was broken, she had seen horrors in the house she grew up in, and she had a job that had to be done. Her emotions were changed every few seconds, which was logical. She needed to use what her father used to call her "prodigious brain" rather than the gut feelings she sometimes let push her forward.

Her brain needed to help her through what was clearly going to be one of the most challenging periods of her life.

She opened the vehicle's compartments, finding her way to the most hidden one. It glowed, ever so slightly, which she had never seen before. She hoped that was because of the lightstone lanterns that were lit all around her.

But the light really didn't look like lightstone had created it. The light was bluer, threaded with reds and golds and purples and greens as well. It undulated, like she was looking at reflection on the surface of lake on a windy day.

She placed her hand over the undulating light, but felt nothing. No warmth, no pricking that sometimes came with heat, no tickle against her skin.

So, with her forefinger and thumb, she grabbed the compartment's handle and twisted it. The compartment's door fell open as if the satchels didn't quite fit and needed extra room.

The strange light flared and then faded as if it had never been, except that it left runnels across her vision—little stabs of color just like she would see if she stared too long into the sun.

She was beginning to hate this day more and more with each passing moment.

The runnels faded as she blinked. She reached inside the compartment, and grabbed the handle of the nearest satchel, pulling it out.

It was the nicer satchel, the one that contained her grandfather's notebooks. She had put that into the compartment last, just in case someone or something stopped her and demanded the satchels.

She had planned to claim she only had that one and she would have shoved it at the person.

But there was no person to shove the satchel at, and as she tugged it out, she realized that she might have made a mistake. Maybe her grandfather's spectral urgings had been right; maybe the notebooks had more value than she realized.

Maybe the notebooks were the only things that would teach her exactly what she had been missing—what she had ignored. She hadn't listened to her father at all, and now there was no one left.

No one except her.

She set the notebook satchel down beside her. Then she reached into the compartment and removed a second satchel.

It felt lighter than it had before, but it looked no different. She pulled it out and set it beside the first satchel. It took a moment for her fingers to untangle from the satchel's handle, something that made her heart rate increase.

She was doing what she could for these satchels. They didn't need to be a bother. They *shouldn't have been* a bother.

Irritation filled her. She shook off the handle, then reached inside the compartment a third time. The third satchel came into her hands easily. It also felt lighter as she dragged it out.

She set it next to her other foot, feeling even more unsettled.

She glanced around the entire area, still expecting someone to see her, someone to know she was there.

But she really was alone.

She leaned forward and stuck her hand inside that compartment, feeling around on the leather interior, as if she could find what had fallen out of those satchels.

Apparently, nothing had. She wasn't finding anything at all. She leaned over the edge of the vehicle's seat as best she could and peered inside the compartment.

Nothing. She saw nothing out of the ordinary.

The compartment looked completely empty. As she leaned back, she had the odd feeling that the satchels were lighter because they were happier.

She shook her head again. If that thought was any indication, she wasn't in her right mind. And why should she be after what she had been through?

But she wasn't done.

She squared her shoulders and shoved the compartment door closed. Then she stood up. She made sure the windstone vehicle was not running, and much as she didn't want to, she shut down the lightstone lanterns in the front of the vehicle. Her father had left lightstone lanterns inside the entrance, and she would use them.

There were also lightstone fixtures, but she had no idea if they worked or not. They were very old.

She picked up the satchels. Once she was done with this task, she was done. She wasn't sure what she would do after she left here, but she would worry about that later.

She would worry about all of this later.

Right now, she needed to continue trudging through this day, through this task, until she finished it.

Then she could stop and think.

Then she could stop.

Whatever that meant.

TWENTY-TWO

Yris couldn't sit inside any longer. The iced-over portals throughout the apartment made the entire place frigid. She was cold. It was probably warmer outside.

The only good thing about the chill was that it stopped the itch in her hands that had been constant since the night before. Nothing had helped, not even Gem's special salve. Just this cold.

The conversation flowed around her and no one listened to anything she said. The other five Infantry members had become talkers, not that it mattered. The Infantry, under Rodderc's leadership, would go wherever he directed. Right now, he was willing to wait until Atrü told them to head out.

She needed action regularly. The action she had experienced so far in this unpleasant place hadn't been enough to satisfy her.

She loved the thick of things. Sometimes, she was too deeply in the thick of things which was, she suspected, why Rugar had put her on the team that he sent to Dorovich. She had gotten into trouble one too many times—picking fights in Nye, nearly killing that idiot restaurateur because he had the temerity to question an order she was making for a superior officer of hers.

She was aware that she picked fights, which was why she was trying not to pick one now. She wasn't as big or as muscular as others in this small Infantry unit, but she was stronger than most of them.

She'd win a physical fight, but she wasn't interested in physical fights. She was interested in those artifacts. They glinted with magick.

They seemed like the key to the magick here in Dorovich, at least to her. If only the team had a Spell Warder who could figure everything out.

Maybe if the team caught and tortured one of the mildly magickal Trinovantians, the team might learn how the artifacts worked.

It would be a risk: that Trinovantian might actually activate one of the artifacts and harm one team member.

But that risk would be mild compared to failure. And if the team learned how the magick worked, wasn't that something valuable to bring back to Rugar?

Yris wanted to ask that question, but she didn't. No one seemed to understand the implications of what they were dealing with. And no one seemed to remember how the Black Family dealt with long-term failures.

If this mission failed, well then, that was probably expected. But if the mission failed and most of the team returned, then Rugar—maybe even the Black Family—would see everything that happened here as a major failure.

Major failures were punishable by death.

Unless the team managed to change the way they talked

about what happened. Rather than the fact that they had failed in learning information or getting the maps or saving Hadley's life, the team could discuss what they had learned: that the Dorovicians were just as magickal as they had been in the past, that they were a very big threat, and that now was the time to come after them, because they had essentially gone to war against themselves with those Purges.

Yris had tried to tell Atrü that this was an opportunity for them. Instead, Atrü (and Hadley, truth be told) had seen it more as a threat to the Fey, because they used magick.

Yris sighed. The conversation in this room was going nowhere. This mission was going backwards. And she was getting very tired of listening to people who were in charge and knew absolutely nothing about what they were doing.

Yris eased herself off the long chair in the main room, as far from the artifacts as she could get.

If Yris had her way, the artifacts would be stored away from the team. She had understood bringing them here to sort through them. They had found a lot of gold coins in vases and jewelry boxes. This culture used a lot of gold, not just in its coins, but in its jewelry, so she supposed some of the gold could be melted down and sold or traded for actual coin.

She let the Spies worry about that, though, now that she had helped provide some of this wealth.

But the rest of the artifacts—the ones that hadn't held jewelry or coin—needed to be kept elsewhere, especially since the team did not understand what the artifacts did.

It was clear that the artifacts had magickal powers, and that nothing the Fey had done so far had activated those powers.

Over the years, Yris had seen some magickal items that

worked whenever anyone touched them. But some that she had seen, those that were not part of Fey culture, required some kind of knowledge of how to make or use them. She wasn't certain if the artifacts were a mixture of those.

What she was most afraid of, though, was that the Infantry had been lucky so far. They hadn't touched the artifacts in a manner that activated them. And she worried about that. Some of the things she'd seen at the various estates had been disturbing, and those disturbing things had happened because of artifacts like these.

But, no one had listened to her all day, so why would they listen now? She was the one who had asked that someone—anyone—open another portal onto that street where Hadley died, and send Infantry through. No one seemed to hear Yris when she suggested that.

They had all been shouting at each other about ways to get Hadley back.

Sometimes Yris deeply resented her lack of magick. During that horrid moment this morning, she would have opened a new portal, brought the Infantry through it, slaughtered whoever was holding Hadley, and then brought Hadley back into this house so that Gem could heal her.

But that was probably too tactically difficult for Atrü.

Yris or Rodderc should have been in charge. Neither of them had Vision, but they both had fought alongside some of the best in some of the skirmishes around the edges of Nye.

At least Yris and Rodderc understood tactics.

Atrü seemed to believe anyone could think their way through a crisis. Which might have been true for some crises, but this kind—the kind that killed people? That required less Vision and more tactical awareness.

Yris moved slowly toward the door. As she did, she watched a shadow float across the wall opposite her.

So Slumber had been in the room after all. Someone should have quizzed him about what he had seen in the Kirilli brain during Slumber's partially successful Dream Ride two nights ago. Hadley had spoken to Slumber about it, but Hadley was dead.

Slumber was young and inexperienced. Yris believed he might actually grow into his powers. But no one was helping him. Rodderc at least monitored him. But Rodderc didn't much like Dream Riders, so Rodderc was doing his best to make sure that Slumber didn't mess up, rather than actually helping Slumber improve.

Maybe, if they all ended up with a lot of free time on their hands again, Yris would help him.

But not right now.

She slipped out the front door and onto the area that the Trinovantians called a lawn. It was dying grass in no discernible pattern, broken only by a sidewalk that disappeared into the fogbank that Sirocco had established around the house.

A blur caught the corner of her eye. She looked to the right, and saw a small man walking with purpose across the lawn. The man's features and his hands seemed indistinct—and that wasn't caused by the fog.

That was Qurzi, the second Spy, the one everyone thought wasn't interested in doing the work. Qurzi had done what was asked of him and nothing more.

But Yris knew for a fact that Atrü hadn't asked Qurzi to do

anything on this day. She wasn't sure if Atrü had forgotten that Qurzi existed—again.

Which meant that Qurzi had an idea of his own, and he was going to execute it. That idea had to be a lot more interesting than whatever argument was going on in the house.

The Spies knew the culture better than anyone. If Qurzi thought leaving the team important, then he might actually know something—or he might be able to bring ideas to their plans, such as they were.

She didn't call attention to herself. She just fell in behind Qurzi, determined to use her tracking skills to stay with him.

If she did it right, he wouldn't know she was following him.

If he was actually doing something interesting, she might be able to provide assistance to him—the kind that Spies never admitted that they needed.

He disappeared into the fogbank, which made her curse slightly. Following an indistinct man into fog would make him even harder to see.

The better for her, then. She needed this kind of practice.

And if he had no idea she was following him, then she would be honing skills she might actually need to return to Nye.

Because, unlike Hadley, Yris wasn't going to die here. She certainly wasn't going to die for a mission led by one of the most incompetent Visionaries she had ever met.

She stepped into the cool fog, and smiled.

Finally, she had something to do today that was worthy of her skills.

Finally, she was doing something that might actually benefit the Fey.

TWENTY-THREE

The constabulary closest to the financial district was a hub of activity. Cilka brought the wagon there, and then let the constables take it, and the horse, to the stables.

She stood outside the building. It was made of stone blocks made from the mud of the Tamsi River. The Tamsi had a reddish-brown color that she had never seen anywhere else.

That reddish-brown color came from the mud—or so the experts said. Which was how it was always possible to recognize bricks made from Tamsi mud.

Cilka probably should have returned home to change. Or at least gone to her Procuratorate. She kept an extra set of clothing there.

But the strange events of the day had given her a sense of urgency that she hadn't felt in a very long time. She had to shake that feeling that she didn't understand what was going on.

Someone had murdered Augustus Kirilli, and that someone

had apparently had help. Those hands, reaching out of that portal, belonged to people she couldn't see, people who had some kind of plan.

The constabulary and the area around it was filled with people, but no one appeared to be anything like the stranger who had attacked Kirilli. She found herself peering a bit too intently at faces, which would get her a sideways glance

People were always in a hurry here. Some wanted to report something. Others, clearly under arrest, were being led in by constables. Some constables were leaving, pulling off their caps and running their hands through their hair or loosening their coats as they walked out. A handful of people walked out, one or two of them crying.

It looked like a typical day, even though it didn't feel like one to her.

Cilka brushed the sleeve of her coat. It wasn't even damp, and there were no longer any blood stains. She hadn't checked her own image—she had no idea how she looked.

She wasn't even sure it mattered.

She walked up the stairs into the building, keeping her head up. No one was going to notice her. No one was going to think twice about why she was here.

As she went through the double doors, she saw one scrawny man gesturing broadly. He looked terrified, saying something about a dozen people dead.

She wasn't sure she had heard that correctly, wasn't sure she wanted to know what he was talking about. So she didn't stop and listen.

Other conversations were going on around her—discussions about arrests, destroyed valuables, thefts.

She knew the layout of this and every other constabulary. They were all the same. Jail cells in the basement. Arrest centers on the main floor. Administrators on the third floor, and meeting rooms on the fourth, along with larger offices for some of the most important members of the constabulary.

The size of each building varied, based on its location. The constabulary here in the financial district was medium sized because no one believed that crime—*street* crime—would happen in this part of town. Some believed that anyone who worked in any financial position would have no compunction about committing a crime or several of them.

She pivoted and headed up the stone stairs, going up the middle two at a time, not holding the railing as she went. Now, she was getting looks from people who were heading down, most of whom were members of the constabulary.

Some were frowning, trying to recognize her. Others gave her a sideways glance. The farther up the stairs she went, the less she belonged.

She had once been a member of the constabulary, but was no longer, and it showed.

She reached the third level and found the building administrator. The building administrator was a slender woman with thinning hair that sat on the top of her head like a pelt. She had a lined face and an air of gloom that her regulation dark clothing did nothing to dispel.

Cilka introduced herself.

"I know who you are, Procurator," the building administrator said. Her voice had an edge of blame in it—apparently, she believed that Cilka should know who the building administrator was as well.

"Well, then," Cilka said. "I can skip some of the preliminaries. I need to see Desmond M'ndue. I was told he was usually here at this time of the day."

"May I tell Chief M'ndue what your business is?" the building administrator asked, confirming, just with her question, that Desmond was in the building.

"No," Cilka said. "This is for him only."

"You've been dealing with the Kirilli matter," the building administrator said.

The Kirilli matter was a strange way of referring to it. Cilka didn't acknowledge though. When she told someone that a topic was none of their business—no matter how politely she did so—that person should respect that position.

"It's urgent," Cilka said.

"Urgent is a matter of perspective," the building administrator said. "If you would tell me—"

Cilka waved a hand at her, pivoted again, and went up the next flight of stairs, the administrator yelling at her as she went. Cilka did not have the time to wait and if Desmond was anywhere, he would be up these stairs.

The fourth floor of this constabulary had wide hallways and small meeting rooms, probably because when this building was built, it was not supposed to house an important part of the constabulary.

But the financial district had become increasingly important over the years, which required the overall head of the constabulary to spend part of day dealing with financial crimes. Most people in charge would force his underlings to report to him in his main office, but Desmond M'ndue wasn't most people. He believed in seeing his staff where they worked.

He used to surprise them, showing up at odd hours and making strange requests. For all Cilka knew, he still did that. But he had a lot to manage now, and he had to become more organized rather than less.

Crime had risen in Trinovante in the past decade, but this crime was different from the crime that the city used to see. Petty crime had mostly ceased and some major crimes had ended as well.

But as Trinovante grew and the constabulary made its presence known throughout the city, criminals became more sophisticated. Theft still occurred, but successful theft often occurred in the form of embezzlement.

Those were the kinds of crimes that Cilka had worked with Augustus Kirilli off and on over the years. He'd had a gift for looking at a string of numbers and finding the error almost immediately.

She walked swiftly past the meeting rooms, and saw a number of offices with the doors closed. Only one had the door open, meaning someone was inside.

She stopped at the open door and rapped her knuckles on it, then peered inside.

Desmond M'ndue stood in front of the large window overlooking the neighborhood. Each window in the building had three panes of very thick glass, making it almost impossible to see detail through them. This window was located near the entrance to the room, away from the seating area, so that no one could shoot anything through the window and catch the inhabitants of the very large room unawares.

Unless, of course, they were standing right in front of the window.

Desmond turned slightly. He was wearing a light-green uniform, with trimmed sleeves and pants that gathered inside his boots. He had no obvious weapons, though, and the belt that usually wrapped around the waist of the tunic in this uniform style was nowhere to be seen.

He tugged at the tunic as he turned, a typical Desmond move. He had put on some weight, so the tunic was a bit tight, which probably explained the lack of belt.

There were other changes as well. His tight curls had been trimmed so viciously that it almost looked like he was bald. He had a triangle of hair on his chin and two matching triangles on the upper edges of his mouth.

It had been a long time since Cilka had seen him. He looked worn and less vibrant than he usually did.

At least, until his dark eyes caught hers and his entire face brightened. Then he looked just like the man she had met at Serebro Academy, when they were both eighteen and feeling out of their depth.

"I'm sorry I didn't speak to you before I assigned you Augustus Kirilli's death," Desmond said, his voice deep and slightly raspy as if he'd either been talking too much or had some kind of cold.

It was just like him to apologize rather than ask her what she was doing here. It was also like him to understand how difficult he had made her day, and maybe even her next month or two.

"We need to talk privately," she said. "Do you feel that we can do that here?"

Sometimes, staff listened in. She often took private conversations outside of her Procuratorate. She also knew that there was a lot of politics in the constabularies these days. Rumors had risen, saying that Desmond had had the job too long and was missing details.

She had seen nothing like that, but she was no longer as close to the constabulary as she had once been.

"Here, yes," he said. "Some of my other offices, no."

His smile was sad. He waved a hand at her, then walked over to the grouping of upholstered chairs.

She pulled the door closed, which made the room slightly darker. The light that came in through the three-paned window was diffuse, and not helped by the fog.

There were no lightstone fixtures here, which she found unusual.

Without saying anything, Cilka and Desmond both sat so that the light from the window illuminated their faces. They were good friends, such good friends that sometimes it felt like they read each other's minds.

But there had never been anything else between them. They both liked to say that their friendship was too important, but Cilka had always felt that, deep down, the two of them were too different to have a relationship other than the one they already had.

"You went to the iron tombs," he said as he leaned forward, elbows on his knees. He often assumed that position so that he could look whomever he was talking to in the eyes.

"I did. We put the body there." She took a deep breath. Might as well start with the thing he would like the least. "It was Judita's idea."

"Judita." His voice was dry. He thought her a bad influence. In fact, when he was working his way up the ranks, he believed that associating with her would lead to the destruction of his career and Cilka's.

Judita never tried to hide her magic, which was dangerous for anyone, especially in the dark times of the Thaumaturgical Purges. She had been investigated several times, but her friendships saved her.

Cilka hadn't really stepped in, although when she was a constable, she had slowed a few investigations until someone else (the actual guilty party) got accused.

But Cilka also suspected that Desmond had actually interfered with a few investigations, making certain that Judita did not get charged with excessive magic use or flagrant disregard for magical controls.

"I needed her," Cilka said. "The entire area reeked of magic."

Desmond frowned at her, but said nothing.

"Which you knew already, because you brought me onto the case," Cilka said.

"I'd heard a few things," he said. "There's been a lot of suspicious activity across the city and I was worried."

"Because we're dealing with a Kirilli," Cilka said.

Desmond pressed his lips together and nodded. That was the best she was going to get, at least right now.

"I need to tell you what happened." Cilka's voice didn't tremble, even though she had thought it might. "And then you can decide what to do about me."

Desmond raised his eyebrows. "You?"

"Yes." She flattened her hands against her knees, then rubbed a little. Yep, no blood at all. That was so odd. She'd have to tell him about that as well.

She took a deep breath, and launched into the story of the morning, beginning with the strangeness of the fog, the way that the body looked, and the unease she had felt from the beginning.

He nodded.

"You were right," he said. "I stopped briefly on my way here."

"Before we arrived?" she asked.

"I told one of the constables to stay far enough away so that he wouldn't be contaminated." Then Desmond ran a hand over his mouth. "I needed someone I trusted, Cilka."

"I thought you needed the training that I've had," she said. It was a sideways way to mention her magic.

"That too," he said. "I couldn't investigate without attracting attention."

Cilka nodded, then told him about her decision to bring Judita in, and how they were simply going to review the crime scene.

"Something in the magics intersected," Cilka said. "And when we got to the point where the killer arrived, she came through a portal and saw me."

"You?" Desmond leaned back.

Cilka nodded, then described, as carefully as she could, the change in the scene. How Kirilli escaped with two satchels. How the strange woman had attacked Cilka instead of Kirilli.

How Cilka had captured the woman.

And how Judita had killed her.

"So that's the body you took to the iron tombs," Desmond said. "Well done."

"No," Cilka said. "It is not."

She then described what happened next—the hands coming through that portal and taking the dead woman back, the fact that Kirilli's corpse had returned, only without the satchels. How there had been a third satchel not far from him, brought by the strange woman.

The one thing Cilka didn't tell Desmond was that she had taken the contents of the strange woman's pockets. Cilka wanted to look at those items on her own later. If he asked about the knife, she would tell him that she had it, but she wasn't planning to say anything else.

"I've never heard of anything like this," Desmond said. Then he took a deep breath, as if he was stealing himself for this next question. "What is Judita's take on it?"

"The reason Judita wanted that woman dead is that Judita believed the woman was Fey," Cilka said.

"Did you say *Fey*?" Desmond asked.

Cilka nodded.

"Fey," he repeated softly to himself. Then he blinked and frowned at her. "*Local* Fey?"

There were small Fey communities, but as far as Cilka knew, those communities were composed of mixed-race families. She didn't know of any pure Fey living in Trinovante.

But then, she was beginning to realize she didn't know a lot about the Fey at all, particularly what the history of the Fey was in Dorovich proper.

"I don't think so," Cilka said. "Judita was terrified. *Is* terrified. I don't think she would be if the Fey were local."

Desmond grunted, his frown growing even more prodigious.

"I was going to talk to her about this all tonight," Cilka said. "After I dealt with the body. You can join me."

"Oh, yeah," Desmond said sarcastically. "That's just what I need. A consult with Judita Ilyn about magic."

Cilka was a little offended.

"I didn't say it would be about magic. She wanted to talk about the Fey." *And what we needed to do about them*, Cilka prudently did not add. "She's frightened. She says the Fey have been trying to invade Dorovich for centuries."

"Trying and failing," Desmond said. Apparently he knew more about this than Cilka did.

"Judita believes they're a danger to us all," Cilka said. "She's afraid we don't have the ability to defeat them."

"Yes," Desmond said, his irritation apparent. "She thinks the Thaumaturgical Purges have left us especially vulnerable to anything the Fey might do. No wonder she killed that person. Fear does not make for a good investigative tool."

That was true. Cilka knew it. She had already told him that she had wanted to interrogate the woman.

"Judita thinks we don't have the luxury of investigating them. She thinks we need to find them and kill them."

"Judita thinks," Desmond repeated. "Well, Judita managed to destroy our only real lead."

Cilka shared his irritation about that. "There is the magic itself. It can be traced."

"But you said that mixing that magic with ours created something new." He looked at her.

Cilka nodded. She had said that. She had *seen* that. She shuddered just a bit.

Desmond sighed. He must have seen the realization on her face. "Well, at least we have a few answers now."

"We do?" she asked.

"Yes." He threaded his fingers together, then unthreaded them, a nervous habit of his that she hadn't seen for years. "We've had a rash of break-ins. They focus on the Old Families."

The Old Families were the de facto ruling class of Trinovante. Of Qavner really. The Old Families ran the major organizations, maintained some of the oldest businesses in the city, and often held positions in the seats of power.

Every one of the Old Families had a seat on various boards. The most influential was the Board of Regents for the academies scattered throughout Qavner.

There was often talk about divesting the Old Families of their positions of power. But it was mostly that—talk. All of the Old Families had enough money to buy most of the buildings in the city, let alone all the other businesses.

Now it was Cilka's turn to frown. "Why haven't I heard about this?"

For the first time since they started talking, Desmond smiled just a little. It was his *Really? You just asked me that?* smile.

"Cilka," he said quietly. "You're no longer part of the constabulary."

"Yet you use me to do your dirty work," she said, resisting the urge to rub her hands on her coat again. She was beginning to think the feel of that woman's blood would never come off her.

Desmond's smile had faded. Apparently, Cilka's tone was a bit too sharp. She'd let just a bit of her anger out. She was beginning to realize that there was a lot more anger behind it.

"I needed you on that," Desmond said. "I'm probably going to need you on all of this."

"It's no longer my job," she said. "I prosecute now."

"You investigate before you prosecute," he said. "You might as well get it all done in a package."

"That's not why you put me on Augustus's murder," she said. "You put me on it because you knew about the magic. You just said so."

"I did." His voice was quiet now. He glanced at the door, a Desmond way of reminding her to keep her voice down as well. "I had a feeling that there was more to these break-ins than simple destruction."

"Destruction?" Cilka asked.

He raised a hand, stopping her. "I'll give you the details in a moment. I didn't realize, until you told me about Judita's comment, that we might have a larger problem. I was thinking that we might be dealing with some kind of Rogue Magic Users. But this might be Fey."

Rogue Magic Users. Cilka shuddered at the term. It had come from the Thaumaturgical Purges, and had been used as a weapon to get rid of anyone without "designated" magic.

She had lost family members to that. The pain in her family about those losses was deep and long. Desmond had experienced the same thing. She had thought he would never try to use that term or that attitude in his work at the constabulary.

"What would you have done to Rogue Magic Users?" she asked, her voice hoarse.

The ground was shifting beneath her feet—here, every-where. She had never been afraid of the way that Desmond would answer a question before.

She had always assumed he was on the side of right, and for a moment here, she was afraid he wasn't.

His gaze met hers. The man inside those eyes looked like the man she had always known, and yet, she was beginning to wonder if she knew anything about anyone. Anything about anything really.

"If a Rogue Magic User killed someone," he said slowly, cautiously, as if he saw the doubt in her eyes, "they would need to be prosecuted."

"Yes, of course," she said, her voice still sounding strange to her. Maybe that was because she felt strange. "Anyone who commits murder would need to be prosecuted. But would you prosecute them under the Rogue Magic Statutes?"

He continued to study her, as if he was trying to determine where she was coming from. His expression became guarded.

"For that kind of killing," he said, "I'll do whatever it takes to bring the perpetrator in."

She nodded, not reassured.

He probably saw that too, because he added, "Your office is the one that determines how people are prosecuted."

"Generally," she said. "But we usually follow your recommendations."

He stared at her for another long moment, and then looked away. It was almost as if he broke eye contact so that he could reset his expression.

She'd seen him do that several times in the past...with other people. It hurt that he was doing that with her. But she was the one who had tried to pin him down with the Rogue Magic Statutes.

"Do you believe this is Fey?" She wasn't quite throwing him

a bone, but she was reaching out to him. She didn't like separation between them, not like this.

"I hadn't thought about it until you mentioned it." He turned toward her, his expression clouded. He was deeply, deeply disturbed by whatever he was about to say. "The break-ins at the Old Family estates, they were...unique."

"What do you mean?" she asked.

"The break-ins were more about destruction than theft," he said. "And in a few cases, someone working in the house or the yard was killed trying to stop the break-in."

"More murders," she said. "When did these break-ins occur?"

"They started a week or so ago." He was sitting up straight now, his discomfort showing in his posture. "We don't know exactly, because you know the Old Families. They have so many houses that they're not always in one."

"Wouldn't the servants report what was happening?" she asked.

"You'd think so," he said. "But we were investigating several of them. After the break-ins, in at least two of the houses, the servants fled."

Cilka thought about this for a moment. She didn't blame the servants. Some families treated them poorly. No one was going to stay to get paid to die just to prevent a theft.

"Explain to me why the mention of the Fey intrigues you," she said.

"I hadn't considered it," Desmond said. "I hadn't even considered the Fey communities in the Qavnerian Protectorate."

"Why would they go after the Old Families?" Cilka asked.

He looked at her in surprise, and then he smiled—the old, familiar smile of a good friend.

"I forgot how much you avoided history at the Academy," he said.

She felt a thread of irritation. That was twice today someone pointed out that her lack of historical knowledge was a problem. She wasn't blaming the people who pointed at her; she was blaming herself.

She hadn't realized that a choice, back when she was a student, would become so important later in her life.

"A lot of scholarship points to the fact that it was the Old Families who defeated the Fey the first time," Desmond said.

"No one knows for sure?" she asked.

He shrugged. "It was a long time ago, and you know how the Old Families like to burnish their reputations."

"You're saying that the Fey hold centuries-old grudges?" Cilka asked.

Desmond shook his head. "The Fey—the ones in Nye right now, the ones that came out of the Eccrasian Mountains—they have more magic than anyone knows how to handle. They don't always win every battle they fight, but they eventually win the war."

"I thought that was because they're a superior force," she said. "A culture of warriors who know how to fight better than anyone else alive."

"Perhaps," Desmond said. "But the weapons they wield are magic."

"All right." Cilka frowned at him. "They wouldn't attack us, would they? I mean if they're going to leave Nye and go after the rest of the world, wouldn't they go to Leut first?"

"If they came across the Infrin Sea," he said. "There are stories that they arrived near the Hidden River, centuries ago."

"Stories." Cilka rolled her eyes. She didn't have time for stories right now. She had a killer and maybe something even bigger to consider.

"No one knows exactly how a large troop of Fey got to Dorovich," Desmond said. "Before that part of Dorovich was in the Qavnerian Protectorate. No one knows. The Fey just arrived and attacked. There was a war, one that destroyed a lot of communities along the river."

"It was that serious?" she asked. "I thought it was skirmishes."

Of course, she didn't really know. She had hated history in school.

"Depends, again, on the scholarship," he said. "It's not my specialty. I know that your friend Judita studied the magic used back when she was in school."

"*My* friend?" Cilka said. "She was your friend once too."

Desmond smiled thinly. He was using his smile as a weapon today, always a sign of discomfort for him.

"My memory is that she was asked to leave Serebro Academy because she wanted to study the history of magic in the Protectorate," Cilka said.

"Which had never made sense," Desmond said, "since there is an entire department dedicated to the history of magic."

Then his gaze narrowed. Cilka knew that look; it meant he was about to get very serious.

"Well, you learned today what a dangerous person Judita actually is," Desmond said. "We're going to have to arrest her."

"For what?" Cilka asked. "There is no body."

"You saw her kill someone," he said. "Your word would be enough."

"I was holding that person when she stabbed them," Cilka said. "If Judita is guilty of murder, then I am an accessory."

"You were attacked by the person. Your own testimony to me backs that up," Desmond said.

"What I said to you wasn't testimony." Cilka's nerves were getting frayed. She didn't like this conversation at all. "It was a discussion with a friend."

His gaze skittered away from her. She had succeeded in making him uncomfortable.

"We have a lot of work to do," he said. "There are entire groups who could have attacked Kirilli. Rogue Magic Users, some dissident group in the local Fey communities, or the actual Fey themselves."

"Why would the actual Fey—the ones in Nye—attack Augustus Kirilli?" Cilka asked.

"What was in those satchels he was carrying?" Desmond asked.

"I don't know," Cilka said.

"What about the satchel they left?" Desmond asked.

"We haven't had a chance to examine it yet," she said. "Besides, that came from the attacker."

Desmond nodded. "Something is going on here," he said. "We're only seeing pieces of it."

Cilka hesitated to say what she was thinking, but this was Desmond. And he needed to know.

"Judita was talking about creating a magic circle," Cilka said.

Desmond let out an exasperated breath. "I trust you talked her out of it."

"Not exactly," Cilka said. "I wanted to deal with the body, so I told her I'd meet her later."

"That's like giving her permission," Desmond snapped.

Cilka almost said, *Probably*, but she stopped herself just in time. He didn't need to know her level of frustration. He didn't need to know that she was actively considering joining a magic circle to find out what had happened to Augustus Kirilli and to the woman that Cilka herself had fought with.

"Look, Cilka," Desmond said, leaning toward her. "We have enough troubles right now in Trinovante. The last thing I need is word to get out that there was a major magical occurrence involving one of the Old Families. The Purges have left everyone skittish and distrustful of magic. If we solve what's going on, without magic, then life will be easier here."

"If we solve it without magic," Cilka said, "and it was all caused by magic, how do we arrest? How do we handle the magical? There will be magic, Desmond, whether you like it or not."

A knock on the door made them both jump. Irritation flashed across Desmond's face. He started to say something when the door opened, and the building administrator leaned in.

Cilka was about to express her own irritation when she actually looked at the administrator's face.

She looked greenish gray, as if she were about to get ill.

"We have a situation, sir," she said.

Desmond stood. Cilka stood as well. With those words, she knew, the meeting was essentially over.

"Apparently Mr. Kirilli, he wasn't the only one to die today," the administrator said.

"What?" Cilka asked before Desmond could speak.

"A man's here," the administrator said. "He's reporting murders at the Kirilli estate."

"Murders?" Desmond asked.

"Yes, sir," she said. "And that's not all. He's saying that Augustus Kirilli was there. This morning. After he was...you know... dead."

Desmond closed his eyes for a brief moment. The secrets he had wanted to keep were going to prove impossible.

Everyone was going to know about this morning's magic, maybe before this day was through.

"Let me talk to him," Cilka said to Desmond.

"You're not doing this alone," he said.

"I know," Cilka said. She would need him beside her.

They would have to make decisions together.

TWENTY-FOUR

Atrü stood in his room, wishing he had the ability to recreate magick he had seen. He wasn't in any of the rooms with portals. He didn't want to watch Sirocco ice them over—or fail to ice them over.

He was terrified of failing. Or rather, failing worse than he already had. Hadley's death had shaken him, and the fact that Rodderc seemed to want to take over the leadership of this small team had shaken Atrü even more.

While he was in here, he packed his clothing into his kit. He traveled light, and he had gained nothing on this trip, just the way a military leader should.

But he felt like he hadn't done anything more than that.

He sat on the edge of the bed, careful not to lean back too far. The mattress had little support and was much too thin.

The room also had a wardrobe, but no closet. He had used the wardrobe for his clothing, and had just removed it all, leaving the wardrobe doors open. He preferred wardrobes to closets—closets always looked like doors into another world.

But wardrobes made him just as uneasy, and this one had some designs on it, little representative hearts, that Hadley had said had no magick at all. During the night sometimes he thought he had seen small faces in those hearts, and that had disturbed him.

He had asked Hadley about that, and she had seen nothing. But she hadn't given it much of a look, either. And he sometimes wondered if his Vision manifested in tiny moments, like faces in hearts, rather than in big grand Visions, like the great Visionaries in Fey history had.

Right now, Atrü was trying to use a skill he really didn't have —not a magickal one, anyway. He dug into his memory, trying to see if he could mentally recreate those maps that the team had lost.

The maps had flowed into each other, and he thought if he could bring them into a flat image, he might be able to see where they led.

He had the sense that the locations in those maps were less about towns and villages and streams and mountains and more a map of the magick itself, as it was scattered throughout Dorovich.

But he hadn't had enough time to figure that out, and he knew that the maps were incomplete. They were part of a much bigger map, or series of maps, something that some Dorovicians understood.

Something he needed to understand.

He wasn't succeeding though.

All he could see in his mind was the way that the maps

attached to each other, then rose off the table, and became something other. They almost looked like a multicolored river, or some kind of Domestic-designed scarf that flowed in a nonexistent breeze. They glowed in a way he had never seen before, and the glow interfered with his attempt at rebuilding them in his head. They—

"Atrü?" The voice sounded like it had risen out of a nightmare.

Atrü shuddered before he turned around. Slumber stood in the doorway. He was half-in and half-out of his shadow persona, which meant he had probably just detached himself from the wall.

At the moment, he did not reflect any light. Light absorbed into him, and made him seem strangely flat and strangely solid.

"I thought you were helping Gem," Atrü said, although he hadn't given Slumber any thought at all. That was probably obvious from the tone of Atrü's voice. He always worried that people could hear his lies.

"I need you to listen to me," Slumber said. His voice was actually shaking.

For the first time, Atrü wondered if Slumber was afraid of him. It certainly seemed that way.

"Can this wait?" Atrü asked. Then, without waiting for a response, he answered his own question. "I think this can wait. We have to get ready to leave here—"

"No," Slumber said, and then he looked appalled at himself. "I mean, we should leave, but before we do, as we pack up, you need to listen to me."

Atrü resisted the urge to sigh. He found Slumber tiresome. And then Atrü tried not to smile at his own private pun.

But he did find Slumber difficult to deal with. He was undertrained and terrified of everything, which was odd for a Dream Rider. All of the others that Atrü had met had been terrifying figures in their own right.

"What?" Atrü said, being deliberately curt.

"The artifacts, they—"

"We'll bring them with us," Atrü said. "We'll be able to study them at the new place, and maybe figure out—"

"*No!*" Slumber shouted.

Then he looked appalled at himself, started to clap his hands over his mouth, and finally stopped before he completed the action. He stood up straighter.

Atrü hadn't moved. He had never heard Slumber yell before.

"When I was in the Kirilli's mind," Slumber said, lowering his voice, "I saw so many artifacts, and they all had strange abilities. I thought..."

Then he stopped, shook his head, closed his eyes as if he was irritated at himself, and sighed.

Atrü waited until the little fit passed, wishing that Slumber would get to the point.

"I—when we learned about all the magick," Slumber said slowly, "I figured we'd better talk about this. Those artifacts, they have magick of their own."

"That's obvious," Atrü said drily.

"But it's dangerous magick," Slumber said. "I think the musical instruments might have Charm magick, and the goblets —they were glowing when I saw them. And then there are the statues, which are like actual people that can come to life—"

"The Infantry have already told me about that," Atrü said.

"I think it's dangerous to have the artifacts anywhere near

us," Slumber said. "I told Hadley that. She said we'd figure out which we could store and study and which we could destroy when she returned. But she didn't return."

He said that last as if Atrü didn't know it, as if Atrü wasn't acutely aware of what had happened that morning.

"We don't have time today," Atrü said.

"Then we leave them here," Slumber said. "They're *dangerous.*"

He had a point. A good point. Why take enemy weapons to the safe house? And there was no denying that anything with that level of magick could be used as a weapon.

Still, Atrü wanted to know what they were and how they worked.

"All right," he said, mostly to get rid of Slumber. Atrü had better things to think about. "We'll find a place to store them, and if we can't, we'll destroy them. Although..."

Slumber straightened. Light was beginning to reflect off him. He was returning to his full Fey form.

"The question is will they harm us if we destroy them?" Atrü said.

"You know they won't," Slumber said, looking as agitated as he sounded. "You know it. The Infantry destroyed a whole bunch of artifacts all over the city, and there were no ill effects."

"Really?" Atrü asked. "Because the magick swirling in the area where the Kirilli was had been strong enough to kill Hadley."

Slumber stared at him, as if he didn't quite understand what Atrü was saying. Or maybe it was some kind of disbelief.

"That area was nowhere near the destroyed artifacts," Slumber said quietly.

So, disbelief it was.

"Magick travels," Atrü said.

"Not like that," Slumber said. "You know it. You know that. Why are you saying these things?"

Why was he? Maybe because it was one more thing to worry about, with an entire raft of things to worry about.

Best to change the subject.

"What did the Kirilli know about the maps?" Atrü asked.

Slumber stared at him, as if he had never seen Atrü before. Atrü knew they had discussed the maps when Slumber returned from attaching himself to the Kirilli, but Atrü had left the magickal decisions up to Hadley.

"I told you," Slumber said.

"Tell me again," Atrü said.

"He knew they were important," Slumber said. "He believed that it was better for him to have them than it was to have them fall into the hands of someone who didn't under-stand them."

Atrü remembered that. "But what about the magick?"

"He didn't use the word *magick* ever," Slumber said. "I *told* you."

"You told Hadley," Atrü snapped.

"He knew that the maps held a history that had been banned in many parts of the Qavnerian Protectorate. He had been raised to believe that the maps should be kept separate, but he was starting to change his mind on that. He was having some kind of issue with a Regent." Slumber shrugged. "Hadley and I couldn't figure that out. We have no idea which country in Dorovich has a Regent."

We have a lot to learn about these maps, Hadley had said as she looked at them undulating over the table. *Slumber said there are many more of them. And they're important.*

Important enough for the Kirilli to somehow revive himself and recapture them, whatever magick he used.

"Can you recreate them with Gem's help when we get to the new house?" Atrü asked.

Slumber was shaking his head before Atrü even finished asking the question.

"You know that what I see in dreams isn't representative," Slumber said.

"But you're arguing for me to destroy artifacts based on dreams," Atrü said, letting his irritation out.

"Because danger usually threads through dreams properly. Imagery does not. Dreams are metaphors, more than anything else."

"Yet you want me to glean information from them," Atrü said. "To make decisions based on a dead man's dreams."

Slumber's face grew dark. The entire wall around him darkened as well, as if he was removing the light from the hallway.

"He wasn't dead when we went after the maps. And that had a feeling of truth," Slumber said. "I know you don't respect me, but Hadley did. She believed in me. She—"

"And look where that got her," Atrü said.

Slumber inhaled sharply. Then he pivoted and walked away, without saying another word.

Atrü stared after him. Rugar wouldn't let anyone talk to him like that. Rugar wouldn't let anyone try to dictate what he did either.

Atrü knew he wasn't Rugar, but maybe he should try to take some lessons from Rugar.

The artifacts hadn't hurt them so far. And the artifacts that they had, the Infantry had already touched.

There was no need to destroy them. Slumber was overreacting, probably from guilt at causing Hadley's death.

Atrü made the decision: they would bring the artifacts with them.

He glanced around his room. The kit was full and there was nothing left. He wouldn't be able to concentrate on those maps, not after this little emotional episode.

He would tell Gem to make sure the artifacts got to the new house. Slumber wouldn't like it, but Slumber was an incompetent Dream Rider who seemed to think he understood the magick of this city, just because he'd spent time in the mind of a dead man.

Atrü left his kit on the bed. He would instruct Gem to take that too.

It was time he took full control of this group. He had allowed Hadley to do much of the communicating and, if he was honest with himself, a lot of the decision-making.

He was going to take that back. He would make them listen to him.

He would do what Rugar used to do.

By doing so, Atrü would make the team respect him.

They had to, if they were all going to survive.

TWENTY-FIVE

Gussie felt like she had been walking forever. She didn't remember the Vault being this big when she had walked it with her father. But then, they had been having a lovely conversation.

He had pointed out various statues and carvings that lurked among the boxes. He had even shown her images of her great-grandmother's face, carved into stone by craftspeople from the Razbitay Mountains.

There were other carvings throughout this entire walk—many of them on the same kind of wood that had decorated the door to the manor. All of them had figures that seemed to leap out of the wood's surface, and all of them looked vaguely familiar.

The cinnamon smell faded the farther back Gussie went, replaced with the faint sent of anise. Once she went through that, the smells became richer—less food and more cut wood.

The lightstone lamps were different the farther back she

went as well. They were held in place by a different stone, a clearer whiter stone, that somehow remained white despite the dusty odor of the boxes near her.

Only back here, there really weren't boxes. There were crates, many of them with the shipping labels still attached. Some of them had paper tags, identifying the owner of the crates.

She wasn't looking at ownership at the moment. She hadn't stopped at all, not since she started walking. She knew the stone bins were ahead of her, but she didn't know how far ahead.

And she was getting impatient. Or maybe just tired. The events of the morning were catching up with her.

It didn't help that the lightstone lamps this far back weren't as bright. Their light was brownish, as if something coated the outside of the lamp itself—which didn't surprise her. She was actually kicking up dust as she walked.

She had sneezed half a dozen times already. She knew once she left here that she would be coated in dust.

She sighed at that thought. At least it would cover the blood.

The lightstone lamps weren't as responsive back here either, which slightly unnerved her. Rather than lighting in anticipation of her appearance, they would light after she passed them.

Sometimes the lightstone actually groaned as she moved through it as if some mechanism inside it cranked to life unwillingly. Or, more accurately, as if it had been dormant and was just now remembering how to work. Rather like people who woke up after a deep and heavy sleep, moaning unconsciously as they moved and stretched.

When she reached the very back of this particular section of the Vault, she nearly bumped into some lanterns piled on top of the crates. The lanterns had a completely different shape than anything she had seen before.

As she reached them, the lanterns flared to light. It almost seemed like they were filled with fireflies, only once she peered at them, the fireflies looked more like people, trapped inside the glass.

She was getting so exhausted she almost believed those people she saw—glowing and increasingly bright—were pounding on the glass, their mouths open as if they were yelling at her.

Her skin crawled. She had never seen anything like that before.

She clearly hadn't come along this path with her father. She would have remembered those lights and asked him about it.

He had had an answer for almost everything, at least, until they had reached the very back. Then his expression had grown serious.

There are a lot of questions about what your great-grandmother did up in the mountains, he had said. *And it wasn't just her. Her husband Magnus had been involved too.*

Gussie hadn't cared back then. She had heard the rumors, but she had dismissed them as tall tales.

Her father, however, had seemed very disturbed as he looked at the old crates, some of them falling in on themselves. The air smelled dank back here, almost as if everything had been dipped in water.

I wouldn't touch the artifacts back here, he had said. *They were stored here for a reason.*

What was that reason? Gussie had asked.

I don't know exactly, her father had said. *But my father told me to let them stay here. I got the sense they were dangerous.*

Gussie was getting the sense—those gut feelings again—that everything back here was dangerous. The air was colder here, and she could almost imagine a different kind of fog rising—not the strange fog of the morning or the yellowish-green fog from the burning coal all over Trinovante.

This fog smelled of river water, and had a ghostly whiteness to it. It rose out of some of the crates, and hovered near her.

If she were a fanciful person, she might even believe that what she was seeing were spirits, not fog, rising out of the crates that they had been trapped in.

But given how much death she had seen this day and how many of her personal beliefs had been challenged, she was unwilling to concede that spirits could actually come out of those crates. She was much more willing to believe that she was misreading dust or dirt or maybe even a bit of a miasma from the oldest part of the Vault.

She was growing uneasy, though. She had walked a lot farther than expected, and she didn't see the stone bins. She remembered them vividly. They had haunted her sleep for years.

She almost set the satchels down here—surely no one else would come this far—but she didn't.

The path turned slightly to the left, and finally she saw the stone bins, blocking the middle of the path. No one had stacked crates or boxes or furniture or sculptures or anything else near them.

They looked just like she remembered, as if someone had built them in the middle of this wide section of the Vault at the same time as they built the rest of the Vault. She had looked inside one of the bins a long time ago. It had looked to her like they had risen out of the floor, rather than being built on the floor.

That was because each bin was built up from a series of stones. The blocks matched, inside and out. The only part that did not match was the cover, which was—in each instance—made of the wood.

The covers were plain. They had no carvings, unlike the wood she had seen earlier. She wasn't even sure what kind of wood this was.

If someone came this far into the Vault looking for the maps, they would look in at least one of these bins—or maybe two. And if she had to predict, she would think that made-up investigator would look in the bins on the edges of the paths—the bin closest to her, and the bin farthest from her.

So she walked a few more yards to one of the bins that was less predictable—or so she hoped. That bin was in no real pattern. It was two away from the middle bin, and four from the bin closest to her.

It would take a bit of concentration for her to remember where she had stashed the satchels.

She kept her gaze on that particular bin as she walked to it. The cover was on tightly. There was a chance that her plan wouldn't work, that something was already stored in this bin.

It wouldn't surprise her. She had always been surprised that the bins she had looked in were empty. They looked like natural storage containers to her.

When she had told her father that, he had responded that he thought the bins looked like coffins.

She didn't see it. Nor did they look like crypts. No coffin

would be made of perfectly measured brick, and no crypt would be that nondescript.

She finally reached the bin she'd had her eye on. She had to set the satchels down to push the cover off. It felt odd to let go of the satchels yet again. Each time she held them—or rather, each time she was forced to let go of them—it almost felt like they were attached to her, like they were part of her body.

She didn't like that feeling. In fact, she didn't like how she was feeling at all. Her skin had started to crawl. A faintly fetid smell, almost like an overabundance of rotting plants, rose around her. As the smell grew, it felt like a physical presence, one that could reach out and touch her.

She might have made the wrong choice of bin. She made herself touch the cover—which was surprisingly smooth. She had half expected the cover itself to be rotted.

The cover was easy to lift and move. The smell did not come from inside the bin. A cold draft rose from the inside, almost as if the interior had been made of ice.

She hadn't expected that either. The chill made her shiver. Her hands were instantly cold.

She couldn't put the satchels in there. She had no idea what was causing the cold or the smell, but she didn't want anything to ruin the satchels or their contents.

Besides, she couldn't stand to be near the bin any longer. She pulled the cover back in place, then grabbed the satchels and ran to the path she had just walked on.

She couldn't bear to open any more of the bins. Maybe they did house something, something that she couldn't see. Maybe that was why they were lined up like that.

Whatever the reason, she couldn't put the satchels in there. She needed to put them somewhere else.

If she went deeper into the Vault, she would find the oldest items. She had no idea what condition they were in, and she wasn't sure she wanted to find out.

It might be logical to go as far into the Vault as possible, but she couldn't face it. Everything felt off, and she was getting so tired.

She turned around and headed back, thinking maybe she would put the satchels with her grandfather's satchel after all.

But that felt wrong too—and didn't just feel wrong. It was wrong. She had made the correct decision; she needed to keep her grandfather's notebooks separate from these satchels.

So she walked back, looking at all of the crates, trying to figure out how to distinguish one from the other. She needed to look inside these satchels at some point, when her head was clear, and all the problems of this day were far in the past.

And when she was ready, she had to be able to find the satchels again.

The light from the lightstone lamps was brighter as she got farther from those bins. She passed some of those strange lanterns again, the ones with fireflies in the shape of people. As she walked past, they came alive once more, and her skin crawled again.

Those things were not natural. They disturbed her, and she didn't want the satchels anywhere near them.

Light came out of one of the crates just past those creepy lanterns. That light undulated, waving like water on a windy lake, just like the maps had done in the compartment.

She started to walk toward that crate, but pain shot through her palms almost as if the satchels she was carrying bit her. The pain radiated up her arms into her shoulders.

She cried out and tried to let go of the satchels, but couldn't. Instead, they seemed to tug her forward, away from this part of the Vault. The satchels were not quite perpendicular to her body. They were almost on end, and she wasn't sure how long she could hold them that way.

She staggered along behind them. She really wasn't in control any longer. She couldn't let go of the satchels and they forced her to move.

Her heart was pounding so hard that she thought it might burst. Mixed with the fear that was creeping out of the pit of her stomach, along her spine, and into her every thought, she was sure that at some point, she would die.

But she didn't. She continued stumbling, her arms extended now, the satchels leading her.

They took her past crates, all the way to boxes. Light grew around her, as bright as sunlight. Sometimes black-gray-sickly orange light rose out of some of the crates. Other times, she thought she heard voices, calling to her.

She'd never had an experience like this in the Vault. Was that because her father was not beside her? She wasn't certain. She wasn't certain of anything.

This day had completely demolished everything she knew about herself, her family, and the world they lived in.

And she didn't have time to contemplate any of it. She couldn't even stop.

Finally, the satchels descended a bit as she reached the very edge of the crate-box piles, where the wooden carvings were.

Unless she was mistaken, the carvings crowded closer together than they had before.

Maybe that was just because she was viewing them from a different angle. She *hoped* that was because she was viewing them from a different angle.

She reached the edge of the pile of carvings, and the satchels immediately fell to the floor.

She continued forward, finally able to let go of them, and tripped on the lines between the bricks, nearly falling. She managed to catch herself with her right hand, scraping the palm as she did so.

That little bit of pain made her furious. She managed to stand, ready to punch something, or scream at someone, or throw her entire body against the piles of boxes, kicking and yelling—and maybe crying.

All right, then. It wasn't the pain in her palm that was making her react that way. It was the fact that the near fall had been the last straw.

She blinked back tears and swallowed hard, trying to stem the emotional tide.

Then she turned around.

The satchels remained behind her. They looked like regular satchels that would sit beside someone's desk. Except for the maps peeking out of one of them, nothing was different about them.

Nothing at all.

Clearly, though, they wanted to be here. Somewhere. But she wasn't going to leave them in the middle of a path. That wouldn't be sensible.

She went back to them, and with great reluctance, picked them up again.

They moved slightly forward, and she growled. She didn't think she had ever growled before, but she didn't even have words any longer for what she was feeling.

The satchels pulled her into the carvings, which—she could have sworn—leaned toward her, as if they were examining her.

"I'm all you got," she snarled at them. "Either you let me put the damn satchels here or leave me alone."

The carvings froze in place. The satchels eased back to her side.

She was in the middle of the carvings now, unable to see the boxes or the crates or the path she had walked. The looming carvings felt menacing. She didn't want to stay here.

She needed to get out of the carvings, away from whatever was in these boxes, and head home. Her home. Where she would crawl into bed and pull up the blankets...

Which, of course, wasn't going to work. Nothing was going to work—except getting out of here. Getting away.

She set the satchels down. She no longer cared about the perfect place to keep them. She wouldn't forget these carvings or the wood or the fact that she had once thought they were lovely, like the ones on her father's house.

That made her wonder what had happened there. She had always thought the carvings beautiful. She had never thought of them as alive.

Until now.

The carvings were crowding her again. She held up her hands, and backed out the way she came in.

"You have the satchels," she said. "I might want to visit them. Please let me visit them."

One of the carvings turned its well-molded head, its smooth eyes seemingly looking at her. Then the head went up and down, very slowly.

"You will protect them, right?" Gussie asked "If someone breaks in here? You'll make sure the satchels are all right?"

The head nodded again, that slow movement. Then a nearby carving's hands reached out toward her. Gussie ducked and almost backed into another carving.

Its hands were outstretched. Other carvings made the same motion.

Then the hands came together, palms touching. They rose so that the fingertips touched the chins of the heads on the carvings. The heads then bowed forward, as if they were bowing to her.

It was the most frightening thing she'd seen all day, and she had seen people she'd known since childhood slaughtered.

When facing other cultures, her grandfather had said repeatedly, *show them the respect they show you.*

Maybe this was respect. Maybe his advice applied here.

She raised her hands, put the palms together, and noted that they stuck to each other. That dried blood wasn't completely dry. It was tacky.

She raised her hands, touched the underside of her chin with her fingertips, and bowed just a little.

The carvings behind her moved, scraping against the floor as they did so. She backed all the way out, and took a gigantic breath.

The air was cooler here and didn't smell of wood. Nor did it smell fetid. It almost smelled fresh, like the wind on a fall day.

She bowed again, and then she pivoted, and ran as fast as her slippers would let her. She headed toward the main entrance, not caring that she looked terrified.

She was worrying about looking terrified in front of *statues*, carvings, wooden carvings—what she had thought were inanimate objects.

She had been wrong.

Not just about that, but about so many things.

She hurried, hoping against hope that she, at least, would be able to escape.

TWENTY-SIX

Sirocco approached the final portal. She had built it in her bedroom. That way, she had been able to augment the fog any time she had felt it fading. She had gone in and out of that portal dozens of times, setting up fogbanks all over the city.

It had been the first portal created, the one that she had made shortly after the team had moved into this house. She had used a wide and ever-changing portal to add strength to the fog that had already blanketed Trinovante.

Apparently, the city usually had big inversions, where the air became stagnant. It was filled with moisture and then that, with the burning coal across the city, would create a fog.

It wasn't like the fogs she usually created. It didn't come from cold or from the river or from too much humidity. It came from the damp air mingling with the smoke.

The mixture was toxic, but only over time. Still, it created a yellow haze that had settled over the city.

She was the one who had changed that haze into fog because she could travel through fog. She could send magick through it, so that she could control the fog, making it thicker in some places and thinner in others.

Closing the portal entirely meant that her portion of the fog would fade away.

She was reluctant to do that, but she was going to do it anyway. Right now, the team had no need for fog.

It was her portal. But she still had to ice it. She didn't want to. Her hands were so cold that they had turned blue. Closing the other three portals had been hard work, leaving her a bit woozy. She could feel the magick drain.

She put her hands on her hips, and then cried out in pain. She held her hands up. They were swollen and cracked, with lines along them that were black.

Frostbite? She supposed that was possible. She would have to talk to Gem about it, after icing this portal.

She took a deep breath and forced herself to move her swollen fingers. She put her hands up like she had done before, and pulled moisture out of the air. There wasn't as much as there had been before, so she had to reach outside of this apartment. She was probably pulling in some of the remaining fog.

She didn't want to do that, but she had no choice.

She had to work quickly because each movement sent shooting pains up her arms and into her shoulders. She hadn't realized how much pain she was in.

Finally, she covered the final portal in ice. Then she sat down hard on her bed, wanting nothing more than to fall back and close her eyes.

But she didn't dare. Not with the condition her hands were in.

She made herself open the door to her bedroom. Voices carried down the short hallway, discussing the artifacts and the magick and the loss of Hadley.

It seemed like most of the team was there, and none of them were happy.

Sirocco walked down the hallway, her arms crossed over her body, her elbows braced against each other. She kept her arms rigid so that her hands didn't bounce.

She needed Gem's help to heal the frostbite—or whatever this was. Gem might not have a lot of Domestic experience, the kind that helped her make a home, but she did have a lot of Healing experience.

Sirocco peered into the main room, saw most of the Infantry there, and Rodderc holding forth. Yris was quietly making her way to the front door, and Slumber was working his way back to the kitchen.

Sirocco didn't see Gem at all.

Either that meant she was still outside, or she had gone to the kitchen.

Sirocco slithered around the group, so that no one would say anything to her. The door to the room where Hadley died was closed. Maybe Atrü was there.

It didn't matter where he was. Sirocco didn't want to see him, not right now.

She had been on several campaigns in her life, and during all of them, the teams had blamed their leader whenever anything had gone wrong. She had always thought that the teams were overreacting, but now she was beginning to realize that she might have been wrong.

Because she certainly blamed Atrü for the mess they were in right now. If he had been a bit more forceful, if he had given the teams more guidance, if he had *researched* Trinovante, for pity's sake, then maybe everything would have gone better.

It wasn't like they lacked time. The Infantry had been destroying artifacts for nearly two weeks now. And then they had brought some of the artifacts back against the express wishes of Rugar.

Sirocco shook her head and stepped into the kitchen. Gem wasn't there either, but something glistened near the door.

Sirocco looked, then stepped backwards, startled.

Another portal.

It glistened in the kitchen's strange half-light. The light seemed to come from the main room. Sirocco followed it with her eyes, and saw that the light seemed to originate on the artifacts table.

Of course it did.

She grabbed a wooden spoon and put it into the light, half expecting the spoon to catch fire. But it didn't. It just looked like a spoon in a ray of sunlight.

Tentatively she stuck the tip of her index finger—her blackened, injured, ice-cold index finger—into the light, expecting some kind of reaction.

She felt nothing, not that she could feel anything anyway.

Maybe the fact that she had closed the fog portal meant that the sun could shine across Trinovante.

She was going to worry about the light later. Right now, she had to figure out what was in front of her.

She paused, looking into the main room. Normally, she would have told someone what she was doing, but everyone seemed more invested in their arguments than in caring about the rest of the team.

So, she squared her shoulders and peered into the portal.

The light changed immediately. The air smelled of pitch and green grass tinged with the faint scent of blood.

She leaned back, frowning. This portal led somewhere. And it wasn't clear whose magick made the portal. Certainly not anyone on this team.

Hadley's magick had a certain signature, one that Sirocco had taught herself how to recognize. This portal did not have that signature.

The only other person on the team who could make a real portal was Sirocco herself. And she knew she hadn't made this one.

So where had it come from?

She turned toward that light again. Did one of the artifacts do this?

She ran her sore fingers along the portal's edge. If an artifact had done it, surely she would have noticed before now. Unless it just happened.

But this portal felt like it had been built a while ago. Days maybe?

She didn't know.

But she needed to know where it came from, and why it existed.

She leaned around the door to the kitchen.

"Hey," she said, stopping the conversation in the main room. "I need someone in the kitchen right now."

Xevkin slipped out from behind one of the chairs. She looked eager to get away from the conversation.

Sirocco felt a slight disappointment that the person who had joined her was Xevkin. Sirocco knew that Xevkin was a hell of a good fighter, but she was also so thin that she looked insubstantial.

They'd never had more than a cursory conversation.

Xevkin came into the kitchen, skirting alongside the beam of light. Sirocco couldn't tell if Xevkin had seen that light or not.

"What happened to your hands?" Xevkin asked.

"Wasn't prepared for a spell," Sirocco said. "I'll get Gem's attention in a few minutes."

Xevkin raised her eyebrows, as if she didn't agree with the decision. "I'd do it now."

"We don't have now," Sirocco said. "We have a rogue portal."

Xevkin straightened, looking around until her gaze alighted on the edges of the portal. "How did we miss that?"

"I don't know," Sirocco said. "It's not one of ours."

Xevkin put a hand on Sirocco's shoulder. Pain coursed through Sirocco's skin. She really had hurt herself.

"I'll get Atrü," Xevkin said.

"No," Sirocco said. "You'll stay here while I go through to see where this leads. I won't be long. If the portal closes or I'm gone for an hour, you'll get Atrü."

Xevkin shook her head slightly. "I should go. You're injured."

"If this portal closes," Sirocco said, "can you open a new one so that you can return?"

Xevkin's mouth formed a thin line. It flattened everything about her face. "Of course not."

"Then you need to stay here and follow my instructions." Sirocco took a deep breath. "I'm hoping this portal came from one of the other teams. We were connected to them through Hadley. Maybe someone noted what happened to her and tried to contact us."

Xevkin tilted her head slightly, her eyes narrowing. "But that's not what you think."

Sirocco stared at her for a moment. It was hard to put anything past Xevkin. Sirocco hadn't realized that when she called her in.

"No, it's not what I think," Sirocco said. "It is what I hope."

And with that, she shrouded herself in a layer of fog and stepped into the portal, uncertain what she would find on the other side.

TWENTY-SEVEN

She was driving too fast.

Gussie had left the Vault at a full run. She had climbed into the windstone vehicle, started it, and driven out of the tunnel as fast as she could.

She bumped along the road inside the estate, barely missing some fallen limbs and some of the trees. The vehicle seemed to be more in control of the drive than she was.

Her heart was pounding so hard that it hurt. She could barely breathe. And her eyes kept filling with tears, making it hard to see.

At least the fog had receded. The thin sunlight had taken over, apparently, but it seemed wrong somehow. As wrong as the fog had been. Like make-believe sunlight. Like sunlight she had imagined or sunlight through several panes of thick glass or sunlight like a child would draw it against a glass-covered sky.

She manipulated the driving sticks, but it felt like she was doing so underwater.

When she reached the edge of the estate, she had enough presence of mind to slow down. She had to look at the road before turning on it.

She had to close the gate.

She had to get as far from here as she possibly could.

The windstone vehicle slid to a stop, the wheels turning slightly. The vehicle ended up sideways near the gate. She really had been going too fast.

The thought didn't upset her, though, like it should have. She was already upset enough.

She got out of the vehicle, pushed the gate open, then peered down the road. The road was dark. The thin sunlight hadn't really penetrated here.

She couldn't hear other vehicles or the clip-clop of horses' hooves. A chill ran down her back. It had grown colder here. She felt very far away from the city, even though she was on its edge.

If she died here, no one would know where she was.

That thought caught her. She climbed back into the windstone vehicle, and slowly manipulated the driving sticks until she got the vehicle out of the gate.

Then she climbed out again and closed the gate.

Part of her hoped she would never have to come here again, but she would. She knew it. She would have to show one of her siblings where the Vault was. This was a secret too important for just one person to hold.

She crawled into the vehicle and put her face in her hands. She was so tired.

But she couldn't stay here. She didn't dare. She couldn't lead whoever it was who had attacked her family to this place.

Gussie took a deep breath. Her grandfather used to say that

when the days got difficult, concentrate on the next hour. If the next hour was too difficult, concentrate on the next minute.

The problem with that was that before Gussie could concentrate on the next minute, she needed to know where she was going.

She couldn't just drive—even though she wanted to.

She took another deep breath, then raised her head out of her hands.

She had to go back into the city. She needed to see if Zeitsev had listened to her and gone to the constabulary.

Then she shook her head. It didn't matter if he had listened. *She* needed to go, to report what had happened to all of those people.

To her father.

Except she didn't exactly know what happened to him.

Her head ached, but not as badly as her heart did.

She drove through the overhanging trees, slower this time. She had started shaking, which couldn't be good.

She gripped the driving sticks hard. Her grandfather used to tell her that in times of great conflict, the great marched slowly through it. *Make a list of what you must accomplish*, he said, *and then accomplish them, one at a time. Do not focus on the crisis. Focus on what* you *can do in the crisis.*

She had done part of that already. She had taken the satchels to the Vault. Now, she had to contact the constabulary. Maybe they would tell her what to do next.

But she couldn't leave it all up to them. She also had to let her family know—and she would, as soon as she figured out where she was staying. She didn't feel safe staying at home, and she couldn't go to the manor, which was what she would have done in the past.

There were hotels and rooming houses. She could stay in one of those. The family had property in several other cities. She loved Windswept Cottage in the Serebro Mountains.

Then her breath caught. She hoped that home was all right.

She didn't know.

For that reason, and that reason alone, she needed to contact her family. And she couldn't just send something through the post.

She needed to send a messenger.

She had to find a messenger.

Someone who could handle themselves on a trip.

Someone that these attackers—whoever they were—did not know. Someone who was strong and fearless.

Someone who could handle a windstone vehicle.

Someone who had their *own* windstone vehicle.

She needed to find Lucinda Barkson, and she needed to do so now.

TWENTY-EIGHT

It was not a beautiful day. There had been no beautiful days in Trinovante for months. But there was a hint of sunshine and the fog didn't stink like it usually did, and for Lucinda Barkson, that made the day worth celebrating.

Or maybe, at least, worth a drink or two.

She sat outside at Mallankam's Public House, her leather car coat wrapped around her. She had pulled off her driving cap and placed it on the scarred tabletop. Her driving goggles rested beside it.

Her boots rested on the chair across from her, and she held a mug of Mallankam's palest ale, figuring it was too early in the day for stout. She might change her mind soon, though. She had forgotten that Mallankam's palest—which was really a light gold —was a little too sweet for her.

Maybe she would have to move to stout sooner. That was the ale that usually brought her here.

But she had thought she'd be adventurous, which was pretty

sad, really, when adventurous was choosing what kind of ale to have and whether or not she should celebrate the thinnest sunlight she'd ever seen in her life.

Maybe she'd just get in her windstone vehicle and take off for parts unknown. She needed to name this one, but she didn't have the energy. She had just purchased it, so it was the latest model. She always had the latest model, but she had grown tired of naming them.

She peered over her shoulder at the open doors of Mallankam's. She wasn't the only patron, but, if she had to guess, she was the only paying patron.

She held up her mug, trying to get someone's attention without standing up. Because even though it was a bit chilly out here in the lingering wisps of fog, she was comfortable.

"Lucinda?"

Barkson put her feet down, reached for her pistol, and turned around so fast that she had completed the movements before her brain told her that only one person still called her *Lucinda.*

Gussie Kirilli stood behind her, looking small and alone. Gussie Kirilli, the strongest, primmest woman that Barkson had ever had the displeasure to know.

Somehow, they'd become unlikely friends in boarding school, and as much as they rubbed each other the wrong way, they had remained friends. Casual friends. Gussie had consulted with Barkson before buying a windstone vehicle, and Barkson— well, Barkson loved to torment Gussie and try to change her rather rigid ways.

Only now, Barkson regretted every harsh word she'd ever said to Gussie. Barkson let go of her pistol, making sure it was firmly in its holster, and set her pale ale on the tabletop. Surprisingly, even with that swift movement, she hadn't spilled a drop.

She swept a hand toward the chair her boots had just vacated. "You look like you need to sit."

"I probably do," Gussie said.

She walked over to the chair, her skirts swishing. They were stained with something that looked suspiciously like drying blood. There was something drying-bloodlike smeared along her chin, and her hair—usually styled within an inch of its life—was tangled and matted.

A brown handprint that had to be blood stained the back of her blouse.

She sat, slowly, as if her entire body ached, and then her hand hovered near the pale ale.

"Mind?" she asked.

Barkson shook her head.

Gussie picked up the mug, took a long drink, and then wiped the back of her hand over her mouth.

Barkson had never seen Gussie drink ale, never seen Gussie guzzle, and never seen Gussie wipe her mouth with her hand.

But Barkson didn't say anything.

Gussie banged the mug down, and some of the liquid threatened to bounce out of the top.

"Goodness," she said with a bitter laugh, "that stuff is foul. It's *sweet*."

"Yeah, I was just thinking that," Barkson said. "I was going to get something darker. You want something?"

Gussie shook her head, but it was clear she needed something. She looked done in. Her eyes were sunken into her head, her mouth was thin, and there seemed to be fresh lines around her rather prominent nose.

Barkson had seen stress manifest on people's faces before, but never quite like this.

She stood and walked through the open doors into the public house. No one looked up as she entered. The publican was rinsing off glasses—something she'd seen him do before. It was one of the reasons she came here. He wasn't the kind of man who figured the alcohol would clean out the glassware.

She leaned against the wooden bar and grabbed a gold coin from the interior breast pocket of her car coat.

"Two stouts," she said, tossing the coin on the wood. The coin spun, making little noises, and then toppled loudly on its side.

The publican, a tall man with a nose that rivaled Gussie's, nodded, but didn't say anything.

He poured Barkson two stouts and handed her the mugs, taking the coin and not offering any change. Barkson wasn't sure if any was owed, and she didn't care.

She carried both stouts out of the public house, and blinked a little at the light. The sunlight had changed from thin to pale.

Gussie hadn't moved. She still hunched in the same position, her hand near the original mug. Barkson had never seen her so motionless, so *small*.

Barkson sat down and moved the original half-empty mug. Then she slid one of the stouts in front of Gussie.

"Drink something," Barkson said.

Gussie started, as if she hadn't even realized that Barkson was there until that moment. Gussie took a deep breath and seemed to gather herself. She sat taller in the chair, and finally bore some resemblance to the Gussie that Barkson both liked and loathed.

Gussie wrapped her hand around the new mug but made no move to drink it.

"What happened?" Barkson asked.

Gussie shook her head. "You wouldn't believe me if I told you."

"Try me," Barkson said.

Gussie closed her eyes for just a moment. Whatever had happened had aged her a decade or more. Then Gussie opened those eyes, picked up the mug, and took a tentative sip—the way that Barkson would have expected Gussie to do.

"I'm pretty sure my father is dead," Gussie said as she set the mug down. "And his house has been ruined. The staff has been murdered."

Barkson leaned back slightly in her chair. Gussie was telling her all of this in a flat, no-nonsense tone.

"I am not certain if whoever is doing this is going after Kirillis or if something else is going on," Gussie said. "I left my house. I will not return until we solve this."

"We?" Barkson asked. Even though she hired on for odd jobs, she wasn't really an investigator.

"Me, the constabulary, others." Gussie waved the hand not holding the mug. Now, she was starting to sound exhausted. "I'm worried about my siblings."

Barkson nodded. She could understand that. It seemed to be the only thing she could understand. She had no idea how Gussie was even standing at this point. She and her father were close—ridiculously close. Barkson had never understood it, since she had abandoned her family as soon as she had had the chance.

"I need to send them word about what's going on here," Gussie said, "and I think I need to insist that they leave their own homes, until we figure out what—or who—is doing this."

Barkson nodded.

"They can't stay in other Kirilli properties either," Gussie said, as if that was the key to everything.

Barkson finally understood why Gussie was talking to her. It wasn't because of the friendship—or whatever it was that they had. It was because Gussie needed her help.

"You want to tell them quickly," Barkson said.

Gussie nodded. "I can't send a letter. I have to get to them fast, and I can't go."

"Why not?" Barkson asked. It sounded to her like it would be better if Gussie left town.

"I...can't." Gussie gave her a thin smile. "Something is happening here, something..."

She shook her head. Closed her eyes. Looked even more exhausted.

Then she did that little squaring of the shoulders thing again, and said, "I can't explain it. I can't. I don't dare."

Barkson stayed very still, waiting. She had learned that sometimes, if she remained very still, someone would confess something or do something or surprise her.

Gussie surprised her by ignoring her stillness.

"Lucinda," she said, "if I give you directions, can you drive to my family? All of them? I have seven siblings and some nieces and nephews, and if they end up like my father..."

Her voice thickened. Tears filled her eyes.

Then she squared her shoulders again. Barkson could almost hear the internal dialogue.

I can't collapse right now. I need to keep moving.

"I understand," Barkson said. "Why don't you come with me?"

Gussie shook her head. "I'm in charge of the family now. We just lost our entire staff. My father's entire staff. I have to tell their families…"

She swallowed, blinked at those tears, trying and failing to prevent one from escaping. But she didn't brush at it. Barkson wasn't even certain that she had noticed.

The tear carved a pattern along Gussie's cheek, making Barkson realize that in addition to the brownish bloody streaks, Gussie's entire face was covered with a light layer of dirt.

"Surely, the constabulary could do that," Barkson said.

Gussie gave her a tight smile. "Surely they could, but the constabulary can't make certain they have enough food or enough money to make it for the next month at least."

Barkson stiffened. Gussie was going through hell, and still had time to think of the families of her murdered staff? Barkson really had never liked Gussie's fastidious, precise nature, but this proved that Gussie had depths Barkson had never even realized.

"I'll pay you," Gussie said into Barkson's silence. "But I need you to travel fast and light. It'll take three days of straight travel, maybe more, to reach my brother Emberto. He's living in my great-grandmother's house in the Forbidden Valley. The others are more or less along the way."

Depending on where he was in the Forbidden Valley, the drive there alone would take three days without sleep. Barkson thrived on difficult challenges, but she needed sleep. She couldn't travel straight through.

Besides that, she would have to stop, talk to the other Kirillis, let them know what was going on.

"You'll have to get them out of their houses," Gussie said. "That'll be hard. I'll give you letters to deliver…"

Her voice trailed off. She had turned even grayer. The exhaustion was weighing on her.

She needed more help than a hired driver could provide. She needed a friend.

And she was Gussie, so she didn't have many of those, and the ones she had had a lot more in common with Barkson than they did with the laughing giggling friends who had clustered together in boarding school.

"I'll help you," Barkson said, "but you're going to have to let me help you."

Gussie blinked at her. "What does that mean?"

"It means I'm going to ask a few questions. I'll organize you. And then we'll see what happens next."

Gussie was shaking her head before Barkson was done talking. "I need to warn my family. That's the most important thing, Lucinda. I can't lose more of them because I waited. Please."

Barkson nodded. Fair enough. "Have you gone to the constabulary yet?"

"Not me," Gussie said. "I sent my man, Zeitsev."

Barkson almost said, *But I thought your people were dead,* and then she realized what Gussie had said. *Her* man. Someone who worked for her.

"I'll go as soon as we're done here," Gussie said. "I need the constabulary's help. I want to get back to my father's manor, but I won't do it alone. I'll need them."

Smart, Barkson thought but didn't say. Complimenting Gussie in the middle of a list was a sure way to get Gussie to snap at her, and that wouldn't be constructive for either of them.

"Your place is compromised," Barkson started, and Gussie said before Barkson could continue.

"I think all the Kirilli properties are compromised. I have to act on that."

"I agree," Barkson said. "Which is why you'll stay at my place."

"Yours?" Gussie shook her head. "That'll endanger you."

"Not at all," Barkson said. "I'll be traveling to find your family."

Gussie was shaking her head again.

"You're not going to argue with me," Barkson said. "You'll need a place to lay your head. You'll have to be careful about it, though. You're going to have to make sure no one follows you there."

"I can do that," Gussie said tiredly. "I've been doing it all day."

"Good," Barkson said. "We're going to go there now. I'm going to make you something to eat. You're going to clean up. We're more or less of a size."

"No, we're not," Gussie said. "You're—"

"I'm sure I have something that will fit you for now," Barkson said. "You can buy more clothing in a day or two."

"No," Gussie said. "You—"

"You will listen to me," Barkson said. "You will do as *I* say right now. Because we need to get you through this."

"You don't—"

"You'll go to my place. You'll clean up. You'll write your letters. You'll write down the directions. You might even close your eyes for a few minutes."

"I'm scared to close my eyes," Gussie said. "After what I saw today, I might never close my eyes again."

"You'll be safe in my place," Barkson said, deliberately misunderstanding her.

Gussie's lips thinned.

"Then," Barkson said, "I will leave on a route you determine. I'll take papers with me, and I'll send you letters at my place as I find each one of your family members."

Gussie stopped shaking her head. Those tears were lining her eyes again.

"I will take care of them," Barkson said. "You will do what's needed here."

Gussie nodded. "Bless you," she whispered.

"I feel awkward leaving you alone," Barkson said, surprised to hear the words come out of her mouth. She didn't feel "awkward." She felt frightened, which was even more unusual.

Lucinda Barkson was almost never frightened.

"I won't be alone," Gussie said. "I'll have the entire constabulary."

How do you know they'll help you? Barkson almost asked, and then she realized the flaw in the question. Gussie was a Kirilli, one of the Old Families. Of course the constabulary would help her.

That was understood.

Still, Barkson felt a little uncomfortable.

"You won't tell them what I'm doing," she said.

Gussie frowned at her. Then blinked as understanding reached her. "You think they might tell the wrong person?"

Or the wrong person might be working for them. But Barkson didn't want to put that in Gussie's already cluttered head.

"Yes," Barkson said. "I don't know how they work with other local constabularies."

Or if they did. She had no idea.

"I will drive you to my place in my vehicle," Barkson said. "Then, when we're done there, I'll drive you to the constabulary of your choice. You'll have to pay attention on the drive, because you'll need to find my place again. And you won't tell anyone where you're staying. Not the constabulary, not your man…"

"Zeitsev," Gussie said.

"…or anyone else," Barkson said. "Got that?"

"Yes," Gussie said tightly.

"Good," Barkson said. "On the drive to my place, you can tell me exactly what happened."

Gussie looked at her, eyes sharp for the first time. "You won't believe me."

Barkson barely believed that Gussie was here, now, looking like she did.

"What little you've told me already strains my belief," Barkson said. "It almost sounds like we're in the middle of the Purges again."

Gussie started. Barkson wished she could take the words back.

"I hadn't thought of that," Gussie said. "It *is* like the Purges, isn't it? All this death. God, Lucinda, what if someone is trying to purge the Old Families?"

Barkson put a hand on Gussie's. It was sticky with something (blood?) and cold.

"Then your instinct to protect your family is right," Barkson said. "And I'll help you with that."

Gussie's lower lip trembled. "Thank you," she said thickly, sliding her hand away. "Thank you. I'll never be able to repay you."

Barkson gave her an insouciant smile, not because Barkson felt it, but because she needed to lighten the mood somehow.

"You told me up front you'd pay me," Barkson said. "Money will do. It always does."

Gussie took a deep, shuddery breath. "Nice try. But you used to tell me that money didn't matter at all. I can't believe that you, of all people, would change your mind."

Barkson hadn't changed her mind. But she shrugged, as if she hadn't given it any thought at all since her schoolgirl pronouncements.

She slapped a hand on the tabletop and looked at the untouched stouts with a bit of regret.

But she didn't pick one up.

She stood. "Let's go," she said. "The sooner we leave, the sooner I can get on the road."

"All right." Gussie struggled to her feet. She still looked small. "You're the best, Lucinda."

Barkson smiled, a real smile this time.

"I know," she said.

TWENTY-NINE

The slender man in the small room looked terrified. His hair stood up on all sides, he had a smear of something dark along his chin, and he kept rubbing his hands together.

The room itself was cold. It had no windows and was made entirely of stone. It was on the half level between the first floor of the constabulary and the cells in the basement. If this room was ice-cold, Cilka suspected the cells in the basement were even colder.

At least this little room didn't smell, not the way that a cell stank after someone had spent every waking hour in it. Still, the man pacing the room's length gave off the pungent odor of sweat.

He was standing, even though there were two chairs pushed up against the wall. He'd clearly been pacing, head down.

He looked up when he saw her come in, and was about to speak, probably to ask for Desmond. Desmond followed her in, though, and with the wave of a hand, told one of the guards outside to close the door.

The door closed with a meaty thunk. No one was going to hear what this man had to say except Desmond and Cilka.

"Did ya fin' Miss Gussie?" the man asked. "I tol' the woman we need ta make sure Miss Gussie's all right. She drove off on us, she did, even though I tol' her na ta."

He sounded as terrified as he looked.

Cilka glanced at Desmond to see if she should speak or if he wanted to. He bobbed his head to her, a movement so small she wasn't even sure the man in the room could see it.

"Miss Gussie?" Cilka asked.

"Miss Augusta Kirilli." The man's voice rose. "How many a ya do I need ta tell? She shouldn'ta gone off on her own, but she willna listen to the likes a me. Maybe she'll listen to the likes a you."

"We will find her," Cilka said, the knot in her stomach growing. What was happening with the Kirillis? She could feel Desmond behind her, his body the only warm thing near her.

The man didn't look like he believed her.

"We weren't briefed on any of this," Cilka said. "So you're going to have to tell us again what's happening."

"I dunna know ya," he said to her. "I wanted ta talk to the chief there. Sir, please."

Desmond took a step to the side so that he was no longer behind Cilka.

"Procurator Lupei and I are handling all matters connected to the Kirilli estate," he said. "That's why she is here. Assume her questions are my own."

Silently, Cilka thanked him. He was making this her investigation, and she was glad for it. That way, she wouldn't really have to think about all she had seen on this day. Or about the way the world changed beneath her, since this very moment.

"We dinna have time for this," the man said.

"We're going to have to make time," Cilka said, falling back into a role she hadn't played in years. She'd interrogated a lot of people, but lately with a firm perspective—one side or another in a prosecution.

They weren't to a prosecution yet. They were just figuring out what was going on.

"If we handle this wrong," Cilka said, "then others will get hurt."

"That's what I been tellin' yer men," the man said to Desmond, not to Cilka. "Others ha got hurt. Dead, all of 'em what worked at the Kirilli manor. All..."

His voice broke, then he cleared his throat.

"Dead how?" Desmond asked quietly. He glanced at Cilka sideways, almost an apology for taking over the questioning. She didn't need the apology. They needed answers, and it seemed this man wasn't going to talk to anyone except Desmond.

"I dinna know, precisely," the man said. "I dinna get close enough to parse it all. They was tied. They was bloody. They was all in the kitchen, 'n' it smelled something awful, 'n' they was all dead."

His voice rose on that last bit.

"People you knew," Desmond said.

"The staff!" the man said. "The whole staff of the manor. *All* of them."

"How many people would that be?" Desmond asked.

"A dozen? Two dozen?" the man said. "Maybe more. I dinna

count them. I never counted them. They was people, don't ya know. People. Aren't ya understandin'? They're dead. Murdered."

Cilka put a hand on Desmond's arm.

"Let me," she said quietly.

He gave her a sideways glance and for a moment, she thought he wasn't going to let her ask her questions.

She'd learned a long time ago how to avoid getting caught in another person's emotions, particularly when they were claiming that something was going wrong or that a crime had been committed.

Too many times, she'd found that no crime had been committed at all.

The man was breathing hard. He said, "Miss Gussie—"

"We will find her," Cilka said. She didn't use a placating voice. She spoke low and calmly, but in a normal tone. She didn't want this man to think that she was humoring him. "I need to know some things first."

He straightened. "They already asked me questions when I come in. We're wastin' time."

She wasn't going to address the time-wasting part.

"Please," she said. "Tell me your name and your connection to the Kirillis."

He leaned back. "They dinna tell ya?" Then he shook his head. "Ah course they dinna tell ya. My name is Fanis Zeitsev. Augustus Kirilli hired me to be his daughter Gussie's driver. *Carriage* driver. She willna let me drive her infernal windstone vehicle."

And neither would Cilka if she possessed such a vehicle. Not when this man—Zeitsev—called the vehicle "infernal."

"Thank you, Mr. Zeitsev," Cilka said. "How did you discover what happened at the Kirilli manor?"

"Miss Gussie was meeting Mr. Kirilli for breakfast," Zeitsev said. "I drove her there, but we knew right off there was a problem."

His voice broke.

"I been workin' for the family for years. They've been good ta me. I've never seen nothing like this, 'n' then Mr. Kirilli..."

"What about Mr. Kirilli?" Cilka asked.

"Ya just need ta get to the manor," Zeitsev said.

"Please give us a minute," Cilka said, and turned to Desmond. "Let me talk to you in private for a moment."

He didn't need her to repeat that. He stepped out of the room and into the narrow hallway. Cilka followed, pulling the door closed.

They walked down the hallway, until they were out of earshot of the guards.

"Something is seriously wrong here," she said.

"Yes," Desmond said. "Throughout Trinovante."

She heard the rebuke in his tone, but didn't allow it in. He probably owed her anyway, considering the way she had spoken to him earlier.

"We need to send people to the Kirilli estate," she said. "We need to secure the scene."

"I want you to go with them," Desmond said.

"I will, after I know what I'm going to see. But their arrival can't wait for me. I need to be here for a while. This man is upset, but he knows something. I want to find out what that is." Cilka poked a finger at Desmond. "And you're not going either until we know."

"All right," he said.

That was too easy. He had probably been about to suggest it. He walked back to the door, and spoke to one of the guards.

Cilka followed, just as the guard agreed to bring the building administrator down here.

"How many people are you thinking of sending?" Cilka asked softly.

"The Kirilli manor is huge," Desmond said. Apparently he'd been there before. Cilka hadn't. She'd only gone by it, and saw all the trees and the long length of the property. "I'm going to send a team of constables, and they'll remain outside until you arrive."

Desmond probably thought that was a compromise. She really wanted someone inside right now, but then, she didn't know what exactly had happened there. So she would acquiesce to his numbers and not argue, not yet.

She put a hand on the door.

"Ready?" she asked him.

Desmond nodded, and made a shooing gesture at the guard he had spoken to.

"Make sure you let me know when she arrives," he said.

The guard hurried. The other guard looked a bit startled, but true to his training, said nothing.

Cilka opened the door.

"I canna wait like this," Zeitsev said. "You have to find Miss Gussie. I made the mistake of letting her go on her own."

As if he could control a Kirilli. Cilka walked all the way inside, with Desmond following. He closed the door.

"We're sending people to the estate now," Cilka said. "Chief Constable M'ndue will be leaving briefly to make sure everyone follows our instructions. I'm going to go as soon as I speak to you."

Zeitsev did not look impressed. "And Miss Gussie?"

They would have to deal with her, so they might as well start there.

"Was she taken?" Cilka asked. "Harmed?"

He looked pained. "She took her windstone vehicle and went off to..." He stopped, as if he was about to reveal something he shouldn't.

"Off to what?" Cilka asked.

"I'm tellin' ya this all wrong," Zeitsev said, more to himself than to her. "Her father—he came this morning and done give her some satchels, told her to put 'em somewhere safe. So she's doin' that, and she wouldna let me help."

"Her father?" Desmond asked. He sounded incredulous. "Her—?"

Cilka put her hand on his arm, stopping him. Perhaps he had forgotten that she had told him that Kirilli's corpse reanimated and ran off as if it hadn't died at all. Perhaps he didn't understand that the satchels he had initially held had gone with him.

"What time this morning was this?" she asked.

"I dinna look, ma'am. Madame Procurator. Miss." The fact that Zeitsev couldn't figure out her title seemed to distress him as much as anything. This man was about to break down. "We got ta the manor 'n' it had been vandalized. The main entrance was demolished, 'n' the decorative things inside was smashed, 'n' the lightstone lamps in the hallways was ruined—"

"Lightstone lamps?" Desmond asked in a tone that said that detail meant something to him.

"Yessir," Zeitsev said. "We was lookin' at the destruction, 'n' Miss Gussie, she wouldn't stay away, 'n' we picked our way to Mr. Kirilli's study, 'n' I was thinkin' it was odd that no one was helpin' us or pickin' up the mess or even there to talk to, 'n' then we found the bodies, and I swear, Mr. Kirilli showed up. He was bloody too."

"Yes," Cilka said. "I saw him this morning as well. He'd been badly injured."

For the first time, Zeitsev looked at her. "Yer people upstairs, they said I couldnta seen him, that he died last night."

She paused. She hated it when constables gave witnesses information that they should have kept to themselves.

"I'm sorry to tell you that Mr. Kirilli is indeed dead," she said. "But when his death occurred and even how it occurred is something we haven't determined yet."

Zeitsev's expression changed. He looked relieved. He still wasn't calm, but he became calm*er*.

"I was beginning ta think I'm losin' my mind," he said. "Mr. Kirilli, I didna see him leave the manor."

But something in Zeitsev's tone told Cilka that he had indeed seen Kirilli leave. Zeitsev just didn't want to tell them how Kirilli left.

"Ya seen him too?" Zeitsev asked.

"I did," she said, but added nothing else.

"We saw him after we found the...staff..." Zeitsev cleared his throat. "Miss Gussie, she was very strong. When her da give her the satchels, she just took 'em and we left."

"You were with her at that point?" Cilka asked.

"We went ta her home, Miss. Missus. Madame Procurator.

We did, because she wanted to see if the same had happened there."

"Had it?" Desmond asked.

"Na then," Zeitsev said. "She made her people leave, though. Told 'em it wasn't safe, 'n' she'd let them know when ta come back. So God knows what coulda happened since."

"How long ago was this?" Desmond asked.

"Hour? Maybe two? Longer than I been here," Zeitsev said. "I wasn't gonna come, even though Miss Gussie told me to, so you'd have a chance to get to the houses, but I was gonna go after her, ta make sure she was safe. Only she drove off so fast. Them infernal windstone vehicles, they make horses obsolete, they do."

"You're worried about her," Cilka said.

"She shouldnta gone off alone!" He started rubbing his hands together again. "I couldna stop her."

Cilka almost told him that Augusta Kirilli was an adult and knew what she was doing, but Cilka didn't know that for certain. Particularly if Augusta had seen all the dead staff members, and talked with her dying father.

"Where will she go when she's done with those satchels?" Cilka asked.

"I dinna know." Zeitsev's voice rose in a wail. He looked alarmed at his own panic, cleared his throat again, and said, "I was hopin' she'd come here. This isn't something the family can handle alone."

A knock on the door made all three of them jump. That was the second time Cilka started in an hour, and she usually wasn't the kind of person who startled easily.

Desmond reached around and pulled the door open. The building administrator peeked in, yet again.

"You sent people?" he asked.

"Yes," she said. "But—"

"I'll be right out," Desmond said, then pulled the door closed.

Cilka caught a glimpse of the woman's face. She did not look happy. There was some kind of politics going on here, but Cilka didn't know what they were, and she really didn't care.

Cilka took a deep breath to settle her rapidly beating heart down.

"Do you know what was in those satchels?" she asked.

"No," Zeitsev said.

"Was she upset?" Desmond asked.

Cilka blinked, surprised. She should have asked that question. She hadn't thought of it. Every time she thought she was doing well on this day, she realized she wasn't.

That was an important investigative question, and she hadn't even touched it.

"Miss Gussie?" Zeitsev sounded shocked. "A course she was upset. Some of them staff, they was her family. They helped raise her. She's just..."

He shook his head. His voice had started trembling again. He clearly felt a lot of emotion as well.

"Just...?" Desmond asked quietly.

Zeitsev looked down. "Stronger 'n me. If she hadna been there, I might've, I dunno, fallen to the floor wailing."

He gave them both a thin smile.

"I barely lasted five minutes after she left. I dinna wanta

come here, but I dinna want her by herself neither. And now yer all talkin' 'n' not doing nothing."

"We're actually doing something," Desmond said without sounding defensive, which Cilka thought an amazing feat. "I've sent a team to the Kirilli manor, and we'll be going as soon as we're done here."

"What about Miss Gussie?" Zeitsev asked.

"Where do you think she is?" Cilka asked.

"I dinna know. Her pa said something to her real quiet like, 'n' I dinna hear it exactly."

"What did you hear?" Cilka asked.

"Just that he said she had to go right quick 'n' it was important 'n' she had to take them satchels. Then he just..." Zeitsev shook his head. He stopped shaking it, then he started again, as if he couldn't believe what he had been about to say.

"He just what?" Cilka asked.

Zeitsev shook his head again. "I dinna see him leave," Zeitsev whispered.

"This bothers you," Desmond said.

"Aye, yessir," Zeitsev said.

"Why?" Desmond asked.

Cilka already knew the answer. She suspected Desmond did too.

"Because he was standing right in front a me," Zeitsev said. "He was there one minute 'n' na the next."

"He vanished," Cilka said.

"They're not magic, they're not," Zeitsev said. "Dinna accuse the Kirillis of that. They're good folk. Mr. Kirilli, he made sure we was all paid 'n' our families were taken care of 'n' we liked our work. He made a point of it, 'n' Miss Gussie too.

Once we got back in the carriage, her first thought was the staff at her house. She was terrified that they was dead too."

"But they weren't," Desmond said.

"Then," Zeitsev said ominously. "Ya need to send yer people there too. And maybe to the other Kirilli households. This is murder, plain as day."

"How many Kirillis live in Trinovante?" Desmond asked him.

Zeitsev swallowed hard. "Just Miss Gussie. But she has seven brothers and sisters, 'n' some a 'em are married 'n' there's grandchildren and they're little 'n' why is someone killin' Kirillis?"

"Why indeed?" Desmond asked quietly. But the question was more for Cilka than for Zeitsev.

"We'll figure this out," Cilka said. "Do you have family that needs protection?"

"Naw," Zeitsev said. "It's jus' me."

He actually sounded relieved at that. Apparently, he hadn't thought that part through.

"I think it would be better if you stayed here," Desmond said.

"I need to find Miss Gussie," Zeitsev said.

"We'll find Miss Kirilli," Desmond said. "We can protect her."

"You're her driver," Cilka said. "Tell us where she goes when she's upset."

"She goes home. 'N' she's too smart for that right now," Zeitsev said.

"Where else would she go?" Cilka asked. "A friend's, maybe?"

"Miss Gussie, she has charities, not friends," Zeitsev said.

That was an interesting distinction.

"So you have no idea where she might be," Cilka said.

Zeitsev let out a small breath. "I'm scared she might go back to the manor. Maybe see if she can salvage more."

"More what?" Desmond asked.

"Her grandfather's things," Zeitsev said. "That's what's gone. Her grandfather's things."

Cilka looked at Desmond. Augustus Kirilli's father was instrumental in protecting the Old Families from the Purges. He was also instrumental in preserving his parents' legacy, and preventing them from being charged long after the fact with theft of antiquities from smaller members of the Protectorate.

"Lemme help ya search for her," Zeitsev said. "Please. I shouldna have let her go alone."

He was afraid she was dead, and he would forever blame himself for it.

Cilka wished she could comfort him, but he might be right.

"We don't know who or what is after the family," she said gently. "We can't legally put you in the middle of that, not after there has been a murder."

"Several murders," he said sullenly, or was it sadly? She couldn't tell.

"We can find you a more comfortable place to be," Desmond said, reaching out a hand toward Zeitsev.

"Ya need this room?" he asked, as if he hadn't even heard the word "comfort."

"No, not right now," Desmond said. "But there are nicer places in the constabulary—"

"This here is fine," Zeitsev said, and sank into the chair in the corner. "So long as you keep the door open 'n' unlocked."

"We can do that," Desmond said.

"I'm na a prisoner here, right?" Zeitsev said.

"You're not," Cilka said. "But we'd prefer it if you did not leave. We need you to be safe."

"I dinna wanna be safe," Zeitsev said. "I dinna deserve it."

Cilka did not know how to argue with that, so she didn't. She patted Desmond on the arm and left the room, leaving him handle the niceties.

She was shaking. She hadn't realized it.

Kirilli had come back from the dead—if that was the way to discuss what she had seen—and he had run home, just like she expected.

His body had returned to the place where he had initially died, but the satchels had not.

She wondered if the satchels he carried had disappeared when his body returned or if Augusta Kirilli had managed to save them somehow.

No matter what this Zeitsev said, the Kirillis had magic. The question was if they knew how to use it.

Desmond joined her in the hallway. He put a hand on her back almost possessively as he moved them down the hallway. It was probably the only thing he could safely do, instead of putting his arm around her, which would compromise the investigation, no matter how nice it would feel, how comforting it would be.

"The power of the magic we're dealing with here worries me," he said softly as they walked down the hallway.

"Me too," she said. "That man saw Augustus Kirilli after he was already dead."

"So did you," Desmond said.

She nodded. "This is the kind of magic our parents feared."

"Not *our* parents," Desmond said. Their parents had looked the other way when magic happened. Their parents probably practiced more magic than they let on. "But yes, their generation. And the older one too."

"Now do you understand why I needed Judita?" Cilka asked quietly.

"Maybe," he said. "But she's a stopgap. And clearly just as dangerous as our killers here."

Cilka couldn't argue with that, so she didn't even try.

"I'm heading to the Kirilli manor," Cilka said. She half expected him to stop her.

"I'm coming with you," he said.

PART THREE
THE NIGHT BEFORE

THIRTY

The manor had magick. Yris could feel it.

She flanked Rodderc, whom Atrü had chosen to lead this small team of six Infantry members. Rodderc was a good man, if a bit unimaginative. If Yris told him that she sensed magick, he would have quizzed her as to how and why she sensed it rather than simply taking that sensation for the gift it was.

Besides, Qurzi, one of their Spies, had already visited the manor, claiming to be a friend of one of the Kirilli sons. Qurzi said he had waited in what he believed to be a parlor and, yes indeed, the manor had been filled with what he called wild magick.

Yris didn't believe the magick was wild at all. It felt tamed and focused. It wasn't Fey magick, which concerned her. It was something else, something refined and targeted, something she had never felt before her arrival in Dorovich.

Since then, she had felt that same magick faintly through

every house, manor, and great house they had attacked in the past week.

But nothing was as strong as what she felt here. The team had just reached the edge of the property, and the magick assaulted her, enveloping her like one of the fogs that Sirocco had been creating.

Only this magick wasn't cold and damp and weather-related. It was something else entirely, rather like a banked fire, something that would take just a gust of wind to ignite it and make it very powerful.

The team waited underneath a small grove of trees. All of the trees—some pines, some birch, some a type she had never seen before—were cultivated and large and beautifully trimmed.

They were part of the estate, which was larger than she had expected.

Larger than Rodderc had expected as well, because he was hesitating. They only had six hours to destroy the magickal items in the manor, and given the size of the grounds, those six hours might not be enough.

Through the trees, she could see at least four outbuildings, and she suspected there were even more. Some of the outbuildings made sense; she'd seen others like them in Trinovante.

A large carriage house sat on this side of the property, probably housing two or three carriages or maybe one of those strange magickal vehicles that the Qavnerians believed ran on wind power. Behind the carriage house was a small stable.

From her vantage, she could only see part of the manor, hidden among plants and trees and a lot of fog. Sirocco had overdone the fog, and Yris wished she had the ability to let Sirocco know to bring the fog back down to something approximating normal.

But behind the manor, on this side, was a little building that housed some kind of well—maybe even a pump or some kind of contraption that siphoned water into the building. Mechanics didn't interest Yris.

The mission interested Yris.

One building did catch her attention, though. It was shaped square with no windows, and it seemed to be filled with some hay. She'd seen buildings like that in other grand homes in Trinovante.

They called the buildings icehouses, and they stored ice to use in ice boxes to keep food cool. Only the iceboxes were unlike any she'd seen in other countries. Those were always big, with a large compartment for ice. The ice compartment in most iceboxes here was the size of a hatbox, and there wasn't a lot of ice in it.

The iceboxes in most grand houses had the same magickal feel as the vehicles that were supposedly powered by wind.

She had spent the last few weeks trying to figure out what kind of magick the Qavnerians had. It seemed like a mix of magicks—natural ones that used some of the elements (water, wind, light)—and others that seemed to require items to make the magick work.

Maybe the elemental magicks required items as well. There might have been components in the wind vehicle that made it run or in the icebox that kept it cool.

She hadn't done a study of it, but she wanted to. There was something intriguing about Qavnerian magick that she hadn't encountered anywhere else.

"What are you thinking about so intently?" Rodderc asked, and the question wasn't kind. It led her to believe that he had asked her something before.

She almost told him about the sense of magick here, but he would say something about Sirocco's fog or leftover magick from Qurzi's visit a few days before.

None of that would be valid, but Yris couldn't tell Rodderc that. Rodderc believed he understood magick—and he did, up to a point. He understood magick because he had studied it from the outside.

Yris tugged on her jerkin. She wasn't cold despite the fog. No one else seemed cold either. They were all laden with rope and knives, things that traveled easily.

And none of them seemed to be in a hurry. None, except Yris.

Yris peered through the branches of a nearby pine. Through it, she could see shrubs and the big red and pink flowering plants that seemed to be on every bit of property in the wealthier neighborhoods. That was how Qavner divided its homes—by wealth. Not by lineage, although there was some of that, and not by royalty, since the government here was chosen by some method she didn't understand.

Some of those gigantic flowers blocked her view of the house, but what she did see bothered her. Faces peered at her from the edges of the windows.

"There's something strange about this manor," she said to Rodderc. It wasn't a direct answer to his question, but it was direct enough.

"I would be surprised if there wasn't," he said. "We have to tread carefully. Even on a quiet evening like this, there are dozens of servants inside."

She wasn't going to contradict him; he was right about the servants. But she was going to hold her own.

"Let me scout," she said. "I'm seeing something that bothers me, and rather than explain it—"

"The manor has already been scouted," Rodderc said.

"But not tonight," she said.

He frowned at her.

"There's movement, Rodderc," she said. "I don't like it."

He hadn't become team leader by ignoring his team. He frowned at her, but he nodded. Then he held out a hand so that the four others did not follow her.

Yris crouched near some underbrush, not that there was a lot. Everything on these grounds was carefully cultivated, sometimes pruned until there was nearly nothing left. She didn't like the manicure. She didn't think it pretty and she didn't like the fact that it failed to provide cover.

She didn't need much, though. She went around the bend in the path, staying low so that no one inside the manor could see her. She huddled beneath one of the larger flowering plants and stared at the windows that were bothering her.

Wooden shutters covered the glass as if someone expected a bad windstorm. Or expected someone like her to peer inside.

The shutters themselves weren't the problem. Nor were the blocked windows.

What bothered her was that each reddish-brown shutter had carvings on them. Not carvings that went inward on the wood, but carvings that were more like sculptures. She'd seen things like that before—some kind of art, which she did not understand. Not just the little sculptures, but also a tiny pattern of hearts and crowns and swords.

That sent a shiver through her. The Black Family's crest was that of a sword piercing two hearts.

Hearts and swords.

She had no idea if that was important. She doubted Rodderc would either. For the first time, she wished she had paid attention to art and decoration. She'd been raised in Nye where everything was decorated, and the worst displays of art were cooed over as if they were someone's precious child. Even clothing had decoration—ruffles or lace or some kind of stitchery.

She hated all of it and for that reason, never tried to understand it. She never learned the language for it. Now she wished she had. Because the carvings, they weren't small and delicate or even pretty.

They were carvings of heads, and they protruded from the wood.

More eerily, they were all facing the grove of trees where her team stood. The etched eyes, carved inward slightly, like eyes in a person's head, but flat and without pupils.

Yet Yris had the odd sense that they could see her, that they were watching her and the team.

She decided to test that theory.

She scrambled across the path—directly visible to anyone who was looking out those windows, not that anyone could with the shutters closed.

She slid underneath another bush.

And at that moment, all of the heads swiveled.

The hair rose on the back of her neck. Those heads were some kind of magick.

She made her way back to the grove of trees, one perfectly manicured bush at a time.

When she reached Rodderc, she said, "There's some serious magick protecting this manor."

They had already seen some magick in some of the other great houses they'd been to—artifacts that tried to repel them when they attempted to touch them. Lights that came on mysteriously and had nearly killed Haevner. His skin was still mottled from the way the light had burned into it.

Rodderc didn't argue with her, didn't ask her to prove it. Instead, he asked her to explain, and she did, as best she could.

She ended with, "It has to be the wood itself. Like the wind vehicles. Something that the Qavnerians have developed to channel their magick."

"Or embody it," Haevner said quietly.

Rodderc nodded, just like Yris was. Haevner had more experience with the Qavnerian magick. It had touched him, and he had survived it.

That gave him some authority.

"You're sure those heads are made of wood?" Rodderc asked Yris.

"I didn't get close enough to test it," she said. "But that's my guess."

"A guess will have to be good enough," he said. "We won't touch them."

Haevner had turned around without Rodderc instructing him, and removed his knife. He hacked some branches off the nearest tree—the kind Yris couldn't identify.

The sharp scent of sap rose. The wood was brown, even on the inside, and it was thick and hard.

Haevner handed her one branch. It felt like he had given her a cudgel made of stone. The skin on her hands itched at its touch.

She resisted the urge to drop the branch. She had already touched it. She couldn't undo the action, so she was just going to hold the branch, unless it burned her.

"Don't hand out the branches just yet," she said. "We need to put on our gloves."

Vidso, the quietest in the group, looked at her in alarm. He was slight and smart, the kind of person who had more victories because of his stealth and intelligence than because of his fighting abilities.

Haevner looked down at his own hands. The mottling glowed where he had touched the wood.

"Good call," he said.

He slid the knife back into its sheath and pulled gloves from his pockets. He slid the gloves on one hand and then the other.

The rest of the team followed suit.

Yris tugged on her gloves, but that didn't make the itch go away. She just forced the itch aside. She didn't want to think about it while she was fighting.

They had learned in the past two weeks that some of their equipment—their knives, swords, and even one of their battering rams—had no real effect on the artifacts. Sometimes the artifacts repelled the Fey-made items, and sometimes the Fey weapons made the artifacts stronger.

It had been Uryek who had, in frustration, pounded one artifact with another. She had hated the way the items attacked the team. She had kicked the door, knocked over a table, and finally had grabbed what looked like a paperweight and slammed it onto one of the tableside lamps that had ended up hurting Haevner.

The paperweight had completely destroyed the lamp, and then the paperweight had disintegrated in her hands.

Uryek was big enough—and strong enough—to crush apple-sized rocks with her bare hands, but she hadn't destroyed that paperweight.

Rodderc had been the one who understood first. He grabbed a book and slammed it onto something that looked like a set of dishes, only it sent heat in the direction of the team.

When the book hit the dishes, they exploded into tiny bits of glass and dust.

Fey tools and weapons couldn't destroy anything that the Qavnerians had in their homes, but the items the Qavnerians had could demolish each other.

Haevner had been the first to remember that, which was why he was cutting more branches, now that he had his gloves on.

Yris peered around him, looking at those shutters. The heads seemed to be watching everything the team did.

She wished she had the time to create arrows out of the wood. She'd send them flying into those heads, and see what happened then.

She bent her knees so that she could reach the branch she had dropped without taking her gaze off those heads. She was afraid they'd turn into some kind of creature, free themselves from those shutters, and hurry across the grounds.

So far, nothing like that had happened, but she wouldn't put it past this magick. It was stronger here than anywhere else she had been in Qavner.

"The magick is growing here," she said to Rodderc.

"How do you know?" he asked, and her breath caught. She'd been so wrapped up in figuring out what was happening with the magick that she forgot to couch what she saw in terms an Infantry person would understand.

Not that it mattered right now. If the team was going to go into that manor, they had to do so tonight, which meant she might have to sacrifice personal secrecy for clarity.

"I can feel it," she said. "Can't you?"

Vidso looked at her sideways, as if he couldn't believe what he heard. Uryek seemed blithely oblivious.

"I don't feel anything," she said.

"I do," Haevner said. "In my hands. Those wounds, they're aching more the closer we get."

Yris let out a breath. Haevner had saved her from explaining, but had upset her even more. He was feeling magick in his hands? Because the light had burned him on a previous mission?

What might happen on this one, particularly with the itching caused by the branches?

"Do we need to go back and get Hadley?" Rodderc asked.

They almost never traveled with the Enchanter. Hadley had other duties. She was supposed to be following Kirilli. She already learned that he carried magickal items in his satchel, so she had prepared one to swap out.

That had been her focus these last few hours, not helping the Infantry team destroy yet another cache of artifacts in yet another great house.

"Hadley's already on another mission," Xevkin said. She was close with Hadley, something Yris found strange, especially since Hadley and Gem seemed to have a budding relationship.

Xevkin was so thin that she could slide in and out of tight spaces. She also had great strength in her arms and hands, just like Uryek. They'd trained in the same unit, and shared a fighting style.

"That mission is important," Vidso added.

"So is this one," Rodderc said tightly.

"Besides," Yris said, "if this Kirilli man's house has a lot of magick, maybe he does as well. Shouldn't we warn Hadley?"

"If this Kirilli had magick," Rodderc said, "then Qurzi would have discovered it on his scouting mission."

"Provided he was a good Spy," Haevner muttered.

"You don't think so?" Rodderc asked.

Yris held her tongue. She had thought most of the people that Rugar had assembled into this team were mediocre at best.

"I think Omriseu is better," Haevner said, which really wasn't an answer to Rodderc's question at all.

The heads seemed to have extended further. Yris could see necks and the beginnings of shoulders.

Maybe she hadn't been wrong. Maybe there were figures in the wood that could escape and attack.

"We can discuss this at a different point," she said. "Look."

She swept her gloved hand toward the heads.

The team followed her movement, and Rodderc actually made a sound of surprise.

"We're going to have to blitz," he said.

It was his favorite formation—with him in front, where no commander should have been, followed by Uryek and Xevkin, then Yris and Haevner, and Vidso bringing up the rear.

Just that one word—blitz—gave them a play. They would go in fast and violent, destroying anything that got in their way.

It was inefficient. When Rodderc had first proposed it, shortly after the team had arrived in Trinovante, Yris had been the one to question him.

If we're going to do that around the houses and artifacts, she had said, *why don't we just burn the houses instead?*

I'm told that fire can augment some magick, Rodderc said.

Yris had never heard that before. She didn't challenge Rodderc, though. Not to his face anyway. Instead, she spoke to Hadley, who confirmed it.

Fire has a power to enhance certain kinds of spells, Hadley said, *particularly ones that were not created by anyone Fey.*

Which was why Yris hadn't known. She understood a lot about Fey magick, and she hadn't thought—until Hadley told her that—about the differences in magick from other places.

Not that Yris had encountered a lot of magick in other places. There didn't appear to be any in Nye, except Fey magick. But she wasn't certain of that.

Here, though, in Dorovich, the magick seemed to flow in the air.

Yris looked at those heads. She thought she was seeing more of the shoulders than she had before. It almost looked like small creatures were trying to get out of that wood.

"Whatever we're going to do," she said, "we need to do it soon."

Vidso was giving the heads a side-eye. "Wish we had more than six of us."

Rodderc didn't seem to mind criticism that came through such muttering. He never really ignored it either.

"I wish we had more than six too," he said. "I also wish we

had magick to help us, but we do not. Are you nearly through, Haevner?"

Haevner handed out three more branches. Everyone on the entire team had at least two, some more.

"I am now," he said.

"All right then," Rodderc said. "Remember, do not use anything Fey."

He gripped his own branches. They looked like thick stout clubs. Not quite weapons, but not anything lethal.

Yris raised her own branches. She clung to them a bit more tightly than she usually would hold a weapon.

Those faces were getting to her.

"We're blitzing on my count," Rodderc said, his voice soft. "One...two...three..."

And then they were off.

THIRTY-ONE

The run through the grounds took less time than Yris expected. The team moved fast, staying on the path, Rodderc in the lead, Uryek and Xevkin behind him. Yris kept pace with Haevner, both of them clutching their branches, not even using them to brush some of the shrubs aside.

She couldn't hear Vidso behind them, like she usually could.

This blitz was being conducted in complete silence, because there was no reason to let out the Fey battle cry. The enemy wasn't here, so it couldn't be intimidated by a yell.

The heads were pulling themselves out of the wooden shutters. The bodies were appearing faster now. Half of the torso was visible on each, with lines for the arms. Once the arms were free, they would attack.

These magickal creatures—or whatever they were—were small, the size of little children, only much thinner. Their mouths had changed into some kind of feral grimace, and a few of these creatures bared some vicious-looking teeth.

Rodderc reached the nearest window, and slammed his branch into the heads with all of his strength. The sharp slap of wood against wood echoed, with something behind it—a moan, maybe? A groan?—and then the heads tumbled off the necks, bouncing onto the ground even as Rodderc moved beyond it.

Uryek and Xevkin reached the first group of heads and paused just long enough to smash each one with a branch. Yris noted that, noted the caution, loving her team. They were smart about most things—knowing better than to stomp the heads.

The heads shattered into tiny pieces. Uryek and Xevkin moved past the first destroyed group, and hurried to the next.

Yris and Haevner arrived just as Uryek and Xevkin moved on. Yris slammed her branch into the shutters, clubbing those headless necks and torsos into more pieces.

Haevner worked on the wood itself, dismantling it quickly, getting it out of the way so that he could smash the windows beyond.

They worked in silence, the only sound more slapping of wood against wood, and finally, breaking glass.

Then they ran forward as well, doing the same to the next set of shutters, and the next and the next.

Yris didn't even check to see if Vidso was using his branches like a broom, making certain that the pieces were far enough apart that it would take some kind of external magick to reassemble them.

Or at least, that was the hope.

It got harder to get near some of the shutters. The perfectly manicured plants seemed to grow larger, as if they were protecting the building.

But that might simply have been Yris's paranoia. She didn't like this magick. It made her entire body tingle.

Rodderc didn't seem bothered. He was hitting the heads with such power that some of them rolled across the path and disappeared into the trees.

Uryek and Xevkin were disciplined enough not to follow those, at least not yet. That clean up would happen after the initial threat was destroyed.

They smashed the heads, and then Yris and Haevner stepped in, completely ruining each set of shutters.

Sometimes that meant standing in the shrubs, feeling twigs dig into her back, feeling like vines were creeping around her legs, feeling like something was grabbing her and trying to hold her in place.

She said nothing, though. She just continued to work, hitting, slapping, breaking, destroying.

And each time she stopped, she looked up, to see if the shutters on the windows on the upper stories were the same.

They didn't seem to be. They were a different color, and so far, no heads protruded out of them.

Just on the ground level.

And for that, she was grateful. She had no idea what would have happened if there had been faces, sculptures, *creatures*, above her, with all the advantages that kind of thing brought.

She was breathing raggedly through her mouth, slivers of wood flying toward her. But using the branches felt delicious, moving her arms with great force, connecting and damaging, and finally destroying.

She loved this work. She loved fighting. She loved the destruction.

She lived for it.

The bang-smash-smash-shatter continued as she and Haevner worked their way across the grounds. She had splinters in her hair, and wood chips on her skin, and flower dust on her clothing. Her arms felt stronger than the wood she was destroying. Each hit sent a shiver up her bones and into her shoulders.

She rounded the corner, heading toward the main entrance —and realized that Rodderc had stopped.

He was standing near some stairs. Uryek and Xevkin reached him, and stopped behind him, close enough to look like they were holding him up.

They all clutched their branches, and the three of them were as covered in wood debris as Yris was. She reached their sides, just as Haevner did, and followed their gazes.

The entrance was composed of the same wood. It was taller than all of them and wider than two doors. The wood was covered with entire bodies, creatures that were moving—in the process of freeing themselves from the wood entirely.

"It's going to take all of us," Rodderc said, "and we haven't even gotten to the second half of this building with the shutters."

He seemed almost distraught. She had never seen him like that. It was almost as if he had gotten tangled in the magick.

Then she reached forward and brushed the wood pieces off his face. Some of it had gotten too close to his eyes.

"No," Yris said, "it won't take all of us. They're not freed yet."

Rodderc blinked and shook his head. Wood pieces fell around him like water droplets off a wild dog. The other team members brushed the wood off themselves too, and she did as well.

Rodderc still looked confused, though. So she shook Uryek and Xevkin.

"You continue. Take his job and add it to yours," she said.

Somewhere along the way, Vidso had joined them. Yris turned to him.

He was the only one who wasn't covered in bits of wood at all.

"You have to help them. Destroy and sweep," Yris said.

He nodded, then gave a sideways glance at that entrance, as if it unnerved him as much as it unnerved Rodderc.

But Vidso didn't say anything. Instead, he clapped Uryek and Xevkin on their backs and almost pushed them forward.

He clearly could sense the urgency. This bit of fighting had to happen quickly.

"It's a blitz," Yris reminded Rodderc. "We have to blitz."

He shook himself, nodded, and took a deep breath. She wasn't going to wait for him to go forward.

She went first. He could run with Haevner if he wanted.

She stormed up the stairs, using her branches like swords—hitting and slapping and stabbing and pounding the creatures that were trying to come out of the wood.

Somewhere along the way, she emitted a guttural Fey battle cry, and that seemed to revive Rodderc. He was beside her—not close, but on the other side if the entrance, clubbing whatever he was closest to.

Haevner joined them. He brought the tops of his branches

down as hard as he could on the heads, shoulders, arms, and actual torsos beneath him.

Some of the creatures had been carved with legs, and those legs were moving, slithering on the entry like snakes.

Haevner was bludgeoning them, grunting with the power of each hit.

The banging in the enclosed space of that entranceway was loud. Rodderc seemed revived as well, shouting and yelling in every language he knew, telling the creatures to die in vicious, horrifying language—

And then the doors swung inward.

A man stood there. He was older, hair neatly trimmed, eyes narrow, his mouth in a thin line. He wore a black uniform, and in each hand, he held lanterns, like the ones that had nearly destroyed Haevner before.

The lanterns were beginning to glow. The light would grow and then it would shoot forward, if these lanterns acted like the ones that the team had encountered before, light would shoot out of them and burn anyone near them.

She glanced at Haevner. His skin was already turning orange where the light touched the previous wounds.

Yris wasn't going to let that happen again. She brought her largest branch forward like a battering ram, and hit the man in the face so hard that he fell backwards. The lamps tumbled out of his hands.

She climbed through the doors, and demolished those lamps with her branches. The glow faded and finally went out. Her eyes ached from all of it.

Then she bent over and yanked the man up by his shirt. He

wasn't dead, but his nose and cheekbones had been shattered. He was unconscious at the moment.

She grabbed one of her ropes, and tied his hands tightly behind him. She didn't tie his feet, though.

She hadn't expected this kind of defense from someone who lived in Trinovante, although she should have.

"You two handle the doors," she said to Haevner and Rodderc. Rodderc nodded. Haevner looked unsettled, the glow still outlining his previous injuries in orange.

"What are you going to do?" he asked.

"There have to be others," she said. "I'm going to find them."

Then she grabbed the man by his shirt and dragged him along the floor. Lights flared as they reached the actual corridor, and she realized that there weren't just lanterns with that weird glowy light, there were also light fixtures.

So every time she saw a light fixture, she smashed it, just as it started to glow.

It made going down the corridor a bit difficult. The farther she dragged him from the doors, the darker the corridor became.

The man was a dead weight, but she didn't mind. She dragged him with one hand, and destroyed lights with the other.

She thought she heard rustling and voices up ahead, which told her she was on the right path.

The team had encountered a handful of servants before in some of the great houses, but none of those servants had attacked back. Rodderc had given all of them the chance to run, and they had taken it.

He had also told them if they went to the authorities with

what they had seen, he would hunt them and their families down and slaughter them.

Apparently, the servants had believed him, because Yris hadn't heard a whisper from any of them.

But this great house, with its vibrating magick, was going to be different. And she wasn't going to let it defeat her.

She walked in the darkness, smashing lights as she went, the man's heels thudding behind her.

Magick seemed to surround her, reaching toward her, calling to her from behind closed doors. There was going to be a lot to destroy in this place, but the team couldn't start the destruction until they had gotten rid of the servants.

And if they all had the same understanding of magickal objects that this man had, then the entire team was in trouble.

She could hear the pounding and breaking glass from the rest of the team. The sound soothed her, made her feel like she was doing the right and most constructive thing.

At about the point she was going to drop the man and go in search of other servants, the flooring changed. It went from some kind of smooth slate to wooden planks. And pocket doors marked the transition to the back of the house, as she had learned that it was called, somewhere in her days here in Trinovante.

The voices were louder here, but then they stopped as they heard the thudding of the man's heels. The air smelled of spices —cinnamon and cardamom and something she couldn't identify—as well as baking bread and something roasting.

Yris's stomach growled. All this pounding and slamming was making her hungry.

But she didn't focus on that. Clearly, she was on the way to the kitchen. And if her experiences in the previous houses were correct, then the entire staff would be huddled in there.

She had no idea how many people she'd be facing, but judging by the voices, it would be quite a few. This house was surprising her. It was grander than the others, and it seemed to have more knowledge of its own magick.

She saw the edge of the kitchen just ahead of her. It was warmer here, which meant that a large oven was working. And she saw the flash of skirts—two kinds. Whispering started.

She set down her branches, then grabbed the man under both his arms. She reached the edge of the kitchen and swung him like a gigantic bedroll, tossing him into the room.

He knocked into four people as he flew, and then hit the top of a gigantic table in the middle of the room, sliding across it, sending dishes and cutlery flying. The crashes were deafening.

Yris rolled back, grabbed her branches, and looked for more of those light fixtures. She didn't see any.

Of course not. She was in the servants' wing. Why give them any magick?

She stopped at the wide door opening. A dozen people looked at her in terror. None of them had lanterns. None of them had the presence of mind to pick up the cutlery and come at her.

She smiled at them, as if they were misbehaving children.

"He tried to attack us," she said in their language. She had learned enough of it to manage threats. "Should any of you try the same, you will end up as he is."

The servants huddled together. They were mostly women, and many of them older. There were a few men, some of them boys. They didn't seem threatening though, or even magickal. They were watching her with big eyes.

Behind her, the pounding and shattering continued. She let her smile soften at those sounds.

Her people were doing just fine.

No one made a move toward her. She grabbed the rope off her right shoulder. Then she pulled bits of rope out of the pockets of her jerkin.

"You," she said, pointing with the rope at the oldest women, "will take these ropes and tie up your friends. I will be watching. If you leave the ropes loose, I will kill you. Is that clear?"

One of the old women burst into tears. Another put her arm around the crier. Why were there always criers? The sound got on Yris's nerves every time.

"Shut her up. Tie her up first and stuff a rag in her mouth," Yris said.

The woman who was holding her shook her head.

Yris slammed the branch on the table, and it wobbled. The sound echoed in the large space.

"*Now*," she said. "I will not give orders twice."

Several of the old women scrambled for the ropes, then started tying up the others. The woman who had been holding the crier was the one to tie the crier's hands behind her back.

Then she carefully stuffed a handkerchief in the other woman's mouth, apologizing the whole time.

Yris hated the whining and the apologies and the tears.

"Hurry up," she said, waving the branch.

The woman finished, then faced Yris.

"All right," Yris said, pulling out the last of her rope. "Half of you will tie the other half, and you will continue to do so until one person is left."

"And then what?" the woman facing Yris asked, voice wobbling.

"Then I'll tie you, and check all the others," Yris said.

The woman nodded. The remaining group proceeded to tie the others up. They all looked red-faced and terrified. The crier was still sobbing, snuffling air through her nose. At least she wasn't as loud.

They finished as the pounding seemed to ease. Yris went to the remaining woman, tied her hands back, and then checked the ties on everyone else.

They were all tied tightly.

She smiled at them.

"Your friend here," she said, shoving a boot on the still-unconscious man, "thought he could attack us. He was wrong. Now, I need to know two things. If I don't believe your answers, I will kill the person nearest me. Then if I still don't believe your answers, I will kill the next. Is that clear?"

The crier snuffled so loudly it sounded like she was going to choke. Yris would start with her.

"First," she said, "is this everyone in the building? Or are there more of you?"

No one answered, which was not a good sign. She slammed the branch again, creating a dent in the table.

"Are. There. More. Of. You." She said the words precisely but quietly, so that the entire group had to lean in.

"In the outbuildings," said the woman whom Yris had tied. "Our families. Children."

Yris didn't care about the children. They were not a threat.

"If we find that you were lying," she said, "and that there were more adults around here, then I will not only kill you, I will do so slowly and painfully. Are we clear?"

The crier moaned. Someone else started to snuffle. She was beginning to loathe these people.

"Yes, ma'am," the woman said. "I'm telling you the truth."

Her voice was soft and almost defiant.

"I hope so," Yris said. "For your sake."

She let those words sink in. Some of the group leaned against the others.

There was still a bit of pounding, but the shattering sounds had ceased.

"Where are the..." she paused. She almost said *magickal*, but she wasn't going to give these people ideas. She tried to remember the words Rodderc had used in some of the previous houses. "...artifacts? I'm looking for the antiques, any maps or papers, and delicate items from the Razbitay Mountains."

The crier moaned and looked down. Another moan echoed.

Yris followed her gaze. The man who had attacked them was waking up.

"No," he whispered.

Yris grabbed a knife, rounded the table, and stood behind him, shoving him sideways so that he faced the group.

Then she slit his throat.

The hot blood sprayed all over the servants and a couple of them screamed. All of them put their heads down.

She slammed the tip of the knife into the table.

"Are there artifacts?" she asked again as she dropped the man. Blood still oozed from his neck, but the worst of the spray was over.

She wasn't sure, but she didn't think she had gotten any on herself. Not that it mattered. She would be coated in blood when this night was over.

"They're all over the house," one of the other women said. She had a handkerchief in her hair. She was far enough back from the now-dead man that she only got a small smattering of blood on her face. "Every room has some."

"Most are in the study, though," said one of the boys.

"And some are in the main living quarters," said another woman, younger, and so terrified that her voice was shaking.

"What about the outbuildings, as you call them?" Yris asked.

"No," the handkerchief woman said. "They're too valuable to be anywhere but the house."

"And more wooden carvings like the shutters?" Yris asked.

Two of the boys glanced at each other, as if they were confused by what she meant. Everyone else stared at her blankly.

They didn't know about that magick. So they didn't see the shutters as anything more than decorative.

"Hidden compartments?" Yris asked. "A safe, maybe?"

Everyone was shaking their heads. Either they didn't know or they hadn't seen any.

She wasn't sure which she believed.

It sounded like she had a lot of work ahead of her, though. The entire team did.

At least the magick in this place had not saved these people... yet, anyway.

But she had to do something with them. She couldn't leave them alone. She hadn't tied their legs, and she didn't have enough rope to do so. Eventually, someone would get out. Some of those children had to be old enough to untie even the best knots.

"Whatever should I do with you?" Yris asked, putting her hands on her hips.

She could go and get reinforcements. She could waste one of the team by using that person as a guard.

Or she could take care of this on her own.

Then she chuckled, deep in her throat. There had been no doubt about what she was going to do.

She wasn't going to let any of the others join in the fun.

She would get rid of these people all by herself.

PART FOUR
NOW

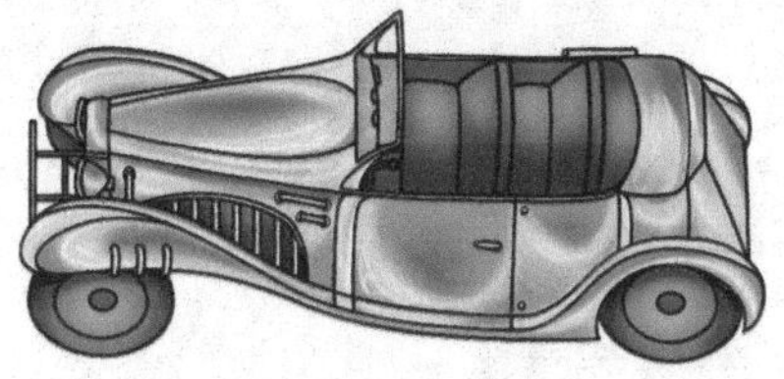

THIRTY-TWO

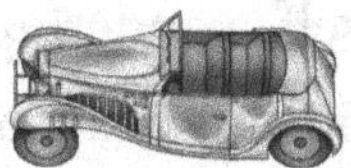

Desmond drove Cilka to the Kirilli manor in his personal windstone vehicle. He clearly hadn't wanted to deal with carriages or formalities or horses, for that matter.

The Kirilli manor sat on land that the Kirillis had owned for generations. The Old Families all had property in this area, not to mention property elsewhere in Trinovante. Miles and miles of land, often forming what looked like parks in the middle of the city.

Unlike parks, when someone who wasn't part of the family or who didn't work for the family showed up on the land, they got unceremoniously kicked off or someone held them while another servant went for the constabulary.

From what this Zeitsev had said, that hadn't happened at the manor. No one had stopped the interlopers—murderers, thieves, whatever they were—from crossing onto Kirilli land.

Cilka had traveled this windy road quite a few times, but she had never stopped at the Kirilli manor. Now, all sorts of vehicles were parked street side, with a few drivers monitoring the horses. Other horses were tied to trees.

The carriages all had the constabulary's ornate gold "C" along the top. Cilka recognized many of the drivers, and would have waved to them had the circumstances been different.

The gates were open onto the main road leading into Kirilli manor. Cilka found herself wondering if Augustus Kirilli—or his shade—had run along this road or if the family knew of other ways to arrive.

She wasn't sure she'd be able to figure that out on this day.

More carriages, one black windstone vehicle, and some equipment lined up alongside the road leading into the manicured estate. Even the trees looked like someone had tamed them, and not really lovingly. The trims were harsh, making the trees and the shrubs and even the flowering bushes look like someone had forced them into a design they had not wanted to assume.

As the road wound around more trees, a handful of constables stood in small groups. Some of them looked pale, others a bit gray, and one or two bent over, hands on the side of a tree for support.

Cilka had seen behavior like that at her earliest crime scenes, usually with beginning officers. She had no idea if Desmond had sent newer officers here, but she doubted it.

Desmond sped up. He didn't seem upset by the constables, although he clearly noted them. He drove around one small group.

He drove like he knew where he was going, as if he had been here before. He probably had. The Kirillis were known to fund almost everything in this city, and it wouldn't surprise Cilka to learn that they had put money into the constabulary as well.

The road turned slightly to the right, and then created a circle in front of the carriage house. Two carriages with the constabulary's "C" were parked there. Desmond kept going, and ended up close to the manor.

More constables roamed around the exterior, but they really weren't what caught Cilka's eye. What caught her eye was the damaged windows on the lower level. Almost all of the windows on this side of the manor had been knocked out, and the area around them destroyed as well.

From what she could tell as the vehicle drove past, there was debris along the edge of the manor, and some shrubs that looked like someone had deliberately destroyed parts of them.

Desmond skidded to a stop, his mouth a thin line. He got out before Cilka could even open her door, and walked toward the nearest constable.

"Why is everyone outside?" Desmond demanded.

"'Tis a lot to take in, sir," the constable said. "We sent for coroners."

"More than one?" Desmond asked.

The constable nodded. "Yessir. As many as could come. You'll see. The worst of it's in the kitchen."

The heart of any house, large or small. Cilka got out, slammed the door, and leaned back, looking at the manor.

"We did find some children," the constable said. Cilka's breath caught. "They were hiding in one of the outbuildings. We've already sent them back to the Constabulary. They dinna see what happened, but they heard the screaming."

His words hung in the air for a moment. There was nothing to say to that, not yet, anyway.

Cilka made herself take a deep breath. The air did not smell like sulfur anymore. It was almost fresh now.

The white walls of the manor glistened in the sunlight, which had grown stronger as the day went on. Still the side of the building was damp from the several days of fog, and what had once been white was really yellowish, with touches of brown.

"We'll start in the kitchen," Desmond said to the constable, while Cilka was looking at the manor.

She had learned a long time ago to look at the entire scene before she focused on the small details. And the entire scene here included the whole manor.

"Lor', sir, I would not start in the kitchen," the constable said. "There's plenty to see throughout the place."

"That's where the bodies are, right?" Desmond asked.

"Yessir, but—"

"Then we start there," he said.

The upper stories looked untouched. The windows were intact. They had standard brown shutters that were open. The window glass glinted in the light.

But the manor felt odd. It was clear that no one was on those levels. How Cilka knew that, though, she wasn't sure.

"Has anyone examined the upper floors?" she asked the constable.

"We're investigating now," he said. "Looks like, though, nothing's been touched above the first floor."

Had something interrupted the attackers? Was that why they had quit? Or had they found what they were looking for?

She craned her head back. The upper levels seemed sad. The lower level—the ground level—made her deeply uncomfortable, the same kind of uncomfortable she had felt that morning, looking at Kirilli's body—before it had gotten up and run away.

She rarely had feelings like that as Procurator. She'd had it twice in one day here, and it was all based on the Kirillis.

"Are you coming, Cilka?" Desmond asked.

She nodded, and pivoted, following him along the path. The manicuring had been upended here.

The broken limbs and twisted branches seemed worse up close. There was mud along this path that she was certain the gardeners would have cleaned off. Some of the mud was in the form of footprints.

She walked alongside them. Boot prints that probably belonged to Zeitsev seemed the freshest, although there were tiny prints that might have been Augusta's.

The older prints were also boot prints, but of a type she didn't recognize. She had once known most of the boot types in Trinovante, but that had been years ago. It had been a good skill to have, however.

Desmond was walking slightly ahead of her, looking at the broken branches as well as the debris on the ground around the windows.

The constable led them across a wider path, which was the formal entrance to the house.

"My goodness," Desmond said, looking at the doors.

Cilka followed his gaze. The entrance had been destroyed. Bits of wood were everywhere. There didn't even seem to be doors, although she knew that hadn't been true.

"Those doors," Desmond said, "they were works of art.

Literally. With the Kirilli family crest visible when they were closed."

"The crest?" Cilka asked.

"A sword, a heart, a crown, if I remember right," he said.

She frowned. "Well," she said, "someone didn't like it."

The constable waited on the other side of the main path. "We'll be using the servant's entrance near the kitchens," he said.

"Is it destroyed too?" Desmond asked.

"No, sir, it is not," the constable said. "'Tis why we've been using it. Figured an investigator would want to look at the destruction as it is."

Desmond nodded. Cilka frowned at the doors. Then she looked up again.

"What's got you so fascinated about the upper level of the manor?" Desmond asked.

"It's different than the rest," Cilka said. "It wasn't meant to be seen, like the lower levels were. The upper level seems functional."

"And how is that important?" Desmond asked.

"Do you remember if there were designs on the lower-level windows?" she asked.

He shook his head. "Why?"

"I'm not sure yet," she said. And she wasn't. She hadn't seen all of the destruction. But she had a theory, considering all the magic she had seen this day.

The Kirillis had magic. Maybe their doors and windows were warded. Maybe they believed they didn't need wards on the upper levels.

She would have warded the entire manor, but she had seen a

lot of awful things. She wasn't sure this current generation of Kirillis had seen anything bad at all.

It took a good ten minutes to walk around the manor. The destruction remained the same—shattered windows, lots of smashed wood, and lots of broken branches and leaves on the manicured plants. Some of the plants gave off a fresh minty scent, which surprised her.

It seemed that the entire estate's exterior had been designed to make someone feel calm and in control.

It didn't look in control right now.

They rounded a final corner. Two constables stood outside a plain door, as if they were guarding it. But guarding it from what, she had no idea.

She caught a faint foul scent. She had a hunch it would grow worse once she got inside.

"You dinna have to see this," the constable said, his accent emerging as he became more distressed.

He wasn't speaking to her. He was speaking to Desmond.

Desmond gave him a faint distracted smile. "It's all right. You don't have to go in with us."

To Cilka's surprise, the constable didn't argue.

"Thank ye, sir," the constable said, and stepped aside. Then he leaned forward as if he had forgotten something. "'Tis through the door and to your left."

Desmond thanked him and stepped over the threshold, pausing a moment as if something caught him. Then he turned to the left.

Cilka followed, and understood immediately why he stopped. The smell hit her like a brick wall. After doing this, she would either have to destroy her clothes or find some creative way to clean them.

Although she probably would have to do that anyway, considering that morning's blood.

Her eyes watered as she walked. She breathed shallowly.

Nothing was destroyed in this narrow little hallway. It probably had nothing to destroy. Desmond rounded another corner, and stopped again.

This time, he didn't move.

Cilka came up next to him.

They had reached the kitchen. Bodies next to each other, hands tied, throats slashed or worse. In all her years in law enforcement, Cilka had never seen anything like it.

Three, four bodies at a time, yes, and some of those cases tragic—families slaughtered by one angry member, for example —but nothing like this.

The kitchen was warm, which was why the bodies already had a stench that would only grow worse as the day went on.

"How long do you think they've been dead?" she asked.

"I don't know," he said. He waved a hand toward the oven. There was no fire inside now, but there clearly had been. Otherwise, the room would not have been this warm.

Cilka just stared at the carnage. She had no idea how anyone could do this. And now, she finally understood why Zeitsev had been shaken and afraid. He had known these people.

She glanced sideways at Desmond. He might have known them too, although he might not have paid a lot of attention. The constabulary and procurators always found themselves in-between the upper classes and the lower classes. Not servants, people with their own money, but not upper class either.

Often, though, the constabulary and procurators had a lot of power, sometimes more than members of the upper classes. Connections were everything.

And for Desmond to become the chief constable, he needed a lot of connections.

His face had gone very still. Only his eyes moved, taking in everything. He was breathing shallowly, just like Cilka was.

"All right," he said after a moment. "We'll leave it for the coroners."

Cilka probably should have objected. Coroners tended to destroy evidence. But she wasn't sure what they'd find here. Whoever destroyed the exterior of the building had killed these people as well. She could find evidence elsewhere.

She pivoted and headed out the way she came, resisting the urge to pull off her coat to get rid of the stink.

She knew from past experience that removing the clothing would not get the stink out of her nostrils.

She stepped outside first and knew better than to take an immediate deep breath. She removed a hankie from her pocket and blew her nose as she took a few steps toward the trees.

The constable who had been waiting for them handed her some leaves.

"Rub them against your nose," he said. "They'll help."

She didn't recognize what kind of leaves they were, but she remembered seeing them just before entering. These were the leaves that smelled of mint, even though they hadn't been mint.

She rubbed them against her nose, and saw Desmond do the same. Then she thanked the constable and took a few steps away from him, hoping that Desmond would follow.

"This was not personal," she said. "None of it was."

He frowned at her.

"I saw Kirilli's body, and now these," she said. "Whoever did this did it for a purpose and the purpose was not revenge and it certainly wasn't in the heat of the moment."

Desmond nodded, then indicated the manor with a slight tilt of the head. "Those deaths were precise."

"Whoever did this has done it before," Cilka said. "You can't kill that many people that quickly."

And it clearly had been quick. There was no real sign of a struggle in that kitchen. *Someone* should have fought back, and it seemed no one did.

"Practiced and precise," Desmond said. "I haven't heard of anything like it in Trinovante."

"Not in a civilian household," Cilka said.

He looked at her.

She said, "I've seen the artwork—and so have you—depicting battle scenes from the formation of the Protectorate."

He half-closed his eyes. She hadn't even mentioned which pieces of art she meant. She didn't need to. So many of them looked the same.

Qavnerian soldiers, ordering the local population to get on their knees, hands behind their backs. Ordering them to remain that way or someone would die.

Sometimes it hadn't mattered whether the locals held that position or not. They were slaughtered anyway. And the deaths came quickly.

"Soldiers," he said.

She nodded.

"But I don't remember hearing that the Kirillis fought in any wars."

Sometimes Desmond was so literal.

"I'm not saying they did," she said. "But whoever attacked them here, those people had been soldiers."

"Warriors," Desmond whispered.

He really liked that Fey theory. She still wasn't convinced. There were a lot of old soldiers in the Protectorate, and not all of them fought for Qavner.

The Kirillis were known for looting artifacts from many ancient and historical sites across the Protectorate. The Kirillis were the ones who created the Forbidden Valley Antiquities Service ostensibly to vet candidates who wanted to study the valley, but really to make sure that no one the Kirillis deemed inappropriate actually had access to the valley's treasures.

Not that citizens of Qavner should have had access. A number of cultures lived in the Forbidden Valley, and some said that the locals should have retained ownership of their own items.

An argument that was well over a hundred years old now. Had that argument come to bite them, finally? Was that what had caused this?

But the main question always was: *Why now?* What made this happen right now?

And she might not be able to find that out until she investigated Augustus Kirilli.

The timeline was important. Did he die first? And if not, were these attacks coordinated? Certainly what happened here could not have been done by only one person.

"I thought you said that other Old Family homes had been attacked," Cilka said, as a way to push against Desmond's warrior comment. Not that he was necessarily wrong, but she wanted to make sure he was thinking of more than the Fey.

"They have," he said. "Not like this, though. If someone died, they died…"

He caught himself, frowned, and looked over his shoulder at the manor.

"Died how?" Cilka asked.

"Quickly," he said quietly. "As if they had caught someone in the act."

"Did the other homes have fewer staff members than the Kirillis?" she asked.

"I don't know," he said. "I don't know a lot about the details of those investigations. You'll have to wind them into this one."

She would. He still wanted her to investigate this.

"I'll need a large staff," she said. "This is too much for one person."

"I know," he said.

She straightened. She wasn't going to make the investigation follow narrow trails or find a designated culprit. Not with something this severe. She needed to know what exactly happened, in all of these places. Not what someone guessed had happened.

"You still want me to investigate, even with what happened with Judita this morning?" she asked.

Desmond looked at Cilka. "You're the best investigator I know. You have a number of skills my other investigators don't."

By that, he meant an understanding of magic.

"I think all of those skills will be important," he said.

"So you're sanctioning some magic use?" she asked, voice low.

He stepped back. She had to follow just to talk with him. Clearly, he didn't want the other constables to hear.

"Use whatever tools you need to make this investigation go quickly," he said. "I have a hunch we don't have a lot of time."

The air shifted around them. Fog grew in the trees just past the corner of the manor. Yellow fog.

The hair rose on the back of Cilka's neck.

She nodded toward the fog.

"You see that?" she asked quietly.

He turned ever so slightly, so that he could use his peripheral vision to see what she was indicating without moving his head. His lips thinned.

"The fog was thick this morning," she said quietly. "And yellow. That's localized."

"Ground fog," he said just as quietly.

"Except we've had no rain and the day was starting to dry out."

"You think someone is using magic to watch us?" he asked.

"It wouldn't surprise me," she said.

"You believe this is magical, but you don't entirely agree with Judita, do you?" he asked.

"I am willing to entertain a variety of possibilities," Cilka said. "This could be connected to the Protectorate, to the Purges, to something else that we don't understand. Augustus Kirilli had a way with numbers, and he might have found something."

"Something that would affect all of the Old Families?" Desmond asked.

Cilka shrugged. "I won't know until I investigate. You're

telling me these crimes are related, but I'm not sure. No one in the other Old Families died, did they?"

"None of them were in residence," he said.

"Neither was Kirilli," she said, but she did get Desmond's point. When a family was in residence, they had a full complement of staff. If the others were not in residence, then the bulk of the staff either traveled with them or they were allowed to take time away from the homes.

She glanced at the fog. It was fading now. And it was no longer yellow. Just a pale white that reminded her of a ghostly spirit.

She frowned at it, trying to remember the portal from the morning. Had it looked like that fogbank had looked? She seemed to recall that it had formed a hole in the fog. Had she missed that? Had someone come through the fog or was she simply reacting to the day's events?

"You know," she said softly, "Zeitsev was right. We need to find Augusta Kirilli. We need to figure out how to protect her."

"You think they'll come for her next?"

"You don't?" Cilka asked.

He studied her for a moment. "I don't know what they'll do," he said. "I don't know who they are."

A small victory for her. He was opening his mind again to other possibilities besides Judita's Fey comment.

"Precisely," Cilka said. "We don't know who they are or what they want. Until we know, we're going to have to protect everyone we can think of."

"I have no idea how to do that," Desmond said. "The constabulary isn't set up for this kind of protection."

"If you haven't notified the Old Families of the break-ins,"

Cilka said, "notify them and warn them to stay away until we resolve this, citing ongoing danger."

"All right," Desmond said uncertainly, and she could almost hear his thoughts. He had no idea where these families were.

"Anyone who is in Trinovante needs protection," she said. "And maybe the partners at Kirilli, Capalidi, Konstandt, & B'Levin."

"They're not all Old Families," Desmond said.

"But they might be the source of the problem. Augustus Kirilli was more than a member of the Old Families. He was an in-demand accountant and money manager, a member of the Board of Regents, the heir to a large family fortune, and one of the most creative minds in the city," Cilka said.

"And the only surviving parent of eight children," Desmond said.

"You think this could be about them?" Cilka asked.

"I don't know," Desmond said. "But you're right. We need to investigate all avenues here. I only wish there weren't so many of them."

"Me too," Cilka said. "Me too."

THIRTY-THREE

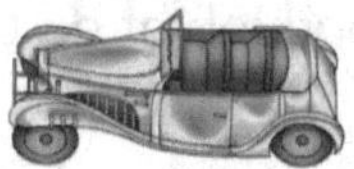

They wouldn't let him help with Hadley's body, so Qurzi snuck here, to the Kirilli place. It swarmed with constables and law enforcement. The Qavnerians were obsessed with punishing each other for crimes. The Fey were much more straightforward; let the Black Family figure out punishment, or let a local leader do so. It didn't matter which.

The manor looked very different than it had the first time he had come here. Then he had been a curious visitor, pretending to be a friend of one of the Kirilli sons. Qurzi had gone inside the manor.

He had walked through that now-destroyed entrance, with its curiously familiar family crest, and he had waited in an entryway filled with artifacts that had emitted so much magick he could hardly sit still.

The magick had been powerful, and he had thought, at that time, that the magick was wild, drawn from the air and the ground and untapped by the Kirillis.

He was revising that opinion now, after Hadley's death.

And the fact that the manor's crest had been obliterated by the Infantry the night before. The crest had been everywhere, and it too had reeked of magick.

But the stench of magick remained here and the crest—with its sword, floating heart, and the surprising crown—was gone.

Much of what Qurzi had seen on that day was gone now. His people had done a good job of destroying the magick he had identified.

He was just worried he hadn't identified enough of it.

And now, he was unable to investigate further.

Oh, he was trying. Once he had seen the law enforcement, he had left the area and walked to the nearest constabulary. He had a map of Trinovante in his head. One of the first things he had done when he arrived in this god-awful place was walk the city.

It was his pattern everywhere he had gone. Knowing exactly where he was helped his magick. Spies had the ability to vanish into an area, to mimic others, and to go unnoticed or unre-marked, but they also had the ability to retain vast amounts of knowledge.

Visionaries never thought of that aspect of a Spy's reper-toire. Sure, a Visionary or a Leader sent a Spy somewhere to learn about that place, but rarely did anyone figure out just how much information a Spy could retain.

Qurzi assigned himself all kinds of tasks, and he never told the group's nominal leader, Atrü. Atrü wasn't the worst leader that Qurzi had worked with, but he was nowhere near the best either.

Already Atrü had missed all kinds of important signs of

magick here in Dorovich. Atrü had to be slapped over the head with it before he believed that Dorovicians had magick, although, if he had thought about it before he had come here, he would have understood that the good people of Dorovich had to have magick.

They had defeated the Fey once, after all.

They could do so again.

That was what Rugar was afraid of. Maybe even that was what the Black King was afraid of. That was why the Fey hadn't come directly to Dorovich again, even though they knew there was a Place of Power here.

It was a Place of Power they didn't control, one that had nearly destroyed everyone who had tried to travel through it. Curiously, no one knew exactly where it was, so it couldn't be approached from the outside.

There was also no urgency about taking over this Place of Power, not yet. Because no one had found a third one.

The legends were clear: Whoever controlled all three Places of Power could create the Triangle of Might, and that would allow them to control the world.

But Rugar wanted to be prepared. He believed he could travel here and control this Place of Power, with a little planning.

This team that Qurzi was a part of was part of that control. That was why Rugar had sent high-level Spies, and low-level—damn near incompetent—Enchanters and Visionaries.

Rugar didn't want the Visionaries to think they could overthrow the Black Family, not with the assistance of an equally good Enchanter.

Sometimes Rugar did not think things through. His odd caution interfered with the success of this mission, at least. It would have been easier if Atrü had been able to build a Shadowlands. Instead, the troop was hiding out in rentals, which they could afford only because they had stolen so many items.

The thefts and resales, and Qurzi's nervousness about them, were the reason Qurzi had learned so much about the legal system in Trinovante. He didn't want anyone from the team to get caught up in it all.

And that was how he knew where to go inside the constabulary to get bits and pieces of a uniform. He'd done so three times before, mostly to test himself. He'd slipped in, stolen parts of a uniform, wore them about the city, and then returned the uniform. Fortunately, a lot of Trinovantians were tall enough that their clothes fit him.

He hadn't expected to wear a uniform on this day, not when it started anyway. He had thought everything had gone well.

And then the entire mission had fallen apart.

He and the others were going to have to put the mission back together. They still had a lot of work to do, and information to get back to Rugar. The loss of their Enchanter couldn't hold this up.

And that was why Qurzi had come to the Kirilli estate twice now, this time in a stolen uniform.

Because he was a Spy, people didn't really see his face, although he had modified it to be a bit paler and a bit rounder. The features were rounder too, because to him, at least, the Trinovantians always looked slightly surprised.

He had gone with that look, and he had assigned himself a place near the front of the manor, so that he could watch the comings and goings.

Mostly, he had seen a variety of constables. If they noticed him at all, they nodded at him and didn't question his presence here.

He stood near a tree to the side of the main path, near the front entrance which the Infantry had completely obliterated. Even destroyed, that entrance was a magickal focal point. All it would take was someone with a bit of Vision or the ability to reassemble other magick to repair all the damage that the Infantry had done.

The destruction seemed to grab the attention of everyone who passed it, but that really wasn't where Qurzi's focus had gone. Those upper levels seemed quietly ominous. He wasn't certain if the Infantry had spent a lot of time up there.

Part of him hoped they had and another part hoped they hadn't.

Because if they had, then the vibration showed that the magick here was more potent than he had imagined.

Voices speaking low caught him. He pivoted slightly and saw two people, a man and a woman, coming around the manor from the back of the building. The man wore a dark green uniform with the constabulary logo, a uniform that Qurzi hadn't seen before. The woman wore a coat that might have been perfect for the morning, but was probably too heavy for this afternoon. Both people were tall, and one was familiar.

He had seen the woman before, when he had helped the team pull Hadley through the portal. Hadley, already dead and battered.

He shuddered.

The voices grew. The two of them seemed deep in a quiet conversation, one he had to strain to overhear. He couldn't quite make out the words, but he wasn't sure if that was due to the softness of their voices or the fact that he wasn't as fluent in the local language as he had wanted to be.

They seemed to be talking about an investigation about what had happened here. They walked fast enough to stay ahead of the constable who was trailing them, and they didn't walk anywhere near the other constables.

If Qurzi moved toward them, he would call attention to himself. None of the other constables were approaching them.

He thought he heard the Qavnerian word for "magick," which was odd in and of itself. The Qavnerians did not like discussing magick. Perhaps that was why they kept their voices so very low.

Then the man said something about "warriors," and maybe —just maybe—Qurzi heard the word "Fey."

That took him aback. He hadn't expected these people—so far removed in both distance and time from their first Fey encounter—to even think the Fey could be involved.

The woman gestured, hard, as she made a point that Qurzi couldn't hear. He wanted to step closer, but he felt very exposed.

Then the woman froze. She turned and peered right at him. He held very still, until he realized that she really wasn't looking at him.

She was looking at the ground fog near him. It swirled and had elements of yellow and brown—Sirocco's work. Qurzi's breath caught. She wasn't supposed to do anything here. She should have been working on hiding the rental house.

But maybe Yris's suggestion had gotten to her. Maybe Sirocco wanted to see if the side buildings here could be protected.

Qurzi resisted the urge to wave a hand at the fog, to tell her to back off or go away.

The woman who had been there when Hadley died could sense something about that fog.

To her companion, the woman said, "You see that?"

The man answered her, and then she spoke, even softer.

Qurzi had to strain to hear the words. He only caught every other one.

Then the man said, slightly louder, "You think someone is using magic to watch us?"

The woman glanced Qurzi's way again. He remained very still. If he did it right, she shouldn't have been able to see him at all.

"It wouldn't surprise me," she said.

He let out a thin breath. They suspected magick. They had a lot more sophistication than he expected.

Rugar wanted the teams to destroy artifacts so that they couldn't be used against the Fey, but he hadn't said that the Dorovicians had actual magick or a memory of magick.

He had figured that they might know how to use the artifacts, but not why the artifacts were important.

It was a gamble on his part, a way of taking away tools.

The woman had returned to her conversation with the man, her focus no longer on the ground fog beside Qurzi.

He took a step back toward the tree, as the woman looked over at the fog again.

She could sense the magick. He was certain of it. And that changed everything.

It also explained what happened to Hadley. A mixture of two different kinds of magick, something Hadley hadn't expected, had created a situation where she had become vulnerable.

Qurzi let out a small breath. The fog was still swirling, which meant that Sirocco had opened a tiny portal against orders. He could go through it and tell everyone what he learned.

Or he could follow the woman who had helped kill Hadley.

Qurzi needed to follow the woman. Atrü had assigned the team to kill those who had killed Hadley.

Qurzi couldn't do that—if he caused harm to anyone, he would lose his magick. If he killed someone, he would lose his magick forever. But he could let the team know what this woman's habits and patterns were.

Besides, she might lead him to the other magickal (missing word?) inside of Trinovante.

He hadn't realized until right now that there were tiers of the magickal in Trinovante—those who didn't dare use magick and might be arrested and punished for it, and those who did use it, those who found it necessary for their work.

He wasn't sure how to make the distinctions, but this woman might lead him to the others.

And he could mark her home or her workplace. Once those places were marked, the team could kill her.

Maybe, before they did, he would be able to find the maps that the Kirilli ended up with.

The maps had been the most valuable thing Qurzi had found in Trinovante. Surely, Rugar would want those. He would want a lot of things.

He would definitely need to know about the magickal tiers.

This team couldn't obliterate all of the magick in Trinovante, and judging by the way the magick was dispersed, they probably couldn't even see all of the magick in Dorovich.

No wonder these people had turned back the Fey hundreds of years ago. The magick here was not slight. It had power.

It terrified Qurzi to consider that the magick wasn't wild, that some in Trinovante—maybe even some in Dorovich—had control of it.

That made Dorovich a dangerous place for Fey.

Somehow Qurzi had to let Rugar know that. Destroying artifacts was one thing; trying to obliterate magick that threaded its way through entire communities was another.

Qurzi tried to remember the tales of battles won and lost. He couldn't remember hearing of anyone defeating the Fey enough that they hadn't tried again for centuries. Sure, there were the battles against the Co, but their magick had been subconscious. They couldn't tap it unless they felt threatened.

The Fey had found a way around that, like they always did. It had taken years, and a lot of death, but they had.

The magick here did not seem to be subconscious. The Qavnerians used magick in many things. They pretended they did not—those lightstones and the windstones had more power than they wanted to admit.

Initially, Qurzi had thought they didn't understand their magicks at all.

But watching this woman, seeing her sense magick in the fog, maybe even sense Qurzi's presence, knowing that this woman had helped kill Hadley and was now quietly discussing magick with a man who seemed to have some authority, all of that made Qurzi reassess his assumptions about the magick here.

It was more powerful than he had realized.

It was more dangerous than he wanted to consider.

The team couldn't obliterate the magick here, but they could certainly figure out how it worked.

Once they knew how it worked, and where its power came from, then they could report back to the entire Black Family on this.

It took a true Visionary to destroy an entire culture's magic. Atrü was not a true Visionary. He was barely a functional one.

Qurzi, and by extension, Omriseu, would have to gather as much information as possible, and figure out how to get it back to Rugar. That would take cunning, because Rugar was safely in Nye, and no one here had any real Links with him.

Qurzi was a Spy. He had no real Links with anyone.

He leaned against the tree and watched the woman wind up her conversation with the man.

Maybe he should follow this woman and see what she led him to.

There were ways to handle magick other than destroying it. In the past, the Fey had used all of those methods, from learning it and turning it against the culture that had it, to using it to destroy that culture, but some of the magick had remained alive, to absorbing it entirely and making it part of Fey culture.

He was not a leader. He was an information-gatherer. He could make suggestions as to the best course, but he couldn't choose it.

And right now, he was in no position to make a suggestion. He needed more information.

He only hoped that he would be able to gather it quickly, because he had a very odd sense that time was running out.

THIRTY-FOUR

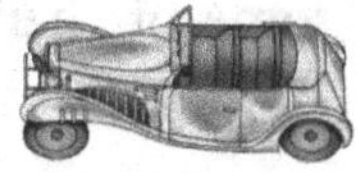

The trip through the strange portal was shorter than Sirocco expected. She kept the fog wrapped around her, all except for her eyes, and stepped out of the portal at the other side.

The air smelled of pitch and fresh grass, mixed with something faintly foul. The foul smell was one she recognized from her years with Rugar's army.

Blood. Somewhere nearby there was drying blood. She didn't yet catch a whiff of decomposing bodies, but that didn't mean there weren't any.

Her feet were on uneven ground. She looked down, saw grass and dirt and some kind of low-hanging branches, apparently from shrubs. Voices spoke near her, but they weren't speaking Fey.

She thought she'd recognized Qavnerian, although she hadn't been around it enough to know for certain. She had stayed with the team throughout much of their travels, letting the Spies handle the communications.

A shiver ran through her, but not from the air. The air was warmer than she expected. The shiver came from a new kind of magick, something she had only felt in fleeting moments.

She looked to her right, saw a gigantic house of some kind, with a destroyed entrance and ruined windows. Dozens of constables milled about, some of them working, while others conversed or leaned against trees.

The constable closest to her seemed indistinct. She blinked hard, thinking maybe the fog was distorting her vision. While the blinking cleared her line of sight—she saw more trees and some bushes she recognized—it didn't allow her to see the one constable any clearer.

She frowned, focusing on him, and then she realized she was looking at a Spy.

He was thin and small, but that was the only thing she could tell about him. If he belonged to their team, he was Qurzi, because Omriseu was taller. But this person might be a Spy for one of the other teams.

The Spy seemed to be focused on two people walking down a path from the back of the building. The building was too big to be a house. It was some kind of mansion.

The destruction caught her eye, but she didn't entirely understand what she was seeing. The two people seemed agitated.

One was a man, who was tall enough to be Fey. He looked vaguely Fey, but from this distance, Sirocco couldn't quite tell. He was dressed in a green uniform though, and seemed to be someone well respected.

He half-hid the woman beside him, at least from Sirocco's point of view. The couple stopped, and stood on the path that led to the destroyed entrance of the building. The woman was gesturing.

Something in her movement caught Sirocco's attention. Sirocco had seen her before.

Sirocco's entire body understood what she was seeing before her conscious mind did. This was the woman who had been holding Hadley. Sirocco and Atrü had taken Hadley from this woman.

The woman was wearing the same coat, which was probably still covered in Hadley's blood.

Sirocco felt a sudden and fierce fury that stirred up the fog beside her. She tried to control it so that she wouldn't be seen, not yet anyway, but the woman looked up and over at her.

The woman seemed concerned, but she didn't move from where she was at. And then she turned her attention back toward the man she'd been talking with as if Sirocco didn't matter at all.

The Spy turned ever so slightly. Apparently, he noted the woman's interest as well and wanted to see what or who caused it.

Sirocco still couldn't tell who the Spy was. His features were too blurred, but his movements seemed familiar. He looked directly at her, and then turned his attention back to the woman near the entrance.

The fact that the Spy seemed to know her convinced Sirocco she was looking at Qurzi. As if he heard her thought, he turned around again and made a small motion with his hands, as if he was shooing her away.

But he didn't know—he couldn't know—that the woman he was looking at was one of the two who had murdered Hadley. Sirocco wasn't sure how to tell him without calling attention to herself.

She wasn't sure what to do. She could go back into the house and grab the Infantry, bringing them here, but they were outnumbered. Not that she doubted they could fight.

Still, with what had happened around the Kirilli and to Hadley, who had the most magick of all of them, Sirocco was leery of bringing anyone else here.

Maybe she should tell the team where the woman was. Maybe let Qurzi follow the woman and figure out what was going on.

Then Sirocco froze.

She was standing in someone else's portal. Had the woman created this portal? Was the woman so very strong that she felt Sirocco enter the portal? Had the woman been spying on them all along?

Sirocco had no idea. She also had no easy way to communicate with Qurzi.

Something told Sirocco she needed to stay where she was. She needed to see what the woman was going to do.

Sirocco rubbed her injured hands together, wincing at the pain. She had to be prepared. She had a lot of weather spells at her disposal, but anything that would injure the woman would call attention to Sirocco and the portal.

So, she would wait to see what Qurzi had planned.

And then she would decide what to do next.

CHAPTER
THIRTY-FIVE

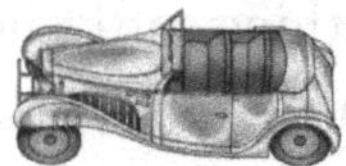

Yris stood in the trees, not far from the place where the entire Infantry unit had hidden the night before. She was careful not to touch any broken branches. The itch in her hands had returned, worse than before. She was trying to ignore the itch, but it was hard.

The Kirilli manor looked different than it had then. The damage that the unit had done was visible in all parts of the building. The fog left trails down its white sides, making the manor look like it had been weeping. The open windows with the broken glass and destroyed shutters made the building look older than it was, as if the damage had existed for a generation rather than a few hours.

There were constables everywhere, but none of them noticed Yris. They didn't notice Qurzi either, but they weren't supposed to notice him. He was very good at blending into whatever he was standing next to. At the moment, he stood in another copse of trees, right inside her line of sight.

The constables were traipsing all over the property, talking with agitation and pointing at all the destruction. A few stood quietly, like Qurzi was, and watched the proceedings instead of keeping an eye on the roads and paths like they should have.

These people knew precisely nothing about protecting themselves or their people from a dedicated military attack.

Yris had slinked (slunk?) right by several groups of constables, moving quietly, breathing softly, her head down. She didn't have Spy magick like Qurzi. She blended in using her own tracking talents and her own ability to make herself seem insignificant.

When she had followed Qurzi to the nearby constabulary, she had debated whether or not to go inside with him. She hadn't, because she had an idea as to what he had been about to do.

When he emerged not five minutes later, clutching a constabulary uniform, she mentally congratulated herself on being right.

The uniform actually made him more visible, not less. His face was still impossible to distinguish unless she focused on it, but his body had a solidity with the uniform that he hadn't had before he had gone into that building.

Given the way the other constables had nodded at him and then ignored him, though, Yris had to admit that Qurzi's decision to get the uniform had been the right one.

Then the two leaders had appeared—at least, that was how she read them. They dressed slightly differently from the rest— the woman in a heavy coat and the tall man in green who had pointed ears and who looked like he might have had some Fey blood.

Everyone deferred to the couple, and they conferred with each other as they stood near the manor's entrance.

Yris watched them, feeling irritated. For once, the others on the team had been right. This would be a bad place to stay, despite all of the outbuildings. Apparently, the Kirilli was even more important than the team realized.

It looked like half of the city of Trinovante was here to figure out what had gone so badly wrong.

She smiled softly to herself. *She* had been what had gone wrong. The *team* had. Maybe when she saw Atrü again, she would remind him of the Infantry's successes.

This clearly was one.

Qurzi leaned against a tree, arms crossed. His entire body was tense, but Yris had to focus on him to see the tension.

She had never really watched a Spy at work before. It was amazing to her how much he vanished.

He was staring at the couple, who were still talking. The woman glanced over her shoulder at something in the trees, and for a moment, Yris thought the woman had seen Qurzi.

But the woman seemed to be looking past him. Yris followed her gaze, and realized the woman was looking at the fog.

The fog was thick in one area. The fog was also threaded with yellow and black.

Yris had no idea why Sirocco was here. Was she trying to see what was going on? Or had Atrü made another stupid order?

Then Yris actually understood what she was seeing. The woman—the Qavnerian woman—had seen Sirocco's fog, or felt it, or knew it was magick. Was that the same woman who had brought Hadley through the portal? Was that why Qurzi was watching her? Did he know who she was?

The thought of Qurzi made Yris turn her attention back to him.

She couldn't see him. The area around the tree appeared to be empty.

Then she squinted, and there he was. He hadn't moved. Arms crossed, shoulder pressed against the center of the tree, one ankle crossed over the other.

Yris had nearly lost sight of him, not because he moved, but because her attention had waivered.

She was gaining a lot more respect for Spy magick as the afternoon went on.

Yris could see the woman and the man if she focused on Qurzi. The two seemed to be finishing up their discussion.

Yris moved slowly, so that no one would notice her either. She wanted to be able to follow Qurzi and if she was careless, the constables would see her, not him.

The woman touched the man's arm, speaking intensely. The man nodded, but appeared to be looking at other things.

Qurzi hadn't moved.

Yris made herself focus on him. He seemed to have some kind of plan, and if she had to guess, she would guess that he hadn't consulted with Atrü. Was that why Sirocco had shown up? To see what Qurzi was doing?

That didn't sound like Atrü. He would be concerned with moving locations and getting away from whatever threat he perceived.

If he were to see the constables everywhere, the woman's harsh gaze as she had looked at the fog, and the way that the Qavnerians seemed to sense magick, he would be even more frightened than he already was.

Yris let out a small breath. So that was why she didn't like Atrü. The idiot was constantly terrified.

The Fey—especially their leadership—should never be terrified. Cautious, yes, like she was right now. But terrified? Never.

Qurzi slowly stood up. Yris really didn't see him stand. His movements were an actual blur, as if someone had smudged the area around the tree.

She would have to follow that smudge. Right at the moment, it wasn't moving, but she had a hunch it would.

And sure enough, as the woman started down the main path, the smudge moved around the tree, looking like fog being blown by the wind.

For one brief moment, Yris wondered if she should follow the woman or follow Qurzi.

Then she remembered that she had only assumed that Qurzi was following the woman. He might have another target in mind, one that Yris couldn't readily see.

That woman was intriguing though.

This entire scenario was intriguing.

Yris wished that Atrü could see that. She wished he and the others could understand it.

Rugar had sent the wrong team on this mission.

Although some of them were doing the work. Yris, Qurzi. They would have actionable intelligence for Rugar when this was over.

If they didn't allow Atrü's mistakes to kill them.

Qurzi slipped between the tree and some bushes, heading toward the path.

Yris kept him in her sight, and followed as cautiously as she could, using her peripheral vision so that she would know if someone was watching her.

The day had just gotten a lot more interesting.

She would have to let it play out.

THIRTY-SIX

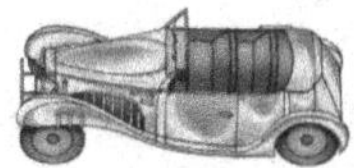

Cilka's skin was crawling. Someone was watching her. Someone with magick. She could feel it.

She and Desmond still stood on the path, finishing their conversation. Her coat felt heavy in the growing warmth of the day. The fog was receding everywhere, except by that tree.

Conversation swirled around them as the constables tried to figure out what had happened here at the Kirilli manor. None of the Kirillis seemed to be among the dead.

Augusta Kirilli did not appear to be here, which relieved Cilka. Nor was there a second version of Augustus Kirilli's body.

From everything Cilka was hearing around her, no one had seen satchels, but that meant nothing. There was too much destruction—and too many knickknacks—to know what was here and what was not.

She'd been paying attention to everything, the surrounding conversations, the other constables, and Desmond, of course.

But that fog near the tree bothered her, and so did something else, but she couldn't quite tell what.

She needed to focus, and she wasn't exactly sure how.

She felt around her back and found that knife, the one that killed Kirilli. She unsheathed it, and held it in her right hand.

"What's going on?" Desmond asked. He knew her well, and realized that her concentration had shifted from the conversation to something else.

"We're being watched," she said quietly.

"Cilka, there's a dozen people here. Of course—"

"*Desmond*," she said with enough emphasis to shut him up. "You might have to back me up."

"You can't use magick here, Cilka," he said.

"We might have no choice, Desmond," she said, then looked directly at him. "You and I. Together."

"Do you realize what kind of crisis that would create?" he asked.

"Do you realize what kind of crisis we already have?" She tilted her head toward the manor. "Augustus Kirilli dead, his staff murdered, this place destroyed. You've told me that this has happened elsewhere. Think about it, Desmond. You don't fight magic with force."

"Sometimes you do," he said. "I think the events this morning have you on edge."

Of course they have me on edge, she almost said, and then realized what he meant. He meant she wasn't thinking clearly. Anger flared through her, but she tamped it back.

She had asked him several times if he wanted her off this case because of the morning's events. Then, after he saw what had happened in the kitchen, he thought she was *on edge*? She wasn't the one on edge, not anymore. She knew something had to be done.

Desmond was the one who was off-balance now. She wasn't sure if he knew that or not.

"Look," she said quietly, so that the anger she felt didn't leach into her voice. "That fogbank near the tree. The fog is isolated, and sometimes it flares with yellow and brown."

"We've seen that all week," he said.

She nodded. "But I think there's a portal in this one."

She didn't add that she thought she had seen a face.

He turned again, that slight turn that he had perfected long ago. "It's a stretch," he said.

After what we're going through? she almost said, but again stopped herself. He needed time to figure out what they could do within the law. She understood that. She also understood how unsettling all of this was.

She had experienced that since the morning.

"But," he said, "do you recognize the constable a few yards from that fogbank?"

She frowned, looked. "I can't see their face."

Nor could she figure out gender. The constable was small, but seemed unfamiliar somehow. And the constable's face seemed...unstable.

"Neither can I," Desmond said. "Do you think it's an illusion?"

Cilka let out a small breath of air. Maybe she had judged Desmond too harshly. Maybe he was thinking clearly, just about different things than she wanted him to.

"It could be," she said. "Because that face seems to be changing. One minute, I see a man with round cheeks, another—"

"A blur," Desmond said. "I see a blur, and then it resolves for just a moment."

"Let's stop speculating, shall we?" Cilka asked.

She didn't wait for his answer. Instead, she strode across the grounds, her hand tightening on the hilt of the knife.

As she got close to the constable, she looked beyond them at the fogbank. Cilka was definitely seeing a face in it. The face was weathered, with a narrow shape and upswept features.

Her gaze met that of the face, and instantly, that face got wrapped in fog.

The blurry constable didn't move. Now Cilka was using her peripheral vision. When she wasn't looking at that constable, the constable's features were blurry.

When she looked directly, which she had as she started to walk, the constable's face seemed rounder each time, with only a hint of upswept features.

Even with features on that face, Cilka did not recognize the constable.

When she got close to the constable, she whirled. With two moves, she was in front of the constable, whose face went from distinct to impossible to see.

But his body—and she was guessing it was a man—was solid enough. She grabbed the front of his uniform and pulled him forward.

"What are you?" she asked.

He didn't fight her. His eyes became clear—black and narrow like the face of the person in the fog.

He shook his head. She put the knife's tip underneath his chin, poking into the skin.

"What are you?" she asked again—only to get blown backwards by the most powerful gust of wind she had ever felt.

She stumbled, but pulled the constable with her. He tripped over her legs and jammed his own chin into the knife.

More wind hit, but Cilka managed to hold him. She wanted to question him, not kill him.

But hot blood started flowing across her hands and wrists. She still staggered backwards, still holding him by the shirtfront, still pulling him with her.

She was in a wind tunnel now, and she heard thunder. She steeled herself. Lightning always followed thunder. She wasn't sure where that thought came from, but it felt true and terrifying.

Voices came on the wind, some speaking a language she didn't understand, others familiar, shouting commands.

She kept holding the man, but he was sagging now, about to fall on her. For the second time that day, she was trying to hold a dying person upright.

Then something hit her from the side, so hard that she fell over. The man fell on her, and someone—something—started pounding her head while grabbing for the knife.

The knife was stuck in the man's chin.

The wind was blowing so hard that dust and dirt and bits of tree branches swirled around Cilka. She couldn't see at all, nor could she see what was attacking her.

The voices got louder—Desmond yelling, "Get over here! We have to stop this now!"—and someone else answering and shouts all mixed into the whistling of the wind.

The body toppled onto Cilka, holding her down. She tried

to crawl out from underneath it but whatever—whoever—was hitting her pushed her back.

Cilka finally pulled the blade free and slashed into the direction of whatever was hitting her.

Something—someone—snarled. Cilka stabbed and stabbed, hitting something—someone—almost as often as she continued hitting the dying man. There was very little air in this whirlwind, and the dust and dirt and debris kept hitting her cheeks.

Cilka needed to be shielded from that. She needed the weather to stop bothering her.

And as quickly as she had that thought, the wind moved back, still swirling around her, but not touching her.

A muscular woman with a narrow face and fierce eyes growled at Cilka, reaching for her. Cilka slashed at the woman, but the woman knocked the knife away.

Then something grabbed the woman and yanked her away from Cilka. The woman turned to fight whoever—whatever— it was and as she did, Cilka climbed out from underneath the man's body, pulling herself backwards with her arms.

Each time she moved, the wind kept moving away from her, leaving Cilka in a little bubble.

Cilka needed to find the source of that wind.

She put up a hand, which was dark with dripping blood, and waved, trying to see.

As she did, light erupted from her fingers, traveling along the wind, burning it all up.

The fog near the tree evaporated, leaving a woman in robes looking shocked. Then the woman ducked backwards into the air, and vanished.

The wind was gone. Other constables were fighting the

woman who refused to be knocked down, despite being cut and bleeding from several places on her body.

More constables hurried over, some carrying weapons.

Desmond shouted, "Don't kill her!"

The constables swarmed over her, ten, twenty, thirty of them, until they finally got her down.

No shackles they had would hold her. Cilka could clearly see that.

So she took that light that had eaten up the wind and conjured some restraints. She'd done light magic years ago, but never at this scale, and never to create restraints.

They floated toward the woman, then latched to her wrists, pulling her wrists together, one on top of the other, and holding her in place.

The woman cried out in pain.

"Was that magic?" someone asked.

"It was all magic," Desmond said. He waved a hand, as if to shut up everyone.

The woman fell to her knees, her skin gray with pain. The restraints seemed to be cutting into her wrists.

"Get her out of here," he said. "And be careful with her."

Someone—Cilka didn't see who—said "Yessir," and the entire group of constables pulled the woman away.

The man was sprawled on the ground. His face had settled into something now. Something narrow. His ears were pointed, his features sharp and clear, black eyes open.

He was clearly dead.

Desmond poked him with a shoe. "Remember those history books we hated? The ones with that glittering gold representational art?"

Cilka looked up. Blood was drying on her hands. She didn't remember books or art, but maybe that was because her mind was trying to process what had happened.

"The creatures that had come out of the mountains near the Forbidden Valley. Remember that?" Desmond asked.

Cilka nodded. She did. The Academy at Serebro was filled with all kinds of art from several of the cultures on the Hidden River depicting that ancient battle.

Every professor she had said that the paintings were not representational, especially of the creatures that came out of that mountain.

But those professors had been wrong.

"I hate that your friend Judita was right," Desmond said, poking the body once more. "These people are Fey."

CHAPTER
THIRTY-SEVEN

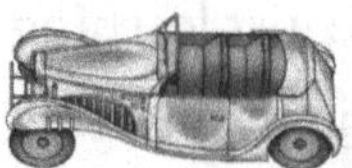

Sirocco stood outside the portal, her hands aching all the way to the bone, her body shivering. She had released even more magick than she had thought possible. And it had done nothing.

Qurzi was dead. The constables had somehow subdued Yris. And the woman—the horrible woman who had killed Hadley—had killed Qurzi too.

Now, Sirocco was standing outside a portal that she had not created, with no fog protecting her. She had sent wind and weather and every spell she could think of to defeat that woman, and nothing had changed.

Except that some of the constables had looked at Sirocco in horror.

She stepped backwards into the portal, ready to use a wind spell again if someone else tried to follow her into this thing.

She probably shouldn't leave Yris, but Sirocco wasn't certain she had enough energy left to defeat that woman who held Yris.

The woman had sent a spell at her, destroying the fog. Destroying it.

Sirocco had felt that fog melt away as if she had stuck her entire body into the heat of the midday sun.

She had no idea what that woman was—she clearly wasn't Fey—but she had power, even though she seemed surprised by it as well. Sirocco had seen that expression on the faces of young Weather Sprites who were just learning their magick.

And if Sirocco was right, and this woman was just learning her magick, what else could this woman do?

Sirocco tripped. She clutched at the walls of the portal, but her hands wouldn't bend. She had destroyed them with the frostbite and the magick and the spells.

She fell backwards, tumbling into an emptiness that she couldn't see. She couldn't twist around to see where she was, and she couldn't stop the fall. Hands grabbed her, and pulled her into a warm room.

She blinked. She was in the kitchen at the house, balanced in Xevkin's arms. Sirocco had no idea Xevkin was so strong, although it made sense. She was Infantry after all.

"What happened to you?" Xevkin asked.

"Not me," Sirocco said. "I need to talk to everyone. Right now."

She moved her feet underneath herself, and managed to stand up, even though she was so exhausted her head was spinning. She couldn't use her hands at all, but she was going to have to.

"I don't think I should leave you," Xevkin said.

"I don't care what you think," Sirocco snapped. "Get everyone."

"As you will," Xevkin said, her voice thick with irony. She let go of Sirocco, who nearly fell again.

She had no balance right now. She had nothing except sheer determination.

Xevkin had moved into the main room. Her voice was reedy, hard to understand. Or maybe Sirocco wasn't able to hear clearly. She was having trouble concentrating.

She could see the rest of the kitchen around the portal—the table, the oven, the fireplace. She made herself focus, and then she gathered the rest of her strength.

She had to close that portal. She really should destroy it, but she was afraid to, given how much magick she had seen this day. She really didn't understand the magick, and she was afraid that she might do something to aid the magick rather than destroy it.

Or, the magick might have even more power than she expected, and it might reverberate in this small space and explode. It might destroy the house and everyone in it.

She would worry about destroying the portal later. Right now, she had to make sure it was closed.

She raised her hands in front of her. They throbbed. She felt like she was wearing five layers of mittens over skin with nerves exposed. The pain made her eyes water.

But she ignored it. She gathered what moisture remained in the air, maybe pulling some from the fog outside of this house, and she sent a stream of ice from her hands.

Ice as thick and strong as any she had ever created. The most solid block of ice she could imagine.

She coated the entire portal in ice, and then did it again, and did it one more time.

When she finished, she sank to her knees.

Soft hands grabbed her.

"Get her water," someone said. Gem? Was that Gem?

Sirocco had to tell them about Yris. About Qurzi.

"Let's get her to her room." Gem again.

"No." Sirocco said, the word small and wobbly.

No one seemed to hear her. Hands lifted her onto her uncertain legs.

"No!" Sirocco said, using all of her strength to get the word out. "No. You have to listen to me."

She nearly toppled over after she spoke.

"Get her a chair." That was Atrü.

A chair screeched as someone moved it across the floor. That was when she realized she really wasn't seeing much of anything.

She was losing consciousness whether she wanted to or not.

"That portal," she said, inclining her head at the block of ice, "is not one of ours."

"Who made it?" Atrü asked.

"I don't know," Sirocco said, or thought she said. She had to focus. She had to concentrate.

It was so hard.

Someone shoved a glass at her mouth. The liquid smelled of orange. She made herself sip. It was sweet.

She knew what that was. It revived people who had expelled too much magick. It was a last resort.

Although maybe not, considering how inexperienced Gem was.

Gem—or whoever—had a light touch with the glass. Sirocco didn't feel like she was drowning in the liquid nor did she feel like she couldn't get enough.

She made herself drink, felt the liquid go straight to her

head. She still couldn't see much more than shapes, but at least she recognized those.

Atrü. Gem. Xevkin. Uryek. Vidso. Haevner. Rodderc. Maybe someone else, lurking near the wall. Slumber?

"They have magick," she said. "They have too much magick."

"Who?" Atrü asked.

The Qavnerians. The Trinovantians. Everyone in Dorovich. She didn't know. She shook her head.

"The portal opens at the Kirilli place," she said. Her voice didn't sound like her own. It was raspy and thin, ragged, her words slurred. She hoped the team could understand her.

None of them spoke. If she hadn't seen their shapes looming around her, if she hadn't felt the hands still supporting her, if she couldn't feel something poking at her fingers, she would have thought she was alone.

"Qurzi was there. Spying. Yris, too." Sirocco licked her lips. "I did what I could."

"What do you mean?" Atrü asked.

"I used wind. Lightning. Thunder. It didn't stop anything. Ow!" Pain skittered up her right arm. Gem had done something, twisting the fingers or maybe just touching them a bit too much.

"I didn't tell them to go there," Atrü said.

"Oh, for..." Rodderc's voice rose over Atrü's. "What couldn't you stop?"

"Qurzi." Sirocco licked her lips. They were dry and chapped. Her entire skin felt dry and chapped. Maybe that was what she had done. Maybe she hadn't found moisture in the air for this last bit of ice. Maybe she had had to pull the moisture from her own body.

"Qurzi wasn't supposed to be there," Atrü said. "I'll tell him—"

"He's dead," Sirocco said. "They killed two of ours today. *She* killed two of ours today."

And she'd had Hadley's knife. Sirocco just remembered that, but she wasn't sure how to say it. She wasn't sure if she could say any more.

"What were you saying about Yris?" Rodderc asked. "Is she dead too?"

"I don't know." Sirocco said. "They have her. They took her."

"They?" Rodderc asked, urgency in his tone.

"Constables," Sirocco said. "And that woman."

That horrible, horrible woman. The one who killed everyone she touched. That woman.

Sirocco could picture her, for all the good that did the others. In fact, that woman seemed clearer than they all did.

She couldn't really see them anymore.

Her head slipped back.

Someone said her name. Rodderc? Atrü? She didn't care. Pricks of pain ran through her hands, but they weren't as bad now. Or maybe they were but she couldn't really feel it.

Any of it.

She'd tell them the rest when she woke up. She'd tell them.

She closed her useless eyes, and let go, feeling nothing for the first time in forever. Nothing. So wonderful. Nothing.

Nothing at all.

CHAPTER

THIRTY-EIGHT

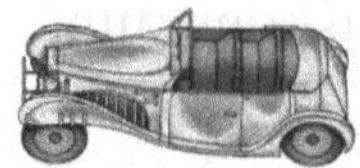

Atrü had come into the kitchen late. He had heard Xevkin shouting that she needed help, she needed Gem, she needed people in the kitchen and fast.

Atrü had hurried in, but five of his Infantry were already there. Sirocco was on the floor, with Vidso supporting her head and shoulders, trying to keep her sitting up just enough to talk.

Her eyes were iced over, something Atrü had never seen. Her face was gray and sunken in on itself. The skin was flaking off.

Her hands—her hands were an abomination, all swollen and black and purple. The fingertips had split, but they weren't bleeding.

The kitchen smelled of suppurating flesh. It was cold inside the room, because another gigantic block of ice floated near the door. Sirocco had created three blocks of ice in the other rooms, closing the portals like he had asked, but he hadn't known about this one.

And then she was babbling about magick and Qurzi being

431

dead and the Kirilli and Yris. Atrü didn't understand any of it. He hadn't even noticed that Qurzi was missing until Sirocco had mentioned his name.

Atrü remembered seeing Yris earlier, but he didn't see her now.

"She's dying," Gem said. "I don't think I can help her. She's used too much magick."

"She's trying to tell us something," Rodderc said. "Do you know what it is?"

He looked at Xevkin, although Atrü had no idea why Rodderc was looking at her.

"She found that portal and went through it. I was supposed to wait for an hour and then get help, but she hadn't been gone for an hour. She fell backwards out of it, and I caught her. Her eyes were fine then."

Xevkin's voice shook.

"I got help, and by the time I came back, the portal was iced shut and she—"

Xevkin waved her hand at the portal, at Sirocco.

"We have to know what she knows," Rodderc said. "Can you roust her?"

He directed that last at Gem. Stupid Infantry. Rodderc clearly didn't know as much as he had claimed he did. Because if he really did know, he would understand that rousting someone took the wrong kind of magick. Rousting spells could kill as easily as they succeeded. Spell Warders and Enchanters did them best, and this troop had neither now.

"That won't work," Atrü said before Gem could answer Rodderc. "Where's Slumber?"

A shadow on the wall slithered toward the main room. Bastard was trying to leave.

"There you are," Atrü said. "You can't escape this. We need you."

The shadow formed into a man. Slumber was so young that his face still had spots sometimes. Right now, his black hair flopped over his forehead and his eyes, black against his skin, were wide.

"I could die," he whispered.

So he knew what Atrü was going to ask. Dream Riders could go into the unconscious mind, could find information, and could bring it back. But if they were inside when someone died, the Dream Rider could die as well.

Especially an inexperienced one.

"Then you better not wait," Atrü said.

Slumber shook his head. "I can't."

"You'll die if you don't," Atrü said.

"Are you threatening him?" Gem asked as if she had a stake in all of this.

"No," Atrü said. "Something happened. We have to know what it was, because whatever it was, it scared Sirocco and turned her into—that."

All of the most magickal people on his team were dying. No Hadley, when he needed her. He'd used Sirocco, and now this.

And then she'd said something about Qurzi. There was no Omriseu here either. Maybe he had listened. Maybe he was off doing the job Atrü had asked him to do, getting them a new place to stay.

They clearly needed one.

"I think we have a better chance of surviving whatever's

coming if we know what happened, don't you?" Atrü asked, and then mentally kicked himself for making that a question. "You will go in there and get the information."

"It doesn't work like that," Slumber said.

"Then wake her up!" Atrü snapped. "Do what you have to do."

Didn't anyone understand that this was an emergency? Didn't they realize that something had gone very wrong on this day?

They had no backup. No one was going to come to their rescue. They were on their own. That was why Rugar had sent in teams. If one team got wiped out, the other teams would maybe find out what was going on.

But the other teams might not have the same knowledge that this team did. The level of magick—that was a surprise. That was new.

Atrü had expected magick—it was in the old stories—but not like this.

Never like this.

"I don't want to," Slumber whispered.

He sounded like a child. If he added, *and you can't make me*, like little kids often did, then Atrü had no idea what to do next.

Because he really and truly did not have the magick to make Slumber do what he wanted.

"I don't want to die like Hadley did," Atrü said. He'd almost used Sirocco as an example, but caught himself just in time. The boy was scared enough of going into Sirocco's dying brain. He didn't need to be reminded that she—and he—might not survive.

Slumber made a face, then he shook his head.

He looked like he was about to run. But, instead, he flattened himself and plastered his entire body on Sirocco's, covering her face. He sank into her, like Dream Riders did, and her body stiffened with the shock of it all.

Slumber disappeared.

"That's an attack," Gem said. "I don't think she can survive an attack."

"It's too late." Rodderc's voice was flat. "Besides, she wasn't going to survive anyway."

"I was trying to help," Gem said. "But she's as dry as leaves on a late fall evening. I'm afraid to touch her. Her skin crumbles like it's made of dust."

Atrü shuddered. He couldn't help himself. What kind of magick did that? What was going on in this place?

He was beginning to think they couldn't counter it. They needed to stop thinking about destroying artifacts. They had to figure out how to return to Nye and give the message to Rugar that this place will require a full invasion force.

No half measures. No attempts at shortcuts.

There was something very powerful in Dorovich—or at least in Trinovante—and whatever that was, it made the smaller magicks of his little team insignificant.

Sirocco's body jerked once, like people did in bad dreams.

"Can we get him out of there?" Gem asked.

"Not if she dies," Rodderc said.

"Then don't let her die," Atrü said.

"I don't have control over that." Gem's voice was filled with tears.

"You're the only one with a hope of keeping them both alive," Atrü said. "So stop whining and do your job."

Gem gave him a sideways look so filled with hatred that he felt it viscerally. Then she placed both hands over Sirocco's heart.

"I need water," Gem said to no one in particular. "We're going to do what we can to keep her from crumbling."

"Water?" Uryek asked.

"As much as you can find," Gem said.

Her gaze met Atrü's.

"I can't promise anything," Gem said to him.

"I'm not asking for promises," he said. "I need results."

She shook her head, but kept her hands hovering. Sirocco didn't move.

Rodderc and three of his team went in search of water. Atrü didn't help them.

He needed to be here if Sirocco woke up. *When* Sirocco woke up. Or when Slumber returned, so that he could tell them what, exactly, was going on.

The room got colder.

Atrü could see his breath.

He could only wait—just like the rest of the team.

Wait and hope that things weren't as bad as they seemed.

THIRTY-NINE

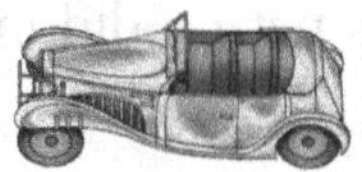

Sirocco's brain was shutting down. The shutdown was methodical, as if someone was walking through a house and blowing out candles in each room.

Slumber stood on the threshold of Sirocco's mind and peered at it. She wasn't dreaming. She didn't have enough energy for that. She didn't have much energy for anything.

He could conjure a Dream, he hoped, but it would take all her remaining light. He wasn't experienced enough to know if that would kill her.

He could maybe give her some of his own strength, but that would be risky. He needed it to escape.

He had no plan. His mentors had always told him he needed a plan before he went into anyone's mind. All he had done here was dive in, without an idea of what to do.

And he couldn't do anything elaborate because there wasn't much here.

So he decided to go for something simple.

He conjured up the kitchen just as it had been a moment ago. The portal was iced over, the room was cold, and there was a thin light coming from the main room.

Three members of the Infantry huddled around Sirocco, looking worried. Rodderc stood to one side and Vidso held her.

Slumber knew that one of the main rules of Dreaming was to make sure the sleeping person didn't see themselves from the outside, but he had no idea how to prevent that here. So he didn't let her see her face or her hands.

Her hands were so awful.

He swept his own mind and focused. He couldn't be distracted. He needed her to help him.

So he stood in front of the tableau, breaking another rule of Dreaming.

"Sirocco," he said. "It's Slumber. I'm here because I need some information from you before you can really rest."

He didn't want to tell her he thought she was dying.

"I don't want you to use too much energy to tell me. If you replay your memories, I can glean the information—"

NO! Sirocco's voice rose above everything else. *No! I can't show you.*

She sat up, pulling away from the image of her with Vidso. Sirocco had taken over the Dream, using too much energy, just like Slumber feared.

Worse, she formed in front of him, thinner, younger, her eyes clear and not covered with ice, her hands small and perfect.

If he wasn't careful, he would break that image by correcting it with what she really looked like.

I have to tell you, Slumber, because I'm dying, she said. *We only have a moment.*

Part of him wanted to lie to her. Lying was his natural instinct. That was usually what Dream Riders did. They lied in the form of nightmares and dreams.

But he held himself in check.

That portal in the kitchen leads to the Kirilli estate, she said, looking over her shoulder. The portal was the only part of the kitchen that remained. *I did not make that portal. Neither did Hadley. I wasn't able to find out who did, but they did so relatively recently.*

He nodded, encouraging her, feeling the energy seep from her.

The Sirocco he could see was surrounded by light. She was pulling energy from somewhere, but he couldn't see where.

I showed up just as the woman who helped kill Hadley attacked Qurzi. The woman was using Hadley's knife. I tried to stop it, but I couldn't. Yris was there. She tried to stop it too, and got stabbed. They captured Yris. Qurzi died.

Slumber held his Dream Self rigidly, setting his emotions into his corporeal self. He didn't dare let himself feel anything. He made sure he did not react.

Then the woman grabbed my magick and sent light at me. She dissolved my fog, Slumber. Her magick attacked mine. She's strong, but not controlled. The magick she used surprised her. You have to tell the team that. She was surprised.

"All right," he said.

I got here, Sirocco said. *I sealed the portals. I'll try to stay as long as I can. I don't know if the ice will vanish when I die.*

"Don't die," he whispered.

To his surprise, she smiled. The smile was tender. *Thank you for that.* Then the smile faded. *You need to leave now.*

"Please," he said. "We need you—"

Now, Sirocco said. *I can't hold on much longer....*

"Thank you," he said, and pulled himself backwards through the path he had made.

The path was closing. The entire brain was dark except for a candle-flame-sized flicker where he had been standing.

The air in here was thick, and he knew that was just an image—a metaphor—for what might happen to him if he stayed much longer.

He bent his spine, rose up, and tried to free himself. It felt like his entire soul was covered in mud and it was trying to pull him under. He grabbed some dark part of Sirocco's mind and used it to leverage himself out of the darkness.

For a moment, he thought he wasn't going to make it.

Then he popped back into the kitchen—the real kitchen— and fell to one side, gasping for air.

The entire team—or what was left of them—watched him. No one said a word. No one asked what he saw.

Behind him, he heard dripping water. He looked over at the portal.

The ice was melting.

Then he looked down at Sirocco.

Her entire body had collapsed in on itself, as if she had been dead for a year.

He had been in there?

He shuddered, terrified and saddened at the same time. She was gone, and he might have hastened that.

But he had done so for a reason.

He sat up.

"We need to leave here," he said, looking at the dripping portal. "We have to leave here now."

PART FIVE
NOW

FORTY

It was the middle of the afternoon. The sun had burned through the fog for the first time in weeks, and with the diamond-like sparkle of the droplets littering their exteriors, Trinovante's buildings looked surprised by the change in weather.

Judita did not like the change at all. The fog had had a magical element that felt foreign, but the sunlight felt unfamiliar, like it belonged to another life, another time.

She stood at the edge of the street where Augustus Kirilli died.

At least Cilka had lived up to one promise: the street was blocked off, and the buildings around its periphery empty. Apparently, Cilka had sent several members of the constabulary to these gigantic houses of finance, told them of the murder, and then implied that they—and their vast wealth—were in danger.

They needed to keep the area clear for at least a day, maybe more, while the law figured out exactly what had happened.

Judita did not know how the initial conversations went, but she did know that eventually the constabulary won.

This place looked amazingly empty for the middle of the day. The only light on the street itself came from the weak sunlight. The windows of the great stone buildings were dark like they were on holidays, and the street itself—as well as the ones nearby—was astonishingly quiet.

No horses, no carriages, no people. Not a single windstone vehicle, and no lightstone lanterns lit.

It was as if, in this small section of the city, everyone had been evacuated and the city abandoned.

Judita knew better than to trust that feeling of abandonment, though.

Her entire body was tense. She didn't want to go back into that street, and she had to.

She was going to call a circle, even though Cilka had asked her to wait until Cilka was ready.

Then Cilka had abandoned her. Judita had been alone to mull over the terrifying events of the morning all by herself, and it was doing her no good.

She wanted to search out Cilka, and she couldn't. Cilka had a body to attend to, which she should have finished with by now.

Judita couldn't lose the sense that Cilka simply said that she would return to placate Judita.

But Cilka knew better than to do that, right? That was what Judita had continued telling herself over and over again. Cilka knew better, and she would arrive soon.

Soon turned into *not yet*, and with each passing moment, Judita's concern grew greater.

The morning's magic was already fading, and if they waited too long, they would never get the answers they sought.

Judita finally couldn't wait any longer. She had contacted five people whom she believed were courageous enough to hold a circle against this kind of magic. They waited in the courtyard of a small public house not too far from the financial district.

She could get to the courtyard in less than ten minutes. She would be able to enlist them and their skills before the sun went down.

Sunset was about three hours away. If she was going to act today, she needed to act in the next hour or so. She wasn't willing to cast a circle spell on a street that had experienced this level of strange magic—not in full dark.

It wasn't that magic was more powerful in the dark; it was that some magic was visible without the light.

If the six of them created a circle in a public street, they could bluff their way past any troubles in the daylight.

But if the magic became visible at night, well, then bluffing was out of the question.

And Judita could no longer trust Cilka should something go wrong.

Judita clasped her hands together. She still felt shaky and off-balance from the morning's events.

That Fey creature had had to die. It had killed Kirilli—not once, but twice. Or at least, the murder had repeated, which meant it was important to the magic.

Judita still didn't understand how Kirilli had walked away during the bungled revisiting of the murder, but he had.

While she had waited for Cilka, Judita had looked up some

of the magic in her books, just to see if there was any mention of something like this, and what she found didn't give her comfort.

There was a possibility that what happened with Kirilli wasn't spirit magic, but magical willfulness.

Magical willfulness meant that Kirilli had had some kind of mission that he felt compelled to complete. His life—or the lives of people that he loved—hung in the balance. If he did not complete the mission, the ones that he loved might be in danger forever.

So his *will* had completed the mission. But only because Judita's magic had gotten caught in the swirling tides on that little patch of street and it had fueled his desire, given him just enough magic to finish the mission, before acquiescing to his own death.

She hadn't spent a lot of time in research, but that had been enough. Maybe after the circle, she would ask some of the others if they thought Kirilli was capable of that kind of magic.

He had never struck her as particularly magical, even though he had come from one of the most powerful Old Families in the entire Protectorate. If anyone had magic, it should logically have been a Kirilli. Judita had just never given it any thought.

Just like she had never given the return of the Fey any thought. They had been two parts of her education—first, the fascinating old histories that she had studied alongside art and architecture she had learned at Serebro Academy, and second, the powerful present-day conquerors whose battles made them feared throughout the world.

She had studied that second part as well, but only because as a young woman she had toyed with going into government.

It was the job of every good politician to understand not just the local situation but the worldwide situation as well.

The Fey were impossible to ignore if one looked at the world, since the Fey Empire already owned half of it—and desired the other half.

When Judita had been in school, the professors had always said the only other culture capable of conquering half the world was the Qavner Protectorate. She had believed it then.

Later, she considered it local delusion.

After this morning, though, when she had stabbed a person to death, a person who was clearly Fey, she was willing to revisit her opinion. She had already removed the word *delusion* from any examination of the Fey.

The Qavnerian Protectorate had already absorbed a goodly portion of this section of the world. She didn't know how much by area, but enough that she would say the Qavnerians had conquered at least a fifth, maybe a quarter, of the world that the Fey had not yet touched.

The mingled magic was another indicator, one that terrified her even more than the Fey did.

So much about Qavnerian magic had been lost, destroyed or set aside. And now, by risking a circle in the middle of the afternoon—risking it without the protection of a Procurator or the constabulary—Judita was risking the loss of even more magic.

Thirty or forty years ago, Judita could have died for what she was thinking of now.

And she wasn't sure if those laws were still on the books. While magic had become something people ignored once again, it still haunted the hinterlands. People there wanted nothing to do with magic and sometimes slaughtered those who used it.

Judita took a deep breath, and pressed her hands together, flexing the fingers as she did so.

So many risks. She would feel so much better if Cilka were here—not just from the law enforcement standpoint, but from a friendly one.

Judita slipped into the shutdown street, standing half a block away from the spot where Kirilli had been murdered. She narrowed her gaze and looked for magical streams, just like she had that morning.

Magical streams showed up like heatwaves on a hot morning. Magical streams had a different thickness. They looked like part of the air, but they weren't part of it at all.

Each stream had its own thickness and its own rainbow of colors. The streams were mostly clear, but along the edges there was usually a series of unrelated colors. Sometimes they were bright and sometimes so faded that Judita could barely see them.

But they identified the stream in the moment for her. She could separate out streams that she created or that were created by a specific spell from streams that someone else created or that were created by a different spell.

This morning, she had seen so many streams, it had been nearly impossible to separate them. She thought she had when she acceded to Cilka's request and tried to recreate the murder.

Judita couldn't tell, even now, if she had grabbed the wrong stream or if, in grabbing the right stream, it had more power than she had ever encountered.

After she had killed the Fey creature, she had looked at the streams again. They had quadrupled, and to her surprise, some of them were not clear. They were tinged with black and brown and yellow and gray, like the fog, and they felt threatening.

She had backed away from them, hands up, worried that they might pursue her.

But they didn't. At least not then.

It took a moment with her eyes narrowed for her to see what was before her now. The dark streams were fading, just like she had feared. No one was feeding them extra magic, which was probably a good thing for the street and for life in Trinovante, but not good for her circle.

If the circle could grab those dark streams, see where they led, then they might end up with a lot of answers.

The streams were still the thickest near the spot where Kirilli died. The streams were layered on top of each other, looking almost like a topological map or a series of rivers stacked one above the other.

Those streams went all the way to the ground. A few seemed to sprout upward from the spot where Kirilli's body had been. And then there were more streams a few yards away, where the portal had first appeared.

Not to mention the gigantic red splotch, almost like a lake of color, in the middle of the air where the Fey creature had died.

Judita blinked and stepped back, surprised and shocked at the angry red of that particular stream. Blinking made all the streams vanish as if they had never been, and she was going to have to work to bring them back.

But she wasn't willing to do that, not without the others.

She was going to need them, and she was going to have to tell them this circle would be the most dangerous they had ever participated in.

She hoped none of them were going to back out, because if

they did, she wasn't sure who else she would find to replace them, particularly now, without Cilka.

Judita took a deep breath, and pivoted, scanning the side street to make sure that no constable, watchman, or Fey creature saw her.

Then she headed back to the public inn to pick up the others—and she hoped they all would survive the day.

FORTY-ONE

Gussie had never been to an Office of the Constabulary before. She had gone by the offices all over Trinovante countless times, even noted how different the buildings were from each other, but she had never had occasion to go inside one.

It broke her heart that she now did.

She stood just outside the main doors. In her memory of this place's exterior, constables were always going in and out, but right now she saw only a handful. The doors were nothing ornate, not like the ones in her father's home.

These were just doors and behind them were people who would have to listen to a fantastical tale. She hoped they would believe her, and investigate. Her staff needed protection. Her home—homes, now, she supposed—needed guards, and someone had to find the culprits.

She didn't have the energy for that.

She didn't have the energy for much of anything.

She turned to wave at Barkson. Barkson had brought her here in Barkson's windstone vehicle. That vehicle was a newer model than Gussie's and, Barkson said, could go much faster.

Barkson had driven like a crazy person, weaving across the roads, going around carriages and spooking horses. Apparently, Barkson didn't care who got injured when she drove, unlike Gussie.

But Gussie couldn't have come here without her. Barkson had taken Gussie to Barkson's apartment, given her clothing—pants!—and made an area for her to sleep that night, if Gussie would ever be able to sleep again.

Barkson had also given Gussie a key, and instructed her to have someone from the constabulary drop her a block or so away when her visit was done. Apparently, Barkson had thought Gussie could walk to the apartment safely, although Barkson again had warned Gussie to make certain she was not followed. Barkson had also warned Gussie not to use her own vehicle for a few days in case she had been followed to the tavern.

Then Barkson had plied her with food, even though Gussie hadn't wanted any, and had made her drink water.

Gussie had thanked her, of course, but there were no words for the friendship that Gussie hadn't expected or asked for. Barkson had just done these things, and had even mumbled something about not getting paid to let Gussie's family know what was happening.

Gussie couldn't abide that. She needed a messenger, and Barkson was the best. So Gussie had given her some gold to start, although Barkson had insisted that Gussie hang on to some.

And then Barkson had brought her here, telling her—no, *instructing* her—to make sure the constabulary was on this.

When Gussie seemed uncertain, Barkson drove her here, to make sure that Gussie would let the authorities know, so that everyone possible could solve these heinous crimes.

Gussie scanned the road for Barkson's vehicle. Gussie could see carriages and a few people on horseback, but no windstone vehicles at all.

Barkson had already left.

Gussie felt a moment of disappointment, even though she knew she had only wanted to see Barkson one last time as a bit of a reprieve before reentering this nightmare.

Gussie mentally wished Barkson well. Then Gussie steeled her shoulders and walked along the entry into the constabulary.

Instantly, the sound overwhelmed her. Dozens of conversations echoed in the large entry hall. Words bounced off everything. Whoever had designed this place hadn't thought about the way that sound reverberated. Or maybe they hadn't known.

Her ears ached right from the start, which told her just how on edge she was. When she was upset, Gussie wanted silence more than anything else, and this place was the opposite of silent.

The constables she had expected outside were in here, hurrying from one part of the large hall to another. A few stood near the door. Some had prisoners, dragging them by their arms. Some of the prisoners shuffled, even though their feet were not restrained.

None of the prisoners had dressed with care. They were all wearing dirty clothing, and many had filthy faces and unwashed hair, all the signs of life lived outside lacked the luxury that Gussie enjoyed.

The high ceiling did help with one thing. The area did not smell as badly as it would have if the ceilings were low.

As it was, she only got a whiff of body odor when someone passed by, not as a prevailing scent.

There were podiums on either side of her, small ones where someone stood or leaned. There were no chairs that she could see. A short flight of stairs led up to a higher level and beyond that, some parts of the building that disappeared into the distance.

The space above her was arched, with some light filtering through. Beyond it, a railing that she could see and probably some more floors, where business got done.

"Help ye, ma'am?" someone asked.

Gussie started. The voice had come from too close to her. She hadn't realized someone had come that close.

A constable with a boyish face and a wisp of a beard gave her a concerned look. He was shorter than she was—so many people here were—and he was rail-thin. His uniform fit well, though, and the buttons down the front sparkled in the thin light through the glass panes above.

"Ma'am," he said, "may I help ye?"

"Yes," she said. Barkson had given her words to say, but Gussie couldn't remember them.

All she wanted to do was say that her father was dead and her family home was ransacked and everyone she had grown up with, except her siblings, was dead in the kitchen.

Instead, she fell onto her training. She drew herself to her full height, and said, "My name is Augusta Kirilli. I need to speak to someone in charge."

"Kirilli," the constable repeated. "Augusta. Related to Augustus Kirilli?"

"He's my father," she said, uncertain how the constable knew her family.

"Come with me, ma'am," the constable said, and swept a hand behind her, not quite touching her, urging her forward.

"Where are we going?" she asked.

"The Kirilli matter is being handled at the highest level," he said. "I've been instructed to bring anyone who mentions the Kirilli family to the Office of the Chief Constable."

Gussie blinked, startled that the chief constable would have an office in this particular constabulary. Had Barkson known that?

Probably.

The young constable led Gussie up that small flight of stairs, then turned a corner. They went up two more flights, reaching the fourth level. A serious woman in an older uniform, slightly frayed, looked up. She was older as well, also slightly frayed, and she seemed tired.

She didn't ask a single question out loud, although her expression clearly showed she was irritated.

The young constable didn't seem to care. "You asked me to bring anyone connected to the Kirilli matter to you."

The woman's eyes changed. They became sharper. And they focused on Gussie.

"Who are you?" the woman asked.

"Augusta Kirilli." Gussie held her chin up a little more, feeling like she was the one being judged.

But the woman visibly relaxed. "Oh, thank goodness. We've been searching for you."

"For me?" Gussie said, startled. "Why?"

The woman stood and walked toward her. The woman's gaze moved toward the young constable.

"Thank you," she said to him. "You may return to your post."

He nodded in an almost military style and headed back down the stairs.

"Come with me," the woman said.

They moved out of the fourth-floor landing into an alcove.

The woman leaned a little too close for Gussie's comfort.

"Your driver said he had no idea where you were," the woman said confidentially.

"Zeitsev?" Gussie asked. "He came here?"

Barkson was smarter than Gussie gave her credit for. She had brought Gussie to the right place.

"He's still here. He demanded that we send constables out to find you. No one knew where to look." Then the woman frowned. "You are aware of the day's events, am I right? Your driver told us you were."

The compassion in the woman's voice made Gussie tear up. She wasn't going to cry. Not yet. She was afraid if she started, she would not stop.

She cleared her throat.

"I came here to report my father's..." She still couldn't say *death*. She was still hoping with an ever so tiny unrealistic sense of hope that he was alive.

So she pivoted mid-sentence.

"My father's home. It's been ransacked and the staff..." She choked. Why were the words so hard? She swallowed, and forced herself to continue. "The staff is dead."

The woman took a slight step back, not out of shock but for some other reason that Gussie couldn't quite fathom. The woman peered around the edges of the alcove as if she had heard something.

"We have people at his home now," she said, returning her attention to Gussie. "They're investigating the crimes. Is your own home all right? Your driver said it was when he left."

"He was there more recently than I was," Gussie said. "I made my staff leave."

"Good thinking," the woman said.

Gussie hadn't expected the constabulary to be investigating yet. Although, if truth be told, she wasn't sure what she had expected.

"Do you know who did this?" Gussie asked. Her voice sounded small.

"I don't," the woman said, "but I am not handling this investigation. Let me take you to the chief."

Gussie wanted to ask if the chief was handling this because her father was involved or if there were other reasons, but she couldn't quite summon the energy. She would probably get the answer soon enough.

The woman led Gussie past the stairs, around a corner, and to an office with a closed door. The woman knocked on the door, and then opened it.

A man swore and said, "How many times do I have to tell you—?"

"Sir," the woman said, as if the swearing didn't bother her at all. "You asked me to let you know the moment I heard from or about Augusta Kirilli."

"Yes." There was a man in the middle of the office. Windows

were behind him, showing a bit more sunlight over Trinovante than Gussie expected.

A woman stood next to him. She looked vaguely familiar. Gussie might have seen her in the offices of Kirilli, Capalidi, Konstandt, & B'Levin. The woman wore a heavy coat with reddish stains all over it. Her face had a bit of spatter across it. She kept her hands in the coat's pockets.

She was wearing pants and shoes that looked mud stained. Somehow Gussie didn't think, though, that was mud on the shoes. She wasn't sure why she had that feeling.

"Chief Desmond M'ndue, Procurator Cilka Lupei," the woman said nodding toward each of them. "Meet Augusta Kirilli."

The woman—Cilka Lupei—let out a long breath. "That's one thing at least," she said. "You're alive."

Gussie had never been greeted like that before. But, of course, there had never been circumstances in her life like these before.

"Yes," she said, because what else did one say? "I came to tell you about my father's estate, but you already know."

"And your father?" the chief asked gently.

Gussie couldn't tell if he was asking if she knew about her father or was going to tell them about him.

"I don't know," she said, "but given what I saw today, I think my father is dead."

This time her voice didn't break.

The chief looked like he was about to say something, but Lupei put her hand on his arm.

"Yes," she said gently. "Your father is dead. He was murdered last night."

"Last night...?" Gussie let her voice trail off. That both made sense and it made no sense. If her father had died the night before, why had his spirit shown up at the manor when she was there in the morning? How had his spirit shown up there?

Had that been his spirit?

And if it had been, how had she been able to hug him?

These people wouldn't have the answer. These people were probably terrified of magic. They were in charge of purging it, after all.

All three of them stared at her. She nodded, then swallowed, and said, "You saw him?"

"I was the one called to investigate," Lupei said. "We've since added the estate into the investigation. We were worried about you. Your driver had no idea where you were."

"I don't tell my driver everything," Gussie said with a small tense smile.

"He said you went off somewhere," the chief said. The man had a way of asking questions without asking at all.

Gussie nodded. "I had to go alone," she said. "My father gave me an assignment..."

Once again, she couldn't quite finish the sentence the way she had started it.

"...should something bad happen to him or the household," she said. She made it sound like he had given her the assignment before he died. In some ways, he had, but she hadn't listened.

Until his spirit visited.

"What was that assignment?" the chief asked.

Gussie gave him her best dismissive look. "I needed to secure certain family valuables in a place that only the family knows about. I'm sure you understand."

"Where is that?" Lupei asked, as if she hadn't understood what Gussie had been implying.

"That's something only the family is privy to," Gussie said again. "These items are important to the Kirillis. No one else."

Obviously, she was lying. Because if the items did not matter to anyone else, then she wouldn't have had to secure them. But she hoped in the confusion of this moment, no one would challenge her on these matters.

The chief studied her as if he was memorizing her face. Then he gave her a half-smile, as if he knew what she was doing.

Gussie needed to change the focus. She needed her most snobbish side. Her *protective* snobbish side.

So she straightened slightly and asked, "What have you learned?"

Lupei glanced at the chief, as if asking his permission to tell Gussie what was going on.

He did not return her glance. He continued to focus on Gussie. His dark eyes made her nervous.

"What do you know about the Fey?" the chief asked.

She started. It felt like a non sequitur, but she knew, in the context of this conversation, it wasn't.

She needed to regain her mental footing. She hadn't expected a conversation about a group she only knew through the news, the discussions of her father's somewhat paranoid friends, and what little she had studied in school.

"I know that they're a major military presence half a world away," Gussie said. "Why?"

"We have one in custody," the chief said.

He was watching Gussie closely. So was Lupei. The other

woman had stepped back slightly as if she didn't want to be included in this conversation.

"We found her at your father's estate," Lupei said.

Gussie blinked, trying to put this information together with everything she knew. Her father's paranoid friends said that the Fey would someday be a threat to Dorovich, but Gussie never expected them to be a threat to Trinovante, and certainly hadn't expected them to be a threat to her father's estate.

"What was she doing there?" Gussie asked.

Lupei's mouth moved in what seemed to be an attempt at a smile. It failed.

"She tried to kill me," Lupei said.

Gussie took a deep breath. "Are you all right?"

"That," Lupei said, "is a question for another time."

Gussie mentally applauded her. Lupei was obviously not going to think about what she had been through.

"You need to know that this Fey was not alone. She was with another man, who is now dead, and a woman who escaped," the chief said.

"You think this has something to do with my father's death?" Gussie asked, choking slightly on the word *death*.

"We think he was killed by a Fey person as well," Lupei said.

"Is there something that your family knows about the Fey? A reason they would come here and attack your father?" the chief asked.

Gussie shook her head. "I don't think I've ever met someone Fey," she said. "I wouldn't know if I had, though."

"Nothing in family lore?" Lupei asked.

Gussie shrugged. "Until today, I thought family lore was just that. Stories told to the children so we would be impressed with the family name."

"And now?" the chief asked.

"Now I'm going to have to reevaluate," Gussie said. "But I'll be honest with you. I'm not thinking as clearly as I'd like to be."

Lupei really smiled this time, as if she understood.

"May I talk to this Fey?" Gussie asked.

"I think it would be dangerous," the chief said. "It's well known that the Fey are a magical warrior culture. She might have abilities that we are unaware of. And these people are targeting your family. We could take you in to see her, and she could kill you with a look."

Gussie took a deep breath. Behind it, she felt a fury she'd never felt before. "I'll take the risk."

"I'll go with her," Lupei said. She gave the chief a look that conveyed something more than what she said, only Gussie didn't understand it.

"I'd be happier if neither of you went into an area near that woman," the chief said.

"She might tell me something," Gussie said, even though she had no idea if that was true. She just wanted to see one of the people who might have killed her father. Who might be attacking her family.

"I'm not sure it's worth the risk," the chief said.

"We might not learn anything without this kind of risk," Lupei said, more to him than to Gussie.

The chief took a deep breath, clearly considering the idea. Then he nodded ever so slightly.

"You'll go in with guards," he said. "You'll stay near the door."

"All right," Gussie said.

"And you," he said to Lupei. "You will do whatever you can to keep Miss Kirilli safe. If something happens, I will run interference for you."

Gussie frowned. She wasn't sure what that meant. Did that mean Lupei had some magic? Or did it mean something else? Had he just cleared Lupei to kill the Fey person?

It couldn't be that. They were in the constabulary, where law ruled. Law, which said that killing was wrong.

Even if it felt right.

Gussie clenched one fist and concentrated on the feeling of her fingertips poking into her palm. She had to stay calm. She had no proof this Fey person had anything to do with her father's death.

She needed to keep an open mind.

She needed to figure out what exactly was going on.

CHAPTER
FORTY-TWO

They sat at one of the four outside tables at Connor's Ancient and Excellent Public House, which was neither ancient nor excellent but did have the advantage of being close to the financial district.

As a result, its ales were overpriced and its décor was lovely, not that the five people Judita had contacted were enjoying the décor. They were sitting as far apart as people crowded around the same round table could be, and only three of them had had enough courage to order one of Connor's Royal Concoctions, which was a vile combination of ale, mint, and some kind of fruit juice.

Judging by the way that the concoction had separated in the clear glass mugs, no one had had the courage to actually drink it.

The five who waited for her had never done a circle together, although she had performed a circle with each of them.

Melba Hammershield had moved to Trinovante from Serebro a dozen years ago. She was short, red-headed, and round, with startling green eyes that missed nothing, and the same kind of upswept features that Cilka had. On Melba, the features looked like they'd been fastened on with loose stitches.

She had ordered one of the concoctions and still had her pudgy hand wrapped around the mug. When she saw Judita, Melba relaxed visibly.

"Finally," she said. "I feel very exposed sitting here."

"That feeling is going to get worse," said Trinity Wallingford, as if she actually knew what she was talking about.

Maybe she did. Even though she was the youngest in this group by a decade or more, she had participated in some smaller practice circles that Judita ran after her early-morning magic classes.

Trinity's magic was terrifyingly powerful. Judita had been working with her to control it. Trinity was a by-blow of one of the Old Families. Her father, who had no heirs, had forced his family to recognize Trinity as a member after his wife had died. At that point, Trinity had changed her last name, but she did not benefit from the Wallingford wealth or the Wallingford history.

Not yet anyway.

Still, she had the Wallingford looks. A narrow face with light brown skin, light brown eyes, and black hair that matched her raven-wing eyebrows. She might have been beautiful, if it weren't for her hooked nose and pointed chin.

Even so, she had a presence and a strength that most of the others here lacked.

She leaned back in her chair, rested a black-booted foot against the table stem, and pretended at confidence. Judita liked that. She also liked Trinity's practical clothing—heavy pants, a thick matching top, and gloves, which she held in her right hand.

"Are we going to get in trouble for this?" Kammie Gaston asked, her voice trembling.

She was the oldest in the group, a woman who lived alone in a small apartment not too far from Judita, and pretended to be poor, even though she was probably the wealthiest of all of them.

She too was from one of the Old Families, but never spoke of it. The family seat for the Gastons was in Mazurkita, and her niece ran it with an iron fist.

It seemed all of the Gaston women had iron fists, even Kammie. While she played at being a scatterbrained elderly woman, she was not scatterbrained in any kind of magical crisis. She could focus, and more importantly, she could send her powerful magic into any kind of artifact that had a tinge of Old Family provenance.

Judita hated doing circles with Kammie because Kammie complained all the way to the circle, but Judita also hated doing circles without her. Kammie had saved the magic in the circle more times than Judita wanted to think about.

This afternoon, Kammie didn't look like someone who could save anything. Her wispy white hair flew around her head in a nonexistent breeze. Her dark brown eyes had sunken into her square, wrinkled face, and her lips were chapped, as if she had been biting them.

Unlike Trinity, who dressed practically for this circle, Kammie wore the same faded dress that Judita had found her in that morning. Then it had smelled faintly of fried food and cat. Given Kammie's predilection for sweating when she was nervous, Judita could only feel sorry for the people sitting next to her.

Trinity didn't seem to notice, though, and neither did Taua Savali, who sat on the other side of Kammie. Although, to be fair, Judita had a hard time reading Savali, as he preferred to be called.

He had come to Trinovante from somewhere along the Hidden River, although he never admitted where. He had ended up in one of Judita's morning classes as if by accident. However, the better she got to know Savali, the more she realized he did nothing by accident.

He was a large man who seemed deceptively doughy. He wasn't. When he wore the clothes he had brought with him from home—some kind of flowing white loose weave shirt and pants, with sandals—his flesh transformed from fat to powerfully muscular.

He just didn't seem to fit into any clothing style but the ones he'd been born to. The Trinovantian clothing styles seemed to shove his skin in the wrong direction.

He wasn't wearing loose weave today. He had on leather that was one size too big. The sleeves covered most of the tattoos on the back of his hands, and the tattoos that rose up along his chest.

He had a few decorative lines along his face, tracing the ridges of his jawbone and encircling his slightly pointed ears.

His large hands were folded across what seemed to be a fat stomach, but which Judita knew showed his abdominal muscles when his shirt was off.

His gaze found hers and asked a quiet question: Could he leave? Or was this going to become something?

She let her gaze move away from his, finding the final member of the circle, a man who went by a single name.

Coulter.

He looked like no one else Judita knew. He was tall, but had yellow-blond hair and sky-blue eyes. His features were round and his pale skin was aging badly, even though he was maybe in his thirties.

He had told Judita when she had finally broken down and asked him about his heritage that his family had made a harrowing escape from Blue Isle when he was but a baby.

They had stowed away on a Nyeian vessel, after fleeing their home in some place called—terrifyingly—the Cliffs of Blood. Apparently, he claimed, the peoples of the Cliffs of Blood did not like children that were born "tall," by which they meant long and lean.

Those children were, apparently, put to death on the mountainside, as some kind of sacrifice.

Or maybe that wasn't why these things happened. She had no real idea, and she was never certain if Coulter was telling her the truth. He had a way of looking down when he spoke, his voice soft, and his manner uncertain, as if he didn't believe anything he said either.

But his magic was pure, and of a type that Judita did not recognize. It seemed to be composed of dozens of magical abilities, in large measure. If he ever learned to control it—and if she learned how to teach him to use it—he might have more magic than anyone here.

She had been reluctant to ask him to come, and he had seemed reluctant to join. She hadn't asked why he was reluctant, but she knew why she had been.

Magic as powerful as his, magic that she found unpredictable, might mingle poorly with all of the magic streams she had seen on that street in the financial district.

He was the only one who had had more than a single sip of Connor's concoction. In fact, it was a third gone, and there was just a bit of green riding along Coulter's upper lip.

At the moment, though, he was hunched in his chair, looking at Judita through his badly cut hair. His fingers toyed with the necklace he always wore. It was a chain with a decorative tiny sword at the end. The sword was of a type that Judita had never seen before.

Coulter always wore the necklace, but Judita had never seen him toy with it before.

Everyone seemed to be waiting for Judita to answer Kammie's question.

"Are we going to get in trouble for this?" Judita asked. "I have no idea. As I told you when I recruited you this morning, this is dangerous work. Things could go wildly awry."

Like they had that morning. She hadn't told them all of what happened. She had said that a Fey creature had died, but she hadn't really said how. She had told them how Kirilli had died, but she hadn't told them Augustus Kirilli's name.

She had told them that their focus would be to trace the unfamiliar magic to its root. She also wanted them to clean that magic out of the street.

"This is the time to quit if you're going to," she said.

She had given them all that option before. Savali didn't move and neither did Trinity. They seemed unnaturally calm.

Coulter's long fingers played with the mug in front of him.

Kammie glanced at all of them, as if hoping they would back out.

"If one of us quits, you won't have enough for a circle," she observed, her voice shaking.

"I'll have to recruit one more," Judita said. And she wasn't sure who.

"How's the magic looking?" Melba asked.

Judita had a hunch that, although the question was directed at her, the information it elicited was meant for Kammie. Melba wanted her to know that time was important here.

Judita wouldn't have lied, though, to save her circle. She told the truth, which ironically was the answer Melba sought.

"It's fading," Judita said. "Just like I thought. If we wait until we're joined by the woman I had hoped would join us, we might run out of daylight. If we wait until tomorrow to hold the circle, we might not get information from the streams."

Still, she didn't beg them to stay. She was asking them all to take a risk, one that could—if the morning was any indication—cost them their lives.

Trinity slid her foot off the center of the table, making it wobble. The concoction in Savali's mug sloshed over the edge and bubbled on the table's surface.

Judita couldn't believe anyone would put that liquid in their body.

"We can sit here all day and debate whether or not we're going to do the circle," Trinity said, "or we can do the circle. Circles always come with risks."

"Do you know anything about the Fey, girl?" Kammie asked with a waspishness that Judita had rarely heard from her.

"Just the stuff I learned in school," Trinity said. "I'm not scared."

"You're too young to be scared," Savali said. "Anyone with a healthy understanding of the Fey would be terrified."

"Great," Melba said. "That's all we need. A circle of terrified people, bungling their magic."

"You're being dramatic," Trinity said, both feet on the ground, hands on her thighs. She was about to stand up.

"No," Judita said quietly. "She's not being dramatic."

Trinity looked at her, her already upswept eyebrows going up farther.

"I can't reiterate enough how dangerous this is," Judita said.

"I get it," Trinity said. "You had a difficult morning. But either we're going to do this or we aren't."

She had a fair point. Maybe Judita was trying to put everything off by talking about it. Maybe Judita was the weak link in this chain, and she hadn't realized it until now.

"All right," Judita said, resisting the urge to offer them yet another chance to back out.

Clearly *she* wanted to back out. But she didn't think any of them had that luxury. The Fey were here, in Trinovante. If no one did anything, then they would accomplish whatever mission they had.

Given her knowledge of the Fey, that mission could only be one of world dominion.

"If you believe it is the Fey," Kammie said, softly, as if she was speaking to Judita without the others around, "then you should tell the authorities."

Yes, she should. She should shout it from every street corner and rooftop. But she would be met with the kind of skepticism she was being met with right now.

She would let Cilka handle the authorities—at least for today—and once Judita had information on the Fey, such as where they were and maybe how many of them there were, then she would go to someone in charge.

Probably someone with a higher rank than Cilka. Someone with real power.

"The authorities already know," Judita said. "They're choosing to do nothing, at least right now. We can't wait for them."

That caught the attention of the entire group. All of them—including Coulter—raised their heads and stared at her.

"So," Judita said. "We're going to hold a circle. We're going to separate out streams of magic. If one looks truly out of place, we will follow it to its logical end."

"We might come face to face with them, then," Melba said.

"We might," Judita said.

"Then what?" Kammie asked.

Judita squared her shoulders. "Then we kill them," she said.

FORTY-THREE

They took Gussie to the lowest level of the constabulary, through back doors that Gussie would never have guessed existed if she had walked the corridors on her own. The doors were almost hidden in the wall and it took special keys to open them.

The chief hadn't come with her, but it seemed like half the constabulary had. She was surrounded by guards. They did not wear the same uniforms as the constabulary on the streets. These uniforms were black with gold piping, and a name sewn into the left breast. There were symbols along the sleeves that she did not understand.

Each guard carried a pistol and shackles, as well as other items she did not recognize. She assumed from the fact that these items were attached to the same belt as the shackles that the items were either weapons or more things that would subdue a prisoner.

Strangely, she was not nervous. She probably would have been on any day prior to this one. But right now, she felt numb.

Lupei walked beside her. This close, it was clear that Lupei had had a difficult day. She smelled of sweat and the faintly iron odor of drying blood. The spatter on her face had turned black, and she hadn't removed it. It looked like someone had taken the time to dot her skin with mud.

Her mouth was grim, her eyes carried no emotion at all, but Gussie got a sense of pure hatred from her.

Lupei had moved into some kind of battle mode.

They marched down a series of hallways, each more secluded than the last. Then they entered an area made of thick brick. The only light came from lightstone fixtures.

The air was ice-cold down here, probably because there were no fireplaces. The walls were slightly moist, either from the perpetual fog of the last several days or because there was some kind of leak somewhere in the building.

The walk took longer than Gussie expected, and no one spoke.

Finally, the first row of guards stopped as the lead guard— the one who had been opening all the doors—took out a large key, and stuck it into a wall that didn't look like a door at all.

When he did so, the entire wall pushed open. Faint light trickled out.

The guards fanned to one side, making a row against the interior walls. Two guards stayed outside. Two shorter guards remained in front of Gussie and Lupei.

The two guards led Gussie and Lupei inside.

Ahead of Gussie was an entire row of bars, separated by

maybe an inch from each other, maybe less. Behind those bars was a long bench, made of stone and jutting out from the wall.

The bench looked supremely uncomfortable, which Gussie assumed was the point.

It took a moment for Gussie's eyes to adjust to the dimness. Then she saw a woman's form in the darkest corner of the cell. The woman had her feet on the bench, her arms wrapped around her knees.

She had lifted her head to see what the disturbance was, but Gussie couldn't make out her features.

"I bring you a Kirilli," Lupei said, as if she was bringing the woman a treat.

A shiver ran through Gussie. She knew that Lupei was being deliberately provocative, but that statement made this moment feel all the more personal.

The woman in the back stood up. She was as tall as Gussie, but very muscular. Her face was narrow, her chin pointed, her eyes dark black. Her hair was black as well, and cut short. Her clothing was stained.

She scratched her palm, then flinched as she stepped into the light. Both movements seemed to be involuntary. The light seemed to make her skin sallow.

"A Kirilli?" the woman said. "You mean we missed one?"

Gussie drew in her breath. Had they gotten to the rest of her family? Already? Was she the only one left alive?

"She's trying to get a rise out of you," Lupei said quietly to Gussie.

"Is it working?" the woman asked.

Gussie stepped forward, nearly elbowing the guards aside.

But they held fast in front of her. If the woman tried anything magical, maybe the magic would hit them first.

"What do you want with us?" Gussie asked.

"It's simple," the woman said. "We are destroying your magic."

"Then the joke's on you," Gussie said. "We have no magic."

"Yet we destroyed piles of it on your property," the woman said. "The windows, the doors, the magical artifacts. You have so much magic that you drip with it. You and that person next to you."

She waved a hand at Lupei.

Gussie let out a small breath. Magic? Her family? They had tools for fighting magic. That was what her grandfather had said.

But she had seen her father hours after his death—or at least the death that Lupei reported.

"Why do the Fey want to get rid of the Kirilli magic?" Lupei asked into Gussie's silence.

"We don't." The woman moved her mouth. It wasn't so much a smile as a baring of the teeth. "We want to destroy all the magic on Dorovich before we invade."

Gussie gave Lupei a sideways glance. But Lupei did not look at her.

"Then you'll have a lot of work ahead of you," Lupei said. "Especially since you seem so reluctant to use your magic."

"I didn't need magic to kill every person in that ridiculous house of yours." The woman said that to Gussie.

Gussie made a sound in the back of her throat and launched herself forward. The guards caught her and held her back.

"Oh, let her come," the woman said. "I haven't killed anyone with my hands for nearly a full day now. I miss it."

Gussie struggled against the guards. Lupei put a hand on her back.

"We're leaving now," Lupei said.

The words were meant to calm, but Gussie didn't want to be calm. She wanted to take on this woman herself.

"Come on," Lupei said. "You don't want to kill her. Believe me."

"Feeling guilt?" the woman asked Lupei.

Lupei's expression changed enough so that Gussie understood Lupei was feeling something unpleasant about the deaths that day. But that expression was fleeting.

"Try anything untoward and I would have no qualms about adding you to my list," Lupei said.

Gussie took a step back and made herself calm down. This Fey woman just confessed to killing her father's staff. People she had known forever. One person couldn't have done that.

So Lupei was right. The woman was just trying to provoke.

But she looked different now. Her skin had mottled where the light touched.

"Do you see?" Gussie asked Lupei. "The light is destroying her skin."

Lupei looked back at the lightstone lamp, dim near the door. Then she followed the light.

"Makes sense," she muttered.

"Why?" Gussie asked.

Lupei shook her head. As she did so, the woman melted back into the dark part of her cell.

"If you turn up the light, she might die," Gussie said. The words sounded bloodthirsty. But she was feeling bloodthirsty.

"Yes," Lupei said. "And as satisfying as that would be, we can't have it. We need to know what she knows."

"Even if it's all a lie?" Gussie asked.

"Even then," Lupei said. "There's truth hidden in lies."

The woman hidden in the dark corner of her cell laughed. "There are millions of us. You'll never be able to stop us."

Lupei gave her a dismissive look.

"It looks like we already have," she said.

Then she led Gussie out of the room and turned to the guards.

"Shut off the light in the cell," Lupei said. "Let her stew in the darkness."

"Yes, ma'am," he said, and reached in to do her bidding.

"Why did you do that?" Gussie asked as they hurried down the hall.

"Because," Lupei said, "we need her alive."

"To talk to us," Gussie said.

"And to show us where these Fey are vulnerable," Lupei said. "Because they clearly are."

FORTY-FOUR

A wind had come up as they walked into the street on the financial district. Judita had to hold her cape in place with both hands. The wind had a chill, but it blew off the rest of the fog.

The air was no longer stagnant. Judita had no idea how the wind might influence the magic streams. The change in weather was sudden, but it didn't feel unusual like that fog had the past day or so.

Trinity walked beside her, as if she couldn't wait to get to the site of Kirilli's murder. It took a bit of work for Trinity to match her long stride with Judita's, but Trinity managed.

Melba walked slightly behind them, side by side with Savali. They didn't speak. No one did, not even Kammie who walked slower and slower the closer they all got to the death site.

Coulter brought up the rear. For once, he wasn't walking with his head down. He stood straighter than he usually did, his expression so focused that Judita wasn't sure he was seeing anything in front of him.

She was doing her best not to look at the magical streams. She wanted to set up before she got lost in the magic and the work ahead of all of them.

The sun was brighter now, even though it was lower on the horizon. It might get dark in this part of the city sooner than she expected. She hadn't really noticed how tall the financial district buildings were. They would create a mountain-like wall that would probably blot out the light ahead of normal sunset.

She tried not to let that thought urge her forward.

She reached the spot where Kirilli's body had lain off and on in the past day. The puddle was still there, but the pile of horse dung had been scattered by people working with Cilka. They apparently had been incautious in their work, which somehow annoyed Judita more than it should have.

With one small flick of her eyes, she looked at the spot a few yards away where she had taken that Fey creature's life. There was spatter on the ground, probably blood, but it might have come from the vicious beating that Cilka had given the creature.

Judita stopped by the puddle. The stench of horse dung wasn't as sharp as it had been in the morning, but it still hung over the area like a faint miasma. It was mixed with a slightly rotted smell, which, for all she knew, came off of whatever fluids Kirilli's body had seeped into the puddle.

Given the rising wind, it was amazing there were any smells at all.

"We'll set up here," Judita said.

"No."

The voice was strong and unfamiliar. It took a moment for Judita to realize she was hearing Coulter.

He was standing a yard or so away from the spatter, looking at the very spot where the portal had appeared in the fog.

"The circle should be right here." His voice was firm.

Kammie gave Judita a glance, as if Kammie expected Judita to contradict Coulter, or to at least remind him who was in charge. Trinity looked at her as well.

Savali squinted. He was, apparently, looking at the magical streams. Melba had a similar expression on her face. But she didn't like what she saw.

Her arms were crossed, and she was looking at the same spot Coulter was.

Judita glanced around the street to make sure the six of them were alone. The buildings were still dark, and she didn't see any watchmen near the street corners.

She knew that watchmen should have been patrolling the area just to keep people away. But she hadn't seen any law enforcement the first time she was here, and she wasn't seeing any now.

She took a deep breath, narrowed her eyes, and looked into the magic.

The streams flowed around the five others. The streams were layers deep, but fading even more than they had before.

Coulter stood only a foot or so from the gigantic red splotch where the creature had died. The splotch didn't seem to attract Coulter's attention at all.

Melba was standing as far from the splotch as she could and still be able to see what Coulter was looking at.

Judita couldn't see much. The streams were thick everywhere, but the black, brown, yellow, and gray streams were nearly gone.

"What are you seeing?" she asked Coulter.

"The hole in the air," he said. "Can't you see it?"

He wisely did not move his hand toward it. Melba nodded once. She clearly saw it.

"I'm not seeing anything unusual except that bloody spot in the air," Kammie said.

"I see that too," Trinity said. "And the body's outline on the street."

Since she said *on the street*, Judita assumed Trinity meant Kirilli's body. But Judita didn't ask.

"I don't see anything else, though," Trinity said.

"If some of us can't see the streams and we make a circle," Kammie asked, "are we making a mistake?"

Sometimes Kammie's caution was annoying, but here, it was right on. Extremely important.

Judita frowned. This morning, she hadn't considered the different types of magic mixing and mingling here. In fact, she had come to the scene at Cilka's request and hadn't even looked at the magic streams, figuring they were the kind she had always understood.

Judita had felt the streams, had known there was magic, and then used a spell of her own devising so that they could see the scene. It was the mixing of that spell with the magic here that— she thought—had opened the door to all the problems they'd had since.

Melba turned toward her. Coulter blinked, and his gaze met Judita's for the first time in the last several minutes. Savali took one step back, as if he felt too close to the magic. And Trinity wrapped an arm around herself, as if she had suddenly gotten nervous.

"The fact that we all see something different bothers me greatly," Judita said. "Coulter comes from a wildly different magical background. Savali's background is different as well, just not as different as Coulter's. Savali hasn't told us what he sees yet."

"I see the hole in the air," Savali said, then glanced at Coulter.

"I don't see any hole," Trinity said, sounding like a student who had just realized she wasn't the smartest kid in the class.

"I don't either," Judita said, "but I know what was there. That's where the portal was, where the Fey reached through and dragged the Fey creature's body away. What exactly are you seeing?"

She directed that last question at Coulter, not Savali.

Coulter straightened, then looked carefully at the spot where the portal had appeared. He didn't turn back toward her as he said, "It's a hole in the air. It looks like a round doorway, with the door closed. The door is black, and the exterior of the doorway a fading grayish brown."

"Yellowish brown," Savali said, as if correcting him.

"*Grayish* brown," Coulter said.

"You don't see any yellow?" Savali asked.

"No," Coulter said in that same forceful, curt voice he had used earlier. It was a powerful voice, one that brooked no disagreement.

He didn't even seem to understand that he was speaking differently.

"Well, I do," Savali said.

"What does this mean?" Trinity asked Judita. Apparently, Trinity was going to default into *student* mode, and right now, the student needed some insight.

Judita shook her head. "I'd be guessing."

"Guessing is all we have," Melba said. "And for the record, I see the hole, but the middle isn't black. It's not there at all, like the surface of a mirror that reflects nothing. I also see yellow around the edges. The yellow bleeds into a fog that I can't see if I look away from the magical streams."

"It's got to mean something," Trinity said.

Judita had never seen this side of her. Trinity had a strong need to have a concrete answer. Finally, Judita had found a problem with Trinity's powerful magic, but that problem was coming too late to resolve it.

"It means if we use magic here, we might create something we've never seen before." Now Kammie was speaking forcefully. She gave Judita a sour look, as if Judita should have said something about this. "Just like Judita did this morning."

"If we don't build the circle," Melba said, "we will not know where these Fey are."

"Maybe we don't build a circle," Savali said. "Maybe we let someone who can see the door try to go through it."

"And then what?" Kammie asked. "The rest of us have to rescue that person, and we won't even be able to see what's before us."

"No." Coulter, again, forcefully. "We follow the magic. It links us to each other, does it not?"

Magic did bind. Judita knew that as a basic principle. But figuring out where the bindings began and ended was a difficult if not impossible task.

"Where did you learn that?" Melba asked. The question wasn't challenging. It was a request for information.

"My parents," Coulter said. "They didn't use the word magic, but they taught me about what they called ties between us. They're strongest in family members, but once you know how to look for the ties, you find them everywhere. They're thick and thin, easy to see if you know what you're looking for, and difficult to access, unless someone opens a door."

"Do you think this is one of those doors?" Judita asked.

"You said it was," Trinity said, as if the question had been posed to her.

"It clearly is," Coulter said. "I can try opening it—"

Judita grabbed his arm. "We're not ready."

He looked over his shoulder at her, then looked at her hand on his forearm. He clearly wanted her to move away, but she wasn't going to.

"We'll never be 'ready,'" he said. "We—"

"I mean," she said as firmly as she could. "*We're* not ready. Us. The six of us. We need to figure out how we're going through that door."

"How can we go through?" Kammie asked. "I can't even see it."

"You don't have to," Savali said. "We can form a circle and pool our magic, as long as we have something to funnel it through."

"Funnel...?" Melba asked.

Judita frowned at Savali. She hadn't taught him that. She hadn't taught any of her students about the ways that artifacts worked.

"Magic," Savali said, "finds a path. Each culture imbues the things they value with some kind of mystical significance. If that culture has magic, then those items can become either magical by themselves or a venue for magic."

Judita shuddered. She had read about this. She had studied it somewhat in her scientific magic classes, but she had never used item-based magic, thinking it was lazy.

"I don't think any of us go around carrying magical items," she said, trying to keep her voice level. She wasn't sure how she felt about the items. His point was good, but it didn't take into account the entire history of Trinovante.

Hundreds of people were arrested during the Purges because they carried artifacts that could be used for magic. Even some of the collectibles that had been so in vogue decades before were considered contraband now.

Only the Old Families had collections of those artifacts. The Old Families, museums, and academies.

To access the items in a museum, you needed special clearance. And only a handful of people were allowed near the collections in the academies. Judita had never applied for the special clearance. She had once taken a tour of the artifacts wing of the library at Serebro Academy, but each student had to remain on a set path as they went through the rooms.

"Do you have a magical item?" Trinity asked Savali.

He smiled at her, then his gaze shifted to Judita.

"I was warned not to bring anything into public here," he said to Trinity, even though he was reminding Judita of her warnings.

She hadn't thought to bring magical tokens to this circle. She had just wanted to see the magic.

"I have something," Coulter said softly, tentatively, as if he didn't really want to admit it.

All five of the others looked directly at him.

His fingers played with that small sword around his neck. Then he grasped the chain that held the little sword and raised it up, letting it dangle.

"My parents gave me this," he said. "My mother made me promise to wear it always. It's the symbol of the main religion on Blue Isle."

"You're religious?" Judita asked. She had never met anyone who practiced religion. Religion was for the superstitious and the stupid, not for someone with a mind like Coulter's.

He shook his head ever so slightly. "My mother said that some of the teachings in that religion claim that certain items have incredible power. She said that this sword, used in conjunction with the right magic, can focus that magic and turn it into a weapon."

"What's the right magic?" Trinity asked at the same moment that Kammie said, "Have you ever done this?"

Coulter looked directly at Kammie. "Have I ever used this sword as a focus of magic? Yes, once. My mother made me channel a tiny spell through it. A decade ago."

Judita frowned. This was new enough to her to make her even more uncomfortable.

"Is your mother anywhere around?" Melba asked.

Coulter shook his head again. "She gave me this just before she died."

The entire group fell silent. Judita's learning on this topic was theoretical. Coulter had done it once. Savali seemed to know about it but he was being silent.

"What *is* the right magic?" Trinity asked again, as if she hated being ignored. Which she did.

Coulter looked at her. Then he shook his head sadly. "I don't know."

"So you don't know if our magic will work with this?" Trinity asked. "We don't believe in that sword."

"I don't either," Coulter said. "I don't even know what it symbolizes, really, if anything."

"But you've done it before," Savali said.

"A long time ago," Coulter said.

Judita studied that little sword as it dangled on the chain. Coulter had worn that little sword as long as she had known him.

"The sword is tied to you," she said.

"Huh?" Coulter swiveled and looked at her.

"Magic binds," she said. "That little sword is wrapped up in you. Or you're wrapped up in it."

"Meaning what?" Kammie sounded frustrated.

"Meaning that we can use the ties to focus magic through that little sword, even if it doesn't have power," Judita said.

She used spells like that often, which was one of the reasons that Cilka had contacted her. Sometimes, touching a possession of a person enabled Judita to recreate the last hours of that person's life. Or to find that person, if the person was still alive.

Judita had offered to train Cilka in that magic, but Cilka could never master the spell.

Melba smiled at Judita for the first time since they arrived.

"You have a plan," Melba said.

"I do," Judita said. "And it just might work."

FORTY-FIVE

Sirocco's body had created a mess on the kitchen floor, and they had no time to deal with her. Atrü knew that some members of the team wanted to, particularly Gem, but he couldn't let her.

The dripping portal bothered him. Slumber's words—that this disaster was because the Qavnerians had more magic than anyone expected—terrified Atrü.

Only Atrü was the leader. He didn't dare show just how terrified he was.

"Get everything together," he said to his remaining team members. "Take as much of those artifacts as you can. But gold and jewelry first."

"Then what?" Vidso asked, looking tired and shaken. "Omriseu hasn't found us anywhere to go."

Atrü felt the words like a rebuke. "Let's hope that Omriseu is back by the time we're packed up."

"And if he's not?" Rodderc asked.

"We get out of this building," Atrü said. Although where they would go was a mystery to him. They'd lost the power of concealment with Sirocco's death.

And, since she and Qurzi had revealed themselves to the Qavnerians, they knew to watch for more Fey. The question was whether or not they would recognize Fey for what they were.

Atrü should have commanded everyone to get Qavnerian clothing and to wear it. But he hadn't. He had never figured that they would come under attack. He had known they might be seen as odd, which was why he wanted this house protected, but he hadn't thought that the oddness would be more than a bother to the others in the neighborhood.

Mentally, he cursed Rugar. Rugar had sent them here with a vague plan and without all the tools they needed.

Although if Hadley and Sirocco had lived, the team wouldn't have as many problems as they had at the moment.

Atrü shook off the thought. He needed to get the team moving. The drip-drip-drip of melting ice told him that.

The growing pool of water did nothing to revive Sirocco's desiccated body, although a small part of Atrü hoped it would.

But they were out of miracles or luck or whatever anyone wanted to call it.

Rugar had warned him.

I have sent a dozen teams to study Dorovich, he had said. *So far, none have returned. I expect your team will be the one that will tell me why the teams aren't coming back.*

Because of the magick here, Atrü almost whispered aloud. Was Rugar that foolish that he didn't understand what was clear from the histories, clear from the behaviors?

Or was he that cunning? Did he want his people to see the magick and then be able to report on it?

This team had already left the kitchen, all except Gem who hovered over Sirocco, hands fluttering.

"We can't do anything to help her now," Atrü said quietly.

"It's my fault," Gem said. "If I was better at my job—"

"It wouldn't matter," Atrü said. "You wouldn't have had time to heal her. She made her choice."

Although he wasn't certain of that. All she had been doing was exploring a portal.

He had no idea how many other outside portals were in this place. Nor did he know how the Qavnerians had found this house in the first place.

He had too many questions and not enough answers.

And he needed to get his team out of this building as soon as he could.

If only he could make a Shadowlands. If only he had the ability to contact Omriseu.

If only the Powers had given Atrü the ability to do something different.

If only...

FORTY-SIX

They stood in a circle in the growing twilight, hands clasped. Judita was standing beside Coulter. His hand was dry in hers. Kammie stood on the other side of Judita. Her palm and fingers were moist and shaking just enough to distract Judita more than she wanted to be.

Judita was looking at the magic streams around her. The dark lake of red where the Fey creature had died almost blocked the portal that Coulter had seen so clearly.

He had moved their circle closer to it. As each person moved through the magic streams, they bounced and floated and reassembled. Some of the magic flowed around each circle member, and some of the magic floated through them.

The white magic stream flowed through Savali all the way to Coulter. The white magic stream floated around Kammie and around Judita as well. That stream didn't get near Trinity or Melba. The yellow stream touched them but didn't go through them. The yellow dipped down near Judita and swirled around her feet.

All of the magic streams flowed upward into Coulter and through that little sword necklace that dangled outside of his shirt. He didn't seem to notice.

The fog was gone, though, which surprised Judita. She could see her breath, though, and the air had gotten cold as the darkness grew.

As far as she could tell, none of the magic was visible to the non-magical, but she couldn't be certain of that.

She also, for reasons she didn't entirely understand, did not want the lightstone lanterns to flare to life, not while the circle was composing its spell.

She squeezed Coulter's hand. "Ready?" she asked him.

He nodded. He was staring down at some part of the streams that swirled into his necklace. She knew the magical posture. He was marking whatever it was he was going to grab.

"All right then," she said, and slowly raised both of her hands. Kammie's hand came with her, as did all of the hands and arms around the circle. Arms turned gold then white and light formed around each circle member.

Out of the corner of her eye, Judita saw the light form around Coulter, but not touch that necklace.

His gaze met hers, and he nodded. He understood the plan. After all, it was mostly his.

He used his own magic to raise the sword and then, not letting go of Judita's hand or Melba's on his other side, he pivoted and followed a magical stream only he could see, heading into the portal that was barely visible to Judita.

She followed, almost at a run, clasping his hand tightly

because she was afraid to let go. Kammie clung to her hand just as tightly, nearly cutting off the circulation.

Coulter stepped up, as if the portal was on some kind of platform. Judita mimicked his movement at the same time as Melba.

The air inside the portal was ice cold, but so damp that it felt more like a semi-frozen lake.

Coulter's necklace sent light ahead, revealing a melting block of ice ahead of them.

Someone had tried to freeze the entrance to the portal shut.

Kammie and Trinity pushed inside, followed at the rear by Savali.

Judita had put him there because he could also see some of the portal.

They continued flowing the magic—their magic—together, and Coulter was somehow channeling it into that tiny sword. The sword sent out a pure white light that made the ice in front of the portal melt even faster.

Finally, large chunks of ice fell away, revealing a mostly dark room. Someone moved inside of it. Judita couldn't see a face, just a general shape—a person who was tall and thin and not anyone she recognized.

That person emitted a squeak of panic and ran. A door opened, revealing more light, and then it slammed shut.

A male voice yelled in a language Judita didn't recognize. But she didn't have to recognize it to understand the intent. Fear-laden words revealing the magical presence of people who did not belong.

Coulter stepped out of the portal. He let go of Melba's hand first, then Judita's, keeping them both close and wrapped in the light the circle had created.

He had said he could do that, although Judita had no idea how, and she had trusted him. She was glad she had.

She stepped out too and moved aside. There was only that door in here. No windows. A table not too far away, and hot close air that stank of blood and death.

Trinity and Kammie emerged, looking around like people who were lost. Savali walked between them, a man with a purpose.

"The magic is strong here," he said to Coulter.

Coulter nodded. "But fading."

He was right: it was fading. Fading the way that something did when nothing was left to fuel it all.

Judita glanced at the portal. The ice had completely melted and the edges were wavering. The portal would not be there much longer.

"Someone saw us," Coulter said.

"Which means they're here," Judita said.

Melba nodded. The other three stood still, waiting for instruction.

The plan was to follow the magic, even if the magic was fading. It was their only chance to find and remove these attackers.

Judita swallowed hard. She knew what her duty was, but she didn't like it. The fear that had propelled her to kill that creature that morning had lessened—well, not lessened as much as become something she was accustomed to. Already.

"Our magic is in the other room," Savali said.

"I don't sense anything," Melba said.

"Dorovician magic," he said. "Not necessarily Qavnerian."

Magic, then, from one of the unconquered countries on the continent. The magic from the other countries in Dorovich was one of the reasons the Purges had been so bad. That magic was even more dangerous than the magic that still lingered in the Protectorate.

"I don't sense it either," Coulter said. "You'll have to lead the way."

Savali didn't lead as much as indicate. He nodded toward the only exit. "There's a pile of magic off to the left. I suspect there are artifacts."

The group hadn't decided whether or not they would retrieve the artifacts or destroy them. And now they actually needed a decision.

It would be up to Judita. It always was.

She glanced at the others, and hoped she could trust them to get through the day.

"I'll go first," she said, and walked through the door.

FORTY-SEVEN

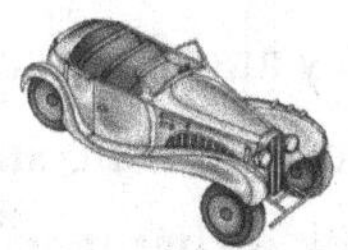

Gem burst out of the hidden room, the room that Atrü had loved so much about this house. She ran into the main room, her hair flying all around her face, her eyes large.

"There are people in there!" she yelled.

Rodderc grabbed her and moved her out of the way. Atrü cursed. He had hoped they would have more time. But Sirocco's death had destroyed most of the ice already, and that meant the portals were opening up.

"We need to retreat," he said to his five Infantry. They would get everyone out of the house—although at the moment, "everyone" only meant himself, Gem, and Slumber.

Rodderc acted like he hadn't heard a word.

"How many people?" he asked Gem.

She shook her head, clearly panicked. Xevkin put a slender hand on Gem's shoulders.

"Just breathe," Xevkin said as if they had all the time in the world. "And think."

"Six!" she said. "I saw six. And they were wrapped in light."

"That could have come from the portal itself," Rodderc said —not to Atrü or Slumber or even Gem. But to his team. "We can handle six Trinovantians. They have no idea how to fight anyone."

"They've killed Hadley and Sirocco," Gem said.

"Luck," Rodderc said. Then he smiled. His smile was feral. "The nice thing about luck is that it eventually runs out."

He stood in front of the narrow hallway that Gem had scurried out of. "This is easy to defend. It's a killing box. Once they leave the room, we have them."

He turned to his team. They were all smiling.

The Infantry didn't like killing as much as the Foot Soldiers did, but it was a fairly close contest.

"You," Rodderc said to Atrü as if Rodderc was the leader and not Atrü. "Clean up these items and go outside."

Atrü nodded, feeling slightly relieved that he didn't have to give the orders in a battle situation.

"You two," Rodderc was saying to Slumber and Gem, "you will help him. You all need to leave here as fast as possible."

Gem inhaled shakily. Slumber pushed against the wall. Neither of them would be very useful in gathering items.

"Remember," Atrü said. "Coins and jewelry. Then everything else."

As he moved toward the table and all of the boxes that Gem had found, the Infantry lined up in front of the door. They all held knives in one hand, their bodies crouched in the exact same position.

It was clear that the moment they saw anyone, they would launch themselves forward.

Rodderc was right; no inexperienced fighters could survive that.

Atrü let out a small sigh. As long as no one came in the other three portals, the group would get out of this alive.

And at the moment, he couldn't ask for anything else.

FORTY-EIGHT

A wall of people faced Judita. All of them had wide shoulders and muscular torsos. All of them were tall. All of them had narrow faces and slightly pointed ears.

And all of them looked furious.

She had no idea how to get past them. She wished that Coulter and the magic-absorbing necklace was in front of her. She raised a hand—

Only to see Savali lift a hand behind her as if he was trying to hold up the sky. Someone cried out in surprise behind that row of people, and a bowl, enshrouded in light, rose high in the air. The bowl was shallow with dozens of little feet.

She had never seen anything like it. It looked like it was made of wood.

One of the men in front of her cried out—some kind of undulating war cry that made the hair on the back of her neck rise.

As he did, Savali slapped his hands together over the top of his head. Bright white light shot from his hands and headed for that bowl, over the heads of all of the people before him.

Those people were so well trained, they didn't even look. Instead, they lunged forward.

"We need protection!" Judita yelled, hoping that someone in their circle knew how to create a shield.

Light rose in front of all of them—a solid wall of light that ran from the ceiling to the floor.

As it did, the white light from Savali's hands collided with that bowl. It exploded and flaming shards flew downward.

"We need to leave," Savali said, but even before he finished the sentence, light and flames rose from the side of the next room.

Someone screamed, and Judita saw a body running across the room—a body in flames. Then the entire room was engulfed in flames, followed by more explosions and blue light and red light and yellow magic streams being consumed by all of those flames and all of that light.

"How do we get out of here?" Trinity asked.

"Follow me," Kammie said. She dove through the door they had just left. The entire interior room was in flame, but that portal still existed barely, mostly because its edges were still damp with ice.

Kammie dove through it, followed by Trinity and Melba.

"You go!" Coulter yelled to Judita.

She shook her head and shoved him. He was valuable and so, clearly, was Savali.

More explosions sounded and the flames grew even higher. Judita's chest hurt.

There was no air.

Coulter grabbed her and pulled her into the portal. As he did, she grabbed Savali and yanked him along with them, wrapping what was left of her magic around him.

They all fell into the portal and out the other side, onto the filthy, blood-stained street of the financial district, along with plumes of smoke and licks of flame.

Judita had the remaining air knocked out of her. Savali landed on top of her, jamming her hip into the street. Behind her someone was coughing.

"I can't close the portal," Coulter yelled.

"I can," Judita said, or tried to say. She had to clear her throat, try to get air into her aching chest, and she said again. "I can."

Savali rolled off her and then helped her up.

It was mostly dark except for the flames trying to escape through that portal. They lit the street like a fireplace in a dark room.

She half-closed her eyes, saw the streams, saw the edges of the portal, and grabbed them, pinching them closed.

Melba saw what she was doing and joined in. So did Trinity. Together, all three of them managed to seal the portal shut.

Judita took a step backwards, still gasping. The air stank of smoke and flame—or maybe she did.

"What was that?" she managed to ask Savali.

He looked at her, eyes wide with wonder.

"A legend come to life," he said. "I never would have believed it if I hadn't tried it."

"The bowl?" Coulter asked.

Savali nodded. "It was supposed to have great power, and if the power was released—well, you saw."

"You mean that was an *experiment*?" Kammie asked as if she was offended.

"It worked," Judita said. "I don't think anyone could have survived that."

"We have no idea what kind of magic they have," Coulter said. "We don't know if they survived or not."

"They didn't." Trinity's voice was soft. "People with magic don't let themselves burn alive. Too much pain."

She was right. They were all right. And they had done what Judita had asked.

They had found the Fey—and killed them.

"How do we know that we got them all?" Coulter asked her.

"We don't," Melba said, looking in the direction of that portal.

"But they'll think twice about attacking us again," Judita said. She wiped her hands on her robe. She was filthy and stank of burned wood and maybe more. "It'll give us time."

"Time for what?" Savali asked.

She looked at him. His words had been the key.

"Time to figure out all of these myths and legends and artifacts. All the knowledge we tried to destroy in the Purges." Knowledge that only she and a handful of others had tried to save. "We have to figure out what it does and how it works, and then we have to deploy it."

"Deploy...?" Trinity asked.

Judita nodded. "We will deploy it. Against the Fey."

CHAPTER

FORTY-NINE

Omriseu heard the explosions three blocks away. He felt the magickal concussion as it rode through the air with the smoke and the sparks.

Omriseu started to run toward the spiraling smoke even before he realized he was running. People came out of their houses. A few carriages stopped along the side of the nearby road.

Everyone seemed shocked at something like this, happening in Trinovante.

The handful of people who stood outside their doors watched Omriseu run by, so he kept his businessman's face and clothing, knowing that his only chance now was to maintain the fiction that he belonged in Trinovante.

He arrived on the block in time to see the house he had rented weeks ago crater. It literally fell in on itself.

There was no fog. There was no protection at all. Not even the vast yard around it made it seem safe.

511

The stench in the air was familiar now. Burning flesh, burning bodies. Like a crematorium without the proper chimney.

He was shaking. He ran to the edge of the street, and looked at the house. Magick sparked off it, more magick than he had ever seen. Explosions continued, and so did multicolored light, rising out of the center of the mess.

It took him a moment to remember the layout.

The center, where the table with the artifacts had been.

They were exploding, giving off magick. Magick that the Infantry and Gem and Atrü couldn't fight. Not even Slumber could fight it. Or Qurzi.

They were gone.

They were all gone.

Omriseu could only hope that they had killed their attackers before their attackers killed them.

He stood at the edge of the street, shaking. Then he touched his pocket. He still had some gold. Not nearly as much. He had just paid for a rental house, one he would not be able to use.

The broker, Yanni Komidas, would remember that Omriseu had rented this house, and Komidas would tell the constables. The constables would go to the new rental house, if Omriseu was in it, even for a moment. They would take him away, and he wouldn't be able to maintain his disguise for days or weeks at a time.

At some point, someone would figure out what he was.

His shoulders slumped. His lungs burned. The smoke was awful.

One of the neighbors approached him—a woman he had seen before. She was slight and too thin. She stood beside him.

She opened her mouth as if she was going to ask him a question. But he couldn't handle questions right now. He couldn't pretend to be someone else.

"I need to see if anyone is still alive," he said and walked across the lawn toward the crumbling house.

"In that?" she asked as he moved away from her.

She was right; no one would be there. But he had to see or it would haunt him.

He reached the edge, the back where they had buried Hadley. The mound of dirt remained, and on top of it, tiny flowering plants.

Gem. Gem must have done that.

His breath caught. His eyes burned. He turned away.

The building was mostly ashes, except for a table that still stood with items on top that were covered in gray dust, but hadn't entirely been destroyed.

If he had been part of a larger team, if he knew he had comrades here, he would have braved that disaster and grabbed some of the things off that table.

But he didn't dare.

His mission now was to get out of the Qavnerian Protectorate. He needed to leave Dorovich, maybe cross into Leut before he caught a ship heading back to Nye.

He needed to talk directly to Rugar, maybe even to the Black King.

Omriseu needed to tell them both that Dorovich had too much magick. If they were going to attack it, they needed a full-scale invasion force.

Before they did that, they needed an entire cadre of Spies. The Black Family needed to learn what this place was, because the information they had was either wrong or terribly out of date.

"It's all I can do," Omriseu said quietly to his team.

It had only been luck that had kept him away from here. Luck that would allow him to report back to his people.

He had to augment that luck. He had to make sensible choices. He had to get back to Nye.

No matter what it would take.

PART SIX
THE DELIVERY

TWO DAYS BEFORE

CHAPTER
FIFTY

ugustus Kirilli sat in his office, staring at the numbers on an account he hadn't wanted to take. The numbers floated off the page, around him, and tried to organize themselves. But they didn't make sense.

He hated that. It always happened when someone was trying to fudge information. Either he would have to confront the client or the client's previous accounting firm.

Then he would have to try to explain why he didn't believe the numbers even if they had been designed to seem perfectly logical.

He leaned back in his chair and stretched. His spine cracked. His eyes ached. It had been a long morning.

The fog outside was thick and yellow. The puke yellow was a new feature, one he found particularly ominous. There was magic in the fog, but he didn't know who to tell about it. Or why the magic existed.

His office was plain, unlike his home. He didn't keep any

family items here, nothing that made the place personal at all. He kept the ancient desk that someone had moved into the office decades ago. It was solid and heavy, but not made of iron-wood or anything truly sturdy.

Nor was his chair, the third one he'd had this year. He tended to ruin them by leaning back too far so that his spine could crack. His office had a window that overlooked the financial district, but he kept the shutters closed—something he had done even before the foul-smelling fog.

It didn't seem to keep the fog out, but it did filter the smell just a bit. He would be glad when this weird weather ended. The gray sunless days and the even darker nights depressed him.

At least he had breakfast with his daughter two mornings from now. It was a working breakfast; he needed to talk with her about family matters.

She kept putting him off, and he felt that these things shouldn't be put off any longer. Part of him felt like it was already too late, and he didn't know why. But he had learned to respect those feelings.

It would be a hard discussion, but an enjoyable one. A man wasn't supposed to have a favorite child, but he did. Gussie was smarter than all the others, more talented, and had more backbone than the rest of them combined.

He smiled at the thought of her. Then he stood just as someone knocked on his office door.

He started. No one knocked on his door. Someone had to go through five layers of office workers just to get to him, and usually the staff warned him ahead of time...unless it was one of his children.

Still, he wasn't going to trust that the knock had come from one of his children. Kirilli remained behind the desk, his hand near a drawer. He kept a few items in the drawer that would have appalled his father, but Kirilli had learned that Trinovante could be a dangerous place, particularly for a man with just enough magic that others noticed.

"Come," he said.

The man who walked through the door was not related to Kirilli. The man was tall and thin, with reddish-blond hair and brown eyes so dark that they seemed like holes in his face.

Or maybe that was caused by the deep shadows under his eyes. His cheekbones were heavy, which also made his eyes recede, and he had a prominent nose, which reminded Kirilli of someone else's, but he couldn't recall whose.

The man carried two battered satchels that were overflowing with materials. The satchels looked like they were about to burst.

"Forgive the intrusion," the man said. "We've never met, but my grandmother spoke highly of you."

The edges of the satchels glowed. Kirilli thought he saw some undulating colors inside, which suggested a powerful magic at work.

His stomach muscles tightened and he had to force himself to breathe normally.

"I'm Josiah Hopkins the Third," the man said. "You knew my grandmother."

"Rosita," Kirilli said. He had known her a bit too well. They had met when he was twenty and new to the Board of Regents. She promised to show him the way that the Regents worked, and she showed him a number of other things as well.

He hoped the flush he felt building in his cheeks wasn't showing.

"Yes." The man seemed preoccupied. As Kirilli stared at him, he realized that the recognizable nose came from the Hopkins side. Every Josiah Hopkins he had known had had that nose. "Do you mind if I close the door?"

Kirilli did mind, but he had a feeling no one in the office should hear this conversation.

"Go ahead," he said.

Hopkins set the satchels down as if they had been weighing on him. Then he closed the door, making sure it was latched.

"I'm sorry to come here unannounced," he said, "but I don't have a lot of time."

Kirilli rested his hands on the desk and waited.

"My grandmother told me that if I needed assistance, I should come to you." Hopkins threaded his fingers together.

"That had to be some time ago," Kirilli said.

Hopkins smiled thinly. "She didn't think highly of my father. She was waiting for the day that I reached my majority so that she could pass him over. Unfortunately, she died before that happened."

Kirilli remembered Rosita's death. It had been unexpected. He'd had to sit in the back at the memorial service because he didn't want anyone to know how emotional he was. It seemed every single member of the Old Families had come to pay tribute to Rosita, who had married into the Hopkins clan.

Because she wasn't from an Old Family, half of the Hopkins (who were the oldest of the old) looked down on her. But she was vibrant and lively and brought a certain magic to everything she did—and not just metaphorically.

Kirilli realized now that Hopkins's eyes had come from her, as did his light brown skin.

"And now your father has passed," Kirilli said, keeping his voice neutral.

"Yes." Hopkins shifted slightly. "The constabulary in Mazurkita is investigating. He hadn't been ill, so I called them. They think I'm overreacting."

"Are you?" Kirilli kept his voice neutral.

"No," Hopkins said. "Some people from the Board of Regents came to him and told him that he needed to donate the Hopkins artifacts to Serebro Academy, specifically the Regents' Tower."

Kirilli leaned back ever so slightly. It was a trick he'd learned long ago to hide shock. He'd heard that other Old Families had donated a few things or offered to give up their seats because no family member was interested.

That was one of the things he had to talk with Gussie about. It was essential that a Kirilli remain on the board.

Hopkins waved his hands at the satchels.

"These are the family artifacts that my grandmother told me to put somewhere safe. My father asked me about them just before he died. He was always short of money, you see, and those people were offering to pay him."

Kirilli let out a small breath. "He didn't know where you put them?"

"No." Hopkins's voice was pained. "Our last conversation was...heated."

"You didn't tell him, then?"

"I wasn't going to let him sell the family heritage for money," Hopkins said.

"But you've brought the heritage to me," Kirilli said.

Hopkins cleared his throat, then looked around the room. When he seemed to feel satisfied that they were alone, he took a step closer.

"For safekeeping," Hopkins said. "Already, someone broke into my father's manor and destroyed every artifact he had there. I think someone has been following me. I shook them off today, but I can't guarantee that I'll be able to do so tomorrow."

Kirilli had heard that the Old Families were suffering break-ins. He hadn't realized that artifacts were being destroyed instead of stolen.

"My grandmother said you have a place to keep...um... forgive me if I'm overstepping, but..." Hopkins looked pained. He stepped even closer. "Magical items. She said you have magical items."

If this was some kind of trick being played by law enforcement, then they already had a great deal of information. Everyone believed the magic that the Hopkins family was protecting came mostly through the male line. It did not. The strong magic—and the most valuable artifacts—had belonged to Rosita.

Kirilli didn't acknowledge anything that Hopkins said so far.

"She said—" and Hopkins was sounding even more nervous than he had before "—that you have a place to keep them where they will be safe."

The Vault. Kirilli had told her about the Vault just once, and had regretted it for the rest of his life. He had learned, as a boy of twenty, that torture probably wouldn't pry secrets from him, but good sex would. Maybe even love.

He had guarded against revealing secrets ever since. His wife hadn't even known. And he had only told Gussie after one of his very first health crises.

He hadn't even begun to explain the items in the Vault to her. Another oversight, one he needed to correct.

"Please, sir," Hopkins said, clearly misunderstanding Kirilli's silence for disapproval. "I have nowhere safe to keep these. I'm afraid that's what these people are after."

"The Board of Regents doesn't kill people," Kirilli said.

Hopkins pursed his lips together as if he wanted to contradict Kirilli, but felt he couldn't.

Then Hopkins shook his head ever so slightly.

"I know it's hard to believe, sir, but they're lying already. They told my father that everyone in the family already disavowed the seat and that there would have to be an election after he died. They told him it would be better to give up the artifacts now."

Kirilli felt chilled. He'd heard at a previous board meeting that the younger generation was not showing any interest in the board. Had that been a lie?

"I need to put these somewhere safe, sir," Hopkins said. "If you don't have this secret place my grandmother mentioned, maybe you know of a safe place? If so, please help me."

Hopkins seemed desperate, and much younger than Kirilli had initially thought. Much younger.

"She would have told you something so that I could trust you," Kirilli said.

Hopkins blinked, as if he didn't know anything.

Kirilli felt his heart sink. He had almost been taken in by all of this.

Then Hopkins frowned. "She said..." He looked up, as if his

memory confused him. "She said something about the old closed-off stairwell to the clock tower at Serebro Academy."

Kirilli barked out a laugh. He hadn't thought of that moment in his life in a decade or more. Leave it to Rosita.

She had found a forgotten entrance to the stairwell. She'd wanted to show him the clock tower workings from the inside, but their relationship had been new and powerful, the perfect pairing of a thirty-something woman who no longer feared having children and a young man for whom the very thought of intercourse inspired an immediate reaction.

That old stairwell had been filthy, filled with cobwebs and dirt on the stairs, and neither of them had cared. The walls were made of thick stone.

My husband could never find us here, Rosita had said, and then she had laughed. *And he never would have thought of* this.

Then she had grabbed Kirilli by the waist and—

"Sir?" Hopkins asked, spoiling the memory. "Are you all right?"

"I'm fine," Kirilli said. He had never told anyone about that day. And he knew that Rosita wouldn't have dared. "I'll take the satchels for you."

"Thank you, sir." Young Hopkins looked relieved.

"Do you know what's in them?" Kirilli asked. He could guess just from the magic swirling around them, but it would be better if he knew.

"No," Hopkins said. "But my grandmother said to tell you that there are maps."

Kirilli felt slightly dizzy. The Hopkins maps were center-pieces of the Hidden River maps. Josiah Hopkins the Second,

Rosita's son, once bragged to the board that the maps showed an area near Mount Vitaki.

Kirilli felt an urge to look at them, which he immediately suppressed. These were not his maps. They were not his family maps.

And the board was not to assemble the maps unless they meant to use the maps, whatever that meant.

"All right," Kirilli said. "You need to fight to get your seat on the board. Then you'll have to come to me to get these back. Or my daughter, Augusta. I will hide these well, and I will tell her where they are, in case something happens to me."

Hopkins nodded. "Your daughter. She will know if I can't ask you. Thank you, sir."

He made a movement toward the door.

Kirilli's sense that something was going to go wrong had gotten worse. But he knew that Hopkins was right to bring him the satchels.

"I will guard these with my life," Kirilli said. If Rosita had done her job, then her grandson would know that this was a solemn binding *magical* oath.

"Thank you, sir," Hopkins said. "I can see why my grand-mother trusted you."

Oh, you have no idea, Kirilli thought. But he didn't say it.

"Please keep me informed as to what's going on with your board seat," Kirilli said.

"I will," Hopkins said.

"And be careful. If someone is following you, then..." Kirilli stopped. He held up a finger and walked to the cabinet against the far wall. He kept his regular satchel in there as well as another satchel.

He pulled them out, removed his possessions from both, and then stuffed them with paper. After doing that, he scrawled numbers—protective numbers—all over two more sheets of paper.

"Take these satchels," he said, placing them in front of Hopkins. "And then carry the papers in one hand. Act like they're important business documents that don't fit into the satchels. Then, when you get home, fold the papers and stuff them into the pockets of anything you wear. You understand?"

"No," Hopkins said. "But I'll do it."

Kirilli smiled. "That's all I can ask," he said. "Now get out and don't come back until you feel safe."

"Yes, sir," Hopkins said. "Thank you, sir."

He picked up Kirilli's satchels, then took the papers and clung to them with the fingers of his right hand, wrapping them around the handle of one of the satchels.

Kirilli took the other two satchels and placed them under his desk. He wished he had a better place to store them. He would figure that out, though. He couldn't go from here to the Vault because if Hopkins was being followed, someone would follow Kirilli the Vault.

Kirilli would have to wait a day or so before he moved the satchels.

Hopkins let himself out, bobbed his head once more, and was about to say something—probably an unnecessary thank you—when Kirilli put a finger to his lips, then waved with his other hand.

Hopkins gave him a pained smile and, with the fingers of his left hand, pulled the door closed.

Kirilli moved the satchels into his cabinet. Yes, that was

where anyone who knew him would think that the satchels would be, but they would think they were *his* satchels.

That would buy a little time.

Time to figure out what he needed to do.

And time to separate himself from Hopkins.

Depending on the magic, Kirilli might have to have Gussie take the satchels to the Vault. Fortunately, he would see her soon.

He would tell her what was happening, although he wouldn't tell her why he had trusted Rosita.

There were some things in life that a man had to keep to himself.

SAMPLE THE NEXT BOOK

BARKSON'S JOURNEY: BOOK 2 OF THE QAVNERIAN PROTECTORATE

CHAPTER
ONE

Lucinda Barkson slowed her windstone vehicle about three blocks away from the Office of the Constabulary. The fog was thinning, but the visibility was still low. There was a lot more traffic here than there had been on the other roads—large carriages, constabulary on horseback, some people walking.

They all seemed to be headed to or coming from the Office of the Constabulary. Barkson didn't want to attract attention here, so she negotiated the large vehicle through openings in the traffic as if the windstone could break.

It couldn't—not easily—but the vehicle did sit lower than the carriages, so was often hard to see in a crowded area like this.

Until now, Barkson had driven, in Gussie's words, "like a crazy woman." There had been a purpose behind that seeming craziness.

Barkson had to make sure they weren't being followed. A

531

carriage couldn't have followed at the speed Barkson had gone, and a person on horseback would have stood out if they tried to keep up with the vehicle.

Barkson hadn't explained that to Gussie. Gussie, who had gripped the edge of the bench seat with a single gloved hand, and hadn't said much after asking if Barkson always drove like this.

Otherwise, Gussie—Augusta Kirilli, the oldest child of Augustus Kirilli—sat primly in the passenger seat of the vehicle. For the first time, maybe in her entire life, she was wearing pants and a loose blouse that she kept trying to adjust.

The clothes belonged to Barkson, along with the boots. Gussie's clothing was stained with blood. When she had peeled it off before washing down at Barkson's apartment, Barkson had quietly gathered the pieces and tossed them in a pile behind the building to be burned.

Barkson made herself pay attention to her driving. She needed to get Gussie to the Office of the Constabulary in one piece. It was probably the only place Gussie would be safe right now.

The neighborhood around the Office of the Constabulary had once been cheap rentals and tiny homes. Now, it consisted of offices and businesses related to the Constabulary.

There were several Offices of the Constabulary throughout the city of Trinovante, but this office serviced one of the richest areas in the entire city. Most of the Old Families lived nearby, in stately estates with massive amounts of land and servants.

Nothing much happened in this neighborhood except petty theft. Until the last few days.

Barkson had heard tell of massive destruction at some of the manor houses, and that was before Gussie had located her at

Mallankam's Public House. Gussie had told her a horrific tale that seemed to get worse as more details emerged. Gussie had sought Barkson out because, as Gussie said, Barkson was the only person she knew who could help.

In the past day or so, Gussie's father had been attacked and murdered, the family estate ransacked, and all of the staff killed in hideous ways.

This morning, Gussie and her driver had found all of the bodies, and had had a strange encounter with her father that had more than a little tinge of magic to it. Gussie hadn't really allowed herself to believe in magic before, even though the Kirillis were steeped in it.

Now, she did, although reluctantly.

Or perhaps what Barkson took for reluctance was utter emotional exhaustion.

Gussie was currently holding herself together with sheer determination. She sat upright, not allowing her back to touch the seat. Even though her hand gripped the bottom of the seat, she wasn't holding herself up with it. She was staring out of the windscreen, as if the road and carriages before her were the most important things in the world.

Barkson admired that. She had never realized just how strong Gussie was. They had gone to school together and had become fast, if unlikely, friends. They were very different—Gussie, prim and proper and concerned with how things looked, and Barkson, breaking every rule as she tried to get through.

Gussie had brought Barkson home several times, mostly on school holidays, until Barkson stopped accepting the invitations because she was so uncomfortable. Still, she had gotten to meet everyone in Gussie's immediate family, including her father.

Barkson hadn't had much time to register his death and how she felt about it. She knew a lot more about Augustus Kirilli than his daughter did.

Now was not the time to tell Gussie any of those things.

Barkson pulled over across the street from the Office of the Constabulary. It was a huge ugly building, with several stories and too many doors. A wide covered walkway swarmed with people, some in uniform and many in everyday clothes. Large posts at the edge of the walkway made sure that no one drove onto it, either with a carriage or a windstone vehicle.

There was a carriage park to the side of the building, but no place for windstone vehicles. Barkson had noted that curiosity before, but she had never considered it a problem until now.

Gussie stared at the building, her lower lip trembling. She had had an impossible day, and yet she hadn't broken down, not yet anyway. Barkson had given her the opportunity at the apartment, and Gussie had not taken it.

Gussie had been on the move all day. After discovering the destruction and the bodies of the murdered staff, Gussie had sent her driver—a man named Zeitsev—to this Office of the Constabulary to report the crimes. Then Gussie had gotten in her own windstone vehicle and driven somewhere—she wouldn't tell Barkson exactly where—to hide some satchels her father had given her, maybe before or (oddly) after his death.

Barkson didn't understand the part about the satchels, and she wasn't sure she was supposed to.

Gussie had told her almost everything, only holding back the location of the satchels because her father had sworn her to secrecy.

Barkson believed her for a variety of reasons. Gussie had

been a physical mess when she found Barkson. Gussie's clothing was covered in blood. She had a bloody handprint on her back. The bottom of her skirts was brown with dried blood, and her hair was coming out of its usually neat bun. Gussie had looked like a woman about to collapse, but she hadn't.

Barkson had taken Gussie home, fed her, clothed her, and demanded that she sleep.

But Gussie couldn't.

I need to get in touch with my siblings, she had said more than once, *and for that I need you.*

That was why Barkson had fourteen letters in the hidden compartment of her windstone vehicle—two letters for each sibling—along with a map that showed her where each Kirilli sibling now lived. Barkson had also brought almost every weapon she owned, from her pistols to nearly a dozen daggers.

They too were in the hidden compartments in the back.

Gussie hadn't seen Barkson pack those. Gussie had been busy writing the letters, calmly penning the same first letter to each sibling, detailing their father's death. The second letter, Gussie had said, was the important one, and she made sure that Barkson understood that no one was to receive the second letter first, ever.

Barkson had had to swear to that more than once, because Gussie seemed able to do only one thing at a time.

That she was still standing after the day she had was a miracle; that she was thinking clearly enough to come up with a plan for her siblings was something that left Barkson in awe.

Gussie still stared out the windscreen, her back rigid. She hadn't moved at all. Barkson wasn't even certain Gussie knew that they were in front of the constabulary.

Barkson put a gentle hand on Gussie's shoulder, hoping she hadn't fallen asleep with her eyes open. Barkson had seen some of the strongest men she'd ever known do that accidentally in her work for the Shadow Company. Sometimes exhaustion won.

But Gussie wasn't asleep. She blinked, smiled ruefully, and sighed.

"I don't want to talk to them," she said about the constabulary. The rich never did.

Had this been a normal day, with normal events, Barkson would have pointed out that class disparity to Gussie. Barkson had liked jabbing at the class differences between them since they'd met at Bekyce School for Girls nearly twenty years before.

"I know you don't want to go in there," Barkson said, "but you need to inform them. They need—"

"I'm sure Zeitsev told them everything," Gussie said.

They'd had this discussion at the apartment, then again when they had gotten into the windstone vehicle, and apparently they were going to have it again. Barkson tried not to sigh.

She needed to get on the road. After hearing what Gussie had been through—what was going on—Barkson knew that time was of the essence.

She had to reach all of the Kirilli siblings as quickly as possible. The problem was that they were scattered across the Dorovich continent, in several different countries. Emberto, the youngest son, lived near Mount Vitaki, and that was at least a three-day drive from here, nonstop.

Barkson wouldn't be able to go nonstop. Even if she didn't have the other siblings to deal with, she would need some sleep. And those three days didn't count road conditions or other problems she might encounter along the way.

"They need to hear from you," Barkson said of the constabulary. "They need to hear *everything* from you."

She had never said that before.

"I can't tell them about my father. It might be magic," Gussie said, staring out the passenger-side windscreen.

Might be magic. It *was* magic. The man had showed up, injured, at the manor house and then had faded away after he had delivered the satchels to Gussie. No one faded away without some kind of magic.

"Then don't tell them that part," Barkson said. "Just tell them you saw him, and get them to that kitchen."

Where the bodies of the staff were. The constabulary would take it from there.

"You just want them to protect me," Gussie said. "But what if they're involved?"

"They're not," Barkson said.

"You can't know that!" Gussie's voice rose. Barkson braced herself. Was this the much-needed, much-anticipated breakdown?

Barkson had hoped Gussie wouldn't have that until Barkson had left on this long trip.

"I can know it," Barkson said as calmly as she could. "You just mentioned magic, and you're right. The constabulary enforces rules *against* magic. They wouldn't sanction this kind of attack. They wouldn't attack an Old Family, and they wouldn't use magic against your father."

Gussie looked at her, eyes lined with tears.

Barkson squeezed Gussie's shoulder. It was so thin, and so much was riding on it now.

"I know this for a fact," Barkson said. "If I didn't, I wouldn't have brought you here."

That convinced Gussie. She took a deep breath, nodded, and then sighed.

"You have my key, right?" Barkson wanted to remind Gussie that she had a place to go.

"Yes," Gussie said. "And you don't have to give me the instructions again. I know them. I'm to get someone from here to drop me off a block or two away from your place. I should be able to make it from there to your apartment just fine. They can't know where I am."

She sagged a little, finally looking defeated.

"I won't be able to sleep," she said.

"But you'll be safe," Barkson said.

"I'll be safe," Gussie whispered, as if she didn't believe it.

Barkson wasn't sure she believed it either, but she did know one thing: she couldn't make this drive with Gussie in the passenger seat. Not that Gussie wanted to come. When she had been thinking just a bit more clearly, she had mentioned that she planned to go to the families of each staff member, tell them they had lost their loved one, and give them enough money to survive for a few months.

That by itself would take days and an emotional toll that Barkson didn't want to think about.

She had made Gussie promise she would not return to her father's property—indeed, to any Kirilli property—until this crisis had passed.

"I need to get on the road," Barkson said.

Being blunt seemed to be the only way to end this cycle of indecision. Obviously, Gussie was getting tired. All of the events of the day were hitting her now.

Barkson wasn't the kind of friend who could comfort a person in a time of need. Barkson was a woman who took action.

Gussie had been right to find Barkson, and to send her with the letters to the siblings. Gussie had no idea who Barkson really was or what she had been doing since they left their advanced studies at Serebro Academy, but Gussie did know that Barkson sometimes took on dangerous "odd jobs" that had once been—in Gussie's opinion—extremely unladylike.

Barkson was actually saddened that Gussie had need of her most unladylike friend. Gussie had long belonged to a part of the world that Barkson had thought untouchable by blood and violence.

Barkson had been so very wrong.

"Yes, yes," Gussie said. "You have to leave. Tell them...well, you know what to tell them."

She was referring to her siblings, none of whom lived in Trinovante. Some of them had children. Others...well, Barkson hoped she could find them quickly.

"I do," Barkson said. "I have all that I need. I'll send you letters as well, just to keep you informed, in case..."

She made herself stop. She had almost made a misstep. She had almost said, *in case I don't make it back.*

That had been a goodbye saying for members of Shadow Company. She hadn't expected it to become so rote that she almost said it to Gussie.

Gussie looked at her sharply. Gussie had probably heard the unstated words.

"In case?" she asked.

Barkson made herself smile reassuringly. "In case it takes me longer to return than you expect."

That was also true. Barkson had no idea what she was driving into, nor did she know how long it would take her.

Gussie grabbed her hand so tightly that Gussie's glove rubbed against Barkson's skin.

"You can't die on me too," Gussie said.

Barkson grinned in her most insouciant way.

"Gus," she said, "that's why you're sending me. I'm indestructible."

A tear ran down Gussie's face. "That's the thing, Lucinda," she said. "No one is. I thought my father was, and you saw— well, you didn't see. You know…"

"I know," Barkson said. She had to stop the emotional breakdown before it happened. "Your father did everything he could to make sure his legacy was protected. I'm going to do everything I can to make sure your family is safe. You have my word."

"I know." Gussie let go of her hand. "You're a true friend, Lucinda."

Barkson laughed, deliberately. "I'm not sure that's true, Gus. You're paying me."

"You didn't want me to," Gussie said.

Trapped by her own words from a few hours ago. Barkson had no response for that.

"Go," she said. "Before someone in the constabulary wonders why we're parked here and their curiosity delays my journey further."

"Right. Yes." Gussie opened the door. Finally. She slipped a booted foot out, then turned.

Barkson half-held her breath, hoping this wouldn't lead to more discussion.

"Be safe, Lucinda," Gussie said.

Since that command contradicted the very point of this journey, Barkson had no option other than a polite lie.

"I will, Gus," she said. "I promise. I will."

Keep Reading *Barkson's Journey!*

Go to *WorldoftheFey.com*

HEAR DIRECTLY FROM KRIS

Sign up for the Kristine Kathryn Rusch newsletter and hear from Kris herself.

Go to kriswrites.com.

Get the latest news and releases from all of the WMG authors and lines, including Kristine Kathryn Rusch, Kristine Grayson, Kris Nelscott, Dean Wesley Smith, *Pulphouse Fiction Magazine*, *Smith's Monthly*, and so much more.

Go to wmgbooks.com.

You can also follow Kris on Bookbub.

We value honest feedback, and would love to hear your opinion in a review, if you're so inclined, on your favorite book retailer's site.

ABOUT THE AUTHOR

International bestseller Kristine Kathryn Rusch wrote seven books featuring the Fey before traditional publishing issues in the United States stymied her. The extremely popular series became a bestseller in multiple languages, including French, Italian, German, Polish, and Czech. When the first book, *The Sacrifice*, first appeared in the United States, it was hailed as one of the best fantasy novels of the year. Rusch took an unintended twenty-plus year hiatus from the Fey after completing the second full mini-saga. Spurred by a successful Kickstarter for a novella featuring the Fey, she dove back into the project. She explains her journey back to the Fey in *Lessons from the Writing of The Fey*. All seven of the books are back in print through WMG Publishing, and have garnered new readers worldwide. Rusch recently published the novella, *The Reflection on Mount Vitaki*, and has completed three new novels, with a fourth underway.

Rusch writes in many genres, from science fiction to mystery, from western to romance. She has written under a pile of pen names, but most of her work appears as Kristine Kathryn Rusch. Her Kris Nelscott pen name has won or been nominated for most of the awards in the mystery genre, and her Kristine

Grayson pen name became a bestseller in romance. Her science fiction novels set in the bestselling Diving Universe have won dozens of awards and are in development for a major TV show. She also writes the Retrieval Artist sf series and several major series that mostly appear as short fiction.

Rusch broke a number of barriers in the sf/f field, including being the first female editor of *The Magazine of Fantasy & Science Fiction*. She has owned two different publishing companies, and writes a highly regarded publishing industry blog on Patreon. She also writes a highly regarded weekly publishing industry blog. Find out more about her work at <u>kriswrites.com</u>, and more about the Fey at <u>WorldoftheFey.com</u>.

facebook.com/kristinekathrynruschwriter

patreon.com/kristinekathrynrusch

bookbub.com/authors/kristine-kathryn-rusch